SOCKEYE

MICHAEL F. TEVLIN

Black Rose Writing | Texas

ISBN: 978-1-68433-465-0
PUBLISHED BY BLACK ROSE WRITING
www.blackrosewriting.com

Printed in the United States of America
Suggested Retail Price (SRP) $19.95

Sockeye is printed in Traditional Arabic

*As a planet-friendly publisher, Black Rose Writing does its best to eliminate unnecessary waste to reduce paper usage and energy costs, while never compromising the reading experience. As a result, the final word count vs. page count may not meet common expectations.

To Diane and a hard-working love.

Thank you, Joanna Rose and Stevan Allred and writers of the Pinewood Table in Portland: You taught me to write with heart and get Joe in trouble. I am grateful to Fishtrap in Joseph, Ore., for the week I spent at the writer's cabin on the Imnaha River and especially to Kim Stafford and fellow campers at the Outpost at Billy Meadows, where I found the aspens and woodpeckers. Mom, thanks for your encouragement. Michael and Sean, you mean the world to me. Diane, you enabled me to spend early mornings holed away without questioning my sanity or dampening my hope

SOCKEYE

"All things on earth point home in old October; sailors to sea, travellers to walls and fences, hunters to field and hollow and the long voice of the hounds, the lover to the love he has forsaken."
~Thomas Wolfe

CHAPTER 1

Even from out in the harbor, he recognized the patrol car on the wharf with the big deputy standing beside it. Only Lloyd could stand out from that distance, like some kind of goddamned freakish uniformed walrus.

Joe piloted the boat in through Sitka Harbor and headed for the ANB dock. He and Cuddyer had hooked and iced and offloaded a hundred kings—a good haul that would fetch upwards of $12,000 for their trouble. He eased the *Jenny Alvord* into the slip as though she were a 12-foot skiff instead of a 35-foot troller.

Cuddyer threw the rope over the gunwale to the deputy. "Got a call," Lloyd shouted over the diesel. The deputy shifted his hat, took it off and looked at it and smoothed his oily hair. He squinted and shaded his eyes. "Family's been looking for you," he yelled. "Sister." Then Joe heard: "father," and "plane" and "down."

His father was dead.

Joe shifted for a moment, as though he'd lost his balance. The evening was clear, and off to the west the snow-capped cone of Mount Edgecumbe poked through the clouds. He wanted bourbon.

They stood for a long time in silence. He left the wheel and turned as Cuddyer secured the *Jenny A*. He held his hands out, palms up, as though he were bewildered that they were his, and then rubbed his fingers together.

When he was alone, Joe got a can of Bud from the ice. There were the islands to the west, and then the open water. Other boats were coming in, and a float plane buzzed off. He hadn't spoken a word to his father since he'd left Sockeye. And his father had returned the favor. Which was fine. Better. What would he have said to him? "Hello, how are you? Thanks for fucking up my life." Which was only part way true, because he had fucked up his life pretty well on his own. He finished the can in a long pull and then crushed it in his hand.

He cracked another beer. Gulls wheeling. Smell of diesel and fish. He'd always thought, maybe things would change with his dad. Maybe he'd come around. But it had to be his dad who made the first move, after what he'd done to Joe, the absolute abandonment when he needed him most. Now it was too late. Now it'd be for his mom, Grace, and for his sister, McKenzie. Not for Howard. The smug bastard, always wanting to believe he was the patriarch-in-waiting. Big brother was getting his wish.

The water pinked with the evening sky. He swallowed. There was something else. All this time in Alaska, he'd felt like a refugee. He'd never thought of it as home. Home used to be the Wallowa country. Jenny Alvord. She was dead a decade. Now his father was dead. Where was home? What did that even mean, going home?

Back at his apartment above the dock store, he picked a juice glass out of the sink and looked at it in the light and rinsed it, and then he poured his second bourbon. He'd never planned to stay long. Now it was 10 years. Old newspapers on the table. Fish-stinking clothes on the floor. Dishes in the sink. McKenzie had left messages. He thumbed her number on the phone and waited.

"I've been trying—. You're coming," she said.

There were kids crabbing from the dock in the dark with flashlights. "I've got a fishing boat and a crew," he said.

"I'll come in to Portland. Pick you up," she said. "Find somebody to take the boat for a while."

He swung the phone down at his hip and blew out and then put it back. "Mom's been schooling you on how to boss me around? Anyway, that's not the issue." He poured the rest of the bourbon into the glass. There were no ice cubes.

"Mom needs you, that's the issue. This is not about Howard."

He swirled what was left of the bourbon. "Last time I saw him I wanted to shoot his fat ass. He getting fatter?"

"I don't expect you to love him. Just be civil." There was the scratch of wind in the receiver. "The funeral is Saturday. Are you drinking?"

"You out on the porch?" he asked her. The old porch overlooked the lake. The vanilla of ponderosa pitch warming in the sun.

A gull flew up outside his window and hovered for a moment as though it was looking in at him. It moved off and up onto the roof.

"Get yourself a ticket and get on a plane," she said.

After she hung up, he sat in the sagging brown couch. He pressed his eyes shut and leaned back. There was an ache in his stomach like hunger. There were things to do, a ticket to buy. Square away stuff with the *Jenny A.* He'd been to a few funerals of guys up here. Now his father, dead. His mom, alone. McKenzie, he'd missed her. Howard, his smirking pig face. And the memories of Jenny— they would return in Sockeye. They had to. He rubbed his face and eyes. He could sleep on the plane if there was enough to drink.

CHAPTER 2

Friday, he sat in her Blazer on the interstate, McKenzie at the wheel. She'd brought Buddy, the black lab who'd been his before he left, now gray-muzzled. They'd driven mostly in silence, Buddy's head on his lap, through the gorge and up the flats past Pendleton, where they stopped for gas. She raised an eye when she saw the six-pack but left it alone.

"You going to stick around?" McKenzie asked him. "There's a lot of work. Stuff dad had going."

"You think it's easy?"

"I never said 'easy,'" she told him.

"Plenty of work in Alaska."

"Don't be such a prick," she said, and she punched him on the shoulder. "Lighten up, for God's sake. Mom could use some help."

"Christ," he rubbed his shoulder but laughed. "You taking up boxing? Mom's always needed help, but she's never taken it when offered. I suspect that hasn't changed much. Right Bud?"

Now in the back, Buddy wagged his tail and offered his wet snout.

McKenzie had come up to see him in Sitka six years ago and she'd sent him her high school graduation picture since then. She was 22 now and she looked a hell of a lot more like pictures of their mom when she was young. Those high cheekbones and blue eyes but their dad's wide face and thick torso. McKenzie was always strong as a diesel, and she'd gotten stronger, with broad shoulders and a steel pipe of a middle.

He closed his eyes, and then he was back on the *Jenny A.* No one to bother him or bring up the past. No one telling a person what to do, or not to do, unless it had to be done. Where the world was boiled to the bones: ocean, sky, rain, wind, cold.

When he'd left, he didn't look back. Swore he'd never come back as long as his dad was alive. Back to where his father had abandoned him when he needed him most, and then kicked him when he was down. "You're not my son," Clark had said after the trial. And that was it for him.

And now this. His father, the shit at the end. And finally Jenny. Goddammit. Jenny. Gone dead, murdered. Goddamn Kyle Macy, Jr. Goddamn him.

In the rearview, the Blues purpled in the summer evening. Ahead, the south slope of the Wallowas rose out of the hay fields of the Grande Ronde Valley.

"There they are," he said.

The summit glowed salmon pink as it caught the last rays of the sun. Even though she worked as a nurse, McKenzie still had a rancher's tan from riding. That was a difference between McKenzie and their mom—as much time as mom spent outside in that high country, she had always kept her face out of the sun and stayed as pale as the belly of a suckerfish.

"I assume the Macys are still interbreeding," he said.

"The Macys." She said it with a measure of disgust.

"The old man still around?"

"He's hanging in there somehow. Cody, the little brother, he isn't so little anymore. Nothing like his brother. Still. The apple doesn't fall far. It wasn't your fault. I hate to say this, but he deserved everything he got." She touched his arm. "It's Jenny, isn't it?"

"I don't know," he said, but he knew she could tell.

"We all miss her."

McKenzie grazed his face with her fingertips and looked at him but he was silent. The way Kyle Macy, Jr., had bloodied her. The sight of her body. How could a person get over something like that?

He'd had plenty of women in Alaska, but none of them could ever hold a candle to Jenny. He saw her now, in her bedroom, the light from the window in her brown hair. She was smiling and laughing at herself for spilling some wine on her Madras top. She was as real and kind and smart as they ever came.

McKenzie stared at him. "Joe, I understand you don't want to talk about any of this. We're burying his ashes tomorrow. You don't have to say anything. Mom doesn't want anyone saying anything at church. No eulogies. Lucky you." She hesitated, then added, "I don't know everything that happened between you two. I know it was bad. I was lucky, I guess. I saw him change the last few years. He was different without liquor."

He rubbed his face and then his eyes. "What do you want me to say? That I'm happy he went out sober?"

She shuddered and tossed her head as if she were going to bang it on the steering wheel. "Uh! I wish—."

"Watch the goddamned road, girl."

"I'll fucking watch the road if I fucking feel like it." She punched the dashboard and the car swerved and ran over the corrugated warning strip. He grabbed the steering wheel but she pushed him away. He angled away from her, holding up his hands in front of his face, half-pretending, half-serious. Buddy sat up in the back and barked, scolding them. She let off the gas and got control of the Blazer.

"Oh Buddy, I'm sorry. It's alright. Everything's okay," she said. She reached out to him, and the whimpering dog hopped forward and stuck his cold nose between the seats and sniffed. She patted his head. "This is not going well."

"Look, maybe we can just put the whole thing to rest for now," he said, and he put his hand next to her on the seat. "Maybe some other time?"

She put her hand on his. "Some other time," she said. She exhaled and looked at him sideways. "You're going to have to talk about it sometime."

"Okay."

"Will you promise to talk to me? Will you get help?"

"I'll think on it."

"You'll think on it."

***

Outside Elgin, they climbed the grassy rise of Minam Hill, the landscape soft and sculpted. The river bed fell away behind them, meandering north until it struck the Blues again and pushed west, scrambling up against the hills. The treed foothills of the Wallowas rose on the right. He found himself holding his breath as the Blazer climbed the grade, the bottomless blue of the evening sky big in their windshield.

They crested the top. Behind them lay the grassy hips of the south-leaning hill. Ahead, the road traversed steeply into the great dark glacier-carved gorge of the Minam River. The exposed rock was brick red, the steep hills gold, and the big trees in the draws almost black down into the timbered bottoms.

McKenzie steered the Blazer into a gravel pull-out, a dust cloud erupting under the chassis. Buddy stretched, yawned and then plopped his clunky frame out onto the ground.

Joe drifted to the edge of the lot. The Minam scraped across the rocks below, a series of straight reaches interrupted by sharply angled changes of direction. There was white water but no sound. Then the low rush of the water came, but it seemed separate from the water itself, floating in the failing light.

He let her put her arm around his waist and lean her head against his chest. Her head reached his shoulder. The smell of her hair was the smell of the Wallowa Valley, the smell of their mother. He closed his eyes. Then he let out his breath in a long blow and let his shoulders and arms hang loose.

"It's been a while." She looked up at him.

He toed the gravel with his boot and forced a hand in the pocket of his jeans. "When we were kids, this was the dividing line, this spot here." He squinted. They were facing east. "Anything between here and the Snake, that was home. Anything to the other side of it was just someplace out there."

He picked up a rock and side-armed it into the air. Buddy wagged his tail and looked up at him like he would throw him a ball to retrieve. The rock arced out and then down and disappeared soundlessly into the canyon. "They had this country to themselves. Nobody came over these mountains. Then one day these guys show up with horses and cattle and sheep and metal tools for cutting the bunchgrass. Shit, if they'd've known then, they'd've cut them down right on the spot."

McKenzie kicked gravel at him. "The Joseph line."

"The what?"

"Old Joseph wouldn't sign the treaty of 1863," she said. "So he and his men put up a line of poles marking the Nez Perce lands. The line was right around here on the divide so they'd see it when they'd bring their wagons into the Wallowa country."

He bent to find another stone. "A lot of good it did them."

She knelt beside him. "What's going on in that head of yours? Coming home now."

He stayed on his haunches and picked up an egg-sized chunk of granite and weighed it in his hand. Buddy wagged his tail and waited for his throw. "Thought I'd left this place for good. Thought I never wanted to see it again."

McKenzie squeezed a rock between her thumb and forefinger and then opened her hand. "But that isn't true?" She spread out like she was a catcher making a pickoff throw from a crouch and whipped the rock hard. "I mean."

She grunted as she threw it. "I could never leave here. This place gets in your bones."

He put his hands on his knees and took time straightening out. "Let's go, Bud. Let's go, then." Buddy sat up and then grunted and pushed up on his hind legs and wagged his tail and followed him to the Blazer.

She got up. "Joe?" She stood behind him.

He kept walking.

"It was him, wasn't it? You didn't ever want to see him again."

He broke his stride for a moment, lowered his head to the side, and Buddy stopped. "You really want to know?" he said.

"I do."

"I never wanted to see the bastard again."

She looked at him and then hung her head and grabbed her temples and cried softly.

He continued toward the Blazer and got in the passenger side and waited for her and Buddy. Before she turned the key, he reached for her wrist. She broke down again, and this time he pulled her to his shoulder and let her wet his shirt. He felt dizzy in the small space of the cab, the canyon beyond their truck, but glad to feel the touch of his sister.

CHAPTER 3

He got up early, before the sun crested the east moraine, and started on the breakfast. He was sweating at the stove. He made the coffee strong, the way his mother enjoyed it. There were small noises from her bedroom—the water running, a brush falling on the sink counter maybe, the old metal medicine cabinet door swinging open and shut, the bed squeaking. Her radio on, as always.

Her door opened, and she was already pretending to complain in that way of hers, croaking in her pre-cigarette, pre-coffee yammering about why he hadn't let her make him breakfast. She sounded the same, but when he turned, his eyes widened ever so slightly. She'd lost weight and had hunched over. She'd penciled on her purple-black half-moon eyebrows the way he always remembered and put on her pink lipstick and had her hair in a net.

"Bacon got me up," she said, sniffing the air.

"Burnt enough for you?" he said.

"You remembered," she said. She stopped and brought her eyes to him. "Good Lord, look at you." She stepped back to appraise him, hands on her hips. "We're going to have to put some more meat on those bones. Don't you eat anything up there besides salmon?"

"Look who's talking," he said.

She kept her hands on her hips and one-eyed him. "I saw you looking at me." She held out her hands. "I've become an old bag. Where's my coffee?"

"Com'ere, Ma," he said, and she softened. He wrapped himself around her. She felt like paper on bones.

"Welcome home, son," she said. She looked in his eyes when he bent to kiss her cheek. "I don't know what we're going to do without him, but we're going to have to soldier on anyway or it'll just get away from us."

The "we" spun in his head and took him where he didn't want to go. He would not think about his father. She could have broken in his arms. She still had the warmth from her bed in her. "We're not gonna let anything get away from anybody," he said. He held her at arm's length. Her eyes were wet and red. She might already have been crying this morning, or did they look like that since he died? Then it was as if she caught herself softening, and she straightened.

"You found the coffee filters? What else do you need? Sugar?" She started for the cabinet.

"Ma, sit. I've got everything. I could've found it in my sleep. Sit. The eggs are getting cold."

She sat at the kitchen table. He'd set the places. He spooned eggs onto a plate, then set down three slices of bacon and two buttered slices of toast. His hands were shaking from the coffee. "You look like you could blow away in a breeze. Go ahead and eat your breakfast. I'd have to lash you to the deck if you were on my boat."

She jutted her jaw and blustered. "Mind your manners. Don't you know that gentlemen never comment on a girl's weight unless it's a compliment? It's hard enough for a girl to keep her figure, let alone at my age." She picked up a piece of bacon and bit off a piece. "Well, come on and sit then."

He sat and took some eggs but he'd already wrecked his stomach with the coffee. He wiped his wet forehead with the sleeve of his undershirt.

"Going to be a scorcher today," she said. "Weather says it should get up over 100 over in Boise. Are you alright? You don't get this heat up there." She started to get up. "Let me get you some water."

"Ma, I don't need anything," he said. "Really. Just sit." He stayed put and tried some bacon.

She ate a little more and then reached for the small purse that held her cigarettes. "I still smoke these awful things," she said. "They haven't killed me yet." She got up.

"Since when do you go outside to smoke?"

"Oh, I don't know. I suppose I got tired of your sister complaining about the smell." She started for the door, and he followed her. "You don't need to subject yourself to my bad habits."

"Oh, I got a few of my own," he said.

The air was warmer outside on the porch than in the house. She sat at the picnic table. He stood and leaned his elbows on the porch rail. The lake sat still. The sun had already topped the east moraine, and its reflection off the lake surface lit the shadows under the trees like shimmering schools of silver fish. She took a match to her cigarette, inhaled and then blew out the smoke in a long breath through the circle of her lips.

"I thought I might stay around a bit, see if I could make myself useful," he said. A jay lighted on the bird feeder.

"Scoot! Scoot, jaybird," she scolded and thrashed her arms until the jay flew off with a screech, sending the big feeder swaying wildly. "Damn camp robbers." She pulled on her cigarette.

"That is, if you could use the help," he said.

She squinted at him while she blew smoke. "I can manage on my own." She said it with enough bluster that he knew to tread lightly. "Besides, you've got that boat and crew to worry about. It's a wonder you were able to break away for the funeral as it is. I'm grateful to you for that, son, you know I am. But don't go feeling sorry for me. I can take care of myself." She dusted an ash off her hollow chest.

The sun had begun to heat the sap in the ponderosas, the scent like caramel. "I know you can, ma. I know. Just think about it, then. The boat's in good hands."

She stubbed the cigarette in the ashtray. "It's going to be a long day."

"Look, ma," he said. He turned to face her.

"Oh, let's not talk about that now," she said. "There will be time for that." She got up from the table. "I know this is hard for you. He made a lot of mistakes."

She looked at him quickly, and then turned for the screen door.

"Ma, I never wanted to see him again." He said it to her back, and she put up her hands. From behind, it was impossible to read her face. He hadn't planned it that way, but now it was out. It was a hell of a thing to say to his mother on this day.

She walked inside, and then a moment later she opened the screen door and held out her hand. "Take this," she said.

"What?" He approached her closed hand.

"Give me your hand," she said.

She placed her bony fist on his palm. She opened her hand and let fall a ring. "It was his," she said.

"Ma?" He stood with the ring in his open palm. He knew this ring.

"Your brother already has one. Take it. You may need it one day."

It was a simple design, a thin band around the edge, with a wider, convex band in the middle. He never saw his father without it. He remembered his father's hand, the freckles on his short fingers. He closed his hand around it.

"Put it someplace safe," she said. Then she let the door close. "Now, let's get moving."

He opened his hand once more. There were small scratches along the surface. From the crash? He closed his fingers around it and bounced it to feel its heft. In his room, he opened the top drawer of the dresser and placed it a lozenge tin filled with coins, a few buttons, paper clips.

He closed the drawer and got dressed, but the image of the ring stayed with him, as if there were a piece of his father in the tin, cool and dense like a piece of animal bone he would have picked up when he was a kid.

CHAPTER 4

The cemetery sat on the moraine looking high across the crooked blue finger of the lake up into the white peaks.

The family—McKenzie, Howard, his wife and two kids, his mom—formed a semicircle around the urn, the preacher facing them. Behind them, old neighbors and family friends shuffled into a rough clutch of mourners, the men with their Stetsons and ball caps in their hands and the women in their wide-brimmed summer hats. Bart Walton had come, his old friend, now a sheriff's deputy.

The urn was a plain slate cube. Nothing to it. It sat black and small and silent.

The old families still used the place. His great-grandparents on his dad's side, the Wallace side, his grandparents—they were all up there. The early families had cleared the spot of as many glacial rocks as they could manage, and what the people couldn't budge they dug around, leaving the big lichen-crusted boulders where they lay.

The preacher came from the Methodist church and made remarks about God and country and family and goodness and heaven. The V.A. had supplied a flag, which now laid folded into a crisp triangle beside the urn. Despite Howard's protest, Grace didn't want a folding and presentation of the flag or playing of taps. Howard would have gone for a 21-gun salute and the Blue Angels.

He squinted into the bleached brightness of the hot day, but he couldn't resist the dark stone. The urn, with its bag of ashes inside, baked in the sun. His father gone, but not gone. His own life a waste. A blackness. Bile. Coffee grounds. His old man a failure to him but not to these people. Not to his sister. Not to Howard.

He shifted on his feet. Sweating through his clothes. He'd been a fuck-up of a son. A coward for running to Alaska. What if he'd gotten to Jenny sooner? Why her and not him?

Grace stood beside him, covered in black, a crow of a woman. Smaller and frailer than ever. The black veil hid her eyes, the light behind the veil purple and dull and still. Her face was marble, her hands beyond the black sleeves bony and blue-white, the fingernails milky.

The brown liquor he'd had this morning left him aching. The morning's coffee and bacon burned his gut. He licked his lips with salty sweat but they dried instantly. The spittle caught in his throat.

He put his clammy hand on his mother's shoulder. She stooped, the bones on her back ridging her dress. His hands shook, stopped, started up again. He tried stopping the shaking but he gave up. The minister's outstretched arms trembled.

McKenzie leaned and whispered into his ear. "You alright?" The world snapped into focus. The gourd-shaped lake was hemmed in on three sides by moraines. It had held a mammoth glacier at one time. Maybe what Alaska would look like in a hundred years. Maybe sooner, the way things were going. Her hand was cool on his. He inhaled, and nodded for her sake, and the shaking subsided. He let his hand drop back at his side but it was a wooden movement.

A bead of sweat stung his eye. His shirt underneath his jacket was soaked. The shaking returned. He clenched his eyes until the dark screen of the inside of his eyelids lit up. The image of the urn came back, a monolith in a blank landscape. He saw his father. He rubbed his eyes, the lights dazzling, but the urn remained.

He opened his eyes but now he was out of his body, looking at himself from somewhere else. Grace, McKenzie and Howard stooped to touch the stone. He bent to do it, but he stopped, his hand repelled by the slate cube. He pressed his hand toward it. He righted himself, but he was shaky, the blood draining from his head, the color bleaching from the sky. He stood with the preacher and his family but it was like looking through a pair of binoculars turned backwards. Everything appeared distant. His hands—they didn't seem to belong to him.

He walked away from them. Aware of every step. Aware of the eyes on him. He wanted to run, the sun screaming in his ears. He could barely breathe. Everything strange. Like he could fall into the sky. His footsteps clumsy. His arms stiff. He found a tree and a rock by the edge of the cemetery, some shade, out of earshot.

The big lake sat breathless. There was a brick-red wooden rowboat, the kind they rented to guests at the cabins, sitting perfectly still and empty in the blue water. He'd spent hours in those boats with his father. Clark taught him how to feel the kokanee through the nylon line, deep, and set the hook ever so carefully.

A motorboat broke the silent, still water, trailing a water skier. The skier, a woman in a one-piece blue bathing suit, split outside the boat's wake as it skidded into a turn. She let go of the tow rope with one hand and waved to someone. Now the boat completed its arc. The skier sank as she slowed. There was a fading black-and-white photo on the wall in the house of Grace water-skiing on the lake when she was in her 20s, in a one-piece suit and a bathing cap, executing a one-legged pose like a dancer.

When the ceremony ended, he crossed the long expanse of parched grass. It seemed wider, as though it had been stretched. The sky relentless. He was walking on bones. The headstones radiated heat. The family stood melting in the glare. He reached them but there was nothing to say. He was watching a movie, and he was in it at the same time. The east moraine rose beyond them, on the high side of the road, its bare shoulders taking the brunt of the sun. Grace was black and withered; she could have been picked up and carried off by birds. She walked ahead, family and friends filing behind, out to the dusty parking lot.

CHAPTER 5

After the cemetery, they had gone to the Bucksaw for lunch, and Bart Walton had come by, still in his cop uniform. He'd hardly changed: jet-black, curling hair; lean and long; skin dark as an oiled baseball mitt, some wrinkles around his dark eyes, which lit up as he came over to their table. He was his only good friend, still was, even though they hadn't talked since he left, the way men do. They'd kept in touch through McKenzie.

First, he took Grace's hands in his big hands. "Mrs. W," he said. "These people treating you okay?"

He hadn't lost any of his considerable BS'ing skills. He moved around the table, stopping first at McKenzie. He massaged her shoulders. "You okay, darlin'?"

She smiled and patted his hands. "We're fine. Thanks, Bart."

Bart reached his hand across to Howard. "Condolences to you both," he said. He nodded to Sue.

"Nice of you to come," Howard said, shifting the toothpick in his mouth.

Joe started to shake his hand, but Bart pointed at his hand and laughed. "Forget it, pal. Ten years and you're getting one of these." Bart came around and bear hugged him, lifting him off the floor.

Joe pounded Bart on the back. "Son of a gun, look at you, all clean and legal."

An hour later they were at the Glacier Tap Room, just him and Bart. Inside the windowless tavern it was cool and dark, the only light the blue glow from behind the bar and the neon Bud and Oly signs on the walls. Duffy was tending bar as if 10 years had never passed. He put the first round on the house.

Duffy proffered the bourbon and set the bottle on the bar. "Sorry for your loss," he said. "A real gem, that old man of yours."

Joe lifted his glass and threw it back in one gulp.

Duffy held the standard glowing assessment of his father, at least the one that was shared publicly. "Good to have you back," Duffy said. "Plan to stay long?"

"As long as you're pouring," he said, and he tapped his glass on the bar.

Duffy poured again. The liquor heated his throat and stomach. He smiled and closed his eyes. It was good to be in a dark bar on this bright day. What had happened up at the cemetery? He knew what it was and he did not want to think about it. Not now. He could not hide from it because he had tried that for 10 years and it hadn't worked. His father, goddamn his father.

Bart nursed a Diet Coke and smoked. Then the daylight streamed in with the open door and another soul came in and passed behind them, trailing the smell of leather and horses. Bart nodded to the guy and said "Macy" to him. He raised his hand toward his hat and nodded but did not touch the brim. He took a seat at the end of the bar and Duffy shuffled over and opened a bottle of beer and put it in front of him without a word between them.

He was small but solid. Looked like a typical ranch hand, except he had longer hair and a look not so much of a hard worker as a hard person. Joe searched Bart's eyes for a clue, but Bart tightened his lips and looked down, shaking his head as if to say, don't ask.

"The little brother?" Joe said, low.

Bart nodded slightly.

Duffy came over. "Another round?"

He pointed to his glass with two fingers and tapped twice.

"Hold that, Duff," Bart said. "We're going."

There was a tightness in his head. It felt like the real world out there waiting beyond the door. But it was over inside the bar. There was no way Bart was leaving without him. It was Kyle Macy, Jr.'s brother.

The kid was barely a teenager when it'd happened. Joe had killed his brother. Those were the facts. Maybe the kid believed or had been fed the lie that said it was just two jealous men fighting over a woman. The brother was old enough now to hold a grudge, and had a right to even if he was wrong. But there was no sign from him that he knew. Maybe he didn't care. Maybe he was grateful for what Joe did to his brother.

Joe moved unsteadily in the gloom. He reached into his pocket, pulled out some bills and laid them on the bar. Duffy came over and picked up the bills and looked at him, but he waved him off. Duffy looked at Bart, and Bart nodded. "Appreciate it," Duffy said, and he nodded without turning. Macy didn't turn or look. Bart took one last drag and snuffed his cigarette in the ashtray. Then the two of them headed for the door and swung it out into the hard light. "Afternoon, gentlemen" Duffy said. "My condolences."

"Thanks, Duff. We'll see you soon."

He visored his eyes. A stream of RVs and trucks pulling trailers and boats rumbled by. There were cars and pickups parked at angles, and families walking up and down Main Street, the men and women in shorts and golf shirts, kids eating ice cream cones. When he was growing up, there were campers from the state park, but nothing like this. Sockeye used to be a place to stop for ice, groceries, beer and gas. There was the drug store, the outfitters that sold everything a person could want for camping or fishing or hunting or ranching, the mercantile. There weren't sidewalks, leastways not paved sidewalks. Now it was a place to walk around and look in windows. There were art galleries. Shops that sold fancy clothes for women. Espresso bars and micro-breweries.

"Let me give you a ride, partner." Bart leaned his hand on his shoulder.

"That's all right. Got my mom's wagon," he said.

Bart stood next to him. "Can you believe this place?"

"What the hell happened?"

"People got money to spend, I guess. Not that I'm complaining. Gives me something to do." Bart angled his gaze at him. "You're coming with me, and you can come get your mom's wagon tomorrow."

"Fuck me. The law now."

They walked to Bart's Cherokee. Bart's knees hit the dashboard. He had a small, perpetually sun-browned and creased face framed by shiny onyx hair he didn't so much comb as finger back behind his ears. He had Indian blood back on his dad's side.

Bart backed the Cherokee out and turned it toward the lake. "I don't profess to knowing much about families," he said. He lit a cigarette.

Joe said nothing as Bart drove through town and made the turn for the lake road. The gray hulk of Bonneville Mountain dominated the head of the lake. Beyond Bonneville, clouds merged with snowy-shouldered peaks in the distance.

"Howard's right about one thing," Joe said.

Bart turned toward him and raised one eyebrow and then looked back at the road ahead of them.

"I'm a goddamned certified nut case," he said.

Bart huffed and looked at him, then looked back at the road. "Everyone's a little crazy."

The Cherokee turned over the cattle guard and up the gravel road that climbed the moraine. He leaned forward, his hands on the dash. "I don't know what the hell I'm doing here. I came down to pay my respects and head on back north. But there's something that isn't done. Something wrong. Something missing. I don't know."

The scarred face of Joseph Mountain gathered like a thunderhead out his window. It had a way of creeping up on a person like a big cat. The Cherokee crawled in second gear.

"Look," Bart said. "A guy's old man dies, he's looking at his own life. Wondering about shit. How it went, how it could've been different. How much time he's got left. Regrets."

He kept his hands on the spotless dash. There wasn't a newspaper, gum wrapper or anything on the floor. He nodded. "Shit. You can say that again." He grunted a laugh that wasn't a laugh. "There's a lot of shit went down between me and my old man."

Bart blew smoke. "You and Howard got some crap there, too."

"Something's up his ass."

"I guess." Bart looked at him sideways and then turned straight ahead. "Cut him some slack. He had to deal with your old man this whole last 10 years. You didn't."

"He's still an asshole."

"I won't argue that. I'm not going to preach to you about families. What do I know?"

At the top of the hill, the road hooked left and crossed a couple more cattle grates. Beyond a locked gate, a jeep track continued up to the top of the moraine, but the main road here joined up with the dirt road that had been carved out of the lake side of the west moraine. The cemetery was across the lake. It was only this morning they'd buried his father up there. What the hell had happened then? It didn't seem real now. Down through the ponderosas, the lake was a deep blue. Bart turned right along the oil-packed road that paralleled the lake and eased the car down the hill.

He crossed his arms. "Thought I could get away from him, but coming back, he just followed me. My dad's in every board in that house. He's under my skin. I can't get away from him."

The Cherokee bounced over the washboard ribs of the road. He pushed back his hair. They passed a Ford pickup coming up the lake road and they raised their fingers in greeting and the driver waved back but he didn't recognize the truck or driver. He uncrossed his arms and rubbed his eyes and spoke into his hands. "My whole life I've been trying to hide from my old man. I tried hiding from him when I was a kid. And when that didn't work, I left for the great white north. And here I am back and he's gone, but he's not gone. What the hell am I hiding from? A ghost?"

Bart drew his lips back across his teeth and nodded. "He was a force of nature, old Clark. No doubt," he said, and he nodded. "Maybe the thing is, you can't run no more. You've come to the end of the road."

The road leveled. He brought his hands along the stubble on his jaw. "End of the road, huh? That don't sound like a whole lot of going anywhere, now, does it?"

"No, I guess it doesn't."

Ahead, a rutted drive cut away and down into a grove of ponderosas. The ball joints creaked as the Cherokee clanked over the ruts, and then Bart steered it down onto a grassy bench and along the double tire track that fronted the guest cabins and led to the old house at the far end. He stopped next to the front porch of the house but left the engine running.

"Thanks for the lift," Joe said, pulling the handle and pushing the door.

"No problem, brother," Bart said. He put out the cigarette and laid his big hand on Joe's shoulder. "You're gonna be all right, my man. It ain't easy coming back. I know it." Bart shook his shoulder. "But you'll be okay. You got family. Friends."

"Friends? Who's got friends?" Bart's hand was still on his shoulder, and he eyed it with mock irritation. And then there was Bart's face playing it up, taking the joke like he knew he would take it. He cracked up.

"Get out of here," Bart said. "Go on." And he pushed him toward the door. "Anyway, you're going back to Alaska in a few days, friend. Talk about end of the road."

Their eyes met and he nodded and then he got out. He still had something to say.

Bart looked across the seat out the window. "You gonna need a ride to Portland to catch your flight back?"

He closed one eye and looked in at Bart. "Nah. Got it covered."

Bart screwed his face into a question. "McKenzie?"

"Taking my old man's pickup. Going up to square things away with the *Jenny A.* Then I'm coming right back with my stuff. Like you said, my mom needs my help."

"When'd you decide that?"

"Just now." Then he poked his face in the Cherokee window. "Hey, what's that kid's name again?"

"Kid?"

"The Macy kid."

"Cody. Cody Macy. But you stay clear of him or any of his misfit family, trust me."

"Oh, I trust you, alright."

***

He got out at the lake house and stood in the clearing as the Cherokee heaved up the hill and out of earshot. He climbed the stairs to the porch, doing a clumsy job of being quiet. Everything so still except for Grace snoring in her living room chair. His head ached, and he got out the bottle that was in the outdoor cupboard. He sank into the deep Adirondack chair on the porch and poured bourbon into a glass.

The lake was still. The decision was made. He would stay and help Grace run the place. She needed him more than Alaska needed him. Fuck Howard's bullshit. Fuck this business with his father. All that weirdness up there in the cemetery—what was that all about? It was almost funny that he was running. Running from what? A dead man? How can you run from a dead man?

He poured another bourbon. He held it in his mouth and let it burn and let his tongue water. He was done thinking about his father. The yellow light on the porch was still burning, and kamikaze moths threw themselves at it with gusto. He got up and shut the light off and then sat back down in the silence. But there was still an ache in his gut, and he knew it was the hole that had been left by Jenny, black as burnt wood.

CHAPTER 6

He crossed the wooden bridge and walked up the old railroad bed until he reached a spot where the river ran deep against the riprap from the rail bed. The August heat had sent the trout to the deep holes. Knowing where they were didn't make it any easier to coax them out, especially the smart ones who'd seen it all before.

He was back in the Wallowas after going up to Sitka to put the *Jenny A.* up for sale and collect the rest of his stuff. He made a deal with Cuddyer to take over the payments and buy him out at the end of the season.

He'd spent all of Sunday after checkout and Monday morning cleaning the cabins, and he'd come down to do a little fishing and to get the river in him. Maybe get a little load on. In this section, the Wallowa canyon was narrow and steep, and the sun had already passed behind the canyon wall on the far side of the river. The rocks still held the heat of the day, and he sweated through his cap and t-shirt.

He sat on the end of a rail tie. There was the smell of heated creosote. The water was low but not too low for this time of year, when the irrigation district usually held more water behind the dam. The river swung around a bend above and then plowed into his side of the bank and ran straight down under the bridge before riffling and pooling again. Then it hit the highway riprap and passed out of sight around another bend.

He got on his haunches. A slot of calm water no wider than the length of a good-sized rainbow or two hugged the edge below him. The faster water slid by mottled and rippled, and where the two sections met there was a waving line and occasional bubbles. The trout would be right under that bubble line, waiting for the sight of a fly. He stayed there, keeping low so as not to spook any fish.

The cooling shade had brought out a hatch of stone flies. They flew drunkenly above mid-river, swirling in bunches and then dropping down to deposit their eggs on the surface film like helicopters playing a game of touch and go. One of them wandered off to the edge of the river. It had barely lighted on the water when a quicksilver flash shot from the olive water. When it was gone, the fly was gone, too, leaving only a few ripples and bubbles that floated down past him.

He retreated back to the railroad tie and picked up his rod. His heart was in his chest and the blood in his veins. He had learned to fish by studying his father. His father would read the water and look for what the fish were feeding on. His every step seemed deliberate. His few words were spoken quietly, evenly, with a quick sideways glance before returning to the task at hand: "Wait on your backcast," or "tip up" or "mend line."

Joe slowed his pace. Those were strong memories, short and happy. Then something changed in his old man. Or maybe nothing changed. Maybe it was his father's own shit that began bubbling up. Maybe it was always in him but just needed Joe to bring it out. Now it was like a knotted rope in his gut, and not even the river could wash it away or dissolve it. Going from dad's buddy to no-good teenaged son. Living with his old man got intolerable. His mother knew, and she tried protecting him from his father. She even lied to his old man about his drinking, making up excuses for him cutting school. But there was nothing he could do to get in the old man's good graces again.

He pulled the line through the guides until he had all of his leader and tippet out past the final guide. It was like he was trying to fit his heart through the wire guides.

His father had humiliated him in front of his friends or to his face, and he had laughed along with the jokes, trying go along. But inside it piled on the hurt. The put-downs. The comparisons to his suck-up brother. The "hurry it" or "do it over" or "what's wrong with you?" comments. The "you don't get that from the Wallace side of the family" bullshit. And yet, he was the one who'd saved his father's drunken butt all those times, covering up for his sorry ass.

He opened his fly box and picked out a stone fly imitation. He tied it on with a clinch knot and spit on it and pulled the free end taut and then snipped it with the cutting tool that hung from his vest.

Someone appeared on the tracks upstream, walking the crossties. The next river crossing wasn't for another five miles or so up by the old sawmill. Must have liked walking. He was wearing a khaki t-shirt, hiking boots and camo hiking shorts. A skinny kid in his early 20s, smoking a cigarette.

Joe started down to the water but then stopped and stood facing the river, his rod in one hand. When the kid approached, Joe turned and nodded.

"Kill any fish today?" the kid said. He smiled or maybe smirked.

Joe raised an eyebrow.

The kid drew deeply from his cigarette and held in the smoke. "Not that there's anything wrong with that," he said, blowing the words out with the smoke. "I mean, people should be able to catch fish and eat them. After all, the natives did it, right?"

The river was dark and silent. The canyon walls were losing light. The kid stood behind him, smoking. He could have told him to bug off, but he kept his mouth shut. He poked his thumbnail into the cork handle of the rod.

"Am I bothering you?" the kid said, and Joe turned. He waved his cigarette toward the river. He smiled and then he screwed his face into a serious look. "Mind if I ask you a question?"

Joe tested the rod a few times, whipping it with the fly still hooked to the cork handle. Then he put the butt-end on his boot and held the rod by the shank. Joe nodded. This kid was nothing if not bold. He had long, dark hair, olive skin and a wispy black beard.

"What are you fishing for?" he asked.

"Nothing yet." He smiled and thumbed his reel and ran the fingers of his free hand through his hair. He turned to face the kid, taking his time. "But that's a good question. What am I fishing for?" This smart-ass kid deserved a smart-ass answer. "The purpose of fishing is not to catch fish."

The kid lit up when he said it. "Hey, that's good. I'll have to remember that. 'The purpose of fishing is not to catch fish.'" He stood there looking at him as if he expected some other smart-ass comment from him. He made to step toward the river but the kid stuck out his hand before he could turn.

"River," he said.

He took his hand and shook it. It was long and bony and soft, cool as the underside of a rock. "Wallace. Joe Wallace," he said. "River? That a name?"

"It is now," he said, and he let go his hand. "So what is it?"

"What is what?"

River stood waiting. "The purpose of fishing, man."

He turned back toward the water. The river was silent but strong against the rocks. When he turned again, River was still looking at him. He shrugged. "Whatever you want it to be."

"Mind if I watch?"

He ignored the kid while he worked the reach between the bridge and the next upstream riffle. He caught two small brookies but no rainbows. They were in there but not interested. The kid said nothing. He returned to where River was sitting to put away his stuff.

River smiled. "You know something about fish," he said. "Did you know there used to be salmon in the lake? Until the dam shut them out?"

He placed the flies from his vest back into his father's old tackle box. "Sockeye? Actually, they were gone before the dam," he said. He kept working but he could see River out of the corner of his eyes.

"Sockeye. Where the name of town comes from, huh?" He was poker-faced. "What else do you know?"

Hard to know whether he was yanking his chain or actually cared. Joe got up and loosened the two ring nuts holding the reel. "I grew up on the lake," he said. "That dam's been there since the early nineteen-hundreds—1919, I think—and likely it'll be there until it falls down."

River reached in his shirt pocket and pulled out a pack of Pall Malls and held it out to him. Joe waved it off but his hand moved down to feel the bottle. "Not if we do something about it," River said. He flipped open the pack with his long thumb and slipped out a cigarette like it was a piece of chocolate from a sampler box and put it in his mouth with his delicate fingers.

River wasn't just some punk. His eyes were cold, the way he was studying him.

"You one of those monkeywrenchers?" Joe said. "People in town've been talking about them."

River laughed and pulled a lighter from a pocket. With his other hand he took the cigarette out of his mouth. "Monkeywrenchers, huh?" he said. He lit the cigarette, inhaled and then blew out the smoke, holding the cigarette in front of him to look at it. "You know what Kurt Vonnegut said about these? A classy way to commit suicide." He grinned.

"Pick your poison," Joe said. He had no idea who Kurt Vonnegut was. He slipped the reel into his pocket. Downstream, the river shone golden, reflecting the bald tops of the canyon walls, still lit in the late evening sun, the grass blonded now. "Where'd you say you're from?"

River said he'd heard about the dam and had come see it for himself. He called himself a "fish person." He couldn't tell a sockeye from a sucker. But he was all about bringing a sockeye run back to the lake. He'd done some research, he said, and he knew about the old sockeye runs and the Nez Perce. Said he wanted to show people how to get along without a dam, but seemed like the last guy in the world anyone around that valley would listen to.

The bottle was still there in his old man's tackle box. His mouth watered. He would wait this kid out, but who knew how much longer he would stick around? He opened the box and held the bottle out to River. "Beats that smoke," he said.

River took the bottle, tilted it and drank. He swallowed and shuddered and handed the bottle back. "Good. Look. Joe," River said. "I'm not one of those people. You know, they call them eco-terrorists so that they have an excuse to go after them like some of those nut-job so-called patriot groups. But they believe in what they're doing, at least, right? And I want to believe that what I'm doing can make a difference. That's all I'm trying to do. That's all anybody can ask for, isn't it?"

Joe nodded. "Sure," he said. "Sure."

He wiped the rim of the bottle with his hand before taking a pull, smoky caramel and vanilla going down and spreading through his body. They passed the bottle back and forth. After a few more pulls, everything was good.

The river slid by and the sun crawled away. "I'm gonna sit right here," he said. "Sit down. Come on." There was a boulder on the side of the rail bed that had fallen from the canyon wall. A train hadn't come through here since the mill had closed three years ago. He sat on the boulder and motioned for River to sit on the rail opposite the rock.

The kid sat. He chattered on about how other dams were going to come down around the Northwest. He said that bringing the fish back would be like bringing the Nez Perce back.

"Don't talk about bringing Nez Perce back around here if you want to make any friends," Joe said. "They like them in the history books, the movies or the rez. That's about it."

The kid said his partner was a Nez Perce, a woman.

"Oh yeah? What does she look like?"

River said that she was beautiful but that he wasn't interested in how she looked.

"Yeah, right," Joe said. "You're a guy, too. Got a girlfriend somewhere? This Nez Perce girl, she your girlfriend?" River narrowed his eyes, and it was like a cloud came over him.

"Don't mean nothing by it. I should keep my pie-hole shut."

"That's cool. You're not the only one who thinks that, just because we're together on this, it means we're together, you know?"

This kid was more than a kid. He could get people to do things, most likely, he could get people to follow along with him. Maybe not the locals, but some of the new people, the people who came out for the summer. The ones Howard sold land to but despised.

The white light of the day was draining away. "You're doing something you believe in," Joe said. The liquor made it easier. "I'm gonna tell you something. I have no idea what the fuck I'm doing. Only reason I came back was to bury my father. We put him in the ground a few weeks back."

River picked a piece of rail bed gravel and thumbed it. "I'm sorry." He said this flatly. He threw the rock, and the river swallowed it soundlessly. He had dark brown eyes that didn't go anywhere.

"We put his ashes in the ground but he's still out there." Joe waved the bottle. "Can't seem to get rid of him." He chose a piece of gravel, cut-edged and gray. River watched him. "He was a good man. Ask anybody. Nothing but good things to say about old Clark Wallace." He flipped the stone to the side.

River lit another cigarette. "Clark Wallace," River said, and blew smoke. "I know that name. Some of the documents I've seen. He was pretty involved around here. Your old man, huh?"

The sun was long gone from the canyon walls. Time was lost in the water and ran out of sight. He lay back with his head on the rusting rail, his hands cupped behind his skull. The sky was nothing but blue. He closed his eyes. "My old man, alright," he said. "Had his fingers in all sorts of stuff. He was quite a guy, a regular pioneer. Built our place from nothing. With his own hands. Raised us out here."

He opened his eyes. He raised up on his elbows. "Hey, where'd you go?" He turned and River was behind him, staring downriver.

River turned back toward him. His hands were in his pockets. "Thought you were falling asleep on me there for a second. Your old man. Sounds like mine, without the dirty hands. Not my dad. Brooks Brothers suits. Manicured nails. The University Club, Yale Club. Wanted me to argue with him just so he could win. A pillar of the community, like they say."

Joe moved his elbows under him like he would get up but then he laid his head back on the cool rail. He was 28 years old and he still didn't know what he wanted out of life, or what it wanted out of him. This River wanted something. All he'd wanted for as long as he could remember was to get away. From his father. From this place. His brother. He'd wanted a life with Jenny but she was gone. He worked to pull himself up on his elbows and looked around. He found the bottle empty and dropped his head back. "Shit."

River walked back to where Joe was lying and sat beside him on the rail. "That was good whiskey. Think I'm gonna have to keep walking and get clear again."

Joe smiled at the sky. "Sober is overrated."

River stood looking down at him. "Look, we're holding a meeting next Tuesday night at the Grange Hall," he said. "You have to come."

The rail bed gravel had begun to make its presence known in his butt. He sat. "AA? I'm not much for meetings."

"No." River offered him a hand up, and he took it. River's hand was as cool as the rails. Skinny as he was, he pulled Joe up with little effort. "We're going to be talking about how to reintroduce sockeye to the lake. Taking down that dam," River said as he let go of his hand. "Maybe that's something you could believe in. We need more locals. You could help us work with people around here."

Joe ran his fingers through his scalp and then rubbed his eyes and laughed. "That's one way not to work with people around here," he said. "Just blow it up and be done with it."

"That's what they think we want. See, that's why we need you." River picked up his pack and slung one strap around a shoulder. "You going to make it out of here okay?"

He was hollow and emptied but he straightened himself. "Don't worry about me." He looped his thumbs under his belt and closed his eyes. He swayed and then jerked his hands out, his eyes wide. "Whoa. Not going anywhere for a while. I'll just stay here and take a nap. Not a problem. You go ahead. Wherever the hell you're walking to."

River took a couple of steps and then stopped. "I do my best thinking here," he said.

"I do my best drinking here," Joe said, and then he bent to pick up the empty bottle. Then the sky and land shifted and he nearly fell but caught himself and cursed and then laughed.

River extended his hand to him, and he took it. "Good to meet you," he said.

"Likewise. Likewise."

River pumped his hand. "Next Tuesday at 7. Hurricane Creek Grange Hall. I'm counting on you."

"I'll think on it."

River walked away. "Don't fall asleep on the tracks. You might get run over."

He laughed. "By a goat, maybe," he said. River walked along the tracks going west until the bridge. Then he called out, "Just how far you plan on walking?"

River waved to him and called back but his voice merged with the sound of the rapids. He waved back. River disappeared where the rail bed bent with the channel.

The evening air had begun to cool, and the scent of the cooling rocks and the sage was in his nostrils. There was somebody standing in the water near where River had passed. Then there was nobody. It was his father. His father inhabited this place. Joe felt it when he'd come through that first day with McKenzie. He saw him now, up to his hips in the water, holding the fly rod clear.

How the hell could he get it right now with his father? Why did he think he had to?

He shook from the cold. He picked up the empty bourbon bottle and smashed it against the rail and it splintered in his hand and stung him but didn't cut him. He thought of cutting himself to feel the pain, because that would be real. He laughed. "Fuck it." He spit and swung his head. He tried getting his mind off his father but he was lying to himself if he thought he could. And then the thought occurred to him to say something. Really say something out loud, as stupid as that might seem.

"Dad?" Joe said. It sounded like he was talking to himself. He yelled louder, "Dad?!" Then louder. "You out there? Son of a bitch." His voice cracked and then it came out as sobs. When he stopped, there was only the sound of the river and the ache in his stomach. Why did he ache for people who were gone, who couldn't hold him anymore?

CHAPTER 7

Grace brewed coffee in the old blue porcelain pot. McKenzie and Howard and Bart had come for dinner. She produced a bottle of Kentucky sour mash with five tumblers. "Don't let an old bird drink alone," she said.

They sat at the table on the porch, and Grace poured the bourbon. Joe threw his down in one draw, and it helped loosen him. McKenzie poured coffee into the matching blue mugs.

"My favorite people in the world," Grace said. "My children, and that includes you, Bart."

"Mrs. W." Bart waved her off but grinned a sideways grin.

Bart produced his cigarettes. "Mind?"

"In fact—where are mine?" Grace said, and then found her cigarettes. Bart lit hers first.

"Got another call from one of those developer types the other day," she said. "Might as well print up maps and brochures and put them down at the Chamber of Commerce."

Howard took the toothpick out of his mouth and pointed at Grace. "I've told you before, ma. We're sitting on a gold mine," he said. "One hundred and sixty acres of some of the most prime real estate in the state, if not the Northwest. Who was it?"

"No idea. Charlie or Bill or Sam somebody." She ran a hand along her stiff-sprayed hair. "All the same to me. They all want what we have, and they all have dollar signs dancing in the eyes."

Howard folded his arms and leaned back. "Dollar signs make the world go 'round."

McKenzie put her hand up. "Let's keep politics out of it."

"It's not politics," Howard said. He twisted his face into a smile. "It's money."

"One and the same," McKenzie said. She sipped her coffee.

"You sound like him," Howard said. "You people allergic to money?"

Grace rolled her eyes. "Save your lecture, son." She pulled her sleeves over her wrists and brushed her pants as though she were whisking crumbs from her lap. She held her cup out to Bart. "A dram for the madame."

Bart poured. "Who else?" he said, and he held the bottle up. He trickled a shot into Grace's mug, then Joe's and his own.

Howard covered his mug and gave a quick shake of his head. But he took a generous second slice of pie with more coffee. "This is good," he said through a full mouth. "You know," he bounced his fork in his hand, "we are blessed."

"Amen, brother," Bart said.

Howard picked at his teeth and nodded. "We're blessed with this land. We own it outright. It's ours to do with—."

Grace raised one finger and cocked her head. "Hold your horses. We *are* blessed, yes. This land's been in our family a long, long time."

"Ma," Howard started.

Joe held his palm up at Howard, and Howard flinched. "She has the floor."

Grace hardened her jaw. "It's my name that's on that deed now. I own these one hundred and sixty acres, not you or your brother or sister. So don't go counting your chickens." Grace wagged her finger but laughed. "I'm not dead yet."

"Mother," Howard chided.

"Oh, quit your prevaricating," she said. "I'll be dead soon enough, and then you'll get what you've got coming to you. And not a day sooner."

"Sheesh, ma," McKenzie waved her hands in dismissal. "Nobody's dying around here, least of all you."

Joe slid his tumbler toward McKenzie and nodded to her and then at the bottle. "Hold on," he said to Howard. "Before you start platting it out with hotels and condos, that's a decision that goes beyond you. Way beyond." McKenzie ignored his silent plea for bourbon. "Besides, there's the little matter of the zoning. You can't subdivide this property the way it's zoned. Hand me that bottle, would you, sis?"

Howard smirked, pointing the toothpick. "Suddenly you're the conscience of the family? And who said anything about subdividing? Please don't give me the argument that we're just caretakers of the land. Because if that's the case we might as well just donate our land to the Democrats in Salem and invite in the Sierra Club, and we can keep mom here in the house and they can all tramp in to the Wallace family museum and peek in her windows to see how quaint it used to be out here."

"They'll come down with a bad case of buckshot in the ass if they do," Grace said.

Howard nodded. "Mom knows her Second Amendment."

"I'm sure they would, too." Bart chuckled, snapping his head emphatically. Even Howard chuckled. But Howard never let go. Everything was personal with him. He was wound as tight as a preacher's ass.

The heat of the day had bled out of the rocks and trees, and the cool night air flowed down the moraine. McKenzie got up and offered more coffee around. Joe reached for the bottle and refilled his glass. Then he held the bottle out to the others.

Grace pushed her tumbler forward. "Just a touch," she said. "And then the bar's closing." She took the glass and eyed the liquid and then drank its contents in one sip. She sat back.

McKenzie laid the coffee pot on the table. "You guys are so pathetic," McKenzie said. "It's like listening to one of those radio talk shows with the people who are always up in arms about their rights."

Grace smiled at Bart. "You're the only one with any sense here," she said. "Should we just sell this place and get out and be done with it? Enjoy our fortune?"

Bart thumbed the rim of his coffee mug. He pulled up his jaw. He lit another cigarette.

McKenzie held out her hands. "You didn't ask me," she said, smiling.

"Count yourself lucky, sister," Bart said. "No way I'm gonna take sides, Mrs. W. It's true what you say about the developers. I've seen more fat cats driving through here in the past year than yellow jackets on a dead coyote. Seen that Wenaha Ranch friend of yours, too, Howard. Might have to consider opening a Mercedes and BMW repair shop in town."

Grace laughed. "They drive those big rigs out here—what do they call them—STDs?"

"Very funny, mom. They're SUVs, and you know it," Howard said.

"SUVs, IOUs, it's all the same, and you can tell it really breaks them up to get them dirty. They're all over at the car wash like it was the state fair and they were getting ready to show Bossie."

Howard sighed and crossed his arms. "Just business people looking for an honest opportunity," he said. "We ought to be rolling out the red carpet for them as far as I'm concerned. Instead, we're throwing up roadblocks. Tell me the last time people with money showed any interest in this county."

"What about those yuppies?" Joe said.

"There you go with the yuppies again," Howard said.

Howard had gotten worse with his free enterprise bullshit, and Joe couldn't abide it. "I'll tell you," Joe said. "It was when the feds told the timber companies and the mining companies and the ranchers to come on in and take what they wanted."

Howard dug the toothpick into the back of his mouth and groaned. "What in the Lord's name propaganda have you been reading?" he said. "I happen to be one of those ranchers, and I haven't exactly seen Uncle Sam helping me make money. I have seen him tell me where I can't run my cattle and how I am supposed to look the other way when a wolf comes loping in from Idaho and mauls a calf."

"If you're a rancher," Joe said, "I'm a goddamned banker."

Grace slammed the table, and that shut them up. "None of that Alaska language at this table. I've about had enough." She folded her arms across her chest. "I'm no fan of our federal government either, but all of sudden, they're the ones to blame for this mess? When we've been feeding from the federal trough for years?"

Howard's cheeks flushed, and he pasted on his shit-eating grin. "Now you? We've let them have too much."

Grace wagged a spoon. "I don't get this notion that the government is suddenly the bad guy. Who makes up this nonsense?" She got up and cleared dishes. "We're the damn government."

"Sit ma," McKenzie said, and she grabbed plates.

"I'll do what I damn well please," Grace said. "I can't sit long anyway." She could be a martyr, and now she was getting cranky, too. Maybe it was her age, or maybe she was in pain. But Grace couldn't tolerate inaction or indecision.

Joe stood and took the plates from McKenzie and a few more. "That's right, ma," he said. "He's full of shit, and he knows it."

McKenzie grabbed his wrist and stuck her face close. "Mom asked you to be civil."

He faked an evil glare for a moment at her and at her hand on his wrist. "Fine."

"Don't fine me," she said, and she squeezed his wrist until her knuckles blanched. She let go and moved on, collecting dishes.

The long August twilight lit the western sky.

Howard pushed around his empty mug. He turned to Bart. "What about these stories you hear? Threats to blow up the dam. Anything to them?"

Bart stretched and yawned. "Y'all don't want to hear what's really just a bunch of rumors, anyway. Let's have some of that cobbler."

McKenzie spooned the dessert on his plate. "There were those Forest Service fires set last year by those—." she said.

"Monkeywrenchers?" Bart said.

"Yeah, monkeywrenchers," she continued. "I've heard the talk, too. People say they want to take down the dam."

"What dam? Who's taking down a dam?" Grace said.

"The lake dam," Joe said.

Grace waved her finger. "That old dam? It's almost older than me. Already been condemned. Got more leaks than an old lady in a nursing home."

McKenzie laughed. "It *is* older than you."

"Not by much," Joe said. "Met one of them the other day."

"What do you mean, you met one of the them the other day?" Howard said.

He held his cobbler over his coffee and watched a few crumbs fall into the mug. "I was down in the canyon fishing, and along comes this scrawny kid walking the tracks. So he starts in talking, and right off he tells me he's trying to bring back the sockeye to the lake and did I want to get involved because they need more locals."

Howard yanked the toothpick out of his mouth and sat up straight. "What did he look like? Did you tell Bart?"

He sipped at his coffee. "I'm telling him now," he said. "And I'm telling you now, he wasn't carrying a monkey wrench. He wasn't even carrying a fishing pole. And if he was, I'm not sure he'd know which end to fish from, no less how to blow off a cap of dynamite."

But Howard was captivated. "Maybe you should have someone keep an eye on this guy," Howard said to Bart.

"Oh, God," McKenzie laughed. "I can just see it now, Bart. You in one of those fake nose things with the moustache and glasses."

Bart looked sideways at Grace. "Mrs. W., you've got some time on your hands for tracking people?"

She dismissed him with a wave of her hand and laughed. "That's all we need. You know, I don't think you've got to appoint anybody to that post. Anyone new or different comes in to this valley, they stand out like a rack of antlers on a cow."

"Ain't that the truth," Bart said from the side of his mouth.

"He asked me to come to their next meeting," Joe said.

McKenzie continued to laugh. "Maybe you should be the spy, then, Joe," she said. "Get yourself a wig and a dress."

Howard was unmoved. "What'd you tell them?" He picked at his teeth and looked at him.

"Said I'd think about it," he said.

"Think about it?" Howard said. "You can't be serious."

"Why the hell not?" he said.

"They're outsiders," Howard said. "They wouldn't know the difference between the rear end of a cow and the——."

"The what?" He laughed.

"You guys are a sorry bunch," McKenzie said. "Why don't we leave it there? I've got to drive Howard home yet and I've got a five a.m. wakeup. Ma, I know you're just getting started, but do you mind if we call it a night?"

"Bar's closed," Grace said. "It's time for this old biddy to hit the hay."

***

Joe and Grace watched the cars pull away.

"You want to sit some more?" he asked his mother. "Maybe a nightcap?"

"I've had plenty of excitement for one night," she said. "You go ahead."

She turned and walked to the door but he said, "You see what he's doing."

She looked over her shoulder. "He's been platting the whole thing out in his head since he was 16 years old, Joseph. It's nothing new."

"He's dead serious."

"You know your brother. Born without a funny bone. He means well. Always has been full of numbers, that boy. Never was much for sentimentality. Sees land the way he sees any object, animate or inanimate. It has a price tag, and the more you fix it up, the more it's worth. So why not get the most you can for what you've got, is the way he thinks. I suppose it's the way to go."

He leaned back against the porch railing. "Sure you don't want a little nip?"

"You trying to get an old lady snockered?"

"Maybe. It wouldn't hurt you none. Here." He took the old Pendleton blanket from the back of the Adirondack chair. "Sit."

She groaned when she sat. He opened the blanket on her lap and then got another blanket and placed it on her shoulders. He ambled to the house and returned with a bottle of B&B and two snifters. He poured a finger of the caramel-colored liquor into both glasses and handed one to her.

"To this house," he toasted, and they touched glasses.

"To this house," she said. Then she squinted at him. "What's on your mind?"

He inhaled. "Oh, nothing. Plenty."

"You've been drinking. You can't hide from me."

"I could give you plenty of excuses."

"Let me tell you something," she said. She sat back and closed her eyes. "What's past is past. There's nothing we can do to bring it back or change it. Your father made mistakes."

"Mom," he said. "It ain't him."

"Let me finish," she said, looking at him. "I left him for a time. I never told you that."

"When? Was it me?"

"We all have our ghosts. They were creeping up on him. His father, your grandfather Wallace. I suppose you made him out to be a hero. He lost his swagger later on, but he was an old bastard. Your father worshipped him. I saw it repeat with you. Your father's son. When you started the drinking and you stopped worshipping the ground he walked, he couldn't abide it. In his heart, he knew he failed you, but he couldn't bring himself to admit it. Then it was too late, at least by his reckoning. You were gone, and he blamed himself."

"Did you?"

"He was miserable after you left," she said. "Miserable to be around him. It got so bad, I couldn't take it. I don't assign blame anymore."

"You visited Aunt Janie that year."

"That's the story." She sipped the brandy. "I took McKenzie and spent that first winter you were gone in Arizona with my sister. Your brother could take care of himself. Your father got himself good and drunk and wallowed in it for some time. That spring, he drove straight through in the station wagon and took us home. Never touched a drop of alcohol again. He made me a promise, and he kept his word."

"But why, mom? Why couldn't he do that with me?"

"I don't know. Fathers and sons. All that stuff you men hold in. You can waste your life wishing it were different. Or you can put it behind you."

"Easy for you to say," he said.

"No. Not easy."

CHAPTER 8

The white grange building sat where Hurricane Creek came flashing headlong out of the mountains.

In the parking lot there were three cars: a beat-up Volvo sedan, a newer Subaru Outback station wagon with a kayak strapped to its roof racks and a dusty seventies vintage Ford F-100 pickup with Idaho plates. The Ford had a bumper sticker on the fender for the Chief Joseph & Warrior Memorial Powwow in Lapwai. He might not go in. He didn't owe anybody anything.

By 6:15, there were a dozen other cars. Maybe 18 people sat in folding chairs facing a table in the front of the plain room. Three people sat behind the table, shuffling papers. One was River, wearing the same fatigues from the day they'd met on the Wallowa. To River's left was a clean-cut guy in a pressed short-sleeve shirt; likely the owner of the kayak and Subaru. Which left the Idaho pickup to the young woman on River's right. Indian—Nez Perce, by the bumper sticker.

He sat in the back, leaving open the possibility of a fast, quiet getaway. Some people nodded his way, people he didn't know. A little too much like a church service. But River's face lit up when he saw Joe. River gave him a thumbs-up and a nod, and Joe nodded his way.

The woman wore her black hair parted in the middle with two double-knotted braids running out of sight below the table. Her skin was cinnamon against her blue denim shirt. She looked up. He lowered his gaze to his hands.

When he raised his head, she was still looking at him. She didn't smile, and she didn't frown, either. But he noticed the upturned corners of her lips before she turned away to her business. It was ridiculous of him to even be wondering if she was interested.

River was in charge. The woman sat quietly with her arms crossed in front of her. The guy turned out to be a biologist from Portland who was smart and well-spoken on the topic of salmon, although Joe found himself turned off by his polished presentation, prep-school haircut and gold wire-rim glasses, a sort of John Denver version of a scientist. Both River and the biologist made a case for restoring the sockeye run to the lake and—blasphemy to seemingly everyone in Sockeye—the removal of the Wallowa Lake dam.

A couple of rowdies in fatigues—guys that might've been vets but were now that curious breed of hippie and don't-tread-on-me wingnut—stood. The one with a bush for a beard said, "We ought to blow it up."

River stood and raised his hands. "I appreciate your passion, friends," he said. "But that kind of talk can only get us in trouble. There's enough people in the community who mistrust us as it is, and we really need folks here to see we're not against them. We need to include a diversity of people in our campaign, and so, come on, tone it down, sit down and please, let's have some respect for each other, okay? And," River made a show of looking to both sides of him and behind him, and then lowered his voice in mock confidentiality. "We're frankly concerned about police infiltrators. You guys aren't narcs, are you?"

River laughed, and the rest of the audience followed along, including the two hippie vets.

"Sorry, man," the shouter said. "Out of line."

"Not a problem," River said. He introduced the woman next to him, and confirmed what he'd guessed about the rez. She was short when she stood, but she looked powerful, her arms muscular, her middle solid. She held her hands by her side.

"River's right. I'm Nez Perce. Which means my folks are from around here, going back. Maybe you know something of the story—the treaty that Joseph and the others wouldn't sign, the forced removal from this valley, all the *Bury My Heart* bullshit."

Nobody twitched. She had a presence, as best as he could figure, some kind of authority about her that made people shut up and listen.

"I won't go into all the failed promises that the government made, except one," she said. "They promised we could harvest the salmon forever, but then they built the dams and allowed the destruction of the habitat and the overfishing to continue. Which brings us to today."

The rush of the creek outside filled the room when she stopped talking. He felt light, the bone memory of a feeling he'd forgotten about.

"We can't undo history," she continued, and her eyes brightened. She brought her hands up in fists by her shoulders. "But we've got an opportunity to make it. We can't restore the past. But we can surely restore a little balance. We can bring them back to where the bones of their ancestors lie. That's a cause worth sacrifice, including the sacrifice of an obsolete dam. The dam can come down, and the sockeye can return."

She stood gazing calmly. And when people applauded, she pursed her lips and nodded. It was like she expected the reaction and maybe even found some satisfaction in it, but she was ready to move past it and on to business. He clapped, too, and then he stood when the others stood and continued to clap. She then put up a hand to quiet them and turned to sit. The group hushed the way a class of first-graders can be corked with one look from their teacher.

He half-listened to the rest. He kept stealing glances at her. It was weird to be so mesmerized by any woman, but then, she didn't seem like any other woman.

A sign-up sheet passed around. He read it, took the pen and signed it. Why not? It didn't commit him to anything. He could always turn down requests later. But he might as well get on their list.

A few people milled around the front table. River, the woman and the biologist gathered papers into folders. He was in no hurry to leave. He approached River, and as he did, her face opened to him.

"Thanks for coming," she said. She extended her hand. "Ana."

Her hand was small and thick, strong and warm. "I liked what you had to say," he said. "There were a few interesting things."

"Just a few?" she asked. She squinted and crooked her lips.

He didn't expect her to be playful. "No, I said 'some,' not 'a few. Some is more than a few."

River touched her shoulder. "How'd you like our evangelist?" he said. "I always have Ana talk right before we pass the hat."

"That sounds crass," Ana said. He thought he saw her bristle when River touched her. "But you're right. We used to have Bake close out the meetings."

She smiled at the biologist, who grinned and ran his hand through his sandy hair. He stabbed his open hand at Joe. "Bake. Afraid the scientists leave them cold," he said.

"Joe. Joe Wallace," he said, but he found himself smiling like an idiot at Ana. He tried to say something smart but could not find words. He mentioned that he signed up for the mailing list.

"Hey man, good to have you," River said. "Maybe you could bring along some of your friends or family members next time."

"That's a tall order," he said. "I'm lucky I don't get tarred and feathered for this myself."

He asked what he could do and he carried a box of documents out to the parking lot. They stopped next to Ana's pickup.

"It takes courage to do this, I know," Ana said.

River stood near her shoulder. "It takes balls, and we're glad you got them, man. It's good to have a local on board," he said. River reached for her again but then stopped short of her shoulder.

"Who are you calling a local?" she said. "I was a local before he was a local." She laughed. And then she shook his hand again and thanked him for coming. He flushed and his stomach caught and he couldn't hold his gaze.

After Ana and River left and the parking lot emptied, he walked to the creek. It had settled some as the day wore out and the snowmelt slowed. He would be back again. The possibility of restoring a sockeye run to the lake had never occurred to him. Now it seemed like a thing he had to do. He'd seen old photos of the huge sockeye catch at the lake. The idea took hold in his mind. He remembered that upriver bright he'd caught at the Deschutes mouth with his dad. He remembered how he'd felt when he looked in the salmon's eyes. Even back then, he'd had a connection, something beyond the everyday. Maybe this would be how he paid it back.

But it was more. He wanted to see Ana again. She did something to him that he hadn't felt since Jenny. It was like being stuck in fog for days and then suddenly coming out into the perfectly blue clear light.

He drove past the airstrip and the rodeo grounds. Something about River. The way he'd touched her like he was trying to signal possession. Joe felt protective about her, even though he had no right and she looked amply capable of taking care of herself. For all he knew, they had something between them. He certainly had no claim on her. There was more to River than what met the eye.

CHAPTER 9

A September windstorm had blown out of the mountains, and it sent boats and docks flying. The morning after, he called Howard to come up and help him work on their dock, which had pulled loose and had to be retrieved from the north shore of the lake. Howard got in a dig on the phone about the sockeye restoration. "Maybe you should just let nature take its course with the dock," Howard said. "It might be bad for the fish."

"Don't try and get out of it," he said. "Get your ass up here."

Howard arrived Saturday morning wearing his designer jeans and polished boots and chewing on his ever-present toothpick. His Suburban looked newly washed. "I've got a meeting in town," he said.

He eyed him. "Well, one of us has got to get in the water," he said. "Don't you ever get that thing dirty?"

Howard walked to the edge of the bluff overlooking the lake. The dock bobbed in the water below, tethered by a rope. "You already got it. Why do you need me anymore?"

Joe stood behind Howard, pulling a rope out of the utility box. "Because we still have to rechain it to the weights, smart-ass. It broke them, too." Howard still wasn't satisfied. "Why don't I just start up the boat and grab the dock from it. That way, nobody has to get wet."

He started down the trail cut into the side of the bank. "Jesus," he said, shaking his head. He stopped mid-way and turned back to face Howard. "You coming or not?" He didn't wait for an answer, but soon Howard was muttering and coming down behind him.

When he got to the lake, he pulled off his work boots and took off his shirt and waded in the water in his jeans up to his waist. The water was starting to lose the little summer warmth on the surface. He gritted his teeth and reminded himself that this would've felt like bathwater up in Bristol Bay. "Throw me that," he said, not bothering to point out any rope in particular.

Howard stood with his hands on his thighs. He was gasping for air, and a wet stain showed through his shirt. "What rope? I don't see a rope," he said, and then he looked behind him and found it.

"I can't believe you're meeting with that bunch of wacko environmentalists," Howard said. "You know this is getting around, don't you?"

Joe fixed one end of the rope to the dock. "Ask me if I care," he said. "Pull."

Howard pulled and the dock drifted toward him.

"That's your problem," Howard said. "You don't seem to realize what's at stake. Or maybe you really don't care."

"I don't," he said, and he waded out of the water and came around to where Howard was pulling in the dock. He stood dripping on the lakeshore trail. "What's at stake is you're planning to run for county commission is what," he said. "You want to get your ass elected, and somehow this doesn't fit the story too nicely. Here, now get in the boat and we're going to have to get that hook on the chain that broke loose. You can see it down there."

The chain lay in 18 feet of water, easily visible. Howard leaned from the dock onto the bow of the boat and tested for purchase with his foot. Then he labored his ass over the gunwale, trying to make it look easy but grunting the whole way. He plopped on the front bench of the boat and wiped his brow with his shirt sleeve. He sat panting. When he got his breath, he slid his butt aft. "Okay," he said, puffing. He pulled out the choke on the Evinrude and yanked three times on the starter and then pushed the choke back in. The motor started after two more pulls. His shirt was soaked. Howard didn't have to go far. He positioned the boat over the chain. Then he swiveled and took hold of another chain with a grappling hook on the end and lowered it over the gunwale. The water was so clear that it was hard to see the spot where the chain penetrated the water's film.

"Don't fall in and get your pretty clothes all wet," he shouted over the sputtering of the outboard.

"Huh?" Howard cupped his ear. He cut the engine and let the boat drift.

Joe dismissed what he'd said with a wave. "Nothing."

"Don't you see what these people want?" Howard said, moving his head side to side to get a better view of the chain on the bottom. "I don't think you do.

You think they'll stop when they get their first win? You think it's just about putting the nice little fishies back in the lake? Come on. They don't give a hoot about that. You think the fish are endangered? How about us?"

"Just keep at it there," he said.

"I got it," Howard said.

"Pull then," he said.

"You think they really care about our way of life?" Howard said.

"Now we have a way of life," he said.

"Oh, come on," Howard said. The chain banged across the aluminum of the boat as Howard pulled it in. "You don't think they'd be happy to see us gone? They've already practically shut down the woods. They'd like to run us out of Hells Canyon for good." He started up the outboard again.

"And now they want the lake back for the fish," he shouted over the outboard as he maneuvered the boat back into the slip. "It wouldn't bother them … saw every last one of us gone … come into this town and put up their—." He couldn't make out what Howard was saying. Not that it mattered.

Howard threw him a line and Joe hitched it to the cleat on the dock. Howard picked up the heavy rusted chain, the other end of which was attached to a concrete slab on the bottom of the lake. He handed the chain to Joe, and Joe walked it over to a piece of rebar he'd driven into the bank.

"Don't kid yourself," Howard said, still sitting in the boat. "You're not one of them. They're just using you. You think they don't know your family owns 160 acres of prime lake real estate? Man, you are so naïve, little brother. Where the hell have you been all your life?"

"You done yet?" he said. He slipped the chain over the protruding rebar and started back to the dock. "Or should I just cut the line and tie you to the boat?"

Howard rolled himself out of the boat and labored back onto his feet on the dock. He brushed off his jeans and looked at his boots.

"And don't tell me you don't care," Howard said. He moved his toothpick to the other side of his mouth. "You better care. Because when the sheriff that they voted in comes knocking on your door to tell you to get off your land because the government that they bought just exercised its right to eminent domain, you better believe it matters now whose side you're on. Because that's what it comes down to, as far as I'm concerned. Them against us. Power against power. And whoever's got the land and the money's got the power."

Joe sat on the dock with his arms around his knees. The sun warmed his muscled back and shoulders. His waist size hadn't changed since high school. He laughed. "So, what are you so worried about? You're the one with the goddamned power."

Howard lifted a finger. "Okay, let me ask you this," he said. "Who's the biggest landowner in the county?"

He stretched out on the dock, his head resting on a life jacket. He crossed his arms over his stomach and closed his eyes.

"The Forest Service owns most of this county," Howard said. "There was a time when we pretty much owned the Forest Service. You know that. But you haven't been around here to see the changes. The environmentalists may still think the Forest Service is a pawn of the big bad loggers and ranchers, but the fact is that the courts are running it, or maybe it'd be more accurate to say that the courts have shut it down.

"If the woods are shut down, and the ranches are shut down, this place becomes a playground for people from Portland. We lose. We're history. So, brother of mine, think about that next time you go to one of your little meetings with your environmentalist friends."

Howard's shadow moved across him, and as he squinted his eyes open, he waited for Howard to step over him. Two seconds later, Howard was thrashing in the water beside the dock, sputtering. "Son of a gun!" Howard screamed. "Dang you!"

Joe stood watching and laughing, hands on his hips. "Don't you be cussing," he said. "It wouldn't be Christian-like of you."

He extended a hand, but Howard spiked the water with his arm. "You just wait," Howard yelled. "You've got yours coming. Just wait."

He laughed and started up the trail to the house. "Okay," he said. "I'll be waiting." He stopped. Howard was sitting on the rocks emptying his boots. "I'll tell my friends you said hello," he said, and he walked away.

***

At the following Tuesday night's meeting of the sockeye restoration group, he waited and looked for Ana. River said nothing about her until the meeting started, and then only that "something had come up" and she wouldn't be there.

At a break, he waited to buttonhole River. He tried saying it nonchalantly. "What's up with Ana?" he said.

River grinned at him, and he knew he must not have done a very good job of hiding his concern. "Look, it's pretty clear you have a thing for her," River said. "That's cool. That can happen."

He wanted to punch him. "What the hell are you talking about?" he said.

River momentarily flinched, stiffening his jaw and pulling back his head. Then, like turning off a switch, he let himself settle into a relaxed pose. "Whoa, man. I was just making an observation," he said. "You seem to dig her. And who knows? Maybe she digs you, too. Let's just remember we've got some important work to do here."

River started to turn away from him, but he caught River's arm and gently squeezed it. "That's my business," he said. "It's got nothing to do with you or this committee."

River returned his stare with a detached grin. His eyes were opaque. "That's exactly what I'm saying."

Joe grinned. "No, I think what you're saying is, you don't like it."

River pulled away. He rubbed his arm. "That's some grip you've got there, cowboy. Remind me not to get in a fight with you." He laughed. "Look, man, relax. You've got me all wrong. I'm on your side."

"Okay," he said. He inhaled and blew out. There were some familiar faces in the room, the young guys in their camo, the older folks in their catalog clothes. "So where is she?"

River walked away again but then stopped and turned. "Left me a message. Some family emergency up on the rez."

He tried acting cool, but this threw him. "Family emergency? Did she say what it was?"

River was laid-back and spoke as he was walking back to the front table. "Nothing, man," he said. "Just a family emergency and she'd be back when she could."

After the meeting, he drove to Ana's place out on the high fields east of town. He walked around the back and looked in. The house was clean except for a few dishes left in the drying rack next to the sink and a pot on the stove. He sat on the back porch and looked south up into the high Wallowas. She'd given him hope, but now he saw he'd spun the story himself.

He leaned back against a porch post, folded his arms across his chest and closed his eyes. His stomach was so tight it ached. He thought hard and tried to keep things clear, tried to slow his thoughts. He tapped his foot fast and then noticed it and stopped. He'd lost Jenny. He'd lost his father. Now there was Ana. Had he lost her before anything had even begun? For the first time since he'd been back from Alaska, he had a thought that surprised him. He missed his father. Or the idea of it. To have a father he could talk to about the things that fathers and sons might talk about. He would've liked Ana. She had guts and smarts, heart and soul. He would've loved her. And goddamn, it hurt that they'd never meet. There was an emptiness in his gut. He opened his eyes and squinted in the brightness, the sun's angle lower now, tilting south over the mountains. The mountains as silent as the urn that held his father's ashes. He pictured his father in his plane again, when he was a kid. His old man, so full of life then. To have that feeling, that must've been something. To have a thing you loved doing, and to do it. To have something worth living for. Was it too much to want, or too late to have?

He could not let Ana go. This much he knew. He would not let that happen. Anything but that.

On the way home, he passed the turnoff for the cemetery. He slowed the truck and pulled over and sat, the engine running. Then he looked in the rear view and drove to the lake house.

CHAPTER 10

Joe began cutting off work on the cabins early to walk the dam or read what he could get his hands on about sockeye, habitat restoration, dam bypass systems, dam removal. He drove in to the county library, a place he hadn't set foot in since grade school. Ana knew about a couple of fisheries biologists who'd been hired by the tribe to study the potential for restoring a lake sockeye run. He got a hold of a report, and it confirmed what he figured: You could bring sockeye back, alright, but there was a huge price to pay. He contacted one of the authors, Norm Kramer, and met him at the dam.

Kramer had the build of an ex-jock—massive chest, thick thighs and beefy arms—with quick eyes and a restless, never-sit-down way about him. He didn't seem to have anything invested in the sockeye, one way or another. He was a scientist, and his job was to discover and lay out the facts, although he didn't mind giving his opinion. But he soon saw Kramer's aloofness as a pose. In fact, underneath it all, he thought, Kramer cared a hell of a lot about salmon. He was just not going to show it, and certainly not to some stranger. Kramer had heard there was a group advocating removing the dam. "Good luck with that," he said, laughing. He had the sarcasm of someone who'd spent a lot of time in the trenches dealing with bureaucrats, politicians and power brokers.

The dam was beginning to spill water for irrigation, and they had to shout over the rush of water booming through the outlet at the base.

The possibility of restoring the sockeye run was "crazy," Kramer said. Never mind that the original run was extinct. The question was whether there even existed a sockeye stock now to do what the Wallowa Lake run had done. "It's 792 miles from Astoria to this fucking lake," Kramer said. "That's a climb of four thousand, three hundred and eighty-three fucking feet. Without eating. And at the end, you've got to fight for a lady and then fuck your brains out."

Kramer was as salty as any Alaskan fisherman he had met. He was the kind of guy they needed in River's group. Someone who could shoot the shit with the boys down at the Bucksaw or the Glacier Tap and hold his own but who absolutely knew his stuff. In other words, the opposite of River.

"They gotta get over this dam first," he shouted.

"That's the least of their worries," Kramer shot back.

They started back to their trucks, Kramer explaining that the dam would have to be modified with a fish ladder or some other way to get fish past it, coming and going.

"Or you could just take it out," Joe offered. "Just kidding."

"That's what that merry band of pranksters you're hanging with are all about," Kramer said. "You must be drinking the fucking Kool-Aid, brother. Especially someone like you, with property on the lake? You take out the dam, you leave everyone's docks up in the fucking air. That ought to go over real big at the family Fourth of July picnic. I'm surprised they haven't strung you up yet or that River pal of yours and run him the hell out of this town."

He laughed. "That could be coming."

They arrived at Kramer's truck. He put his hand out, and Kramer shook it.

"Appreciate it," he said.

"Not a problem," Kramer said, and he got in the cab of the truck and started the engine. He rolled down the window. "I don't mean to be such an asshole. Look, don't get me wrong. It's complicated but it isn't impossible. But it's more than getting some fish past a dam, or around it. You're gonna have to regulate water flow so there's enough of it, and it's good and cold, when they're coming and going. You're gonna have to screen the irrigation ditches in the river below the dam. It's all in the report."

"They're pretty convinced it's got to go," Joe said. "The dam."

"Oh hell," Kramer said. "I'd take it out tomorrow if I could. But I need this job. Keep at it. The more you do, the more reports I'll have to do. I call that job security."

"We could use your help to tone those guys down," Joe said.

"Good luck, friend. I've got to go."

Joe stayed at the dam after Kramer left. It was a mass of concrete and steel, nothing more, nothing less.

CHAPTER 11

The door opened and it was Bart, backlit by the bright daylight. "I saw the pickup."

Joe had come in to town to pick up nails and paint from the general store and a few groceries. He hadn't planned on stopping in at the Glacier Tap Room.

Bart still had his Stetson on.

"You gonna have a drink?" Joe said. "Either that, or I have to get me a different rig. Go undercover."

Bart put a pack of Marlboros on the bar along with his hat. "On duty," he said. He picked up the cigarettes and tamped the pack in his hands like a ballplayer punching his mitt and then pulled one out with his long fingers and lit it and blew out the smoke. An old Ray Price song played on the jukebox, a song Joe remembered hearing on his dad's radio when he was a kid. Like most of the records on that jukebox, it had been there for as long as he had been coming in to the Tap Room. A bony, scarlet-faced patron sat on a stool at the far end of the bar, smoking, nursing a beer and looking straight ahead with the detached look of a regular, or at least a regular to this kind of a bar on a hot Tuesday afternoon in the middle of September. But it was not someone he recognized, a sign that he had been gone that long or that there were new people showing up in Sockeye, even new drunks.

Duffy came in from the back to a smoking cigarette in an ashtray. He'd gotten grayer and more stooped. "Bart," Duffy said. "You drinking for yourself or the town?"

"There's not much difference," Bart said. "Make it a Diet Coke."

They sat through the song about the kid and the old man, "Desperados Waiting for a Train." Bart sipped his Coke. He finished his cigarette and stubbed it out in the ashtray. He picked up his hat and smoothed the leather band.

"You just got here," Joe said.

"Gotta go."

Joe held the empty glass up to the bar light. "Go ahead if you want to. I am not thy brother's keeper." He laughed and watched Bart through the bar mirror.

It was hard to tell what Bart was looking at. Duffy unloaded the dishwasher and stacked glasses. Then Duffy walked down and took away the regular's glass and gave him a new one and filled it. Bart got up to go but then stopped and sat back. "Your sister sent me in here after you."

He looked across his shoulder at Bart. "She's a nurse," he said. "It's her job to worry about people. Talk about her brother's keeper."

Bart fingered his hat. "She's got more sense than I'll ever have, McKenzie," Bart said. "Maybe you should listen to her every now and then."

He shrugged and briefly opened his hands.

"Well?" Bart said.

"What do you think?" he said.

"I think she should be worried," Bart said.

Then Joe picked up his glass and slammed it down. "You know, the service in this place has gone downhill," he said, loud. "I may have to go somewhere else where they keep you filled up and they don't let the local constable harass the patrons."

Duffy made to move but then shot a glance at Bart and stopped. "Clientele's gone downhill, too," Duffy said. A cigarette bounced from his lips.

Bart turned to face him, but Joe looked at his hands and then straight ahead. "What's going on?" Bart said. "You start taking up with a different crowd. We don't hear from you. You come in here in the middle of the day."

He held Bart with one eye and then he turned back to face the bar. "You're in here in the middle of the day," he said. "It's hot out, and it's cool in here."

"I get that you don't want to talk about stuff," Bart said. "You seeing that Nez Perce girl?"

He sat up. Bart was looking at him with that wrinkled brow look of his. "Is that what this is about? And you, with Cherokee blood."

Bart lit another cigarette. The guy at the counter dismounted from his stool and disappeared into the gloom at the back for the men's room. "I got no problem with that. You know that if you know me. But you know how some of the people around here are. I probably shouldn't have brought it up. But I suspect you know you're going to catch hell for it from some of the yahoos around here."

He smiled and laughed a half laugh. "The Macy bunch," he said. "Our good friends. The Macys."

"No doubt," Bart said.

"She's Nez Perce all right," he said. "But I'm not exactly seeing her. She left a couple weeks ago. Some family problem. Who knows if she'll even be back. Not like she told me."

Bart tapped his cigarette in the ash tray. "Look, I should talk. My advice and two bucks will get you a beer. What I'm saying is, we all have our cards we're dealt. We all have to go through shit on our own. But you've got friends and family here that care about you. All I'm saying is, use it. We're here for you but you've got to ask for help."

His stomach tensed and he closed his eyes. Then he opened them and nodded. "Okay," he said.

Bart palmed his shoulder and got up. "Tell you what, have Duffy pour you some coffee and let me take you home," Bart said. "It's either that or I'll have to wait outside and cuff you when you get in the truck. You could probably run that rig on the goddamned fumes."

They stopped at the pickup and grabbed the supplies he had bought. The smell of alfalfa cooling in the evening drifted through the open windows. They passed over the little bridge that spanned the lake outlet downstream of the dam.

"Be careful around some of those people," Bart said. "I've been hearing some things."

He put his hands on the dashboard. "What people? What things?" he said.

Bart looked at him and then looked back at the road. "You know what I'm talking about. The monkeywrenching shit," Bart said. "There have been a few more incidents around. Some yahoo ignited some Forest Service stuff out of Roseburg. Reports of fences cut, tools stolen, firearms popping off. That sort of thing."

Bart seemed weary, his forehead and the skin around his eyes deeply creased. "Roseburg? What's that got to do with these people?"

"Maybe nothing," Bart said. "Look, all's I'm saying is, be skeptical, okay? That shouldn't be too hard for you. Don't believe everything you hear, and don't take everyone at face value. They're not always who they say they are."

"Is anyone?" he said.

They crossed the cattle guard and turned down the lake road. A motorboat towing a skier cut a white swath through the blue water. "You know, I thought maybe things would be different this time," Joe said. He ran his hands through his hair and then rubbed his eyes.

Bart nodded and grunted.

"I thought I could come down here and start something from scratch. Instead, I'm just picking up where I left off. Maybe I should just leave. Mom said as much. Go back North. Just get the fuck away."

The Cherokee lumbered down the road alone, not passing another car or truck.

"Sometimes it's a good idea to leave, sure," Bart said. "Other times you're just carrying your garbage with you."

Bart pulled down the dirt drive and onto the soft dirt track that circled the clearing in front of the house. He stopped the Cherokee and left the engine running. Grace parted a curtain in the kitchen window, and Bart waved. He sat.

"You gonna be alright?" Bart said.

He nodded but kept his gaze straight.

"Well, you know where you can find me," Bart said.

He got out and grabbed his bags from the back of the Cherokee. He started for the porch but then wheeled and poked his head back in the open window. "And I guess you know where you can usually find me," he said. He nodded and pressed his lips in a smile that was more an acknowledgment of guilt. But there was a light of mischief in his eyes, too. "Thanks, bud." Then he turned and picked his way up the stairs, and Bart rolled away.

CHAPTER 12

A day later, he spotted the rusting pickup with the Idaho plates and the Nez Perce reservation permit as soon as he rounded the curve and the grange hall came in sight. It had been three weeks since she had gone. She owed him nothing, neither an apology nor an explanation, and yet he felt like he wanted to put his arms around her first, and then give her hell for leaving without word. But he slipped in silently. He sat and watched and waited.

The talk at the meeting concerned news from places in another world: Portland, Salem, San Francisco, Seattle. Even La Grande seemed far away. There was something about living at the end of the road that did that to a person.

River announced that several environmental groups had joined a lawsuit against the irrigation district, the county and the federal government. The suit would declare the dam a violation of the Endangered Species Act, the Clean Water Act and the 1855 Stevens treaty with the tribes.

River then introduced Ana. She stood, her beads and jewelry clicking. His chest filled. She smiled a smile he'd seen now several times, where you couldn't be sure if she was smiling or whether it was the look of a levelheaded person who'd accepted stuff you couldn't hardly grasp.

"I just got back from Lapwai," she said. "When I was there, I met with the tribal leadership. They have decided not to join the suit." There was a sound as though air were being let out of the room, and Ana nodded. "They know the dam violates the Stevens treaty. This is the only legitimate treaty we ever signed."

Ana showed little outward sign of emotion, but her intensity was only the clearer by her calm. The treaty had guaranteed the right to hunt and fish forever, she said, and it also had promised the Nez Perce their home in this valley. Growing up here, he'd heard the stories about how the government reneged on its word and forced Joseph's people out of the Wallowas. But the treaty's fishing provisions had been upheld, guaranteeing Northwest tribes half of the catch at all the "usual and accustomed" places.

Though Ana spoke softly, she commanded attention. "The tribal leadership is divided," she said. "They want to restore the sockeye to the lake, but they don't want to call for removal of the dam just yet. So we've got to do it on our own." And then she grinned and said, "Let's tell them and the feds, 'Up yours.'"

At this, three people shot up and applauded. "Down with the dam!" they shouted. As they did, more joined them. Soon half the crowd of 40 or so was chanting, "Down with the dam!"

Ana sat, smiling her cipher smile. River returned to the center of the room. He raised his hands to quiet the crowd.

"It's a good feeling to be right," he said. "But we've got to be more than right. What else do we have to do?"

"Fight!" yelled a man from the front, as if on cue.

"I can't hear you. What do we have to do?" River said.

"Fight!" More yelled. And as they did, River pumped his fist in the air.

"What are we going to do?" River yelled.

"Fight!" The crowd shouted back.

Soon everyone was on their feet, chanting, stomping, clapping. He stood when they stood but he kept his hands in his pockets. He wasn't much for religion or church, either, and this felt somehow like it. Pretty soon, they'd be writhing on the floor. He figured River was watching him, but he didn't want to know and didn't look.

But Ana eventually calmed them. Then River announced an "action." The following week, they would hold a news conference at the state park. The conference would talk up the lawsuit against the backdrop of the river delta where it enters the lake. By next week, the river above the lake would be filled with red spawning kokanee. After the conference, all were invited to gather below the dam at the lake outlet. People would walk up along the river banks and, as they moved forward, various groups and individuals would split off, splash themselves with red paint or put on a red vest, and lie down.

"It will be a die-in," River proclaimed. "The more people, the more bodies, the better. Bring your friends, your kids, your parents. Let's give them something for the TV cameras and the folks at home!"

After the meeting, Joe walked to his truck and sat on the open tailgate. The cars rolled out of the parking lot. Then all that were left were his and Ana's pickups and River's old Volvo, parked near his truck. River and Ana walked out of the grange hall together.

"Joe Wallace," River said. "What are you doing here? Were you inside?"

He stayed on the tailgate. "I was keeping a low profile," he said, though he knew River had seen him. "The troops were fired up."

River opened the trunk of his car and dumped in two boxes of papers and books. Ana put two boxes of papers on the ground.

"Wasn't that an inspired performance?" River said. He closed the trunk. He walked up to her and rested his hands on her shoulders. "We just love her, don't we?" He looked at her and smiled, but she stiffened. She pulled away from him, and he let his hands drop. River made a face for a moment, and then he smiled, as though a cloud had passed. He had never seen the two of them like this. There was something between them.

She bent to pick up the box of papers. "Joe, can you get the tailgate?"

"Sure," he said, but he stepped toward the box first to offer a hand.

She showed her palm to him. "Got it," she said, and it was dumb of him to suggest otherwise. He dropped the tailgate, and she swung the box up and slid it in. She grabbed a river rock from the truck bed and placed it on top of the stack of papers in the box.

River hadn't moved. "Well," he said.

She rubbed her hands like she was warming them over a fire. "A performance? You think this is a performance?"

River held up his hands. "Are we a little sensitive? I never said it was contrived." He dug in his pocket for keys. "Nothing wrong with a little theater, now and then. Hey, it's a compliment. We need you to rally the troops." He leaned against the tailgate of her pickup.

She turned from River and lifted a boot onto the bumper. "Okay, then," she said. She banged dust off her jeans. "I'll take it as that." She turned and put her hands in her pockets. "Anyway, you're right. It was a good meeting. We got some things done. Still a bunch more to do. But we're making progress."

River walked to the side of his car and opened the door and then stopped. "Of course, I know that," he said. "You think I'm finished for the night?" He glared at her. His mouth was drawn tight, and he held his head back and his chin up.

"Everybody knows how hard you work," she said.

He acknowledged her with the slightest flare of his nostrils and pursing of his lips. Then he got in his car and started the engine. The window rolled down. He looked at them and nodded with a pasted-on smile. "You kids have fun," he said.

He backed out and drove off, churning up a cloud of dust in the parking lot. Ana stood watching the car leave, shaking her head.

"God damn," she said, and then she tried to grab the other box, but he had already gotten hold of it and slid it in the bed. "You didn't need to do that," she said, and she looked pissed, her eyebrows and forehead knotted. But she seemed to catch herself and let go and then smile. She touched his forearm. "I'm sorry. Thanks."

He pretended not to notice though the truth was that he flushed red. He shrugged. "What's got up his butt?"

Ana leaned against the side of her truck. "Ah," she said. "He's just a little boy who takes himself way too seriously in his playtime. Besides, he's new to this sort of thing. He thinks things happen fast. He hasn't been at it as long as we have."

He sat on the open tailgate. "We? Don't count me in this business. I'm a greenhorn to all this stuff."

She looked out across the empty lot and smiled. "We, as in the real people, the *Nimi'ipuu*." Then she walked back to where he was sitting and looked at him. He wasn't sure what to do next. "Ah, you mind getting off my tailgate so I can close it and get the hell out of here?"

He laughed for being so dumb. "The Nimee-poo?" he said.

"Nez Perce to you," she said.

"Sorry," he said, and he jumped down and closed the gate himself. He brushed his hands together out of habit. "There you go."

She got in the truck. When she turned the ignition key, the engine coughed and turned over four times but then fell dead. She tried twice more, then punched the steering wheel. "Shit."

He came around to the driver's side door and folded his arms. "She's not getting gas maybe," he said. "Fuel filter?"

She shot him a look. "The fuel filter's fine," she said. "Sounds like it's not getting air. By the way, it's not a 'she.'"

He walked in front of the pickup and raised the hood. He took the air filter out and held it out between him and the sky.

"Bang it against the bumper a few times," she said. "I've been driving a lot of back roads. It gets dirty."

She turned the key. The engine sputtered but then died when she tapped the accelerator.

"Maybe there's dirt in the line. How far you have to go?"

Ana got out, walked to the front and kicked the fender.

"That an act of aggression or repair?" he said.

"Both," she said. "It's worked before." Then she took out the air filter again and gave it a good whack across the fender. She got back in and turned the key. It started up.

He stood outside her window, his arms crossed. "I'll be goddamned. You want me to follow you, just in case?"

"No," Ana said. "But follow me anyway. I want you to come to the house. We should talk."

His head reeled. But she was leaving and there wasn't time to think. By the time he ran to his truck, she had already wheeled out of the parking lot and onto the creek road. She sounded her horn, and he answered back and stepped on the gas in pursuit and drove with his heart and head racing.

He was still a good 30 seconds behind Ana when she turned off the highway out near the ski hill. He followed her into a farm compound and pulled his truck next to hers near the barn. The house looked out on Mount Howard, the scars from the old fire still silver with dead trees.

She stood waiting for him in the yard. He got out of his truck. "This is the old Farrell place," he said. There were no other cars. "You staying out here on your own?"

Ana laughed. "Is that going to be okay with you?" she said, walking away from him and toward the house. "Come on, let me show you around."

His heart hammered. She was way ahead of him, wherever she was going, and it was all he could do to keep up. They walked around the yard. There was a big old weeping willow that shaded an irrigation ditch where clear water moved silently.

She pulled the barn door open. It was empty and clean inside except for some hay bales near them.

He kicked a bale. "It needs animals," he said.

"Horses," she said. "Appaloosas." Then she turned and looked at him and his stomach tightened and burned. He didn't know what to do with his hands, so he put them in his pockets.

She looked at him with such honest directness that he felt shy. "You're nervous," she said. "You okay?"

He kept his hands in his pockets and arched his back. "Whatever gave you that idea?" he said.

She stepped toward him and touched his arm, and his breath caught. Then there were her dark, kind, open eyes on him, and this time it was different and he stayed with her. He forgot to think. He took her hand and kissed it and then put it around his waist. Then he took her in his arms and found her eyes and kissed them. He kissed her mouth. He felt light and heavy at the same time, dizzy and certain, the blood in his veins like hot oil. She tasted like coffee and cinnamon. The world shut down and narrowed to her.

They stood holding each other in the empty barn with the sweet smell of hay in their noses. He brought his face to her breasts and breathed in her body, and her sighing when he touched her nipples drove him, and he drew down into them with his mouth and tongue. Her heart raced on his lips. She pulled him in. There was no stopping, only moving on and on, a force unto itself.

She reached and touched him, and he closed his eyes and squeezed them until the undersides of his eyelids flashed psychedelic.

They sank to the floor, on the hay from the open bales, he on his knees in front of her, she sitting. He kissed her neck and her ears. He tried to slow himself but it was no use. He let her unbutton his shirt, and he undid hers and slipped off her bra. And the sight of her was a miracle.

The air was perfectly warm. Barn swallows outside called their soft *kvit–kvit.* Inside was still. They laid out their shirts on the hay and slid down on them. There was no more separation, he in her and she in him. Perfect and whole and light and right.

They lay in the warmth with the smell of hay and sweat, seawater and bleach on them. Their bodies were spent and satisfied and they no longer wanted anything.

Afterwards, they sat on the porch swing eating chocolate ice cream from white bowls. The sun had gone down in the flats, and the mountains were purpling in the fading light. It was as though by giving himself to her he had got himself back again. He felt so clearheaded and calm it was stunning. Even the mountains looked clearer, as though he hadn't realized he'd been looking at things through a dirty window until someone came and cleaned it for him.

"I still don't know what happened in there," he said.

"I do," she said and laughed.

He lifted a spoon of ice cream in front of him. "It was like I was just loping along and then, wham," he said, putting the ice cream in his mouth, "a bolt of lightning just came out of nowhere and jolted me right off my horse."

She held the bowl in her lap and put her arm around him and kissed him.

"So I'm a bolt of lightning, eh?" she said. "If that's so, you're a shark. I was just calmly swimming by myself, minding my business. Then, out of the deep blue sea, you came and bit me. Took a chunk of my ass right off."

"And you loved every minute of it," he said, and he pretended to bite her breasts and then planted his lips on her. She pulled him to her, and her bowl fell.

Soon he was engulfed in her again. They were like opposite poles of two magnets, a force of nature with its own rules.

This time she led him to her bed. And if the first time had been like lightning, this time it was like a long, intense dance, building, changing, building, turning, building. It was pure joy. It was the only thing that existed, all that mattered. He could have died and been happy, not wanting anything more. He never felt stronger yet more vulnerable.

He awoke once in the night and pulled closer to her. The air was cool through the open window, and the curtains shifted in the breeze. Almost despite himself, he was hard again as soon as he touched her, even in his sleepiness. He tried to pay it no mind and go back to sleep. But then she mounted him sitting. He held her breasts and then brought her down and held her in his arms. They made tired, quiet love, hardly moving, until he felt he could give no more. Afterwards, they lay side by side and passed out.

In the morning he awoke to the aroma of frying bacon and coffee. He lay under the sheets as the room brightened. She'd been up for who knew how long, and she was singing out in the kitchen. The room flooded with sun, and the cool fingers of a breeze parted the lace curtains and smoothed the sheets across his skin. He needed a shower and a shave but it didn't bother him. It occurred to him that he had not thought about wanting a drink since yesterday. But now there was that old pull on his body. Why would he ever want to drink again with her in his life? He wanted her more. He could have stayed that way, in that room, listening to her and feeling her presence, for an eternity. He wanted it to never end, and he stayed in bed until she came to him with coffee. She wore a white cotton blouse and blue jeans. He took the white cup from her and thanked her and then reached for her hip with his free hand. She smiled but told him she had to leave after breakfast. She turned and walked. "Come on, get some eggs."

CHAPTER 13

By October, the cottonwood leaves and larch needles had turned gold. The tourists left and, with the exception of a few elk hunters, the place returned to what it always was underneath, a small town at the end of the road. Soon there was ice on the puddles in the mornings. When daylight savings passed and the clocks were set back, he found himself in unfamiliar territory. It had been a long time since he had felt this way about a woman. After what had happened with Jenny Alvord, he swore he would never get involved again; the pain was too high a price. He had loved Jenny, and the way she had been killed had turned his stomach.

But Ana changed the calculus. He could not get enough of her. She liked doing all the things he liked, and she could do many of them better than him. They hiked the mountain trails before the snow buried them. They took horses up to Ice Lake, and Ana showed herself a steady hand. They talked hours about restoring the sockeye run, read the same research, drove to see Norm Kramer together. Even fishing, an activity that Clark had said that Joe was born to do, came effortlessly and beautifully to her.

He thought of Ana constantly. It kept him going when she left now and then to work on paying projects on the rez and to be with her father. When she was gone, he busied himself with cabin repairs and sockeye research and maintenance saved for the off-season. He called her, or she called him, most days. He stopped drinking, but it was hard when she was gone.

They watched for steelhead coming up the Imnaha. There were still some summer-run fish, but the bigger winter run would come later, in January. Still, the smaller numbers were not cause to stay home; if anything, they were all the more reason to go, and they made a game of who could catch more. Besides, the weather in the lower canyons of the Snake was the nicest of the year. It was as though summer could lose itself in the deep canyons and hide out from winter for a while.

They loved to drive down the Lower Imnaha Road. Down there, it was as though the topographic map was turned in on itself. Instead of mountains being the major features of the landscape, what stood out were reverse mountains—gaping canyons that opened out from under them and that, as they dropped into them, rose overhead and engulfed them and felt to him like sinking into the trough of a wave. But this was a wave of red rimrock and scalloped ridges. Here was a place he could feel puny in relation to the landscape yet protected at the same time.

They would take the jeep road, passing more mountain sheep than people (often not passing anyone; having hundreds of square miles to themselves), and suddenly the river was way down to the right, a silver tongue of water. Then just as suddenly they were at river's edge. At Cow Creek, the road crossed the Imnaha and zigzagged away northeast to the Snake. The river continued northwest and entered a sumac-filled box canyon that could barely accommodate a couple of hikers, let alone a pickup. They would park at the bridge and walk the rest of the way to the Snake. It was the same route Joseph and the Nez Perce took in 1877 with General Howard and his horse soldiers in pursuit.

When she was back in town, Ana continued to meet with River. But their relationship had changed. Where they had once been comrades-in-arms, they were now business partners. Where they once met at each other's homes, they now met in town at the home of a supporter who lived in L.A. and was never around. They never met at the Bucksaw or the Glacier Tap Room because those were places where locals ruled and conversations were overheard. They knew they needed each other, and they were good at recognizing each other's strengths, but when the meetings ended, they went their separate ways.

River rarely spoke with Joe. This was not the same kid he had met that day on the railroad tracks. He had seemed younger then, brighter-eyed. He'd been intense, but in a relaxed way. Even when he made a joke now, it seemed forced and calculated. Maybe it was the pressure of leading his crusade on a shoestring budget. The clock was ticking, and he had to show progress if people were going to write checks to keep him going. But maybe it was more than that. Something only River knew about. Some person or some idea driving him.

But there was something else, something about the way River acted around him and Ana. Joe couldn't put a finger on it. A flash of a look when River saw them, and then River would catch himself. It was hardly worth mentioning to Ana, and so Joe held on to it. He even suggested that things would be better if he stayed away from the meetings, but she wouldn't have it.

People in town acted different, too. They were cordial enough. There was still plenty of "Hello, Joe" and "How's your mom?" But then they'd turn and leave. Or, waiting to pay for something at McCully's, he would notice the darting eyes of the cashier, going from smiling at him to locking eyes with another customer.

When he and Ana were together, it was more blatant. People avoided them. One day in November, they had come out of the grocery and were walking up the sidewalk along the storefronts. The sky was oyster gray and threatening snow. The Reeses had started to park their pickup and then swung around and crossed to the other side. Then Bud and Laura Wayne came out of the hardware a block away, turned toward them and then turned around and walked the other way.

He stopped. "I saw that," he said. "Did you see that?"

Ana folded her arms across her chest. "Now you know what it's like to be the town nigger," she said.

"Jesus Christ." He was wearing a Stetson, and he took it off for a moment. "These are people that have known my family for 50 years. I didn't think they had it in them." He smoothed his hair.

Ana laughed, shaking her head in disbelief. "Oh, come on," she said, and kept walking. "*Your* people." Then she stopped and crossed her arms. Her face was intense. "When they couldn't run us off themselves, or kill us with small pox and typhus or booze, they had their army take care of it. They sent us to goddamn Oklahoma, for Christ's sake. Sent us to Idaho. Killed off the buffalo. Obliterated the salmon. And it's a surprise to you that you're a pariah because you're consorting with a squaw?"

"Let's go," he said. He put his hat back on and blew into his hands. They walked to her truck and drove toward home.

Clouds hid the spine of Chief Joseph Mountain for days at a time, and each time they lifted, as they had now, the snow level had crept down. The mountain seemed bigger. Ana's treks into the high country would need to come to an end soon. And it wasn't only because of the snow.

"What's going on?" she said.

"Nothing."

"You're so easy to read. Something's bothering you," she said.

"Maybe it's this stuff about the monkeywrenchers," he said.

Ana glanced at him. "What are you talking about?"

"I don't know," he said as the truck bounced over the lake outlet. "It's dumb."

The monkeywrenchers had left their mark again, only this time they'd struck much closer to home. The ranger station at Bear Springs had been torched. Nobody was inside at the time, but the fire had been so hot that it had melted coins. Bart said Earth First, with an exclamation point on the end—whoever they were—had claimed responsibility through a note from Portland, and had threatened more of the same, or worse.

"You're right," Ana said. "You're letting that stuff get to you. It has nothing to do with us or the lake or the dam."

"How can you be so sure?" he said.

Ana slowed the truck. "Are you serious?"

"Sure, I'm serious," he said. "Maybe a fool, too."

"Do you think I'm getting up at night to burn Forest Service buildings?" Ana said.

"What about River?"

Ana braked and stopped the truck in the road.

"Pull over, okay?" he said.

"The hell I will," Ana said.

"Maybe I should just get out and walk," he said.

"Maybe you should," she said.

The old ski hill road ran up through the trees until it disappeared. "Okay, then," he said as he pulled forward and put his hand on the door handle.

Ana shot her arm across him and grabbed his hand. "Enough," she said. "You're not going anywhere until you tell me what's on your mind."

"Ah, shit," he said. "I knew I should've kept my mouth shut. Can you pull over now?"

"Would you just stop worrying about how I drive," she said.

"It's not how you drive; it's where you stopped," he said. "You're in the middle of the road."

"Ahhhh!" Ana grabbed her hair. "You drive me crazy. Okay, look. If it makes you feel better—."

"Thank you," he said.

She threw the truck into first gear and rolled onto the shoulder. "There. Is that better?"

"Yeah," he said.

"Sheesh," Ana said. "You know, that's your problem."

"What's my problem?" he said.

"Afraid what other people are thinking," Ana said. "Fuck other people. If you're afraid what other people are thinking about us, then we might as well just end it here. Is that what you want?" She turned off the ignition.

He shook his head. "Look, I don't know about River. Can't you see it? He's getting paranoid. He's weird around you, and now he avoids me. I think he resents me. He had you to himself before I—."

"He never *had* me." She glared at him, her face hard. "That's for one. Second, he's harmless. A little crazy? Maybe. But harmless as a mosquito. Third, I know how to take care of myself. Is that what this is all about? 'Cause if it is, let me set you straight, buddy. I could take care of myself before I met you, and I can take care of myself now."

He widened his eyes. "Believe, me, I know you can take care of yourself." Then he sunk and put his boots up on the dash. "This isn't about kicking someone in the balls and running," he said. "I just don't know if I trust him. Especially around you."

"Let's not talk about this anymore, okay?" She touched his hand. "Let's just be together. But let's face facts. People around here, they're not that far removed from 1877. They look at me but they don't see me. They feel guilty for what their racist old filthy forebears did, but what can they do? They live here now. Deep down, they know it was wrong. But they could never admit it, because to admit it would mean acknowledging they'd stolen our land.

"And you, you're just throwing it in their face. First you take up with a bunch of Birkenstock-wearing environmentalists. Second, you shack up with a squaw. You're not endearing yourself to the townsfolk, now, are you?"

He shrugged, then smiled. "I guess not." But there was more to say, and he spread the fingers on his upturned palms. "River? Just what's his deal? I haven't exactly endeared myself to him, either. Honest? I think he's jealous of you and me."

She blew out a breath as if his suggestion was nonsense. "Let me take care of River, okay?" Ana said. "Trust me?"

"It's not you I don't trust," he said. "It's just that I've seen some bad shit go down in my life. I'm not going to let that happen again to someone I love."

She reached for him, and he pulled her to his chest. "I know, I know," she said. "Don't worry about that. Nothing bad is going to happen to me. Ever."

They stayed that way for more than a little while. She still did not know what shit he'd seen, and he didn't know what it was like to stand in her shoes, either. He let her go, and she leaned back and started up the truck and pulled onto the road. Was it that he couldn't trust her? He'd trust her with his life. He was sure of it. But it was life, or the world, or whatever you wanted to call it, that couldn't be trusted. She couldn't say what would happen to her, or what wouldn't. When he let her go, when she was out of his sight, how could he trust that she would return safe? No one could.

CHAPTER 14

"Was I sleeping?" Grace said, low and weak. She moved, but just barely. "I'm sleepy. Whatever they gave me ... what did they give me?"

"Fentanyl and Versed," McKenzie said. She applied the parking brake and gathered their mother's things. "Happy drugs."

"Oh."

When he'd seen McKenzie's Blazer moving along the rutted drive, he knew. He ran down the porch steps and had the door open before McKenzie had rolled to a stop and applied the parking brake.

Grace was pale and sunken. She had looked awful after Clark died, but now she was worse, so thin. She had always eaten lightly, and smoked and did everything as if on an urgent mission. But she'd lost weight and had kept on losing it. Her energy evaporated like mist on the lake. McKenzie took her to Dr. Sorensen in Enterprise, and he'd ordered blood work. And that led to the advice for a colonoscopy in La Grande. Stubborn mule, Grace refused but relented after McKenzie and the doctor came down heavy on her, and she must have known herself to expect the worse.

McKenzie got out and left her door open and stood beside him. The lake had fall fog on it. It swallowed the opposite bank and made the clearing outside the cabin close and quiet and small.

Normally, Grace would have bounded out of the Blazer. But she was waiting, gaunt. Her eyes were drained of life. He pressed his hand on the door handle. She drew a breath and pursed her lips. She sighed and swung her head. "Fenta, fenta verset … what?" she mumbled.

"Just something to control the pain and help you forget," she said. "Come on, dear. Let's get you out." She slid her arm under her mother's elbow.

Joe bent and took hold of her below her knees.

"We're going to get you out and walk you up the steps, mom," McKenzie said. "Put your feet down, let them touch the ground."

"Oh, stop it, stop talking to me like a child," Grace said. But she let them ease her around, each of them with a hand in an armpit. "I … don't remember … I don't remember a thing." She stiffened and it was her resolve moving through her, a pulse of life that was real in his hand. "The damn drugs. I'd rather be alive and feel the pain than be in la-la land like this." She reached her hand tentatively, probing the air for balance. "I can get out of a damn car myself."

He stepped closer and she looked at him. Her eyes were lazy in their sockets. "Joseph?" she asked, as if unsure. "Well, are you just going to stand there, or are you going to help an old lady? It's too high off the ground for me anyway."

"You didn't need my help but you need his," McKenzie huffed and acted annoyed. "I'm crestfallen."

Grace harrumphed.

"Easy does it," he said, guiding her by her forearm till her foot tested the dirt of the drive. She stopped and rested.

"Thank you, son," she said. "Now leave me be. I'm fine. Let me walk." She tugged away from him with her bony arm.

He looked at his sister and she nodded. "Sure?" he said to Grace.

"Sure I'm sure," she said. "I've got Nurse Ratched over there making sure everything is fine, don't I?"

"Mom!" McKenzie faked hurt. "I don't even know who Nurse Ratched is, and I'm still offended."

"She okay on her own, Nurse Ratched? Or do you think we need to knock her out," he said.

"I'll knock you out first," Grace said. She managed something like a hoarse laugh. Then she walked.

"Slow down, woman," he said. "What's the rush?"

"Shut up," she said.

"Okay," he said. He stayed by her side to the porch, and then she let him help her up, one step at a time, without a word.

"We're going to have to think about those stairs," McKenzie said.

"Those stairs are solid. Your father built those stairs, and they're good as the day he put them in."

"I'm just saying, mom, those stairs could be a problem. If you're alone—."

Grace stopped and closed her eyes. She put her hand to her eyebrows and tightened her lips and dropped her head.

"Mom?" he said.

"Ah, shit. Leave me alone." She let her hands fall to her sides and stood frozen. "I'm so ashamed. No better than a child. Get away! I don't need anyone!"

McKenzie widened her eyes as he let her go. She looked down and he followed her gaze. The urine was dark yellow where it ran from her dark-stained pants and across her shoe onto the step.

"Oh, ma, I'm sorry," McKenzie said.

They got her inside and she let McKenzie help get her changed and bathed and put to bed.

He made coffee and they sat at the kitchen table. They were there twenty minutes before Howard pulled up in his immaculate SUV. McKenzie had called Howard from the hospital.

"He pulls that thing any closer," Joe said. He got up and leaned against the sink holding his mug. The door opened.

"I had a meeting," Howard said, taking the toothpick from his mouth. "How is she?" His cheeks glowed slap-faced red. He was wearing a blue blazer, blue shirt, khakis and tie. The blazer, buttoned over his gut, hung like a curtain. He stood waiting with his hand on the door knob.

"She's asleep now," McKenzie said. "They found a growth."

"A—."

"Tumor?" she answered.

"You mean—?"

"Yeah." Joe said.

"There was too much for them to remove during the colonoscopy," she said.

Howard rubbed his hands together. "I can't believe it," he said. "Colon cancer? I would have guessed lung cancer. Can smoking cause colon cancer?" He screwed his face in a frown. "What is she going to do? What are we going to do?"

This was how Howard thought. Joe could see him calculating the risks and rewards. He wouldn't have put it past him to have already factored in Grace's death and how that would affect his plans.

Joe blew into his coffee, sipped it and shook his head as he put down the cup.

"What?" Howard said. "What did I say?"

"Surgery is tomorrow," McKenzie said. She was annoyed now.

"Tomorrow?" Howard was flabbergasted. Or maybe just inconvenienced. His cheeks wobbled. "So soon?"

McKenzie got up. "Not soon enough. It's amazing they didn't just admit her on the spot. You want coffee?"

"I've got a meeting. There's people waiting for me. I can't just … well … you know, drop everything."

"No, we wouldn't want you to go out of your way," Joe said.

"Don't get sarcastic with me," Howard said, running his toothpick along his gums.

"You don't want sarcastic? How about a pop in the goddamned face?" Joe jutted his jaw.

McKenzie spun from where she was standing at the coffeemaker. Her jaw was set and she nodded wide-eyed toward the bedroom. "She can still hear, you know," she said. "Don't you two start." She poured from the pot and set the mug on the kitchen table.

Joe came back to the table and sat. She held the pot to him and lifted her eyebrows, and he let her fill his mug. He thought of going in his room and adding a finger of bourbon from the bottle under his bed. She put the pot back and returned to the table, pulling a chair out before she sat. She nodded at Howard and motioned toward the chair. "Sit," she said.

"Well," he said.

"She said, 'sit,'" he said. "So sit down."

Howard sat with a hurt look and took the mug of coffee she poured. She brought cream and sugar and a spoon. He took two spoonsful of sugar, poured in the cream and stirred. He licked the spoon, stirred again, and then put it down.

"You're the nurse," Howard said. "What's the prognosis? Is she going to make it?"

She smiled bitterly and smoothed the tablecloth, though it didn't need smoothing. She looked at Howard, then back at the tablecloth. "They won't know till they go in and see what they've got to work with."

"Well, then, there's not much we can do till then," he said. "Unless I'm missing something?"

"Wait just a minute," Joe said.

"What, little brother has something to say?" Howard rolled his eyes.

The anger flashed white in his vision but instead of slamming his hand on the table he lowered it in slow motion. "I'm here. I can take care of her, whatever she needs."

"We may need some meals," McKenzie said. "She's going to have to eat something, and she won't be able to fix it herself."

"Sue can cook," Howard said. "She'll be glad to make something and bring it over." He pushed out from the table and kept his hands on top of it. "Now, here's what we ought to do. We ought to've talked about this a long time ago. But anyway, we're all here now, and I've been thinking about this." He raised his chin like a little emperor, the fat of it bulging. The fog was beginning to burn off, the sky outside the window watery blue.

"We're all ears," McKenzie said, her hands folded on the table.

"Good," he said. He surveyed the kitchen. "This was going to happen sooner or later. Mom can't live here by herself any longer. She's been slowing down for a long time. We just haven't seen it till now."

"Mom's best interests at heart," Joe said.

Howard yanked the toothpick out and cut him off. "Let me finish."

He waved him on.

Howard rubbed his stomach. "God, I'm hungry. Is there anything in the refrigerator? I could use a sandwich."

"I need to go shopping," he said. "Have an apple."

McKenzie got up. "I'll fix you something. Just go on."

"Thanks, sis," he said. "Okay, that'll be good. Sue and I have been thinking about this. Praying on it." McKenzie opened the refrigerator and found lunchmeat and bread. "We think it's time for mom to move out. Get into a nursing home. There's some—."

Joe held up his hand. "Hold it right there. Stop."

"See, I knew. I knew you'd have something to say."

"Good then, you know me well."

McKenzie had bread out. "Keep your voices down," she said.

"I will," he said.

"Not too much mayo," Howard said. "Is there any lettuce or tomato?"

"No," she said. "Pickles. You want pickles?"

"Sure, pickles sound good."

The tightness returned to Joe's head and stomach. He inhaled, let his cheeks puff and then blew out. His brother was such a scumbag. "Okay, look. What you're saying could be an option down the road. But for now, taking her out of this house?"

She plated the sandwich and placed it in front of Howard. "I know what Joe is saying," she said. She wiped her hands on a rag and stood beside the table, her arms crossed.

Howard put the toothpick on the plate and grabbed the sandwich and bit in. "Thanks," he said, grunting his approval as he chewed. "I was starving."

"It'll kill her," she said. She leaned a knee on the chair. "This is her life, this house. It's dad. It's everything she ever lived for."

Howard made a sour face and looked at Joe. "What you were going to say, no doubt." He tore into the sandwich and squirreled a ball of food in his cheek.

"No doubt," he said.

She moved back to the counter and cleaned up. Howard finished the sandwich. Then she turned. He could tell she was holding it in, the way she set her jaw and creased her brow. "Let's just get through this surgery for now," she said. "We can have this discussion again if things get worse. In the meantime, Joe's here. I'll be looking in on her."

Howard stood, still mashing his food, and wiped crumbs from his shirt and pants. "Okay, well, you heard me out. I've got that meeting now." He picked up a paper napkin from the table and wiped his mouth and stuck the splintered toothpick back in his mouth. He crossed the room and touched her shoulder. "Thanks for the sandwich." He made for the door and nodded at him as he left. "Keep us posted," he said.

"Go to your fucking meeting," Joe said.

Howard grunted. "That mouth," he said. "It's offensive."

McKenzie looked at Joe and make a zipping motion across her lips. He grinned at her, but she glared. He kept his mouth shut.

The SUV bounced out of the compound and up to the moraine road. Joe got up and took Howard's plate to the sink. "She picks up for him at home," he said. He patted her shoulder. Her eyes were drawn in tightly and her jaw was fixed, holding something back, anger or heartache. When he stopped, she threw her arms around him. He held her as she sobbed. She settled then and blew out. "The little bastard," she said. "Already planning her funeral. He'd just as soon push her in the grave. Nice knowing ya; have a nice life."

"At least we know where he's coming from. All that Christian talk. When it comes down to it, he's out for number one. Such an ass."

She let go of him. "The worst part is that he might even believe what he says." She returned to putting away things. She opened the refrigerator. "If he thinks I will let him tell me what to do, he's sorely mistaken."

"Amen, sister. But you know him. He's going to keep at it until he wears us down."

"Over my dead body," she said. And she laughed. "Bad choice of words."

McKenzie was a rock, and he needed her more than she may have suspected. "You're the only thing keeping me from choking that bastard," he said.

"He better watch himself then. I have my limits too." She got ready to leave, and he walked her outside to her Blazer. She got in and turned the key. "You sure now?" she said.

"Sure?"

"You're her caretaker. You're going to have to get tough with her. Don't let her boss you around."

He laughed. "Since when has she not bossed me around, or anyone else for that matter?" He leaned on the door. "That'll be the day. But yeah, she's got another thing coming to her if she thinks she's not going to do what the doctor orders."

She put the truck in gear. "I'll be back later. Remember, no solid food today. No milk either. No coffee." Then she clutched and took it out of gear and looked at him.

"What?"

"She needs you sober. That's all I will say."

"Mmm." He nodded.

"Mmm? That better mean yes, mister."

"Yes, ma'am," he said.

She raised her eyebrows, but she had the hint of smile on her lips. "I'll see you tomorrow after I get off from work."

He waved as she drove out of the flat. When she was gone, he walked to the shed and picked the tools he would need to begin winterizing the cabins. He could work on that while she recovered. This is why he'd stayed. He hadn't known at the time that Grace would get sick. But now that she was, it confirmed the rightness of his decision. It felt good knowing he could be there for her. And as ornery as his mother could be, he knew she appreciated it. Her fussing and fighting was her weird way of showing it.

There was a bottle that he kept there, in the same place his old man had, above the workbench. He took two quick pulls, nothing much. Just enough. Then another before he left.

CHAPTER 15

The surgery was scheduled for a week later. McKenzie and Joe took her in to the hospital at LaGrande. It was hell waiting, and he wanted a drink. The two of them escaped outside, and they bummed cigarettes from a smoker. They laughed at themselves for smoking, and she stubbed hers out after coughing on the first drag.

They returned to the cafeteria and drank bitter coffee. McKenzie told him everything in her matter-of-fact nurse way. She'd told him before but it didn't hurt to hear it again: They were going to make a long cut down the center of her stomach. They'd cut out the cancerous part of the colon, as much as a third. Then they'd cut out a small part of healthy colon tissue near the cancer. Next, they'd remove lymph nodes to see if the cancer had spread. Finally, they'd sew the whole thing up. Easier said than done.

The surgeon emerged in his green scrubs. He was short and ruddy-faced, with bushy eyebrows and a tired smile. He knew McKenzie, and he extended his hand to Joe. "You must be the good brother," he said.

"That's a matter of opinion," he said. He liked this guy, but he also knew who was in the driver's seat. The man exuded confidence but not swagger.

"Your mom is a tiger," he said.

"More like an old turkey," he said.

The surgeon laughed. "I think that's more accurate."

"You got it?" McKenzie asked.

"We did," he said. "We believe we got it all."

"Thank God," she said.

"No spreading? What about the lymph?"

The surgeon looked at McKenzie, even though Joe had asked the question. "You've educated your brother well, I see."

"I'm a slow learner," he said.

Then the doctor turned to him. "No, no lymph, as far as we can tell."

"As far as you can tell?"

"To the best of our knowledge," he said. "We're a slippery bunch, I guess. Tough to pin us down. We never make promises, but we think she'll be fine. Now, what else can I tell you?"

He explained that Grace would need five to eight days in the hospital, maybe longer, depending on her recovery. She needed time for her plumbing to return to normal and to start eating on her own again. After that, she'd need a good six weeks of recovery at home. That would include trips back to the hospital for chemo to make sure any cancer left would be zapped.

In fact, she needed the minimum five days. During that time, McKenzie and Joe shared the visiting. Howard came a few times, always with Sue, when he didn't have an excuse. Howard always combined visits to LaGrande with business—dinners and lunches with God-knows-who, developers and lawyers and accountants and the rest of the power brokers.

Joe and McKenzie and Grace were in her Blazer on their way home from the hospital. Grace sat in the back. She was dressed in the outfit McKenzie had brought for her: blue polyester pants and a lilac blouse. Purple was her favorite color, but it made her skin look sallow today. McKenzie helped her get made up that morning, her eyebrows penciled in, lipstick on and eyelashes mascaraed. She tied a scarf around her hair.

"There's going to be some people when we get home," McKenzie said. "Not too many, but they wanted to do something for you, a welcome-home party."

"Oh?" she said. "I'm sure it was Howard and Sue's doing. Those people with their birthdays. You'd think a new queen was being crowned sometimes. And my hair. I've got to get over to Louise's right away. How is that girl of yours?"

They were at the bend in the road near the old Elgin Opera House.

"Ana," she said. "How is Ana?"

He turned away from the window. "Ana? Good, ma. She's doing real good." He was surprised she remembered her name.

"What does she do for a living? She seems to be busy all the time."

They crossed the Grand Ronde and started up the Elgin grade.

"She works for the tribe, ma," he said. "She's doing some work on fish."

"That must take some schooling. She have a degree?"

"She went to, what, Wazoo?" McKenzie asked.

"No, over at Idaho. Moscow. Got a degree in biology. And she'd like to get work as a fisheries biologist for the tribes. She's hoping a job will come open."

"You were always interested in fish, Joseph," she said. "For as long as I can remember, you had fish on your mind. We used to say you even thought like a fish sometimes."

He wanted to say that he drank like a fish, too. It would have been funny, at least to him, and true in the past. But he was sober now, for the most part, and he had Ana to thank for that. He smiled and chuckled to himself. McKenzie looked at him, but if she noticed, she didn't let on. "He still does have fish on the brain," McKenzie said.

"Good lord, I'm hungry," Grace said. "I could eat a horse. Why didn't Howard and Sue come over?"

"They came the other night, remember?" she said. "There's going to be plenty to eat when we get home. It's great you have an appetite."

"I suppose," she said. "Depends on what they're cooking. Beef. That's what I crave. Real food. Something bloody. Why didn't they come with you people this morning?"

"There's only so much room," she said. "Besides, they wanted to do this thing for you."

"Oh, they should save their money and not throw a party for an old fogey," she said. "I'd just as soon get my hair done. How do you open the windows in these contraptions? I can never."

"Are you okay, mom?" she said. "Are you hot? I can open your window for you. But it is getting chilly out there. I can bring you to Louise's tomorrow. I already called for an appointment."

"You're a good girl," she said.

"If Howard'd had his way, he would've had a marching band and an Air Force flyover," he said. "We talked him down to some balloons and a cake, I think." He left it at that. The truth is, they'd argued over it. He was sick of Howard's stunts by now. His brother was pathetic in his need for recognition from his mother. Had he been that deprived as a kid? And there was that part of Howard that wanted to have things his way. This party was all about him, but the worst of it was how he'd paint it. He'd wrap it all up in an American flag somehow, as if he was acting in a movie about himself and how he wanted to be shown in it. The film would later be used on TV when he was running for Congress or something. It would be like, "This is what a red-blooded American son does for his mother when she gets out of the hospital." He'd make sure Sue was taking video of it.

Grace was talking about the weather. "It's getting late in the year," she said. "I lost track of time in that damn hospital. They wake you up at all hours. Always some pill to take or some poking around to do. Ana. She's a handsome gal, that Ana. Nez Perce are a handsome people. Strong features. How many people?"

"Nez Perce? Oh, I don't—."

"No, I don't care about the Nez Perce. How many people are going to be there when we get home? Sue and Howard and the kids? Who else?"

"Just a few, mom. Bart will be there. The McGraws, maybe. Some of the ladies from the church."

"Well, okay, Bart's a good boy. Not that minister?"

"Reverend Davis?"

"Davis. I don't like him. Tries to please too much."

"No, ma. I don't think there's going to be any preachers there."

"Good then."

"Amen to that," he said. "Preachers make me nervous."

"They should," Grace said. "You've got a lot to be nervous about, I'd say."

"Speak for yourself, you old sinner," he said.

"The surgery went well, ma," McKenzie said.

"You can speak for yourself, too. I just hope they took out everything they were supposed to take out and left in everything that's still working. And I hope they sewed me up okay. I don't want anything falling out."

They were crossing the bridge over the Minam–Wallowa confluence. The water was clear and low, and the boat ramp was empty.

"Nothing's going to be falling out," McKenzie said.

"Oh, I haven't been up to Red's Horse Ranch in so long," Grace said. "Your father loved flying in there and camping."

"New owners now. Doctor said you're an amazing patient," she said. "Strong as a bull. He couldn't have asked for a better outcome."

They were in the Wallowa Canyon. "I suppose it did go okay. It better have. They took half my guts out. Maybe that's why I'm actually feeling hungry now. I would love a burger. My God, the food. It's so bland. They've got better food in Enterprise. I don't know why I couldn't've had this done there. They'd've taken better care of me over there. That's right about Red's. I remember now."

"I don't know about a burger right now. That might be a little too much for your stomach to handle. They just don't have the facilities there in Enterprise for that kind of surgery, mom. But they did a good job. They got all the cancer. And it didn't spread beyond the colon. That's such good news."

"Well, I guess that means I'll die a little slower."

"Ma!" she said. "Don't."

"You know I'm just foolin'. But when you get to be my age, you start getting used to the idea. No, I'm not planning on going anywhere except my own house for a while. And you can tell your brother that, too."

"Tell him?" she said.

"You know damn well what I'm talking about," she said. Which was true, of course, but McKenzie couldn't be faulted for trying to steer clear of the topic. Grace crossed her arms over her chest. "You think I'm dumb? I know he wants me out and in the old-farts home. I heard him." She set her jaw. "The only way I'm leaving that house is in a box."

"Ma," she said. "You're so dramatic. No one's going to let you leave."

"That's right," he said. "Besides, I'm gonna need you to help winterize the cabins when you get back. You're not getting out of the work just because of a little surgery."

"Hmm," she muttered. "Your father and I cleaned those cabins ourselves for a long time without your help. I could still do it myself if I had to."

"I'm sure you would, too, ma," she said.

"I might let you off the hook a little the first few days," he said. "Seeing as you're a bit gimpy still."

She hit the back of his seat. "If I was stronger, I'd get up there and box your ears," she said. "Gimpy?"

McKenzie and Joe laughed. "I think you'll be just fine, ma," she said. "Just fine."

***

The party turned out to be a quiet affair. Grace lasted a couple of hours before she pooped out. Most people had the sense to drop by with a dish and a card and leave before Grace even arrived, or shortly after. Bart left early. Howard made a speech before the cake candles were blown out. The cake was decorated with American flags, and Sue videotaped, as Joe had predicted. But Ana was there, and she helped him laugh off Howard as best she could.

Grace was happy to be home. McKenzie got her ready for bed while he and Ana helped Howard and Sue clean up. Grace had wanted to clean up, but in fact, she was dog-tired and didn't put up a fuss when McKenzie ordered her around.

When they were done, they walked out to the porch to say good-bye to Howard and Sue. The kids were sugared up and squirmy. As Howard was stepping down, he stopped and turned. "Thought any more about what I said?"

"What you said?" Joe acted ignorant.

"You know. Ma?" He held his toothpick and whispered. "I don't want to say it in front of the kids."

He wanted to punch him. Ana knew it too, the way she massaged his back.

"You mean the nursing home?" he said, loud enough. "Tell you the truth, I haven't thought about the nursing home at all. Not until you brought the nursing home up just now."

Howard's cheeks flushed. He squinted at him. He turned and walked toward his SUV. Then he stopped. "Doesn't surprise me," he muttered, and then he shouted for the kids to get in the car. "We're not done with this, I promise you."

"We are, as far as I'm concerned," he said. Ana's hand was still on his back. "Don't think ma isn't on to you, either."

Sue busied herself with the kids. "Bye!" they screamed. He smiled and waved at them. When Sue was done, she stopped at the passenger side door before getting in. "Gosh, I'm tired. Good-night," she called. "Howard?"

"I'm coming," he said.

"Good night, Sue," Ana said. "Thanks for all the work. It was real nice. Good-bye, Howard."

Howard looked at Joe again before getting in the SUV. "I don't know what you told her. And I don't care what she knows. Think it over. You'll see I'm right." He closed the door and drove off.

Joe slid his hands in his pockets and spat. "Christ," he said. "Will he ever stop? He's going to drive me insane. Either that, or I'm going to have to put a hurt on him."

"Oh, yes. That would achieve a lot." Ana folded her arms over her stomach. "It's getting cold. It's amazing how the old roles play out as adults. Howard is so insecure about his place in the family."

They started back for the house.

"I don't know why. But you're right," Joe said. "When we were kids, he just craved attention. He'd be like, 'Look at me, ma. Look at me, dad.' Whatever he was doing. Riding a bike, fishing, mowing the goddamned grass."

"What did they do?"

"Ignored him."

"Did they give you more attention?"

"I don't know. Things came easy to me for a long time. I did everything good. They sort of expected it from me, I guess. But when I started fucking up in high school, I think it really pissed him off that somehow he still didn't get the spotlight. He was like, 'I've been a good boy all along. Look at me! Look at me!'"

"And they were consumed with your stuff. So he still didn't get their attention."

"You're right. That's exactly what happened."

They stopped at the porch. Darkness and quiet had descended on the lake. It would be good to make a fire in the woodstove. He touched her cheek and brushed her hair over her shoulder. Then he pulled her in and held her.

"I don't know what I did to deserve you," he said.

She looked up at him and smiled. "Nothing," she said. "You just were you. And it's not about deserving anyway. We're all worthy from the day we're born naked and crying and helpless."

He grinned and hugged her tighter. "Naked, huh? I like to think of you naked, but not crying."

She pushed him away. "Hah! Leave it to you to bring it back to sex."

He held on to her hands. "What makes you think I was thinking of that?" But he laughed and pulled her back to him. "But come to think of it?"

"Don't even," she said. "Not with your mother in the next room."

"Hell, we've got 10 cabins to choose from," he said. "Hmm?"

"Oh, God, you're incorrigible. You're devious." But she kissed him on the mouth and then started giggling. There was that delicious longing that takes on a life of its own, closes the world down to the present, and will not rest until it is exhausted. He let it take hold of him.

He took her by the hand. The tall grass that grew in front of the cabins brushed against them. "I feel like a teenager," he said, and he started laughing softly.

"Shhh!" She held her finger to her lips and did a quick shake of her head. "Just shut up," she said, but she laughed while saying it.

They walked up the stairs to cabin 2 in the dark and quietly opened and closed the door behind them. There was a chill in the cabin. He stayed at the front door for a moment. The lights were still off in his mother's room at the main house. The compound was completely dark.

"I'm cold," Ana said from the bedroom. "Come warm me up."

She was already naked when he slipped under the blanket beside her. Ana meant the world. There was no thought. There was just letting go, giving himself over to her and to the night. He imagined a tropical place must be like that, like floating in warm, salty water. He felt nearly whole. Or maybe he'd always been whole, and he never realized it. They fell asleep after making love. In the first light, they tried sneaking back into the lake house. Grace found that very funny and gave them hell about it. "There's a law against that, I'm fairly certain," she said.

CHAPTER 16

River rose from the table at the head of the room and raised both hands. He'd been getting more and more preacherly. Was it real or an act? River seemed to be buying into it himself, and damned if a lot of the group did, too. "Let's pause to reflect," he whispered. The group quieted. He bowed his head for a few seconds and then looked up, smiled and nodded.

It was the best-attended meeting on dam removal yet. Maybe it was the Bear Springs fire that *Earth First!* said was theirs. Or maybe what got attention were the die-in and the subsequent story in *The Oregonian* and on the dam-removal campaign. In either case, a good 50 people showed at the Grange Hall for the Wallowa Lake Restoration Committee meeting.

"What happened at Bear Springs is a reminder of what can happen when people feel they have no alternatives," he said. "What do people do when they feel they have exhausted their remedies in our system? When they feel disenfranchised?

"They strike out, of course. They flout the law. They endanger themselves. They destroy. Thankfully, the people who did this took care not to hurt people but only property.

"We do not condone their actions. Let me be clear about that. Yet we share many of their same goals. Let me ask you. Do we want an end to the cutting of old growth timber on federal lands?"

Some nodded. Some said, "Yes!" Some said, "Right on!" The din of chatter drowned out the rushing of Hurricane Creek outside. River again raised his hands.

"That was pitiful," he said. Pockets of uneasy laughter ignited, and soon the room buzzed. River quieted the room.

"Let's try it again. Do we want an end to the cutting of old growth timber on federal lands?"

"Yes!" the answer came. Joe was not among the faithful. He just didn't like this group mentality. And besides, he'd come here to talk about fish and dams, not trees.

"Better," River said. "Now, let me ask you. Do we want see the return of the Northern gray wolf to these mountains?"

"Yes!" Joe tried staying low. He didn't know how he felt about the return of the wolf. Did he have to maintain an opinion about every contentious issue in this valley?

"Good!" River said. "Now you're waking up! And do we want a free-flowing river and a return of the sockeye to Wallowa Lake?"

"Yes!"

"Let me hear it again!"

"Yes!"

Joe nodded and grunted. It would have to do.

"One more time!"

"Yes!"

"All right," he said. "That feels good. That feels right. That reminds us of why we're here. We're here because we have a historic opportunity. We have a once-in-a-lifetime chance. We can undo the mistakes of the past. And we can allow natural processes to once again assert themselves. Are we going to allow this opportunity to pass without taking action?"

"No!"

"No. I don't think so. We're going to march forward and we're going to take back what's ours!"

Almost as a whole, the people jumped from their seats, clapping and whistling and woo-hoo-ing and right-on-ing. He eventually stood. But he felt awkward. It was too much like a tent revival he'd been dragged to once by an old girlfriend in high school. That had been the last date he'd had with her. He thought about leaving. But he had something to say, and he held his nose and stayed put.

He sat and waited for several others to say their piece. Then he stood. Ana was seated at the front table next to River. She knew what he would say. They had talked about it, and she realized River could take it the wrong way. But it was something he had to say.

River stood at the center of the room behind the table. River's eyes darkened momentarily when Joe stood, and he glanced at Ana. Then he recovered and smiled. "Now let's hear from a man whose family has made its living from development of the lake," River said. He smiled when he said it, but there was an edge to the smile.

There was laughter, murmuring. Ana did not change her expression, but she stiffened slightly and kept her gaze straight.

"Joe understands it's only good-natured ribbing," River said. He grinned, his lips drawn tightly.

Joe stood in front of his chair. Only the naïve or blind would have said it wasn't personal. "I appreciate the introduction," he said. There was no way River would get the satisfaction of seeing him angry or hurt, if that's what he wanted. "This from a guy whose family made a fortune from clear-cutting the Coast Range, had his college paid for by those cut trees, and who now lives on trust-fund checks from that fortune."

River closed his eyes and, when he reopened them, smiled serenely. The room quieted. He didn't know where it had come from, but it felt good to give it right back.

"River can take a little good-natured ribbing, too," he said. The quiet allowed the rushing of the creek back in. "What River says about my family is true. We own a 160-acre land patent that my great-great-granddad got from the feds in 1887, and which the government basically stole from the Nez Perce. But I'll say this: We've taken care of this place. Managed it for the long-term. Never tried subdividing it or selling it off."

River remained standing in front. "Your point?"

Now it was his turn to smile through his teeth. "Sure. All I'm saying is, have some understanding of this community. These are good people. A lot of them make an honest living from the land, and they care about it. I don't agree with all their ideas and ways of doing things, but that don't make them enemies. That don't mean I'd go out and take a torch to their property, or spike a tree, or fuck with their equipment.

"Now, I'm not saying any people in this room here did that or would do that. 'Cause I don't believe that. But what I'm asking for here is a little more understanding and a little more reaching out."

River folded his arms and then pulled away one hand and raised it. "Okay, Joe, thank you. You've had your say, so why don't you sit down."

He put his thumbs in his pockets and didn't move. "I'm not done, is why," he said.

"Let the man have his say," a guy dressed in fatigues in the front row said.

River glared but then drew in a breath and nodded. "All right, all right. You've got a minute and then we need to move on."

He toed a gap in the floorboards with his boot and took a breath. "I'll keep it short," he said. "We ought to come out stronger against that torching. I appreciate that, as River said, you don't condone this monkeywrenching business. But we've got to let the community know. It ain't enough for us to just think it. We've got to send a message that we're law-abiding people, and we're not about to go out and set fire to their means of livelihood, or, to be really ridiculous, blow up their dam, even if we don't agree with them and we're looking to upset the apple cart a bit."

River started to say something but was interrupted by the man in fatigues. His name was Phil Hartnett. He lived over in La Grande, which was more Eastern Oregon than most people in the hall could claim as home. He was the closest thing to a local, besides Joe, in the group.

"I'll sign it," Hartnett said. "You got a statement to that effect, I'll put my name on it."

Several more said they'd sign a statement.

River raised both hands and tried to stop things, but then a young guy in a camo shirt with short hair and faint stubble—Jesse was his name—stood and spoke. "I am for peace, but I am not for silence," he said. "I think it takes courage to do what Earth First! is doing. Maybe we ought to have a statement to that effect."

Five guys around Jesse's age jumped up and shouted their support. Soon, others in the audience shouted for them to sit and shut up. Some people began heading for the door. "Stop!" River yelled. "Stop it!"

The place fell quiet. People stopped in their tracks. They turned around to stare at River. His face had turned crimson and the veins on his forehead snaked out. The whites of his eyes showed, and his lips were drawn across his teeth. "This is bullshit! We can't have this. This is my meeting. This is my program. If you have something to say, wait your turn, raise your hand and let the chair recognize you. That's me. I'm in charge. Understand? I'm in charge."

People were stunned quiet. But then Jesse broke the silence. "Fuck you," he said, and he walked toward the front table. "I don't need your bullshit. I'm out of here."

Joe sensed what would happen next. But it was too late. Before he could do anything about it, all hell broke loose. As soon as Jesse got close, River lunged across the table at him. Ana grabbed River by his shirt but he broke free. She jumped out of the way as the table overturned, sending papers and boxes flying. There were screams and shouts. Some ran for the door. Others flashed to the front of the room, either to watch the fight between River and the kid or to get in a few punches of their own. It was a flat-out brawl, plain and simple.

This was a schoolyard tussle compared to barroom brawls Joe had seen up in Alaska, but he had to work fast before it got any uglier. He got up a head of steam and bore down on Jesse. He lowered his shoulder and dove into the melee on the floor. He broke the two up like a cue ball ricocheting off two billiard balls. Jesse was stunned. In one continuous movement, Joe picked him up, slung him over his shoulder and ran him across the floor and out the door. When he got outside, he plunked Jesse in the gravel.

He wiped blood from an elbow and watched Jesse gulp air. "You need to cool down, my friend."

"Cool down? Motherfucker," Jesse said. "Fucker sucker-punched me."

He turned back toward the hall. A group was gathering behind them on the steps. "Things can get out of hand fast," Joe said.

"That fucker is crazy," Jesse said, wiping a bloody lip on his sleeve. "He's a fucking Nazi. Just some kind of power trip for him."

"You okay?" he said. "Can you drive?"

"Hell, I'm fine," Jesse said. "But they ought to lock that motherfucker up. He better watch his back around here, I'll tell you that."

Jesse staggered to his feet. He had scratches on his face, and his lip and ear were bleeding. Joe handed him a neckerchief, and Jesse pressed it against his ear and then held it out to look at it before returning it to his ear. Friends of Jesse's now ringed the two, making threats against River. "Forget it," Jesse said. "Let's just get out of here. This thing's over."

Jesse and a group of a dozen or so friends made for their cars and left in a storm of dust and gravel. A few laid on their horns as they spun out onto the Hurricane Creek Road.

Ana had come out and was now watching from 10 feet away.

"You've got blood on your shirt," she said, moving toward him. She squeezed her lips sideways in a dry grin as if to say she didn't exactly approve of what he did yet she forgave him.

"I'm okay."

She pressed her hand against his cheek. It felt perfectly cool.

"You learn that move in football or up in Alaska?" she laughed.

"A little bit of both."

Then she knelt beside him and examined his cuts. "You need cleaning up," she said. "Let's get out of here."

Her eyes shone. He forgot about his cuts and felt that sense of peace that surrounded her. "What about River?" he said. "What the hell got up his ass?"

She laughed. "I calmed him down," she said. "I had to keep a few of Jesse's friends there from crucifying him on the spot."

"How'd you do that?"

"I used a little Indian trick," she said. She threw her head back and laughed. "I just told them that I had a few tribal members ready and willing to cut off their dicks and wrap their balls over their heads if they made another move."

He sputtered in a half cough, half laugh, shaking his head. "Injuns," he said. "You think River'll be all right? Son of a bitch, he sure lost it up there. I had a mind to punch his lights out. He's lucky I went for Jesse first."

She stood and reached for his hand. "Let him clean up his mess," she said, and he let her pull him up. "It'll be therapeutic for him."

***

They drove back into town and picked up cotton and peroxide and Band-Aids at the grocery and then stopped at the drive-in for burgers and fries. From the restaurant, the tops of the mountains were obliterated in a hovering cloud.

"Snow's falling up there already," he said.

She'd brought in the peroxide and stuff and worked on his cuts. People watched them in cautious glances, and they were getting used to it. "It's supposed to come down to the valley floor tonight," she said. She patted his forearm where it had been cut. A clean red line traced a roadmap highway across it. "Maybe you ought to stay away from the meetings for a while."

He took her hand. "I wondered about that. So you've come around to that, too?" he said. "But I think River's got worse things to worry about than me. Now he's got a mutiny on his hands. He's not going to be able to control Jesse and his friends. He made himself some real enemies back there tonight."

She blew on the cut where she'd cleaned it. "They're just a bunch of punks," she said. "They'll get over it."

A blond teenager he recognized brought their baskets of food and drinks. "Thanks," he said, and he made eye contact with her.

She smiled shyly. "You get into a fight or something, Mr. Wallace?" she asked.

"What made you think that?" he said, and she stood there smiling at him and then at Ana for a moment. "You're Indian, aren't you?" she said. "You're pretty. I like your jewelry."

Ana smiled at her and then glanced at him. "Thanks," Ana said, and she extended her hand. "What's your name?"

"Emily," she said.

"I'm Ana," she said. "We used to live around here."

The girl seemed stunned. "I better get going," she said in a moment. "My boss." She backed away and turned and left.

Ana stifled her laugh. "Mr. Wallace? Now, that was hilarious," she said. "That kid at least had the balls to get it right out in the open."

He chortled. "We used to live around here?" He slapped the table. "She's right about one thing, though. You are pretty."

"And I have nice jewelry, don't forget," she said, and she rattled the bangles on her wrist.

He bit into his burger, chewed and then wiped his mouth with the back of his hand. He returned the burger to the red plastic basket. "You know, River created this mess. And he's got a bunch of work to do if he wants to clean it up. There's a whole lot of people who don't want anything to do with what just happened back there at the grange. And for him to put up so much resistance about a God-damned petition or whatever it was I was talking about, I've really got to question where he's coming from."

She pointed to the corner of her mouth, and he wiped his mouth with a napkin and then examined the napkin. "Well, I want you to stay clear of River for a while," she said.

He picked a bunch of fries. "I don't know," he said. He shoveled the fries in his mouth. "I'm okay. He can't touch me. Maybe you're the one that should steer clear of him."

She laughed. "Me? Don't worry about me. Don't talk with food in your mouth."

He reached for his burger again. "I guess I won't, then." Which wasn't true. He took another bite. "I'm hungry Let's just eat. Maybe that was his problem."

"What?"

"He was hungry."

***

River canceled the next planned meeting two weeks later, blaming it on his need to be out of town. But right before the meeting, Joe bumped into him out in the parking lot in front of McCully's. River walked up with his hands dug in his pockets and nodded.

He nodded back. River stopped and turned to face out the same direction as him. The mountains were submerged in clouds to their base.

"How much snow do you figure is up there by now?" Joe asked.

"Enough," River said.

They stood shoulder to shoulder for a while longer. "Look, I know you've been staying away," River said. "I don't blame you. I'm sorry about what happened. I get so wrapped up in things. I take things personally. It's a personality flaw."

River looked hangdog. The sky was low and gray, the look of winter and bad weather on the way.

"It happens," Joe said. "We all got our little bullshit things. I should know."

River sank into a droopy posture and hung his head. "I don't think Ana can forgive me," he said.

Joe scraped his boots on the pavement. The color had washed out from everything. He blew into his cupped hands, the vapor from his breath escaping between his fingers. Then he rubbed his hands and put them in his pockets. "Don't take it all so serious. She ain't the one that's quit going to the meetings, is she?"

He made to go but River put a hand on his arm. "I need your support," he said. "Come back, okay? And I need Ana. Can you tell her that? She's my lieutenant. She gets things done."

"Sure," he said. And then he moved away so that River's hand slipped from his arm. But River stepped in front of him and blocked his path. His face had darkened. "You're jealous," River said. "That's what's bothering you. Isn't it?"

What the hell could he say? It was the dumbest thing he'd ever heard, but it also surprised the hell out of him. Where did that come from? There was no way he wanted to have this conversation. It couldn't lead anywhere good. But he was stopped, and River was all caught up in himself again, the way he could take himself dead serious.

"I've gotta go." He moved, but River put his hand out. "Wait!" River said. "You're jealous of me and Ana, admit it."

"Come on now, let it go," he said. River had no idea who he was dealing with. Or maybe that was the point. He wanted a confrontation. The blood pumped in Joe's arms and head. His chest tightened. There was a coiling feeling in his body. This wasn't worth it. But the stupid kid wasn't backing down. Something had got in him.

"That's really funny," River said. "That's what this is all about, isn't it? This is all about the girl."

Joe wasn't about to be cornered. He tried going around River, but River stayed in front of him.

"Answer me," River said.

Joe made a move and almost got by him but ended up having to push past him as River fumbled at trying to grab hold of him. He made for his truck but it felt like he was walking uphill in mud or like he'd been drinking. He was walking but it didn't seem like walking. He threw his elbows to get a stride. His face was hot.

He stopped and turned. River had his hands on his hips, his face drawn up in a stupid grin. "Damn it, kid," Joe said. "You just don't know when to quit, do you?"

"Whoa there boy, take it easy," River said. "Don't get yourself so upset. Your hand's shaking. Your jugular's about to burst. That's not good. Stress is bad for you."

"Ah, shit," Joe said, and he stomped back toward River, his arms heavy at his side, his blood pounding in his ears.

River retreated. "Don't go and do something stupid now," he said.

He planted himself close enough to smell River's garlicky sweat. He clenched his fists and then opened them and stuck them in his pockets. "I don't know what's got in you, but you're barking up the wrong tree," he said. "What you're saying, well, it's just laughable. It ain't worth a person's spit. For Christ sake, don't make this personal. So why don't you go on and get out of here and let's forget about anyone being jealous of anybody else."

He pulled a hand from his pocket, opened it and extended it. He put his hand back. "Christ."

River never blinked. His black-brown eyes told less than stones. It was like walking into a dark house after being out in the sun.

River shifted on his feet. Then it was as if a cloud had passed and the sky had brightened. Like he stepped away from a kind of trance and moved back into reality.

"Well, okay now," River said. "I think you made your point. Would you mind standing a little more outside my American male comfort zone?"

He detected a glimmer of something in River. Mockery. Bullshit. Fear. The kid was afraid of something or hiding something. He wasn't worth getting angry at. He could have picked this skinny punk up by the collar and thrown him if he'd wanted. Maybe it was what he needed. He certainly deserved it.

"Okay," Joe said, "sure." He stepped sideways. "That good?"

"Yeah." There was another subtle change then, a sort of melting. River smiled. "I do get so serious about things. You're right. I'm sorry. Just caught up in it, I guess, and it's a long haul. Ana and I make a good team, though. She keeps me grounded and moving along the path. She's got that perspective from being a Native, you know, she sees the big picture."

"She sure does."

River was almost back to being the same kid he'd met that day fishing along the Wallowa. Or maybe that had been one of the personalities that River could take out of a closet and put on when he wanted.

Joe moved toward his truck. "Gotta go," he said. "Anything else on your mind?"

River ran his fingers through his dark hair. He'd let it get long past his shoulders. Then he put his palms together in front of his chest. "Tell Ana, would you? Tell her we talked, and I'm sorry."

He nodded. "I'll tell her we talked," he said. "Don't know that you need to apologize, but if you feel that way, you ought to take it up with her directly, don't you think? You going to call another meeting soon?"

River looked toward the mountains. He put his hands in his pockets. "I'm not sure. It's getting late in the year. A lot of people have left."

Joe laughed. "You think a lot of people have left now? Wait till December and January. You could roll a bowling ball clear down Main Street without so much as hitting an RV or a tourist. Better get your meetings in while you still have a few warm bodies."

"Maybe I will."

Joe turned and began walking back across the parking lot to his truck. "See you then," he said. He got in his truck and started it and began pulling out of the lot. As he did, River waved.

"Nice talking with you," River yelled. "Hope to see you at the meeting!"

He nodded and saluted lazily with two fingers. There would be no meeting. What the hell was River going to do this winter? The old truck lurched out of the lot. His was the only vehicle on the street.

CHAPTER 17

The October sun was a white ball in the cobalt sky. He came to cut and stack firewood to get Grace ready for winter. After starting off with a Pendleton shirt in the morning, he had stripped to his undershirt. The sweat rolled off his forehead and stung his eyes.

He positioned the wedge and then drove the blunt end of the maul down on it until it bit into the log and held. Then he raised the maul and came down on the wedge hard. The wood split cleanly in two, diving away from the cutting stump. He fell into a rhythm that lasted until he had finished splitting the logs and had a nice pile of cut firewood before him.

The confrontation with River had left him uneasy. River had seemed so head-in-clouds and peaceful at first, a starry-eyed college kid determined to save the world from corporate greed. It was hard to know whether to dismiss his weirdness about Ana as a mere schoolboy crush on the teacher, a naïve romantic's infatuation with her native-ness or something more sinister.

Ana had assured him that she could handle River. He wanted to believe her. But he didn't know if he could trust River anymore. What were his demons? What was driving him? He was deluded, for sure. But dangerous?

Joe had always held a firm grip on the plain truth. He couldn't bullshit himself—except for when he was drinking. He wasn't making this stuff up. He was gravestone sober about it. As sober as he was now for the first time in months.

He stopped and leaned on the maul. The lake was an unbroken surface from end to end, as calm as a bedspread, with not a single boat to cut its surface.

River was in over his head, and that was probably what was making him crazy. The kid wasn't capable of doing bad things. Mistakes, sure. But seriously bad?

He assembled a full load of split wood in his arms up to his chin and packed it up the stairs onto the porch. Now Kyle Macy, Jr.—that was evil. The look in his eyes when he came at him, Jenny's blood fresh on him. And Macy's family. Even after a decade, he could never feel completely safe around that clan. People like that didn't care for the subtleties of justified homicide or jury verdicts. Bart had warned him. It was easy to avoid them, since they lived out in the tules.

A trio of hungry yellow jackets circled him, soon joined by more. He jerked his head. "Bastards." It wasn't the possibility of confronting one of the Macys that put him on edge. What scared him was what he couldn't see—some kind of trap, some way they'd stalk him out in the woods.

When he got to the top, Grace was watching from behind the screen door. She opened the door and labored out. She was stooping even more now, and she forced a resolute smile.

"You're a good boy, Joseph," she said. "Now quit what you're doing and get washed up for lunch."

"Give me a minute." He laid the wood on top of the pile. It was the second row and was about half-way to the top. He still needed to finish that row and add a third today. Before winter came on, he'd need to add a good six more rows. "Have you been taking those pain pills the doctor gave you?"

"I've got more pills than that doctor has brains," she sniffed. She scrubbed the plastic table cloth.

It was typical bluster. She would have done anything the doctor and McKenzie told her. "Here, let me do that," he said, and he started to grab the rag.

Grace spun and eyed him. "Back off, mister. Get away from me with that dirt and sweat," she said, wagging the wash cloth at him. "Go wash up like I told you before I take this rag to your bottom. Hell hath no fury like an old crab on pills."

"Jeez, ma," he laughed, but then obeyed.

When he returned, she had spread the table with enough food to feed four. There was a platter of cold sliced beef, a full bowl of homemade German potato salad, fresh sliced tomatoes, sliced Swiss cheese, sourdough bread, pickles and a pitcher of iced tea. He made himself a sandwich nearly as thick as a piece of split firewood.

"Sit down, ma. You're going to eat something, aren't you?"

"I've been nibbling all along, and I've nibbled myself an entire lunch," she said. "You eat."

"Well, at least sit down. You're making me nervous."

She rarely sat at meals. She always seemed to find an excuse to be up and fussing or serving or fixing. With her cancer in remission, she was getting her energy back. Still, the disease and surgery had aged her yet more. There was no getting around that she was a shell of her once-vital self. Her body had withered, and it made her head seem too big and heavy to support. She was like a battered old ship, listing to starboard after coming through a storm. It pained him to see her like this, but he tried to take her for who she was now.

She slouched on the end of the bench seat opposite him.

"It hurts to sit anymore," she said. "Hurts to stand, too. And I don't like to take things lying down. The only thing I like doing anymore is swimming. I can still swim out to the raft and back. Where's your Ana?"

"I told you, up the Lostine trail. McKenzie told me you were still doing that," he said. "That water's too damn cold. Do me a favor? Do it when I'm not around. I don't want to have to go out and save your bony ass."

"Huh!" she huffed. "I could still swim circles around you, mister! For a boy who grew up around water, you're about as seaworthy as a sack of lead shot."

"Water was made to be drunk and sailed on," he said. "If God had wanted us to swim, he would've given us webbed feet. Besides that, up north, it don't matter if you can swim. You're dead in the water, swimmer or not."

"If God had wanted mothers to be happier in this world, he would have installed zippers on the mouths of our children," she said. "So, just shut your yap for a second and eat. She's up there alone?"

He grinned and spooned more potato salad onto his plate along with extra slices of bread. "She's got Buddy," he said. She rose to get the ice tea pitcher but he jumped up and fetched it and brought it closer. He poured a full tumbler for her, and she grumbled about getting beat.

"I've got to keep my edge up," she said. But she winked and laughed at herself as she said it. He wagged his head and laughed at her. "She's an independent one, that girl."

The porch was shaded and cool, and the sweat dried cool on his face and back. The aroma of sun-baking ponderosas was in the air.

She looked out past him toward the lake. Then she sighed as she swung her head.

"What is it, ma?"

"This goddamned place." She pulled her hands down her mouth and then held them at her chin. "We're going to have to do something with all this land one day, Joseph."

He was used to her directness, but she still managed to surprise with what came out of her mouth. "Where the hell did that come from?" he said.

She drew up on her elbows. "Oh, it's been on my mind these days quite a bit," she said. "You know, this old horse ain't going to go on forever. In fact, we'd all be better off if some good-hearted vet would just take me out on top of the moraine and put a bullet in me and have done with it."

"Cut out the whining," he said. "You want a pillow or something?"

She glared at him but sat back. "You know, I kid about it, but it's true, my dear," she said. "You know it and I know it. I don't know if I will be around sitting on this porch a year from now."

He swiped at yellow jackets around his plate. "None of us knows that," he said.

"True," she said, "but if I were a betting man, and I'm not, I'd say I presented some lousy odds for sticking around to show."

She lifted her glass with a shaking hand. The tea spilled from her lips onto her blouse. "Damn medication," she said. "I can't tell if I'm drinking or not. It just feels numb."

He knew better than to offer to clean it off.

"You've heard your brother's plans?" she said.

"I knew it was him," he said. He put down his sandwich. "Goddammit. I'm sorry, ma, but he needs to back off. He's seen dollar signs on this land for years now, even before dad died."

It was perfectly still on the lake, and it was hot. But there were long shadows and absolute quiet and a crystalline clarity in the air that had in it a sense of the end of things.

"Your brother sees things differently than you," she said.

"Tell me something I don't know."

"Don't get sarcastic with me." She looked at him sideways. "I'm mother to the two of you, just the same."

"Okay, ma, but, I don't think now's the time."

"The time for what?" she said. "Frankly, for a long time, we didn't even know if you cared."

His head tightened the way it did when he felt shame or confusion. "Cared about what? Besides, this ain't about me. It's about him."

"Oh, son, come on now. You were gone all that time. You might as well have been on the moon. We didn't hear from you."

"I wrote you. And McKenzie."

"Every five years. Listen, Joseph, what went on between you and your father was, oh, it was unforgiveable. I understand how hard it must have been for you. How wrong. Your father made so many God-damned mistakes. We both did. But he paid a price. He lost a son he deeply loved. And he never got over it. Never. Oh God, Joe, if only you … if only he—." Tears welled in her eyes. She tried again but couldn't get it out. "Oh, I'm blubbering."

He got up. "Ma." He knelt by her side. He took her bony hands in his and pressed them. "Come on, now. You don't have to do this."

She looked at him hard. He pulled a chair out and sat. Then he put his hand on her knee. He was sweating.

"It is so good to have you back," she said, and she laid her hand on his. "He would have loved it—."

He had to stop her. "Ma, ma. No. Please, please don't go there. I can't do it. I can't talk about him."

She pulled her hands to her face. "Oh, God, Joe. I'm getting old. I miss him. I miss him so much. Damn him!"

"I know ma. I know."

She let her hands fall and she sighed. "But please, don't take it out on your brother. Don't make him pay. He's not … he's not your father. There, I said it."

He fell back in his chair. "Goddamn it." He swatted a yellow jacket around his face.

"I think he sees it as inevitable," she said. "Either we develop it or someone else will develop it for us."

"And you believe that?" he said.

She labored up on her own. Then she walked over to the porch railing at the lake.

He let her be. Chipmunks chattered in the ponderosas. Juncos twittered in the bushes. He got up and stood beside her. The lake was a perfect blue mirror of the sky.

"You've heard this a hundred times before. When your father first saw this place, there were two things he said from the beginning," she said. "One was that he knew where he wanted to live out the rest of his life. And two was he wanted to pass this on to his children and their children.

"Make that three. He knew where he wanted to die, and damn him if he didn't get his wish. He was a quiet man, but I never heard him talk more keenly than when he talked about this place. He never went in for religion, but when I saw how he felt about the lake and these mountains and this place, I knew he had found a kind of religion in it. Like he'd found a home he'd never known, some kind of goddamned lost salmon that finally found its way. It's what drove him to work himself to the bone to build it."

"And now Howard wants to sell it," he said. He put his arm around her. The washboard of bones beneath her blouse still surprised him.

"Joseph," she said. "I don't know what to do. Maybe Howard's right. Maybe we're just lead-headed fools for wanting to keep this. What good is this land to Howard's children? You'll have children one day, God willing, and so will McKenzie, and I hope to God I live long enough to see them. And what good would this land be to them? Maybe now is the best time to sell and get the value out of it. Maybe there'll never be a better time."

He barely turned. Her eyes were wet and scared. "I think you know the answer, ma," he said. Then he smiled. "What's all this talk about God, anyway? You got religion all of a sudden?"

She turned and looked at him. "Pfft," she blew out and appeared annoyed. Then she returned her gaze to the lake. She drew in a breath and then let it out in a sigh that sounded like "mmm." She turned back to him and squeezed his hand and looked in his eyes, and he sensed it coming before she said it, but he didn't stop her. "In your heart, Joseph, in your heart, find a way to forgive him. I'll never bring it up again. Just try to find a way."

"Ma," he said, and he squeezed his temple between his thumb and fingers. She was talking about his father, but she might as well have been talking about his brother. Clark had been the thing that stood in his way all those years, even in death. Now Howard had become like his father. Not that he feared Howard the way he'd feared Clark. But Howard was always there to remind him of his failings, his faults, his weaknesses. He seemed to have a power over him, so that he ended up being the very thing he despised and didn't want to be but that somehow fulfilled his brother's view of him. Clark had made him feel worthless. Or more accurately, he'd let him do it, let himself be dragged down. Howard brought out the same crap in him, stirred up the dark shit.

He rubbed his eyes till they filled with psychedelic flashes of blue and red. "I'm trying," he said. "I'm trying."

"We'll save a plate for your girl," she said.

"She's staying the night," he said. "She'll be starved tomorrow."

CHAPTER 18

The weather came up during the night. At first, he thought it was Grace banging around, unable to sleep herself. But then there was the wind in the trees. There was a bump on the roof, then another, the big cones falling. Soon, drops of rain—or was it hail?—pelted the roof like falling nails.

He got out of bed and shivered. The temperature must have dropped 25 degrees. Maybe more. Why hadn't he checked the weather? He pulled on the cold jeans he'd dropped on the floor and a fleece jacket and tiptoed past Grace's bedroom.

"Joseph?"

"It's me, ma."

Her door opened and she appeared in her robe and slippers. She looked like a dressed skeleton in the half-light coming from the hallway nightlight. "I wasn't sleeping anyway," she said. "Some storm. Cold front's come in."

He looked at his mother but then he jerked his head as though he'd heard something and was startled. He made a desperate kind of guttural sound and his fingers splayed like he would catch a basketball.

She braced herself in the doorway. "What's wrong?"

He pressed both hands to his head. "Ana," he said. "What the hell was I thinking? She's up there."

She put her hand to her chest. "Up where?"

"Remember, ma? Up the Lostine. She took off his morning, her and Bud. They're up there at Minam Lake."

"Oh, dear lord," she sighed. "What is she doing up there this time of year?"

She raised herself like a flag being run up a mast. She pulled the belt of her robe tight and threw on the room light. The light was yellow and dull, absorbed by the aged ponderosa paneling, the worn leather of the furniture. She crossed the room. She had summoned the energy that had always defined her. It was in there still.

At first, he felt like a ship foundering on rocks. But she helped to get him unstuck, and a switch flipped inside him. He sucked in air and set his jaw. "I've got to get up there," he said. "Now."

He threw together as many emergency supplies as he could find into a pack. He settled on a simple plan as he packed: Get up there as fast as he could, as safely, and take only what was needed. Go on foot, ski, or snowshoe. He found the old cross-country skis and boots from the shed and threw those in the back of the truck.

By the time he was ready to leave, Grace had packed a bag of food and had made a Thermos of coffee. She'd somehow managed to get dressed in Wranglers and a Pendleton shirt. No makeup, which was a sin by her Bible, of course. "She's going to be all right," she said. "Did you take the snow shoes?"

His heart rose in his throat. But his head was clear, and he knew what to do. "Thanks," he said, and he was already out the door.

"Call Bart and tell him I'm on my way up the West Fork Lostine trailhead. Tell him—." He couldn't find the words. It wasn't that he couldn't think. It was just that he could only think of one thing. "Call Bart," he said. "He'll know what to do."

She narrowed her eyes and pinched her jaw. It was that determined look that he had seen so many times in the past. It was as though a crisis allowed her to summon her old self out of the wreckage of her broken body. If she had to, she would have gotten in the truck and driven up to the trailhead and gone and searched for Ana herself. And yes, he wasn't much different, he thought. A wreck, too.

He was out the door then and into the pickup and climbing up the moraine road. It was coming down in the headlights as a mixture of rain and wet snow but as the pickup climbed out of the lake and toward town it began spitting snow.

He checked his watch. Six o'clock. In this weather, the sky wouldn't even show the first signs of light until at least 8 o'clock.

All the way up the Lostine River Road it was snowing hard. It caked on his wiper blades and smeared the windshield with ice. He should have stopped and put on chains. He had to get there and up the trail as fast as he could.

"C'mon, girl," he patted the dash. "Be good to me."

He skidded to a stop at the Two Pan trailhead at about a quarter to the hour. Her pickup was there with a good six inches of wet snow on it. There were two other pickups in the lot, both old and battered. One had a horse trailer hitched to it. Poachers?

He got out of the truck. It was quiet the way it only is when it's snowing. Just wind and the roar of the river below. And it was cold—if it had been at freezing down on the lake, it must have been 20 degrees or less up here. He'd felt plenty of below-zero temps in Alaska, but the combination of wet snow and cold could be deadly, regardless of whether it was 20 degrees or 10 below. He worked fast, double-checking the pack and then pulling on the ski boots. They were hard and cold and tight. The laces hadn't been changed since he was a teenager. He should have brought new ones, but he'd get there without laces if he had to.

The trail started in dense woods, making it even darker than usual. But as long as he followed the path of white, he should be all right. It was six miles in to the lake, with plenty of places where the trail switchbacked through steep and rocky terrain, places he'd have to take off the skis and put on the snowshoes. If he was lucky, he'd be there by noon.

The first part of the trail was steep, following the west fork where it spiraled out of the granite as though following a circular staircase. He had to remove the skis and clamp on the snowshoes in parts. Each time he did, he lashed the skis to his pack. It took time, and so he waited until he fell before he stopped to put on the shoes. By the time he hit the first meadows, the sky had begun to lighten enough that, combined with being out from under the trees and in the open, he could see where he was going. He stopped to put the skis back on. His thighs hurt and he had sweat through all his layers. He was hungry but didn't dare stop for fear he'd get cold or lose his momentum. All along, he kept an image of Ana in his mind. He swigged water and moved on.

The snow was deeper in the meadows, drifted in spots, and canceled out any advantage gained by the flatness of the terrain. The heavy snow made breaking trail tough. In the big meadow, it was an expanse of white surrounded by the dark outline of the forest. No tracks anywhere. Ana would have cruised by here yesterday within the first half-hour of her hike. But it had taken him at least an hour, and he was already sore and out of breath.

Still he kept going. He kept telling himself that the faster he got to Ana, the sooner they could both make it out. Between the first meadows and second meadows was the toughest going. There were places where he had to pick his way through boulders using hands and feet, the skis lashed to his back and banging his head every time he raised an arm. He stopped and gulped air. His heart pumped like an old furnace, his clothing soaked through with sweat and with a layer of ice wherever the movement of his body didn't keep knocking it off.

By the time he reached the second meadows, it had stopped snowing. The day was brightening, and the clouds were breaking up. In places, he could make out the dark slopes where it was too steep for snow. Another day, a different circumstance, he might find it beautiful.

There were voices. The sound of another human voice up here sounded so foreign that he needed time for it to register. It was coming from the edge of the woods, but it might as well have been coming from another planet.

He waited. It was easy to hear human voices in things; he'd heard rivers sound like playing children, or far-off geese like laughing women. He lay back in the snow. The clouds scudded like whitewater, but they were breaking up and there were occasional pockets of deep blue. Ana couldn't be far now, and the lightening sky temporarily lifted his spirits.

She will be okay, he told himself. She had Buddy to keep her warm. If need be, she would have pulled the old boy into the sleeping bag with her. But he had to get to her.

He sat facing the trail. A party of three men on skis emerged. One towed a rescue sled, and the others wore heavy packs. There were bursts of static and chatter—the emergency channel of a police radio echoing in the stillness. He stood and waved.

His heart, already pumping hard, spiked with another shot of adrenaline. "Ho! Over here! Over here!" he shouted. He left his pack and skis and took off in his best snowshoe trot toward them. "What in the fuck took you so long!" He laughed and nearly fell on his face, he was moving so fast.

Bart stood with his back to the light, the evaporating sweat smoking off him like a hot springs in winter. He removed his mirrored aviator shades. "Got here as fast we could," Bart said. "You know Engler and Finley from Search and Rescue?"

He recognized the men and nodded. "Thanks, guys," he said.

Bart returned his glasses to his nose. "No time to lose, right?" he said. "Let's go find Ana. You guys leave the sled and go on ahead and we'll pick up the rear."

Bart hooked the sled to his harness and followed Joe to where he'd left his pack and skis. Energized, Joe traded the snowshoes for skis. Then they took off, Joe in the lead, the going easier over the trail that Engler and Finley had broken.

He shouted over his shoulder. "She'll try walking out, especially since it's breaking up."

"She'll be all right," Bart said. "You notice those other trucks at the trailhead?"

He slowed slightly. "Yeah. You know them?" he said.

"Those are Macy rigs," Bart said.

It was a though he'd touched a knife to an old filling, a shot of panic. "Goddammit," Joe said. "God-fucking damn it."

***

The report of a rifle pierced the air and echoed through the mountains. Heading up a rise on his skis, Joe let himself crash to the snow. As he fell, two more shots followed, cleaving the thin air. Then there was silence, broken only by his rapid breathing. He wanted to charge but waited for Bart. Bart had taken cover behind a clump of snow-covered boulders and was already on the crackling radio.

He called to Bart. "What the hell? You okay?"

Bart held up his free hand and with the other held a radio to his mouth. Joe heard every word in the heavy quiet. "You guys okay?" Bart said. "Repeat. Everything okay? What's going on up there?"

There was a long pause, and then the crackle of radio. It was Finley. His heart, already pounding like shit, jumped when he heard Finley say, "Spotted the girl in camp and on our way."

Joe took off up the trail following Engler's and Finley's tracks toward the group of trees that bounded the bottom of the last meadow before Minam Lake. He got through the trees and came out on the other side, followed by Bart, and then there was another rifle shot, closer, but this time he only jerked his head down and blinked. They were surrounded by ridges that circled the lake, and the rifle shot echoed from ridge to ridge.

The ski tracks lead to a camp with a smoking fire off to one side, against the dark trees on a bench above the frozen and whited-out lake. He called them, and Ana stood, wrapped in a dark blanket like an ink blot on a bleached sheet. She waved and called back, and he waved back.

But they weren't alone. Across the lake outlet, in the spot where hunters often set up camp, there was a greater commotion: laughter, banging pots. An old canvas hunting tent was set up with a smoking stovepipe poking out the roof.

Three men stood in front of the tent. Two of them orbited around the third and smallest. They were dressed in camouflage hunting gear, and each held a rifle. Three horses stood hobbled nearby, eating hay spread on the snow.

Bart came up behind him and, though there was no need for it, he said in a low voice, "The Macy brothers." There was a sheen of sweat on Bart's forehead, and his black hair was curlier and shinier as though it'd been greased.

"The little one?" Joe said.

Bart nodded and made a noise in his throat like he was agreeing. "Cody."

"Just like his murderous brother," Joe said. And then he took off in a measured sprint across the snowfield, his head down.

Ana knelt by the fire, wrapped in a blanket and hunched over another blanket. She was drinking from a cup of steaming tea. He kicked off his skis at the edge of the camp and hurried through the tramped-down snow the rest of the way.

She looked up and smiled, but it was a guilty smile. Her skin glowed from the fire and the tea. He grabbed her and took the blanket and wrapped it around the both of them and cradled her in his arms. They stayed like that for a long time not saying a word. Her nose was cold but her lips were warm. He forgot what he would say to her.

She spoke into his chest. "I'm so sorry," she said, and she repeated it several times, almost to herself.

He kissed her hair. "Stop, okay?" he said. "You're okay, that's all that matters."

Bart came up then and put one hand on his shoulder and the other on hers. "How's the dog?" he said.

He'd forgotten about Bud. He pulled back so he could get a sense of what to think, some sign in her eyes. She looked at him and then at the wrapped bundle at their feet. Bud's nose poked through the small opening in the cinched top. He reached to feel the warm but listless dog inside.

"Buddy boy," he said. "Hey Bud, look who's come to take you home."

Buddy's eyes were open and sleepily aware, but his breath was slow and shallow.

"It was my fault," she said. "I made him spend the night outside the tent on his own bag, like he always does. I heard the wind blowing and could feel it getting colder, but I never thought it would snow for some stupid reason. As soon as I found him, I put him in the sleeping bag and then I wrapped some warm stones from the fire and put them next to him in the bag."

Engler came around to the other side of the bag and put his gloved hand on the bag. "He's definitely hypothermic," he said. "There might be frostbite, but I think he dodged a bullet. Let's leave him in the bag."

Bart circled to Engler's side and hunched. He removed his sunglasses and squinted. "You okay to ski out?" he asked her. "We've got an extra pair of skis and some boots that'll probably fit. Or you could hitch a ride on the sled."

She waved him off. "I'm fine."

Bart straightened and replaced his aviator sunglasses on his nose. "Good," he said. "Then I think I'll reserve the chariot for Buddy here." He glanced across the valley and then back at her. "I'm going to go have a word with our friends across the way. They bother you or offer to help at all?"

There was more clattering and wind-garbled voices across the way but no one to see.

"I didn't ask for any help. They stuck to their business," she said. "They could see I knew how to take care of myself. Once they threatened to shoot Buddy if I let him run loose and chase game. But I'm used to that from hunters. I've heard worse. They didn't bother me, although frankly I didn't come up here for company. I would've moved off somewhere else but for the weather."

Bart spit into the fire. "Which of them threatened to shoot the dog?" he asked.

She stared at the sleeping bag and stroked Buddy's head with a grim smile. "All of them," she said. "I can't blame 'em for not wanting the game run off."

Bart watched across the valley. Whatever Bart had in mind, Joe wanted nothing to do with the Macys. There would always be bad blood between them. Better to let it lie. He'd killed Kyle in self-defense, but he assumed they didn't see it that way.

"Fuck 'em, Bart." Joe said. "Don't bother with them. They're not worth it."

Bart toed a spot in the snow with his boot and grunted. "Okay, then, let's pack it up and get out of here," he said. "We'll run into them some other time, I suspect."

***

At the trailhead, they hoisted Buddy into the cab of Joe's truck. They thanked Engler and Finley and said their good-byes.

Bart looked at the Macys' trucks and then turned to them. "I don't know enough to say you dodged a bullet. Everything was fine, and, really, I know you could have—would have—walked out on your own, just the way you got in there. I don't know what those boys are capable of, or what they might've done if we hadn't showed up. Maybe nothing more than poaching game, drinking whiskey, hollering at the moon and putting a scare in people every now and then. That might be their nature. But there's bad blood. I've told you this before and maybe you don't want to hear it. I don't think it's wise. If you're ever in a situation again where you see signs of these boys out there, give them wide berth. Treat them the way you would any feral creature. Leave them the hell alone, turn around and get the hell out of there."

The trees dripped with melting snow. The sky was bluebird blue. The sun was low, and it was cold in the shade.

She touched Bart on the wrist. "I'm sorry. And I will be cautious; you know that. But I do think those boys are full of bluster. Frankly, I think they're afraid of women. They're more comfortable around horses and dogs."

"You're right there," Bart said. Then he got in the Cherokee and rolled down the window. "Just do me a favor. If you ever see Cody or any of his tribe out in the woods alone, even within a mile of you, call me. I don't care what you're doing or what time it is, call me. Don't ever trust him or dismiss your concerns. Will you promise me that?"

She nodded. "Sure," she said. "I'll do that."

They followed each other in a three-truck convoy out of the canyon until the river road met Highway 82 at Lostine. Bart flicked his hand out the window as if he'd just seen them at a tavern. He turned toward Wallowa. They turned east and back toward Sockeye, and drove immediately to the vet.

CHAPTER 19

"Frostbite alright," Dr. Wheeler said. "That right leg of his, below the elbow, I'm afraid."

The vet would do the amputation himself and keep Buddy overnight.

They left the vet's and drove to the lake house, exhausted. After eating the meal Grace had made for them and putting her to bed, they stayed up late in the living room with the wood stove stoked. He stretched out on the sofa and she spooned against him. She was the one who brought up Kyle Macy, Jr. She said she wanted to know the whole story. She knew the outlines, but this time, she wanted to hear it all.

"Haven't we had enough?" he said.

"Tell me," she said.

She broke down when he told her how he had found Jenny Alvord lying in her blood. He stopped and held Ana's shaking body for a long time and said he was done with it but she sat and told him to go on. He cupped his face in his hands, and there was a gripping nausea in his stomach.

"I'm so sorry," she said. "It's awful." She turned and held him and rocked him.

"I can't. It's just—."

"I know. I know." She held his head against her shoulder.

There was something that began to let go in him. So he told it, how he'd come on Jenny's body, how Kyle Macy Jr. had come at him, how he'd seen the blade and reacted. Then the trial and the acquittal. He sweat through his shirt. But then the nausea drained from him. His head cooled.

They lay pressed together a long time. She cried quietly, and he kissed her face, her salt on his lips. They said nothing, and he fell into a deep sleep. In the night, she woke him in the cold after the fire had died and led him to bed.

When he woke in the morning, he felt different, lighter. As though the telling of the whole miserable ordeal had purged his gut of some malignant, toxic lump. He rolled over, and she was there. "Never had cancer and hope I never do," he said. "I kind of feel like I know what mom must have felt like. How it must be to have a tumor cut out. I feel like something has been taken out of me. I feel happy, goddamn it."

She smiled, her eyes still closed. "Good, Joe," she said.

He watched her in her sleepiness. "Do me a favor?" he said.

"Hmm?"

"Never go off by yourself again around here," he said, as he touched and smoothed the warm blanket along her hip.

She squinted.

He leaned on his elbow and stroked her. "I could never forgive myself if something happened to you," he said. "I just couldn't. Don't put me in that position. Maybe I overreacted yesterday. I don't know. But you scared me to hell, the thought of you up there alone, and with the Macys to boot."

She put her hands around his face and then leaned to kiss his eyes and then his lips. "Sorry," she said. "I'm so sorry. I won't do it, I promise."

He kissed her, and then she fell back into the spot she'd warmed and closed her eyes. He watched her breathe. In her, there was the possibility of wholeness. It wasn't that she completed him so much as that she showed him what he could be. After a while, her sleep came over him, and he couldn't keep his eyes open any longer.

CHAPTER 20

In February, they spent a weekend on the lower Imnaha. Down there, it could be pleasant during the winter, sheltered by the great canyon walls and below the snow level. She told him how the Nez Perce had overwintered here, grazing their horses, catching fish in the Imnaha and Snake, and hunting deer and elk in the river bottoms.

The elevation of the cabin was low for around here—below 3,000 feet where the Imnaha joined the Snake. Not much farther south, the Imnaha up in its headwaters was deep in the grip of winter. The cabin belonged to an older friend of Bart's who'd been unable to work on it and had let the place go. It was five miles from the nearest house, 10 miles from the four-building crossroads and was the last house on the road before it turned into a rutted jeep track that fell all the way down to the Snake.

The owner was more than happy to have someone stay there in exchange for work. So Joe and Ana arrived Friday night with an arsenal of equipment, two trailered paints borrowed from Bart, and enough food to last the weekend. It was steelhead season, and there was a pretty good run of steelhead up the Imnaha. So they took along the big steelhead fly rods that had been his father's and a selection of steelhead flies. They pastured the horses and then unloaded the food and supplies.

It was a log cabin with a stone fireplace made from rounded rocks collected from the river. The cabin sat on a hill on the east side of the river. From the living room, the Imnaha below them was green with snowmelt. This reach held some of the best trout and steelhead fishing in the river. Across the river, the canyon rose in pink and brick red palisades.

The cabin was in good shape, the furniture covered with white sheets. When they got inside, his heart raced. He wanted her but he tried slowing himself and taking his time. He took a sheet off a chair and brought it outside and shook the dust out of it. When he came back in folding the sheet, Ana had already made the bed. She was walking toward him with her arm outstretched and a broad, playful grin. "What are you waiting for?" she said.

He laughed with her. "You got me," he said.

She took his hand and led him to the bed. She was the whole world. He wanted nothing more than to please her, and there was no need to think. The smell of her alone was enough. The taste of her. Her skin. Her voice. There was the sense that she grounded him and connected him to the earth, that there was nothing to be afraid of because it was all a part of the same thing.

She put her head on his chest and he held her. The hum of the river filled the room as the light faded. "I could live here, at least for a few months of the year," she said. "It's so peaceful."

He rolled on his side and spooned against her. He traced the contour of her shoulder with his finger. "What about me?" he said, feigning hurt. "Are you including me in your little fantasy?"

She slipped onto her back and smiled at him. "I'm sorry," she said, playing along with him. She pulled him to her and kissed his hair. "Of course I am, silly. Maybe that's something we ought to talk about this weekend. You and I, you know? What are we going to do?"

He laughed. "I thought we were doing something."

She grinned. "You know what I mean."

He got up on his knees and elbows above her. Then he lowered himself to kiss her mouth. "I'm just playing with you," he said, and he ran his fingers from the bridge of her nose to her lips. "Yeah, let's talk about it. But can we talk about it later? Because I'm hungry."

She pushed him away, and he fell beside her. "Hey!" he mock protested.

"Men," she said. "Always the stomach first. Followed closely by the dick. And then something to eat again."

He slid down on her, kissing her. He wanted nothing but to be absorbed by her, taken up in her stream, the boundaries between them dissolved. He cupped his hands around her ass and pulled her up into him. He wanted to be completed and made whole. Surely religion must be about being connected to a thing bigger than you in some way that you lost yourself, you stopped thinking, you let go of who you were and you didn't care any more about protecting yourself because you realized that there was nothing to protect, it was all just a story you made up. He wanted this to last forever, and he tried to slow down and let things come naturally, but another force drove him forward, a desire that wanted nothing but to consume it all until it was gone, all spent. He moved up on her and then she turned him and she was above him.

Exhausted, they lay entwined. A part of him would never be satisfied. The craving. He hated that part of him.

CHAPTER 21

The next day dawned brilliant blue and cool. She got up first and took care of the horses. He got a fire started in the old wooden cook stove in the kitchen. After breakfast, they worked together all morning, clearing brush from around the perimeter of the cabin. It was dry down here, and fire was a real threat.

After a late lunch, they packed food and water and saddled the paints and took off down the trail. The track followed the canyon another 25 miles to Dug Bar but they only had time to go about five miles before stopping. The trail was double-track dirt road and it allowed them to ride side-by-side at a walking pace. It was a trail he had been on many times with his father and uncles to fish and hunt.

On one trip, Clark told him about how Joseph and the rest came down this path to cross the Snake at Dug Bar. He loved to hear how the Nez Perce held off the U.S. Army for months as they escaped across Idaho and Montana. It had seemed boyishly heroic and fantastic. Now he felt their misery and desperation. It hadn't been much more than a hundred years earlier that the entire band had come along this bitter trail.

They rode without speaking, a plume of dust fanning out behind them. The trail stayed above the river for a while, the water flashing like a knife blade in the sun. When the path descended and returned to the riverside, they dismounted and led the horses to water. He let his horse free to drink and then nibble on grass.

He stood at the river's edge. It was flowing hard with snowmelt from the high Wallowas. He knelt and cupped his hands in the water. It numbed his hands, hot from holding the reins. He took off his hat and placed it beside him. He plunged his hands in again and splashed water on his face. He did this twice more. Then he sat in the grass, his legs splayed out toward the water.

She stood with her horse, gazing at the river, her back to him.

He lay back, cradling his head in his hands. The sky was so endless it made him dizzy. He shifted his gaze toward her.

She turned and smiled and lifted her eyebrows. Then she let go the reins, and her horse moved off and followed his horse. She sat in the grass next to him and took her boots and socks off and let her feet dangle in the water. She took his hand in hers and felt along the creases in his skin. The sun was already low on their backs but still warm.

"It strike you funny that here you are with me on this trail?" he said.

She pressed his hand. "It always strikes me funny when I'm with you," she said. "You're a funny guy."

But he was on a track and wanted to follow it. "No, I mean, here we are in this spot. So old Joe and the rest of them came through here and then never came back. And it was pretty much all because of people like me, directly or indirectly. That must bug the shit out of you."

She let go of him and laughed hard. Then she lay back in the soft grass next to him and put her hands over her stomach. "You just kill me," she said.

He rolled his head and turned toward her with one eye open. "You're supposed to hate me," he said.

She looked at him, the sun raking her face. "Let's see," she said. "You're about as white as they come, you're a recovering alcoholic, your people stole my people's land. I must be crazy for being with you. Sometimes I think I am. And yes, sometimes I think I can't do this. I think, 'This *is* crazy.'"

The place and time suited talk about big things. "Would it ever stop you from marrying me and having kids with me?" he said. He hadn't planned to say this. But there it was.

She sat. She grabbed his forearm and squeezed it and looked almost wildly in his eyes for a moment. "You crazy man," she said, and then she got up and made to go. He reached for her and caught her arm, but she pulled away and walked upstream. She bent and found a rounded white stone and threw it into the river. It made a gulping sound and a splash of white and then quickly the swift water erased its ripples.

He pulled himself up and hunched beside her. He picked an egg-sized rust-colored stone and tossed it in the current. "I had no idea what I was doing when

I came home," he said. "At first I thought I'd just come home and go to the funeral and help mom out and then get the hell out. Too many reminders of my old man and all that shit I could never live up to. Which is why I was drinking when I got here and it only got worse. But just being in these mountains again, walking the river, I started to think maybe I'd left a part of me behind, that a part of me was here. And then I met you."

He sidearmed a flattened stone and followed its skittering path. She drew closer to him and lightly touched his hip and smiled. There was energy in her touch, a flooding warmth, as though she could tap into something below the surface and conduct it through her body.

"It's crazy, I guess, but I'm starting to believe that all this was meant to happen," he said. "Like I was meant to come back. Meant to do something here. We were meant to meet and make a life here. And I've never said anything like that before. Not even sure what I'm saying."

The water sighed and hissed as it ran down from right to left. She studied the creases of his hand as though she'd picked up a stone and was fingering its topography. She smiled and cocked her head. "Did it ever occur to you that you are already doing something here?" she said.

The river seemed to get louder as it got darker. "Not until now," he said. "I don't know where all this with River is leading. He's a whack job, but the sockeye restoration, that's bigger than him. It's work that's got to be done, and it needs someone who's going to stick around longer than him."

She punched his ribs. "I've got more skin in this game than any Johnny-come-lately son-of-gun. Your plan include sticking around with me?"

He feigned pain and then rounded his arm across her shoulder and pulled her to him. Her eyes were as dark as roasted coffee. He held her tight but started laughing.

She wrestled free and put on a crazed look. "Is that an answer?"

He laughed. "I already said so. Yeah."

"It better be," she said, and then she grabbed him by the balls and bared her teeth. His eyes widened and he bent and grabbed for her hands. "It better be, or I'll cut these off." She let go and laughed. Then she jumped on his hips and straddled him with her legs. "Make love to me here," she said.

"You mean?"

"You heard me." She squeezed him with her legs and kissed him hard. Then they dropped to the ground and she was on him. Each time they made love, he couldn't help but think it couldn't get better but it always did. This time, it was like dying and being reborn. She cried but it was pure joy, and he remembered holding her hair in his mouth and against his eyes.

When they finished, they lay in the grass. There was only their breathing, the singing of the water and the munching of the horses.

After a while, she said, "You're just like those salmon. Born here. You left—for Alaska, even, for God's sake. And now you've come back."

The sky was draining of light. "So that means now I have to spawn and die?"

She closed her eyes and then, when she opened them, there was a mischief in them. She smiled, and then she let him pull her closer and kiss her lips. "It depends," she said.

He kissed her again. "On what?" he said.

She pulled her chin back and cocked her head, and she wore a teasing grin, her lips pursed against her teeth. "Depends on what kind of salmon you are," she said.

He played along with her. "Steelhead get to spawn more than once. Plus—"
She looked at him with one eye. "Yeah? Plus what?"

He hovered over her face and breathed heavily in mock lust. "I haven't even spawned once," he exhaled. "But I'm looking for a fertile hen, 'cause I sure got some milt to spill." And then he rolled on top of her and began humping her and kissing her face. She broke out in hysterical laughter and finally pushed him off so she could breathe. And then they lay, side by side, laughing under the infinite sky.

They rode back up the trail in the gloaming. On the way, there were mountain goats walking the ancient game trails that followed the contours of the canyon. The goats looked ghost-blue, lit by the failing light. The animals stopped and watched them from a distance and then skittered away and disappeared.

When the goats were gone, there was a difference in the air. He'd felt it before at times in the past, but not for a long time. He slowed. Incense of sage was in the wind. The canyons were enormous, and he had a sudden sense of smallness, of being mere motes in the wind. He rode close to her. "Ever get the sense something's following you?" he said.

She looked straight ahead but nodded. "Lots of times," she said.

The canyon walls had long gone to shadow, bled of color. She kept a closer rein on her horse. "You don't see them but you can feel it," he said. "You can feel something looking at you, tracking you. You can almost feel it breathing down your neck."

They rode in silence a moment longer, and then she said, "Cougar will do that. Follow you."

He nodded and thought about that. "Yeah, wolves, too," he said. "There's been wolves crossing the Snake from Idaho. I haven't seen one, but they say they're out there. My brother and some of his friends are up in arms like it was the second coming of Sitting Bull."

She laughed. "Maybe they're right," she said. "Maybe Sitting Bull will come back as a wolf."

The river left the trail but it was still whispering its river language and singing its river songs in the ancient and immense canyon. They passed through warm drafts of rock-heated air, ghosts of the day, billowing across the trail. The breezes carried the tang of sage and willow. The trail narrowed in slots and they rode single file.

The feeling of being followed continued back to the cabin. But they never saw a thing. He allowed that he could have been wrong but he couldn't shake it.

In the morning, they rose early and took the rods down. They walked the reach in front of the cabin for half a mile downstream until the river turned hard and ripped through a long series of rapids. They caught nothing, the steelhead not yet in the river because it was running too high.

They got back at noon and were hungry so they cooked all they had left for the weekend. They cooked bacon, sausage and hash browns. They sautéed onions and green peppers. And then they made three-egg omelets with it all. They tidied up the cabin and then left as the sun was low over the canyon.

Her pickup lumbered up the long incline out of the canyon. Even as they climbed and extended the daylight by leaving the canyon, they drove up into the cold. By the time they were halfway up the grade out of Imnaha, she rolled to a stop, and they put on their heavy coats. She shook. "I forgot it was still winter," she said.

"No wonder your people spent the winters down there," he said. He grabbed her and pulled her tight. "We must be nuts for living up top in the winter."

She leaned into him. "I've got a crazy idea," she said.

"All your ideas are crazy." He laughed and rubbed his hands back and forth along the back of her coat until he produced heat.

She pushed against his chest and looked at him, her face drawn into a smile. "Why don't you talk to Bart's friend about letting us rent his cabin," she said. She tilted her head and raised her pitch. "Let's move down to the canyon."

He pulled back and examined her in an exaggerated, one-eyed inspection. "You're serious," he said.

"Dead serious, boyfriend," she said. Then she shivered and blew out. "And fucking cold, too. Let's go!" She got in and turned up the heat.

After a minute of silence, he put his arm on her shoulder. She was smiling. "You know, you are crazy," he said. She grinned and nodded at him, hamming it up. "But I like your kind of crazy." Then he rolled down the window, the freezing air blasting in, and her cursing him to close it, and he howled his best wolfish howl impression until his voice broke and he dissolved into laughter.

CHAPTER 22

In May they moved into the cabin. They worked out a deal with Earl Cummings, the friend of Bart's who owned the place: free rent as long as they took care of it. They'd be responsible for paying the electric bill, fixing anything that got broke, but otherwise it was theirs.

They drove both trucks down and took only what they needed. The cabin already had plenty: cast-iron pots and frying pans; an assortment of mismatched cookware, utensils, plates, bowls and cups for the kitchen; a bed draped with an ancient Pendleton blanket; furniture and lamps for the bedroom and living areas. They took towels, blankets, clothes, stuff for the medicine cabinet. They packed a box of books and reports and papers related to the sockeye restoration. She took her dog-eared copy of Josephy's book on the Nez Perce. They took their fly rods and gear, a chest of tools, a chain saw, a generator and flashlights. The rest they could get on other trips up to Sockeye, which was far enough away that they wouldn't be jumping in the truck and going into town to get something but close enough that they could go up for the day or even part of a day—at least that was the thought.

Three-legged Buddy couldn't fit in the back where he normally rode; so he sat up front. He could tell something was up. He paid attention to every curve, every cow, every bridge, every building, as though one might hold the answer to this mystery that was now unfolding for him. They were going somewhere, Buddy sensed. Somewhere for him; somewhere he would like. When Joe slowed the truck, Buddy sprang up, wagged his tail and whimpered, breathing hard as if to ask, "Is this it? Is this it?"

"Slow down, Buddy boy," he said. "We'll get there when we get there."

He led the procession. They passed thirsty fields of mint and alfalfa, the mint oil spicing the air, the rolling irrigators working madly and incessantly. The land tilted up toward the eastern sky like an old table that had been left out in the rain and warped. But they climbed merely to drop more. The only hint of the sudden change ahead was the appearance of the tops of the Seven Devils, jutting up over the horizon like big blue clouds sailing over the ocean. When they reached the top of the rise, it was as though the gods then took hold of the land and changed their minds and decided that now it should point downhill. From here down the 30 miles to Imnaha, you didn't need an accelerator pedal as much as you did plenty of metal on the brake pads and lots of clutch pad. The burnt metal tang of red-hot brake linings came in through the open window. If it weren't for the fact a person had to slow and hang a sharp left at Imnaha to head down the river, he could have coasted the final 12 miles as well.

At Imnaha, they stopped at the general store and bought ice cream bars. The store was owned by Rex Parson, a retired Air Force non-com who said he was born in New York but no one believed because he spoke with a drawl that was as slow and thick as West Texas crude. Rex was not much to look at and went through wives the way some men go through razor blades. He wore heavy black drugstore reading glasses, sneakers in a land of cowboy boots, the same greasy khakis and stained white t-shirt every day and lately had taken to wearing the wisps of his only remaining hair in a wiry, gray excuse for a ponytail.

Rex was watching satellite TV when they came in to the cool, dark, quiet store.

"Y'all gonna be stayin' at the Cummings place for a while?" he said. "That's good, 'cause I need some customers can pay with real money instead of these fellas think they can bring me some meat that they probably poached or dear god ran into on the goddamned highway and call that a payment. I got all the meat I can handle, if you know what I mean?" He snorted.

Rex never said a word that wasn't followed by a question and a sort of high-pitched, squealing laugh. Sexual innuendo was his stock in trade, and Joe figured the porn channels kept Rex occupied. "So y'all going to stay?"

"At least for a while," Joe said. "Till it gets too hot down there."

Rex's eyes kept track of Ana, who was walking the dusty aisles behind them.

"She's not going to steal anything, Rex," he said.

"Never said she would, now, did I?" he said. Then he pulled in close, feigning a between-us-fellas familiarity. "I happen to like them people. Their money's as good as any other long's it's green and signed by the goddamned secretary of the treasury."

She came around behind him. Rex nodded and smiled. "Ma'am," he said. His teeth were stained brown and their roots were exposed in the gums like loose tent stakes.

She wore a wry smile. "You have an interesting store," she said. She looked around again.

"I'll take that as a compliment. That's better'n what I've heard some others call it." Rex snickered like a chimpanzee. "You're welcome to come in any time. Got anything you need down here. No need to go all the way into town. No ma'am. Got it all here. Got buffalo meat, elk meat, cow meat. Even got snake meat. You shoot yourself a snake, why bring it up here and we'll throw it in the ice box and we'll fix a rattlesnake stew what tastes like the best goddurn stew this side of the Snake River. If you know what I mean?"

"We'll think about that," Joe said, and he made to leave, but Rex got going and he stopped in mid-turn.

"Oh sure," Rex said. "Got more stuff 'n your average IGA. You see?" Then he leaned in close again. "Sorry to hear about your pa. That was a hell of a way to go, but you know it warn't so bad in a way if you think about it, no disrespect intended?" Then he made eye contact with her. "You know, I always say, if I'm gonna go, just pack your rifle and take me out in the woods and just goddurn shoot me and leave me for the coyotes and buzzards. I mean, don't put me in one of those goddurned prisons where they feed you baby food and they lock the doors. You get my drift?"

Joe put up his hand as if to signal a time out, but she stepped in and extended her hand to Rex.

"Good to meet you, Rex," she said, and held her hand out. He studied it as though it were a rare bird.

Then he sniggered and smiled his rotten-tooth smile and looked at her and pumped her hand.

"Likewise," he said, and snickered again.

They turned and left, the entire time Rex talking over their shoulder on out to their trucks. He stood on the wooden porch that still had hitching posts for horses.

"We better be moving on," Joe said, and he waved.

"Thanks, Rex," she said. "Nice meeting you, and I'm sure we'll be seeing more of each other."

"Likewise," Rex said. He pulled something from his pocket. "Here," he said, and he handed him a plastic bag full of rattlesnake rattles. "These are good luck. They'll keep your place safe. Just hang 'em over your door."

He shook the bag. "Thanks, Rex. We'll put them up as soon as we can."

"C'mon back and I'll fix you some rattlesnake stew," Rex said. "It'll be on the house. And if you ever miss the outside world, c'mon up and we'll watch us some TV. I've got more channels'n a hog's got hairs, if you get what I'm gettin' at?"

They thanked Rex again and got back in their trucks. He put the bag of rattles on the dash. The road snaked alongside the river for long stretches and then bumped around small farms carved out of the narrow floodplain, each like an emerald in a field of jasper. It was only March, and yet here it was as warm as early summer up at Sockeye.

At the driveway, he got out and opened the gate and let her drive past. Then he closed the gate and drove up and parked on the side of the cabin. She was already out of the truck. As she rounded the corner, she stopped and recoiled, as though she had crossed a rattlesnake.

"What is it?" he called. "Ana. What's wrong?" He left the pickup door open and hurried to her.

She stood before the front porch. He came up and around behind her. It was sprayed on the door in ragged strokes of red paint. At first it didn't look like anything but a tangle of angry slices. But then it resolved itself into a crude message: "SQUAW." And then, below it, "WHORE."

"What the?" he said. He reached for her but when he touched her she shook him off.

He had never seen her so consumed with rage. She bent over and picked up a handful of jagged gravel and heaved it against the door. Then she screamed and picked up more stones and threw them and did this again and again and then she stood panting and sweating, the dust caked on her face and hands. She dropped to the ground and put her head between her knees and her hands over her head and rocked back and forth.

He sank beside her. He intertwined his fingers in a fist before his face and bit hard on his thumbnails, shaking his head. He tried to comfort her again, and this time she let him smooth her back and the nape of her neck. Then there was a tightening in his stomach and head, a metallic smell like blood in his nostrils, a primitive reckoning.

"The Macys," he said. "It's them. I know it."

"Oh, stop it, goddamn it!" she shouted. "I don't fucking care who it is. It's everybody. Don't you see? They're all the same. They're all the fucking same, every last one of them. It doesn't matter. They're all the same."

She shuddered and sobbed against him and he held her. This is what it feels like to be hunted, he thought. It had to be the Macys, their breathtaking stupidity and crudeness. And cowardice, like those midnight taggers in the cities. Whoever they were, they were going to get a fight. They had touched a raw nerve, and they knew it. If anyone tried to hurt Ana, he would not wait for Bart to settle matters. If this was their idea of a trap, they were mistaken.

CHAPTER 23

They moved in to the cabin later that day, but not until after they drove back to the Imnaha store and bought paint thinner, a scrub brush and rags. Rex told them that he personally would shoot the son-of-a-bitch who did it but that he didn't sell any paint to anybody, including Cody Macy, and so couldn't say he'd done it. But he did say that Cody Macy had been in recently. "That ain't unusual, Macy stoppin' in," Rex said. "Does pretty much whenever he's coming through."

"Did he say anything about the cabin or us being down there?" he asked.

Rex scratched his scalp, took off his glasses and wiped his forehead with his wrist. "Nope," he said. He replaced his glasses. "I would've remembered something like that. No. Didn't hear him say anything about that."

Joe narrowed his eyes. "Was he headed downstream on the river road?"

"Not sure, though it was more likely he was going upriver. He might've been up at Freezeout. Spends most of his time up that-a-way."

"Is there anyone else who knows about us being down at the cabin?" she asked.

"Oh, sure," Rex said. "You know how things are around here. Word gets around whenever there's goings on, new people."

They thanked Rex and left the store. They made the long drive up the canyon to the high bench of Sockeye and stopped at the house on the lake to get the shotgun and elk rifle. Grace protested but fell asleep in her chair, looking spent, her skin thin and pale, as he was about to explain what was happening.

***

Summer had come to the valley but the high peaks were still brilliant with snow. They drove up the moraine road with Chief Joseph Mountain high and white over their left shoulder. There were few cars on the road, the summer crowd not here yet. They cruised down Main Street to the city hall and parked alongside Bart's Cherokee. They left Buddy in the bed and stepped in to the office.

Bart sat behind his desk with the newspaper. The air smelled of dust, burnt coffee and stale cigarette ashes. The radio played country music with the telltale lightning-scratched signal. The police scanner spit and popped.

Bart smoothed and folded the paper. He slid out from the desk, got up and came around and hugged Ana. "Gotta keep up with all the news in town." He laughed at his joke. "Coffee?"

She said, "Sure."

But she looked at Joe, and he held up a hand. "Not for me," he said. "Can't stay long."

Bart screwed his face. "The hell's the rush? You got someone you got to meet?" But he smelled the trouble. There were two plastic kitchen chairs with straight backs in front of the desk, and he turned one out. "Have a seat. Ana, why don't you sit?"

They sat. Bart lifted out the metal pot on a Bunn warmer. "I don't know how I drink this. We'll fix a fresh pot."

Joe slid down in the chair until his neck rested on the back. The ceiling looked like it hadn't been painted since 1962. "I'll drink it if you make it."

"So, how's the move?" Bart emptied the swill from his cup into the sink and opened a large can of ground coffee. It smelled good. "Old Rex give you his good luck rattles?"

Joe straightened in the chair and leaned his hands on his thighs. "It's the Macys," he said. "Goddamn cowards."

Ana crossed her arms. "Whoever it is, they're fucking idiots," she said.

"Whoa, whoa, slow down." Bart's back was to them as he filled the coffee pot with water, emptied it into the coffee maker and flipped the toggle on. He turned to face them, leaning against the sink, his arms folded. "The Macys? Let's start from the beginning. What's going on?"

Joe stood and sank his hands in his pockets. He lifted a dusty slat from the blinds on the window that looked out onto Main Street. A ranch truck with a couple of sheep dogs surfing the flatbed rolled by. He turned and leaned against the wall. The coffee pot sputtered on the hot plate as hot water dripped into the grounds, the smell of coffee filling the space. "We got down to the Cummings place, and there was a little friendly greeting for us. Crude but effective. Red spray paint across the door."

Bart looked at Ana and then at him, and then he swung his head and grimaced. "What the? Son of a bitch! Pardon my French." He rubbed his hands. "Graffiti?"

When she told him, he looked at her sideways and grimaced. "Okay, first off, you've got to be careful. Ana, don't go off on your own for very long, or if you do, take Buddy with you. That old dog may have three legs but he's got all his teeth. I'd advise you to get a cell phone but we all know they're useless down in the canyon. I could tell you that having guns around the house is actually not a good idea but I know you wouldn't listen to me and I don't know that I wouldn't do it myself if I were in your shoes. Maybe you ought to think about not going down there just yet."

He pushed off from against the wall and came back and sat. Ana sat stiffly in the chair. He knew what she was thinking, and it wasn't what Bart was suggesting.

Bart unhooked cups from a rack and inspected them in the light. He blew in them and rinsed them in the sink. "Nobody does the dishes around here," he said. He poured hot coffee into them and handed the cups over, and then he poured himself a cup. He sat back behind the desk.

Ana emptied a packet of sugar into her cup and swished. He sipped the coffee black. "I thought about that," he said. "About maybe staying away from there. If that's all it takes to stop us, God help us."

Bart had coffee in his mouth and put his hand up while he swallowed. "Slow down, cowboy," he said. "This is not some John Wayne movie. Nobody's riding around with shotguns out their windows."

She shot up. "I don't scare that easily, and I'm not afraid of some little white boy with a chip on his shoulder. I'll be out in the truck." She turned to Bart. "I appreciate your concern, but we won't change our plans." She headed for the door, walked out and pulled it closed behind her.

Bart tried one more time to talk sense to Joe. He said he'd talk with the sheriff but reminded Joe of the budget cuts and how they were down deputies.

Joe put his cup on the desk between him and Bart. "And as a friend, I'm saying thanks, but no thanks," he said. "We're going back on down there."

Bart fell back in his chair. "Knew you were going to say that. Don't blame you, either. Just be careful. Something else happens, you call me."

Joe got up and looked at his friend and chuckled.

"What's so goddamned funny, Wallace?" he said.

"Now I know why the sheriff's ass is so huge," he said, moving to the door.

Bart got up but stayed behind the desk. "You think it's easy not jumping up and running down there right now?"

Joe left and shut the door but then opened it a crack and stuck his head back in. "Just keep sitting there and the only thing's going to happen is your ass is going to turn to lard," he said, and as he pushed the door shut Bart was cursing him.

CHAPTER 24

For a month, they had peace. They repainted the door a bright red—she said it was so that no one could mistake the place for anything but the home of an Indian—and scrubbed the porch boards clean and resealed them. As the days got longer and hotter, they settled into a routine. They hiked in the mornings and fished in the cool evenings, sometimes keeping two fat rainbows for dinner. During the day, they kept busy with the rebuilding projects he'd promised to do for Earl Cummings and tended the garden. In the evenings she read books on salmon biology and shared things aloud.

On a hot evening in June, they drove up again to Sockeye in his truck, Joe meeting with Kramer at the lake and Ana with River. They'd left Buddy because of the heat and they knew he'd be happy in the shade under the porch until they came home. Besides, he made a great watchdog.

When they returned home, Buddy didn't come out to greet them or even make a sound. There was a wake of turkey vultures by the river. A couple of them had flown overhead, their plumage rustling like velvet drapery in a breeze. She took off down the path to the river, shouting to scatter the buzzards. He followed closely behind.

She stopped short, and when he caught up to her, she had sunk to her knees and was sobbing. He pulled her up and they walked the rest of the way. Buddy had been shot through the head and left to die in the sun along the river. A trail of blood had run from his head where he had fallen and had stained the river sand as it passed the bleached stones and then stopped at the water's edge. The blood was dried and clotted black on his head, and what the vultures hadn't already done, a swarm of flies and yellow jackets was finishing.

He waved a stick to scatter the vermin and then knelt beside Buddy. The stench of the vultures caught in his nostrils and made him retch. Anger like acid erupted in his veins and muscles. He raised his face to the sky and let out a scream that shattered the air and scattered small birds from the nearby brush. Then he bent again and grabbed Buddy's matted fur and stayed there for a long time with his arms out straight over him. She knelt beside him and put her arms around him. Her body shook, and her pain pierced him until the wall of resistance broke in him and he sobbed, slowly at first but then the sorrow took hold and he cried and shook until the tears and sweat mingled and it seemed he would never stop. They held each other in the heat and the dirt until they were exhausted with grief.

After some time, the rushing of the river returned to his ears. He had blood and dirt on his hands and arms and clothes, and the reek of Buddy's emptied bowels and the metallic tang of dried blood clotted the air. A clear-headed calmness came over him, so real it was surreal, and he knew what he must do. He would clean Buddy in the river and bury his body, and then he would find this coward and get justice however that had to be gotten. Someone had sent a warning—no, this was an act of war—and he planned to answer it with a shot of his own. They would pay. There was the law, and there was justice. There were times a person had to take the law in his hands, and this was one of those times. He would do it, law or no law.

And yes, he wanted whiskey. Whiskey to steel him. Whiskey to anneal the rage. Whiskey to hammer the blade of anger and sharpen it.

CHAPTER 25

They washed Buddy in the river as best they could and kept him in a burlap sack in a cool outbuilding to protect him from scavengers and then buried him the following day up at the lake. The grave looked out over the water and at the moraine, which had begun fading from pale green to camel in the June heat.

He drove into town alone and bought a bottle and then found Bart at Long's Chevron with his Cherokee on the lift. Ed Long was under the vehicle and Bart was standing around with his hands in his pockets. He parked and walked into the cool, dark garage. "You keep putting money into that thing and you're going to send Ed off to an early retirement," he said.

"That'll be the day," Ed said, poking his head out and looking above his bifocals. "I'll be lucky if I can retire before I'm 75 the way I'm going. Hand me that torque wrench, chief."

Bart handed Ed a wrench and he walked in under the truck next to Bart. "New exhaust system this time," Bart said, wiping his hands on a rag. "What brings you out of hiding?" Bart gave him a look. "What's wrong?"

He gulped air and then blew out through his lips. Bart would smell the booze, but he didn't give a shit. "We just buried Bud up on the property," he said, looking at Bart and biting his lip. "We found him along the river with his brains blown out."

Bart narrowed his eyes and squeezed his lips into a tight ring. He looked out with black eyes. Ed stopped what he was doing long enough to look at him but then returned to his work. "Ah, shit, Joe. Not the dog," Bart said.

From the other side of the hanging shop light, Ed never stopped working. "Killing a man's dog without reason is a damnable act," Ed said. "I've seen people shot over lesser things."

"We'd been gone and left him down there." Joe traced the tread of the front tire with a finger. "Somebody knew we were gone."

Bart ran his hands through his hair. "Buddy ever harass any of the locals' livestock, kill some chickens, that sort of thing?" he said. "Don't think this is possible, but anyone down there not seem to like Buddy?"

It took effort to answer Bart's dumb questions. "No, never. I would have heard about that. No, Bud was a damn good dog and too old to give a shit about chickens anymore anyway. You know that."

"So who the hell did this?" Bart looked at the floor and wiped his hands on the red rag.

"That's a damn good question, but you're shirking your duties," he said, nodding toward Ed, who was holding up the exhaust pipe and looking at Bart.

Bart helped Ed drop the old exhaust system and carry it off outside and throw it in a pile of rusting parts on the side of the service station. Then they came back in, and Bart wiped his hands on the rag. "Can you take it from here?" Bart said to Ed.

Ed glanced over his bifocals. "Give me half an hour and I'll be finished with this old heap of yours till the next time it breaks down," Ed said, wiping his hands on his overalls. "I'm sorry about old Bud. What's this place coming to? An innocent dog."

They walked to the Bucksaw. Bill Mosey was sitting in his usual corner spot nursing a cup of coffee and needling at his gums with a splintered tooth pick. Becky Hastings came over and poured coffee and took their orders. She wore low-slung jeans and a tight blouse that showed a perfect little navel and slim waist.

"How's the pie today, Becky?" Bart said.

"Oh, it's real good, Mr. Walton," she said, blinking. "We've got peach, apple and huckleberry." Bart took his time, milking it. She took their orders and left.

"Mr. Walton, my ass," Joe said. Then he turned serious. "I want his ass. You and I know it was Macy."

Bart opened a packet of sugar and poured it in his coffee. Then he poured creamer from a stainless pitcher. He stirred the coffee. "Maybe it was Macy," Bart said. "But you don't know that for certain. What do you propose doing?"

Joe took out the pint bottle from his jacket pocket and poured in coffee and then held it out.

"Put that away," Bart said.

"Sure." He capped the bottle and slid it back in his pocket. Then he held the coffee cup in both hands and brought it to his lips. "How 'bout I shoot the son of a bitch first and ask questions later?" he said.

"Give me a break, son."

Becky brought their pie and refilled their cups. They ate and drank silently, and Bart smoked. Then he pushed his plate away and finished his coffee. "I suppose you're going to tell me not to take the law into my hands," he said. He put his cup down. "So you can save your speech. But I've had it. First it was the spray paint business. Now this. What the fuck is next? I've got to do something before it gets worse, because you sure as hell aren't going to do anything. By the time you get involved, it will be too late."

Bart pushed crumbs with his fork. "You don't have much faith in the law, do you?"

"No, as a matter of fact, I don't," he said. He wiped his mouth with a napkin.

"I don't know why not," Bart said. He put his fork down and folded his hands on the table in front of him. He quieted and looked directly at him. "The law treated you okay."

Joe set his jaw. "Don't bring that up if you know what's good for you."

Bart started to say something but he cut him off. "Jenny Alvord would be alive today if the law hadn't let Macy abuse her for so long," he said. "So don't try telling me about the law. About the only thing you guys do is pick up the pieces after they've been busted. If you call that justice, I don't want any part of it."

He threw the napkin on the table and stood. But Bart caught him and put a lock on his wrist and smiled between his teeth. He glared. "Goddammit, Joe," he whispered. "I think I know a thing or two about the way we do things around Sockeye. Now look me in the eye for a second and hear me out."

Joe tried to jerk his arm away, but Bart wasn't letting go.

"You've got a choice," Bart said. "Sit and hear me out, or go ahead and go marching out of here and do whatever it is you've goddamn got to do so bad, and I'll wash my hands of the whole thing. But I'll be the first one on the scene when they're either hauling your ass off to jail or they're zipping you up in a nice and cozy coroner's Zip-lock. Now, which is it going to be?"

The café patrons stared. When he caught their eyes, they returned to their meals. He blew out and sat. Bart let go.

"Okay then," Bart said. He leaned in. He had that no-bullshit look on his face. "Look, I'm sorry about that comment," he whispered. "But what do you want from me? You want permission to go ahead and shoot Cody Macy for allegedly killing your dog and allegedly spray painting your cabin? Is that what you want? You know I'll be the first to clamp the goddamned cuffs on you. If that's what you want, that can be arranged."

"Who's side you on, anyway?" Joe said. He brushed his shirtsleeve and looked at his fingernails. He gulped the laced coffee. "You know it's Macy. Who the hell else would it be?"

Bart slouched in the chair. "Here's the truth," he said. He looked off and down to his side. "I don't know who it is that's done these things. I don't even know if they're connected. But I'd advise you to get out of that cabin for a while and take a breather."

"That's just it," Joe broke in. He raised his hand and then let it fall. "That's where I take issue. Ana's right. I don't want to wait for something to happen again. And I'll be damned, but I am not going to let myself be intimidated. I'm going to live my life the way I want to live it and where I want to live it and who I want to live it with. And if somebody's got a problem with that, I will find out who that is and I will stop it."

Becky came by with the coffee pitcher but they waved her off and she took their plates.

"Don't know if I talked any sense into you," Bart told him. "I should've known better. When have you ever listened to anything I had to say to you?"

"There was that time when we were seventeen and you told me to buy some weed off of you," he said, grinning.

Bart twisted his head and squinted at him. "Got me there," he said. "Never should've asked. It's a good thing they never asked you for a character reference when I was interviewing for this job."

"Oh, I would've given you a character reference, alright."

Becky brought the check and Bart looked at it and reached to get his wallet, but Joe stopped him.

"I got it," Joe said.

"All of a sudden you want to buy me breakfast, after you'd just as soon shoot me?" Bart said. "Where are you getting money to buy breakfast anyway? You must've caught a lot of fish up in Alaska," Bart said.

"Don't you know, I was smuggling pot," he said, and Bart looked at him sideways.

They walked out and crossed the street to Long's. Bart's rig was in front, dripping clean.

"Don't look like the same truck," Bart said.

"Last time it was that clean was probably the last time Ed washed it for you," Joe said. He started for his truck.

"Hold on a minute, would you?" Bart said.

Joe stopped and put his hands in his pockets. "Yeah?" he said.

Bart blew out smoke and shook his head. "You just knock me out," he said. "You know that? You really do."

He laughed. "Somebody ought to knock you out, but it sure looked like it was more like Becky Hastings over there at the Bucksaw that had you blindsided."

Bart spit and took off his hat and scratched his head. "I sure as hell like looking at her a lot better than looking at your sorry face," Bart said. "But you know, you really do crack me up. You come back here after all these years. You start in to meetings with tree-huggers. You take up with a Nez Perce girl who you don't deserve and who sees God-only-knows-what in you. You're all about lost causes, you know that? Sockeye and Indians. They're gone, and there ain't nothing we can do to bring them back."

The motor homes and campers were starting to stream through town, on their way to the state park. "You done your little speech?" he said.

"I guess," Bart said. They stood side by side, the traffic wheeling by and the mountains shouldering over it all.

"Hell, I don't know," Joe said. "I came back here, I didn't know what I'd find. But I sure as hell wasn't going anywhere up in Alaska. For the first time in my life, I felt like I was on to something. And then this shit."

"I hear you," Bart said.

Standing there, he felt loose and free. Maybe it was being outside or being able to look off in the distance. Maybe it was the shot in his coffee. It seemed to give him more space for saying what was on his mind. "Well, maybe I'm not going to go looking for it, but I sure as hell am not going to run away from it, neither."

Bart scuffed the heel of his boot and then brought it up to inspect it. "No, I suspect you won't," he said. "Just don't go and do anything stupid?"

"The only thing stupid I ever did was become friends with a no-account sheriff's deputy," he said, and he grinned and turned and started back toward his truck. He opened the door and paused before he got in and then turned toward Bart.

Bart stood in the parking lot with his hands on his hips looking after him and shaking his head. Then Joe nodded and waited while Bart started the Cherokee and pulled alongside him. Bart leaned out the window.

"Have a nice day," Joe said.

"Yeah," Bart said. "Have a nice day yourself. You just take care of Ana and let the law take its course. And get rid of the bottle."

Joe pulled out onto Main Street and honked his horn and then drove back through town to the house on the lake. He finished the rest of the booze before he reached the parking space outside and then stashed the empty bottle in the workshop garbage.

CHAPTER 26

"It's Rex's truck," Ana called from the porch of the Imnaha cabin.

Joe came out behind her. Rex drove an old Dodge with a dilapidated camper listing to one side. It was unusual for Rex to be away from the store in midday, and even more unusual for him to be down their way. Rex got out of the truck and left the door open and the engine running.

"Howdy, Joe, Ana," Rex said. He tipped his torn drugstore-cowboy hat. "Now, she didn't ask me to do this, but I figured maybe I ought to come on down here anyway seeing that you might not be coming by for another day, if you know what I mean."

"Is there something wrong?" she said. "Joe's mom?"

"What's the deal?" Joe said. He visored his eyes against the brightness. "Spit it out, man."

Rex never did anything fast, but this time Joe wanted to shake him. "Well, I'm getting to it now, hold your horses," he said. He pulled off his hat and ran his hand through the greasy tendrils of remaining hair.

Joe moved to the edge of the porch. He placed both hands on his hips. She moved to his side and put her arm around his waist.

"Well, your sister called down to the store," he said. He flopped his hat back on, adjusting it.

"Please, Rex, what did McKenzie say?" she said. Rex took his hat back off, looked at it and looked around at the porch and then seemed to remember he'd left his truck running. He started to say something, then made to go for the truck, but then stopped and turned to face them. He glanced at them before looking at his feet. He held his hat in his hand. "McKenzie, huh?" he said. "That's right. Well, she says old Grace—your mom, that is—she's not doing too well. I guess the cancer and all. And she says she was going to come by and get you herself but I says, 'No, I'll go down and deliver the message myself.' Wasn't nobody in the store but me and I figured—."

He inhaled and then let his chest cave and his hands hang by his sides. "Thanks, Rex," he said. "Thanks for doing this."

She took his hand and squeezed it.

"Oh, not a problem, not a problem," Rex said. He grinned and put his hat back on, pleased with himself. "I hope your mom's going to be all right. Nasty stuff, that cancer. Wouldn't want to go near it, if you know what I mean—."

"We better go," He interrupted Rex before he launched into another one of his runaway rambles.

"You're right," Rex said. "Anything I can do for you folks?"

"You've been a great help." Ana stepped off the porch and walked toward Rex. Then she stopped. "Keep an eye out on who comes down here, will you?"

"Sure will. Always do. Not a problem, really," Rex said. He turned, then stopped and hesitated. Then he squinted over their shoulders. "Say. You folks ever put those rattles up over your door?"

She looked at Joe.

A splinter of fear stung him. He squinted and looked up and to his side, trying to see them in his mind's eye. He'd left them on the dash of the truck that day and had no idea where they were now.

"Not to worry," Rex said. He pulled another bag from his pocket. "I always carry these with me. For good luck." She came over and he handed the bag to her. "You take these now."

"Thank you," she said. "This time, we'll make sure we use them."

He said good-bye and then got back in his truck and drove off. She returned to the cabin and found thread. She threaded the rattles together and hung them over the threshold on the outside the doorframe. "I was taught not to have snakes come inside because they didn't always know if you were in their family or not, so they could be aggressive if they were confused. So this is a good place for these."

The rattles moved in the breeze, making a dry scratching sound. "Should've listened to Rex from the get-go," he said. "Rattlesnake rattles—why not? We could use all the luck we can get."

They left the cabin to the protection of the rattles and got to the house on the lake an hour later. McKenzie's Blazer was parked outside. They climbed to the porch. McKenzie opened the door and mouthed that Grace was sleeping and brought the screen door to a close without banging and came out onto the porch.

"How is she?" he asked. He wanted Ana near him, and he put his arm around her shoulder.

"Better," McKenzie said, and she walked across the porch and hugged them, first Joe and then Ana. "I guess Rex gave you the message."

"Yeah," he laughed. "Nearly had to strangle it out of him. We came as fast as we could."

McKenzie was in her element, clearly in charge. He was grateful for having a sister who was a nurse. That McKenzie was still single, while bothering Grace to no end, certainly made a difference in everyone's lives. She was able to care for her mother, get the best medical attention in the Wallowas for her, and see to it that her brothers knew what was needed and when.

A boat was slowly passing, below them on the water, trolling for kokanee, the voices of the boaters mixing with the puttering of the motor. It was bright and calm, broken sunlight bouncing off the water.

"She's such a trooper," McKenzie said. "But she had a bad morning. I thought I was going to need you to move her back to the hospital. I could have called an ambulance, but I—."

"Look, 'Kenz, don't worry about it, okay?" he said.

Ana took McKenzie's hand. "We're glad you called," she said.

McKenzie nodded. He put his arm on her shoulder so that they formed a triangle. "The chemo is making her sick," McKenzie said. "She can't eat a thing. Can't hold it down. She's lost more weight. She's in pain. But she gets up every day and wants to do everything she's always done. The other day I caught her helping someone trying to start the Evinrude down on the boat."

"Amazing Grace," he said.

McKenzie told them the cancer was killing Grace faster now. She had a high tolerance for pain, much higher than most people. But even she was beginning to buckle under the weight of the pain wracking her body. He could tell by the way she set her jaw when she walked. Still, Grace was Grace. She took life at full throttle, and if she could get out of bed, by God, she would get things done. If she couldn't get out of bed, she could order people around.

They divvied up a to-do list. Ana volunteered for grocery duty and drove in to Enterprise to the Safeway. McKenzie looked in on Grace again. She was sleeping.

The house needed brush clearing to make it fire-safe. He got the ladder from the side of the house, climbed up and cleared pine needles, twigs and cones from the roof and gutters. He placed them in a bucket attached by its bale to a hook on a rope, which was then strung on a pulley on the ladder. McKenzie let the rope slip through her hands until the bucket was on the ground and emptied it into an old oil drum to burn later.

"She's not going to last much longer at this rate," she said, attaching the hook on the bail to the loop on the rope. "The tumors are growing again in her colon. The doctor wants to schedule her immediately for another colectomy and then put her on an experimental chemo trial."

He filled the bucket and let her take it. Then he descended the ladder and moved it along the gutter. He leaned on the ladder. "Should we do it?"

"You mean, should we just let her die?" she said. She was sweating, and she let him mop her brow with his bandana.

"The surgery could kill her anyway, right?" he said, and he put one foot up on the ladder and then wiped his brow.

"It could," she said. "But just do nothing? That wouldn't be Grace."

He said nothing but nodded, and then he turned and climbed the ladder. "She's going to do what she wants to do in the end anyway," he shouted. He looked, and she had already walked away and was busying herself with some task.

They worked for another hour to finish the gutters. They took a water break and sat in the grass looking out at the water. "All this lake and not a boat," he said.

"It's a weekday," she said, and then she threw him a curve, patting his knee. "What about you and Ana? When is my brother getting married? You know, Howard can't be the only one in this family to do it."

"Speak for yourself," he said. He picked up a ponderosa needle and used it as a toothpick.

She laughed. "Find me a good man first," she said.

He looked straight out. "There's Bart," he said.

"I said find me a good man," she said, and they both laughed. "Bart's nice, but, for God's sake, he's your best friend. He already knows every story about me, and don't you deny it." She laughed and gulped water from a bottle and then untied a blue kerchief from her copper hair and shook it loose. "I'm worried about you and Ana," she said, and touched his chin and turned his head toward her.

"Who isn't?" he said. Her eyes were as blue and clear as the sky. "That seems to be a regular sport around here."

She lay back in the grass and looked up. "I know us Wallaces can be stubborn," she said. "How well I know that. Bart said he asked you to think about moving out of that cabin. I told him he might as well hit his head against a stone wall as soon as expect you'll back down. Is there anything new about Buddy?"

"Nothing," he said. He stretched his legs in front of him and leaned to get at his hamstrings. "We had some boot prints down in the mud nearby, but they could be anyone's, and, let's face it, it's just a damn dog. They're down two deputies from a year ago as it is. They don't have time to follow up on break-ins, let alone dead dogs."

"Buddy was not just some mutt," she said.

"No. He wasn't."

They drank the rest of the water and got up to go back to work. He snuck off to pee in the woods behind the boat house. He'd stashed a bottle there, and he got it and took a couple of pulls. Then he left to get the telescoping pole saw from the tool shed and set up to begin limbing the trees close to the house. She returned to the house to check on Grace and came out 10 minutes later.

"She's awake and she's getting up," she said.

He held the limb saw. "And we'll be getting our marching orders soon, is what that means," he said, and laughed. He made his way up the porch and sawed the dead branches he could reach from there. As they fell, she grabbed them and dragged them off. They were tinder dry.

She returned for more, already sweating through her shirt. "Bart told me about the monkeywrenchers," she said from below.

"He tells you a lot," he said. "What else has he been telling you?" He moved along the porch railing, craning his neck to look for pruning possibilities.

She had gotten the raw end of the deal, but she never said a word. She talked while she gathered. "He says they suspect some of them were involved in those fires up at Bear Creek," she said. "There's talk they're involved with this business about the dam."

Dead branches fell to the ground. "Talk's cheap," he said. "I haven't seen anybody with a monekywrench at any of these meetings."

She was making a sizable pile of dead wood. Later, they would cart it to the fire pit for kindling. "People around town can be pretty paranoid about this stuff," she said.

"Tell me about it," he said. "I see how they look at me and Ana. Like she's the ghost of Chief Joseph come back to avenge General Miles."

He shifted to another tree. He made the first of three cuts about one third of the way through the branch, half a foot out from the main trunk, starting at the bottom. The sweat flowed again, and he stopped and mopped his brow. He wanted a drink. "People in this valley somehow think they can operate out of time or nature," he said. "It's like they think they came to this place the way it was, and they're always going to have it that way. Then they go and do things like dam the lake and cut the trees, and when the sockeye are gone and the trees are cut, they still don't get it. They go around with their heads stuck in a hole."

She busied herself cleaning up small branches she'd missed. She stopped for a moment and looked at him. "Maybe it's not the Macys behind all this stuff at Imnaha. Ever think about that?"

He took the saw and placed it on top of the branch, about an inch farther out from the first cut. This time, he cut all the way through. "Heads up," he said. She danced away as the branch cracked and fell to the ground, and she looked up sideways at him with her hand on her hips.

"Almost," she said, and she took hold of the branch and dragged it off and then returned and watched him.

He cut the remaining stub with one smooth motion from the top down, outside the branch collar. When he was done, he came off the porch and helped her haul away the debris.

She followed him as he made a pile of branches. "I mean, maybe somebody else has a grudge or something," she said. "What about Ana's River guy? Where has he been in all this?"

He looked over his shoulder. "He's been out of town," he said. "Besides, he's about as violent as a poodle. He went to Reed College, for God's sake." He threw the limb on the pile.

She came up behind him and added her armful. "That's not what I heard about him at that one meeting at the grange hall," she said. She brushed her hands together.

"What? That he didn't go to Reed?" he said.

"You know what I'm talking about," she said.

They made their way back to the porch. He picked up the pole saw and looked for new pruning candidates behind the house. "He got carried away," he said. "He's still a kid."

She followed him. "Well, maybe so," she said. "Look, believe it or not, I'm glad you're getting involved in this stuff. It's about time someone from this valley took an interest instead of yuppies from Portland and Eugene. But there's someone who doesn't want you down there on the river, or with Ana, and I'm afraid of what they're going to do next. I just think that, well, maybe you and Ana ought to move back up here, at least till—."

"You, too, huh? You and Bart been talking about that, too? Till what? Till someone burns our house down?" There were a couple of trees left to work on. "We've got more limbing to do." He began walking, but he stopped. She was so much like their father. Those blue eyes communicated a lot without words. Too often with his dad, it was disapproval or disappointment that registered in those eyes. With McKenzie, though, it was genuine concern.

They were not yet out of sightline of the porch when Grace came out. She was like a dragon awakened from its cave. "Who's afraid of whom?" Her voice was like a bare loudspeaker that someone had thrown sand on. Grace pushed open the screen door and let it slam behind her. "Who's afraid of whom?" she repeated. "No Wallace has ever been afraid of anything or anyone in their lives, and they're not going to start now."

He let the saw drop, and they silently hustled back up to the porch. His mother willed herself across the deck to the padded Adirondack chair. He moved forward to help but she saw him through her narrowed eyes and shook him off with a jerk of her head and her uplifted hand. She put her arm out to brace herself on the near arm of the chair, and then, gritting her teeth, she searched with her other hand for the bottom of the chair and lowered herself to the seat. When she reached the chair bottom, she exhaled and caved in to her body. Her skin was see-through. Bruised purple and blue shadowed her wrinkles and creases and the hollows of her eyes. She had still managed to apply makeup, the penciled eyebrows like charcoal chevrons, a sore violet on the edges. Gradually she pushed herself back into the chair. "Don't just stand there," she said. "Help me with these pillows."

He welcomed her cranky invitation. It hurt to see her like this, but doing something, anything, was better. He came across the porch and fluffed the pillows behind her and gently touched her. She was sweating on her forehead, and the sweat had beaded up on the peach fuzz on her upper lip and cheeks.

"You should have on a sweater, mom," McKenzie said. She came across the porch, and he stepped back and sat on the picnic table bench opposite Grace.

Grace held up her hand. "I don't need a sweater," she said. "Don't start bossing me around, young lady."

He scratched his scalp. "She's got a point," he said. "She is a nurse."

"Don't I know that," Grace said. She folded her arms across her ribs. "Someone get me a sweater then."

McKenzie walked inside and returned with her blue sweater. "That sweater?" Grace said.

McKenzie didn't take the bait. "Here, mom, let me help you with it," she said, and she began putting the sweater on Grace, who barely cooperated. "It's cool up here on the porch," McKenzie said.

Grace protested. "You're trying to kill me by overheating me," she said. "I will die of heat exhaustion before I die of cancer." He suppressed his inclination to give it to her, though he knew she was having fun at McKenzie's expense. Even in pain, her wit hadn't abandoned her.

Moments later, Ana returned from town. He swooped down to help her with the bags.

"Mom's out and she's as ornery as ever," he said. "Watch your back." By the time they made it up the stairs to the porch, McKenzie greeted them with her index finger pressed to her lips and motioned toward Grace. She was asleep in the chair.

They snuck the groceries in and then kissed McKenzie good-bye.

McKenzie looked at him. "Call me," she whispered. "And think about what I said, please?"

He began to walk away. "Joe?" she said.

He stopped and turned. "Okay," he said.

They didn't speak until they got out on the road. Ana drove. "She's fighting so hard," she said.

The lake showed blue between the ponderosas. "She's strong, but she's losing it," he said. "I don't know if she's going to make it."

"What did McKenzie ask you to think about?"

"Oh that," he said, and he kept his face turned toward the window. "Just stuff about mom," he said. "You know." He couldn't look at her. It wasn't that he was telling her a lie. It was that he wasn't telling her everything. She was the one who wanted to stay at the cabin, and it wasn't going to do her any good to hear otherwise.

CHAPTER 27

In late June, Ana's period had stopped, and she'd gone in to see McKenzie and her doc, and the test had come back positive. He knew something was up when she took him from the cabin down to the Imnaha. He stopped and gave his head a twist and looked at her sideways and then stepped back and sized her up and down the length of her body. He'd forgotten to breathe.

She started laughing. "Aren't you going to say anything?"

"Well, yeah. Of course I'm going to say something," he said. He thumbed his belt and walked around her. "You're not kidding, right?" he said. "Of course you're not kidding. You wouldn't kid me about something like that."

"Hah!" She kept laughing. "You're hilarious!" Her face lit up with her smile. But there was a slight twist to her lips and a narrowing of one eye. She wanted to hear it from him.

"I'm happy," he said. He didn't know whether to sit or stand. But he jumped and spun, and then he grabbed her and kissed her. "Whoa! I'm ecstatic. Scared to shit, too. I don't know what to say. I'm going to be a father? We're going to be parents? You sure about this?"

"You want to call your sister and see the tests?" She pressed him to her and began alternately sobbing and laughing. She was flushed hot, and he kissed her and held her. The salt of her tears was on his tongue. "I thought you might be mad, or scared. I was really afraid for some stupid reason."

He kissed her forehead. "Yeah, that was stupid," he said. "Scared? You bet. Real scared. But happy, too. Really happy."

She kissed him. "I love you, Joe Wallace. I really do."

She was wet with tears and sweat. "You better. 'Cause I love the hell out of you."

After dinner that night, the power blinked out as usual, and it didn't come back on. They fell into bed. In the candlelight, they made love fiercely and tenderly, both of them crying and laughing, the moment alive, as though they were tapped into a well of energy emerging from the ground below the cabin.

He lay awake a long time listening to her breathe beside him. But he couldn't turn off his mind and finally he got up and walked outside. The full moon had risen over the rimrock at the head of the valley. It flooded the grass and trees with a sharp colorless light. In the distance, the river carried on its endless and unknowable conversations.

He sat on the deck of the porch. Warm breaths of air slipstreamed by, laced with timothy and mint from upriver farms.

It had all come so fast. But there was never a question about the baby. He was sure from the first moment: They would have this baby together. Not that they were trying. They weren't, but then again they weren't being too careful. They had talked about it all: marriage, children, the future. Now nature had taken its course and decided the timing for them.

At the same time, a child meant change. He'd have to think of another life, one completely dependent on him. Where would they live? What about money? What would he do now that there would be medical bills, diapers, strained carrots, winter coats, skis, books, school supplies, fishing rods? Definitely fishing rods. What about schools? What about religion? What about drinking?

There was no way he would sleep. His worst thoughts came at night. In Alaska, he'd wait out the night in a tavern and leave at closing time too drunk to care. When daylight came, he was more relaxed and could fall asleep.

He jumped up and leaned on the front porch post with his left hand and pulled himself in close to it. With his right hand, he covered his face, which was now hot and sweating. It was the finality of it that got him. There was no going back on this.

Why was it that, just when he should be happiest, these idiot thoughts crept in? He realized he'd been holding his breath as though he were under water. He gulped the night air and then released it. He let go of the post.

There was a noise inside and then Ana. "Joe?" she said. "Is that you?"

"Just me, wrestling with a bear," he said.

"Well tell the bear to go home so you can come to bed," she said into her pillow.

"I already tried but he said he wasn't tired," he said.

"What?" she said, and she made some unintelligible mumble as their bed creaked and then silence returned.

The last thing he could do was sleep. He thought of waking Ana to talk but couldn't bring himself to do it. He figured it would do him good to walk. He thought of taking his pistol for some stupid reason, but then he realized he never would have taken a pistol before, and there was no need for it.

The trail was a ribbon of cold light. The shadows were pure black. As he walked, trees, bushes and rocks appeared when they should have appeared, but they were transformed into different shapes. In this lunar landscape, nothing seemed truly familiar.

He navigated to the river, not far from where he had found Buddy. The white water flashed in the inky river. He remembered being on the *Jenny Alvord* up in Alaska at night, how the phosphorescence lit the dark water. He remembered the canopy of stars reflected on the surface of the water, so still that there seemed to be no seam between water and sky, only a curved, star-bejeweled blackness.

The mind played tricks on itself on moonlit nights. He remembered many times getting spooked in the dark woods when he was a kid. After a while, he would find himself running for the lights of home, pursued by an imaginary beast nipping at his heels. Once, he nearly got his eye poked out when he ran straight into a tree limb that had fallen in the path near the house.

The river talked, especially in the quiet of the night. It hissed, murmured, moaned. Sometimes it sounded like conversations between people. Sometimes it was like children laughing. Other times, there was music, as though the river were playing an old AM radio, tuning in and out of fuzzy stations from distant places. Yet other times, the sounds might have been the ghosts of the Nez Perce who had wintered here, Ana's ancestors planning another ride across the Snake or back up the valley to the summer lake and the swirling sockeye, reversing their exodus and returning to the Wallowas.

Now he and Ana would have a child whose blood was a part of those stories. Boy or girl, it didn't matter. Their child would come from these waters, these mountains and canyons, as much a part of them as the salmon, the coyote or the elk.

He sat as the dark water flowed by. Is this how he was, moved by a force over which he had no control? On the far side, cottonwood leaves flickered, reflecting silver. The night air carried the scents of the valley. There was the humid tang of the river when he caught a salmon or steelhead. There was the vanilla of the willow, the oven smell of rocks cooling, the beery smell of skunk, the sweetness of mown hay, the earth smell of horse. The wind picked up and carried these, mixing them as they tumbled along and sending them down these canyons.

A child was a blessing. He had not considered it when he returned to Sockeye. The possibility of meeting a woman and falling in love? Ridiculous. The idea of fathering a child—at least doing so sober and, if not deliberately, at least in an act of love? Even more ridiculous. He had not even planned to stay. Now everything had changed. This was meant to be. He didn't believe in an all-powerful God, moving people around like chess pieces. He had once believed that things happened for a reason. Then he stopped believing. Or did he?

Why had his dad died when he did? Why was it that he had returned to Sockeye and met Ana? If Clark's plane hadn't crashed, he would have still been in Alaska on a fishing boat, getting drunk in port, occasionally bringing home another honky-tonk girl who looked good through the veil of a dark bar and five or six bourbons and a beer or three but who looked like a knotted pile of rope in the morning.

What would Clark have thought of all this? Would it have been cause for celebration, for bourbon and cigars? Or would it have been another embarrassment to the family name, another example of failing to live up to his standards? It occurred to him now, as he brooded in the moonlight, how larger than life his father's presence was to him, like the moon itself, even more now in death than in life. Here he was seeking approval from a ghost. He could spend his life searching for approval from a dead man, but it would never come. Dead men don't speak, except perhaps in the garbled jumble of lost conversations leaking from tumbling rivers. In the end, he not only would become father to his child, but he himself would have to learn to parent the kid inside who had never got what it wanted or needed from his father. And yes, he'd have to put his father to rest, too, or else let Clark's ghost rattle around inside his head until it drove him back into a bottle.

Was his father out there somewhere? Was he in the river, in the wind, in the moon? Could he carry on a conversation with him? What to say? It was stupid, but there was no one around to hear. Jesus. What to say? Yell at him? Call him a bastard? Blame him for abandoning him when he needed him? For all the hurt? "Fuck, fuck," he said quietly to himself, and his eyes watered. But he caught himself and twisted his head down and sideways, angry for being such a fool. What did he think he could do—bring him back and get the love he never got? He ran his hand through his scalp. Then he screamed, "Fuck! Fuck you! Fuck you!" until it was as though he were connected to a well of rage gushing from the earth and through him and out into the night.

When he was done, he let himself sink and sit. He was spent, and he began to feel cold. The river was moving down from right to left in front of him like a living creature whose name he'd known but had never truly known.

Then there was a flash of silver, almost like a shooting star, but this flash shot out of the water and was followed by a splash. Only Chinook made that loud of a splash. Most likely it was a Chinook making its way upriver to the spawning grounds. There used to be thousands of them. Now most of them were hatchery fish, genetic misfits, but there were still a few bull-headed natives that somehow had managed to survive the dams on the Snake. They moved at night, especially on moonlit nights like this. He imagined their muscular silver bodies electric with the scent-memory of their birthplaces. And here they were, fighting gravity the whole way, against the water and yet a part of the water, consumed by another relentless force every bit as strong as gravity. He'd never known that kind of drive, commitment, passion—whatever you wanted to call it. But by fathering a child, he himself was swimming out into a kind of current. He would either let it pull him down or he would swim against it. The choice of standing still didn't seem like an option anymore. It was time to move on.

He was tired and cold and alone, but he was not ready to go back to the cabin. He lay in the grass at water's edge, beneath the dense Milky Way. The three jewels of Orion's belt shone in the southern sky. Sirius, the dog star, shimmered in the blackness. The three stars of the summer triangle beamed. He lay there a long time, long enough to feel the tide of sleep rising in him. Satellites caught his eye in their quiet arcs across the sky. Drifting down, his eyes closed, his hearing switched off.

But then it was jarred back on. His mind had not yet caught up with his hearing. The sound was a snapping. A cracking twig? It was hard to tell over the rush of the river. He opened his eyes. His stomach fluttered. Silence. Just the river, the breeze. He closed his eyes, and his mind turned off. Moments later, another strange sound came to his ears. The sound of someone or something breathing? The soil and rock beneath him vibrated, as though drummed by something running hard. This time he opened his eyes and shot up to his feet. He wheeled in the direction of the cabin, his body taut and his senses alert with animal attention.

"Hey," he said in a low, guttural voice that seemed to come unconsciously, spawned by a cutting fear in his stomach. His mouse-of-a-man attempt sounded ridiculously quiet and frightened to him. "Hey!" he yelled louder, and then louder again. "Who's there!"

The bone and ink landscape lay in silence. He could detect the slightest change of sound or even of wind or vibration, his alert level was so high. The blood rushed in his ears and his heart pounded beneath his shirt. Leaves ticked in the night breeze. There was nothing. Then there was a voice, a woman's voice or a child's voice.

"Ana?" he called. "Ana!"

CHAPTER 28

His only thought now was of her in the cabin alone. He had left her sleeping with the door open. The cabin stood in the ghostly light, as if it were made of marble, quiet and strange up on the hill. He ran for the cabin, but at once the familiar became unfamiliar, and he lost the trail.

He crashed through the riverside sage. Buddy would have protected her. Now there was only him, and he'd done a lousy job. He jumped to clear a bundle of sage, but when he came down he caught his foot, twisting his ankle and falling headlong to the ground. There was the grit and metallic taste of dirt in his mouth and the warm wetness of blood trickling on his knee beneath his pant leg. He had scraped his face and knee on the rocks and he had messed his ankle. He picked himself up and hobbled the pain off.

He slowed at the sight of the cabin. It was too quiet, too dark. No lights: The power was still out. He called her name. His heart pounded, and he sweat cold. His thoughts had wanted to race but now that there was danger, the tunnel vision came over him and he settled.

He bolted across the porch and opened the screen door. It was dark inside. The moonlight flooded through the open door, leaving a bleached path across the floor boards and into the bedroom like frost. There was a flashlight in a drawer in the kitchen, but this was not the time to get it.

This was too much like Jenny Alvord again. This couldn't be real. This couldn't be happening. He approached the bedroom. He did not breathe. His hands trembled. His spine buzzed up his back, up the nape of his neck and across his scalp. Every fiber of him stood on end.

It's Cody Macy, he thought. Maybe those voices he heard were him and his brothers. Maybe they'd come on horseback. Maybe he's waiting in the shadows, just like his brother, just like before.

He moved through the main room and crossed the threshold of the bedroom. He made out a shape in the bed, the shape of a body. He yelled her name, but there was no answer, no movement. He inched closer. His head throbbed along with his ankle.

He stopped and turned, scanning the darkened room behind him. Get the pistol, he thought. No, too late. Ana's curtains moved in the breeze from the open window, throwing shadows across the moonlit floor. Then came the sound of something outside, maybe just the river. His body clenched. He was about to pull back the covers when he heard it again. A voice. Definitely a voice.

It sounded like a hurt child. He couldn't tell where it had come from. What was real or what was a dream anymore? In this goddamned unreal black and white landscape, the world had turned into a negative of itself.

The bed looked different when he turned back toward it, as though the blankets had been moved. Jenny Alvord and Kyle Macy and that terrible night. He'd kept the memories locked but they hadn't gone away.

The voice came again. Calling him? He reached and grabbed hold of the down comforter, cool and light. He knew she wasn't there. He pulled on it anyway, his eyes shut, yanking it clear off the bed. He memory of the dark, bloodied sheet came to him. His body stiffened and he raised his head. *God,* he said aloud. *God.* Tears came, and he sobbed. He opened his eyes. The bed was empty. Where was Ana? Was it her voice? This was a nightmare. He wanted daylight, not this fucking ghost light. He wanted to find her and hold her. How could he have left her?

The sound came again, like crying. But it was gone before he could place the source, in or out. He called her name low, as if she were there if only he could see her. Then he stopped and quieted himself. But there was no answer, only the river down the hill and the wind-blown sagebrush outside. From where he stood in the main room, he pivoted, waiting for something to move or stand out. Nothing. He walked into the bathroom. Nothing. He returned to the main room and reached into the junk drawer and grabbed the flashlight. Strange, the yellow beam like the weak energy of the daylight world. Weak as the light was, he squinted as he scanned the room with it. The table, chairs and other pieces of furniture seemed weirdly real yet not lived-in, like set pieces in museums.

He pushed open the screen door. Her boots were gone. The boards creaked under his feet as he walked to the edge of the porch.

In front of the porch, the gravel and dirt were monochrome, cold and drained. He pointed the flashlight out into the brush, but the immensity of the night swallowed its light. Goose bumps rose on his arms. The moon was approaching the western rim of the canyon, etching shadows on the rocks.

"Ana!" he called out into the brush. "Ana! Answer me! Ana!"

Stay calm, he thought. She's out there. She had to be. She can't be far. She can't just disappear.

Then he heard, or he thought he heard, her voice washed by the night wind. It was a low moan, and then his name and finally sobs.

"Ana!" His heart pounded. There was no doubt this time.

He jumped off the porch and winced when he hit the gravel. His ankle was swelling. He raked the light over sagebrush, juniper and stone, but the light, barely bright enough in the cabin, was useless out here. He shut it off and let his eyes adjust to the moonlight. He called her name again, and this time he was sure she answered, feebly yet clearly. She was out there and she was hurt.

"Ana, I'm here," he shouted. "Keep talking. I'm going to find you."

He located the main trail to the river and followed it toward where he thought he had heard her voice. He stopped and called; she replied but she sounded farther away now.

"Where are you! Don't stop talking, Ana. Keep trying."

The last sliver of moon disappeared over the canyon rim, now silhouetted and outlined in white. The ground darkened, as though a pool of quicksilver had been drained from around his feet. He turned on the flashlight again, and this time its brightness seemed to intensify in the moonless vacuum. He had gone in the wrong direction. He backtracked toward the cabin and scanned the brush again.

Her voice returned, this time to his left. In that direction, a mound of weathered rock rose like the humped back of a spawning sockeye. Then it dropped off about 20 feet into a pit where the bones of broken rocks had accumulated over thousands of years. A smaller trail splintered from the main trail and led up to the rock. He had climbed it numerous times with her, often sitting there and watching birds and deer. In the spring and fall, it was a favorite haunt of rattlers to sun on the dark rocks. She might have climbed it to look for him. He shuddered to think of her climbing it and taking a wrong step.

Carefully, he climbed the dome. Pieces of rock loosened by his feet fell away into the dark, skipping and spinning down the cliff. His swelling ankle throbbed, but he limped and willed himself to the top. Again he scanned the dark with the flashlight.

He swept the light past a white object and his heart jumped.

CHAPTER 29

"Ana!" he yelled. "Ana. Are you all right?"

Below the cliff, in a small depression, she was curled in a fetal position, her arms cradling her shins and her head between her knees. Her hair cascaded over her shoulders like the fronds of seaweed on sand. She was wearing only her nightshirt and boots. She brought her hand weakly to her eyes to shield her face from the light and looked up. She seemed dazed. Her body shook.

"Just hold on," he called. "I'm coming."

He would have jumped if he'd had to. But he scrambled down the shoulder of the dome and then slipped through the broken rock. He felt for purchase with his hands and feet, the jagged edges cutting into his fingers. At the base of the rock, he had to clamber down the boneyard of small broken stones and then back up a slope of sandy soil and sage before he found her.

She picked up her head and stared at him through confused eyes, her eyelashes caked with tears. He knelt beside her in the cool sand and put his arms around her. She was bone cold and shivering. He kissed her salted cheeks and eyes. Her skin was pallid. She looked at him wildly.

"I've got to get you back to the cabin," he said. "What happened? Are you okay?"

"I ... I—" She began to form words but could not finish. She tried to get up, then winced and sat back.

"Did you fall?"

She nodded.

"Did you fall from the rock?" he asked.

She shook her head no.

He felt along her legs. When he got to her right knee she flinched.

"That's it," he said. He held her tightly and kissed her lips and neck and hair.

"I woke up," she sputtered. "I heard noises. You were gone. I thought something ... had happened ... to you."

He would do anything to protect her. "I heard things too," he said. "Don't worry. You're going to be all right now. I'm going to get you back to the cabin and warm you up."

But the thought still occurred to him. "Was there ... anything ... anybody?"

"I ... I," she put her hand to her forehead and shook her head. He held her. "I freaked out. It all came down on me. The baby. I panicked. The baby. Then I started hearing things. I had to find you."

"Don't worry," he said. "Be quiet. We'll get through this. It's all right now." He kept his fears about the baby to himself. She didn't need to hear that. But he was terrified for what they might find. He wanted to ask her if she felt the baby but he couldn't bring himself to find the words.

He helped her to her feet and draped her arm over his shoulder. The pain in his ankle knifed through his body but he pushed on and then pain settled into numbness. The blood from his knee had cooled and dried once, but he reopened the cut and now the blood trickled down his leg. Step by step, they inched up the side of the rock. At one point, it got so steep that he put her over his shoulder and carried her. When they got back to the main trail, he eased her down. His shirt was soaked. It had taken a half hour or an hour to climb; he couldn't tell. But the cabin was ahead. The power had come back on. The light on the porch shone like a beacon. A surge of energy shot through him, and he made the final push.

They stumbled in and he led her to the couch, and she let herself fall. He turned on the light in the main room. The windup clock showed 2:40. Her tears had made a channel through the dirt on her face. Her nightshirt was torn and filthy.

"We're going to emergency now," he said. "I don't care what time it is. We're out of here."

"Joe," she said, cradling her belly. "I'm so afraid."

"I am too," he said. "I am too." He put his hand on her belly.

In the truck on the way up the grade out of the great canyon, the two of them in pain, they tried to make sense of the events of the night.

"I was dreaming," she said. "I was dreaming I was a salmon and I was trying to find my way in the dark. Somehow I knew the moon would help."

"That's crazy. I saw a Chinook in the river," he said. "It might have been at the same time you were dreaming."

"In the dream," she said, "I got to a place that was dark and had no current. I couldn't find a way upstream, and I got scared. That's when I woke up. I don't know if I woke up and then heard the noises or if the noises woke me up."

The pickup rumbled through the night. He drove fast but cautiously, looking for the glow of eyes in the headlights.

"What noises did you hear?" he asked.

"Voices," she said. "Men. Horses. I thought I heard horses snuffling. I could smell them on the wind. Then I thought I heard running."

"I heard voices, too," he said. "A branch break, then running. Not like elk or deer. People."

He shifted through a curve and then rested his shifting hand across her thigh. "I am so sorry I left you," he said. "I couldn't sleep. I thought you would be okay. I decided to walk down to the river. Everything was fine. I was thinking about us and the baby. I was happy."

She leaned against him. "Don't," she said.

"I just got caught in it," he said. "I ran as fast as I could, and it wasn't fast enough. I got to the cabin, and all of sudden it all came back to me, that night, Jenny——." He inhaled and let his shoulders drop. "It was like I couldn't separate the past from what was happening. I was so afraid, so afraid for you. I couldn't bear it. Couldn't bear it again."

He rubbed his temple. They raced past sagebrush and canyons lit only by starlight. "I saw our bed," he said. "I was afraid for the worst."

"Joe," she said, and she reached for him. "I was afraid for you, too. I didn't know what to think. I didn't know where you had gone. We were both scared."

The pickup crested the hill, and the road stretched straight before them on the high grassy benchlands above the canyon. Up here, the moon was still burning cold in the sky. To their left, the dark silhouettes of the mountains massed against the horizon.

"Let's make a pact," he said. "I'll never leave you alone again without telling you where I'm going."

"I'll do the same," she said. "Joe?"

"Yeah?" he said.

"What did we hear?" she said. "Did we really hear something out there?"

"I don't know," he said. "I'm tired of the night. It's like I won't be able to think right until I see the light of day."

They drove straight through Sockeye and on to the hospital at Enterprise and entered through the emergency room entrance in back, which also happened to be the only doors open at 4 a.m.

The first thing the night nurse said to them was, "Well, for God's sake. It looks like you've both been out rolling in the mud."

The second thing she said was, "Looks like it's a Wallace convention. Your mom's in room thirteen, and your sister's been here with her about the whole night. I'm surprised you didn't run in to her on her way out."

She waited for him to say something, her eyes wide as the rim of a coffee mug and her eyebrows upraised in half-moons.

"The baby," he said. "She's expecting. We—"

The nurse cut him off. Her face momentarily registered a shock, her eyes narrowing and her lips drawn slightly back in a frown. Her mouth opened as if to start scolding but she seemed to catch herself. She set her jaw, and she composed her face. "Let's get you in there right now," she said. Within seconds, Ana was being pushed on a wheelchair through the double doors into an examining room.

CHAPTER 30

By the time McKenzie showed for work at about 10 minutes before seven, Joe had been outfitted with a pair of crutches and an ice pack for his ankle. He waited for her in the emergency room lobby, which also served as the employee entrance.

"What in God's name," she said when she saw him. "What are you doing here? Were you in a fight?"

He got up and tripoded himself to where she stood. She was wearing her all–business face, which only made him want to needle her more. "We thought we'd keep you company," he said. "Ana's in room six."

"Stop joking," she said. "What's going on? Where is Ana? No, forget it, you already told me. Six." She turned and started for the doors into the hospital.

"She's all right," he said. "I'm all right. We had ourselves a little scare is all. What about ma?"

McKenzie stopped and turned and set her jaw. "A little scare," she said. "What is she doing in six?"

He balanced on one crutch. In the light of day, the story seemed strange, and he didn't want to repeat it. "We were afraid for her, for the baby, for her being pregnant and all," he said. "I know you know about that. It's a long story. She took a spill. Wrenched her knee pretty good, but the doc says everything else is okay, thank God. Tell me about ma."

"Follow me," she said, and she took off speed-walking through the swinging double doors into the main corridor. He vaulted after her as fast as he could, which wasn't very fast. She waited for him at the nurses' station, where Lauren McKay, an old classmate of his, looked tired.

"Your mom slept pretty well through the night," Lauren said to McKenzie. "It's your brother and his, uh, wife, that have been the entertainment for the night."

The two nurses exchanged looks along with papers and then Lauren left.

"You can bring mom some breakfast," McKenzie said. "Juice, toast and a poached egg. No coffee, whatever she says. I'm going to go and check on Ana."

He got the food from the small cafeteria, using a cart to hold the tray and support himself. He rolled the cart along the hallway and cracked open the door to room 13. His insides jumped. Grace lay with her mouth open and her eyes vacant. In the room's fluorescent light, she was as pale as the moon, her skin stretched across her skull. He didn't think he should try to wake her.

But when he pushed open the door all the way, she said, "I'm thirsty. Get me some water."

"It's me, ma. Joe." She seemed so out of it. He wheeled the cart in.

"I know who you are, damn it," she said. With great effort, she pushed forward with her hands. "Put some pillows behind my back."

He left the cart and hobbled to her bedside and arranged the pillows.

"You're limping," she said. She squinted through one eye. "You've scratched your face. Dammit, son."

"It's not that," he said. He looked at the tiled floor. "Just a little fall down at the cabin. I'm okay."

She patted the bed. "You're a good son, Joseph. Come to see your dying mother," she said.

"Cut it out, ma," he said. "You're not dying. Shut up and eat your breakfast."

He hopped over to the cart and pulled it toward the bed.

"I'm not hungry," she said. "At least not for the stuff they've got around here. Your sister should be ashamed." She hissed and waved her hand as if shooing a fly.

"This is special order, made by Miguel especially for you," he said. He pulled off the plate cover to reveal scrambled eggs.

"I don't want Mexican food," she said. She turned her head and raised her palm against it.

"It's not Mexican food, ma," he said.

"It was made by a Mexican," she said. "That makes it Mexican food."

He took the tray and put it on the bed's little attached food table. "Yeah, that's right, and you'll eat it," he said. "So stop your complaining and eat."

She grumbled but then turned to look at the steaming eggs. "Why didn't you tell me he scrambled some eggs? What do you know, they can make American food." She took up a fork and ate the eggs and toast quickly. When she finished, she reluctantly allowed him to wipe her mouth.

"I'm not a child, you know," she said. She puckered her face.

"Could've fooled me." He put the napkin down on her tray and then picked up the tray and put it back on the cart.

"And I am dying," she said. "Don't believe what they tell you otherwise."

"Ma," he said. His armpits hurt.

"Hear me out," she said. "I get tired fast so listen. I've got something to say to you. Get me some coffee."

"You're not supposed to have any."

"Oh, shit on that. Don't listen to your sister. Get your dying mother some goddamned black joe."

He left for the cafeteria and returned with a cup of coffee. He handed it to her and then sat on the chair next to the bed. "Go ahead and tell me what you've got to tell me."

"Don't patronize me, you little guttersnipe. I'm not joking now. I will tell you," she said. "Stop asking questions and don't interrupt. I don't know how much longer I will live. So just shut up and listen. It's time I said this to you. Where are my cigarettes?"

Maybe it was the egg and toast, but she seemed to will the energy into her being. She sat and held her head high, her withering body dwarfed by the hospital bed. The cup shivered in her hands, the coffee sloshing and dripping over the edges.

"Your brother wants to sell the lake property. You know that. He wants to divide it. Turn it into million-dollar homes and fancy stuff. You know that, too. He's been working me over about it. He's shrewd. He knows he needs me on his side.

"Your father was always the one to say, 'Don't sell the land. Keep it intact. Keep it in the family.' And I'd argue the other side. I'd tell him land is nothing different than money or stocks or gold. An investment. Buy low. Sell high.

"Well, I was wrong. I've come around to your father's way of seeing things. I've thought about what I want to pass on to my children and my grandchildren. Money gets spent. Things break. Old ladies die. But land outlasts everything. That's what I want to pass on."

She fell back in her pillow. He reached and placed his hand on hers. It was cold. She seemed primeval, her face not the face of the mother he had known so many years but more like a face wind-sculpted in stone.

He filled a cup with water from a plastic container. The cup was covered and had a straw in it. He took the coffee from her and handed her the water. "Here ma," he said. "Drink this."

She opened her eyes, inhaled and nodded. He held the cup out and she tried to grab it but her hand wobbled. He moved the cup closer, and she grabbed hold of the straw and sipped the water.

"Howard will try," she said, measuring the words. "But you stand up to him. Don't allow him to call the shots. He will try. You know how."

"Do I ever," he said.

"Don't let him," she said. "I love him as much as I love you. But on this point we are night and day."

He leaned across the steel bedside railing. "You don't have to worry."

She closed her eyes and drew her lips back in a smile and nodded. Then she opened her eyes and pulled her lips against her teeth. "I'm not done with you," she said. "It's time you settled down. That girl is a good woman. Marry her."

He laughed, shaking his head.

"What's so funny?" she said, feigning annoyance.

"You," he said.

"I'm not so funny," she said. "I'm a sad sight."

"The day you stop telling me what to do is the day I'll start worrying about you," he said.

She grumbled and acted miffed. Then she reached for his wrist and held it surprisingly firmly. Her hand was cool and dry. "Marry that girl and have children. Don't drink. Stay away from it. Keep the place going, the three of you kids, keep it like your father and I kept it. And when I die, promise me this: Burn me up. Take my ashes and spread them over the lake. Unless you need a damned government permit for that these days. Take your father's ashes out of that box. Spread him over the lake with me. We ought to at least be good for fish food."

He kept quiet. God, he loved this woman. She was right, on all counts. "I promise, ma," he said. "Do you want a fly-over and a three-gun salute?"

"Very funny," she said.

He rubbed one of the crutches with his thumb and grinned. "Oh, and by the way, he said. "I've already made good on one of those promises."

She looked at him sideways through one pinched eye.

"You're going to have another grandchild," he said. "Ana is—."

"Well for God's sake," she said. "I've got some knitting to do."

She fell asleep soon after that, and he stayed by her side until McKenzie opened the door. Ana sat in a wheelchair behind her. The fright of the past night had worn off and she looked happy. He got up, and they stood in the hallway.

Ana looked back toward the room. "How is she?"

"Tired," he said. "She told me to marry you."

"And?" McKenzie said. She crossed her arms.

"I told her to mind her own beeswax." He said this smiling at Ana. "Just like the other members of this family."

McKenzie punched him in the shoulder. "Goddamn you!" But she laughed. "You're going to get this woman a ring and you're going to get married."

"He already has the ring," Ana said.

"I do?"

"You do," she said. "My dad gave it to me when I went back. My mom's."

"Can't wait to see it," McKenzie said. She turned to Joe. "What did you really tell mom?"

He folded his arms in front of him. "I promised a lot of things, actually."

"Is that a proposal?" Ana said.

McKenzie broke in. "Look, I'm sorry for being a wiseass. I've got to go to work. You've got everything you need?"

Ana nodded.

McKenzie raised a finger to Joe. "Don't let her do anything too strenuous for the next week. Ana, ice that knee and take ibuprofen to keep the swelling down. And you are staying at the lake house. Promise?"

"Promise," Ana said, sending McKenzie a mock salute.

"Do you want me to promise, too?" he said.

McKenzie punched him again and left. Joe looked in on Grace once more, and she was sleeping. Ana left the wheelchair at the exit, and Joe swung out on his crutches. On the way back to the lake house, Ana drove. "What did you two talk about in there, really?" she said.

The sun angled low. He shielded his eyes. "Man, what didn't we?"

CHAPTER 31

From the moment they arrived at the lake house, Ana let him know she wanted to return to the cabin. He told her that Grace wanted them to take the lake house and cabins and run the place after she was gone. She wasn't sure how she felt about running a cabin resort.

But Joe was finding new reasons to stay put at the lake. For one, he could keep a closer eye on Howard.

True to Grace's predictions, Howard had begun lobbying the family harder about the land. He wanted to change the zoning to allow a real resort. Doing so would make the land exponentially more valuable and eventually make them millionaires several times over. Howard had yet to file for the county commissioner election, which meant he could still take every opportunity to twist arms, cajole and influence them. On top of that, he knew all the state legislators, the district's congressman and even one of the state's U.S. senators. He'd written fat checks to them all.

Besides, there wasn't any paying work down on the Imnaha. Up at the lake, he could keep busy with maintenance projects on the cabins. He might also pick up a few extra bucks in town at Long's garage. His Alaska savings were starting to run low, and they were going to need money soon.

There was also the sockeye project. He'd met with the fish biologist, Kramer, a few times, and read his report until it was dog-eared and lit up with yellow highlighter. He even convinced Kramer to consider coming to one of River's meetings. But River was clearly suspicious of Kramer—or simply didn't want any competing viewpoints aired. He said he'd already read the report and didn't see anything new in it. He probably never did read it. So Kramer pulled out, and Joe didn't blame him.

But most important was Ana's safety. Her fall at the cabin had been a wake-up call. They were lucky she wasn't hurt worse. But the what-ifs kept coming back to him. What if she had gone into labor down there and he wasn't around? What if something else happened? At least the lake was that much closer to the hospital in Enterprise and to the ob-gyn in LaGrande. What if something happened to Grace? He couldn't expect McKenzie to take care of everything, even though he knew she would, and without complaint.

One evening after sunset, a week after they moved to the lake house, they walked along the lake trail. The path led through the ponderosas on a small bench above the water. Robins glided through the trees in the failing light.

The day before, they had moved Grace out of the hospital and into a nursing home in town. McKenzie had to play her nurse card to get her to go. She hated it, of course, and she complained of being "stuck with the old biddies and pabulum dribblers." When they moved her in she declared to them that she was "already dead anyway" and that the room was nothing more than a fancy coffin.

He held Ana's hand as they padded across a carpet of dry pine needles. "I want to bring her back," he said. "She loves this place so much. I'm past thinking it would save her. I just think she deserves to die in her own home."

The two of them still limped from their falls. "I understand what you're saying, but I don't know," Ana said. She stopped. "Let's ask McKenzie what she thinks. Can we take care of her? Would we have to get a hospice nurse to come in?"

"I know," he said. "I can make some changes in the bathroom and other things. We can build a wheelchair ramp up to the porch so she can get in the door." He touched her shoulder. "So does that mean you're thinking of staying?"

"Maybe," she said.

He pulled her close and kissed her. She was only six weeks into her term and could still fit into her clothing. But he thought there was a little more flesh in her cheeks and breasts. He had developed a ritual of putting his hand on her stomach and rubbing it.

She held him at arm's length and looked in his eyes in that way of hers, where she cocked her head and squinted. "What's on your mind?" she said. "You're a little preoccupied."

She had him figured out. "I've been thinking of what mom said last week," he said.

"The land?" she said.

He nodded and let go of her and stepped toward the grassy cut bank overhanging the lake. Occasional concentric rings from rising trout were the only ripples on the water. The trout sipped flies from the surface film, their slurps plain in the stillness.

"I must be crazy," he said. He slipped his hands in his pockets. "Mom must be crazy." She was right behind him.

"We're all a little crazy," she said.

"We could be, I don't know, millionaires," he said. He turned away from the lake. There was a healthy stand of ponderosas there, not crowded, leading up the slope to the road. Above the road, the steep slope was mostly grass with occasional pockets of trees. They owned it all, right up to the ridge line and down the other side. "Some people would pay anything to get their hands on this land."

"Your brother seems to think so," she said, turning with him.

"Are we doing the right thing?" he said. "We don't have the money to send our kid to college." He rubbed her belly again. "At the rate we're going, we never will. We could have all our needs taken care of."

She pulled closer to him. "That's a long time from now," she said. "It's getting chilly. We should head back."

She took his hand, and they walked back through the darkening trees. The moon had risen, and it spangled the lake with shards of cold light. They walked slow, holding each other, her head on his shoulder. The ponderosa needles softened their footfalls. She squeezed his hand. "Did you ever think that maybe the land is not yours to sell?" she said.

He hesitated. "What?"

She looked dreamy, a little smile puckering the corners of her mouth. She kept walking, gently pulling him. "Maybe you were meant to take care of it. That's all."

"The day is coming," he said. "We'll have to make a decision."

"And you'll make the right one," she said. "Maybe you should ask your father what he thinks."

He stopped and let go of her. "Now you're the one talking crazy talk. I can't do that."

She let him go but stood watching him. "How do you know?"

He brought his hands palm up and stretched his fingers and then made fists. Then he exhaled and let his hands drop. "I tried. That night down at the river. I did. I ended up cursing him in the dark, like some kind of lunatic. It's over. You can't talk with dead men."

"Look at me." She crossed her arms over her chest. She was intense now. "It's not too late."

"You're crazy," he said. He yawned and scratched his scalp and looked away.

"He's still your father," she said. "Look at me." She touched his jaw and turned his head back to her. Then she took his hand and opened it and traced along the creases of his palm. "There's a reason you still think of him. Maybe you should invite him in. He'll come to you. He'll come if you let him."

He eased up and took in a breath of the vanilla-scented air. "I don't believe in ghosts."

She squeezed his hand and laughed. "Who's talking about ghosts? It's something else. You don't have to believe. They don't need your approval."

The moon lit the path. He wanted to believe he didn't know what she was talking about. The truth was, his father was everywhere, in the lake house, in everything he'd built here, on this path that he'd walked so many times, in the places he'd fished.

Out of the trees, the night sky opened over the lake. There were times standing watch on the *Jenny A.* when it seemed they were a ship floating, not on water, but weightless in the space of the starry night. Then it would be as if he would have to grab hold of something solid so that he could be anchored to the ship, or otherwise gravity itself would lose its pull on him and let him go like an untethered astronaut. He touched her shoulder and then let his hand rest in the curve of her spine.

CHAPTER 32

The summer passed too quickly, like all summers at Sockeye. They moved Grace back to the house, and the improvement in her health surprised everyone but Grace. He built the wheelchair ramp and bought her a wheelchair but she stopped using it after a while. She was soon able to cook for herself again, walk up and down the stairs with the help of a cane, and get in the car and drive to town for groceries, dipped behind the enormous wheel of the old station wagon. She drove it the way she piloted a boat on the lake, in wide, looping turns. The townies who knew better gave her wide berth. Bart and his deputies cringed when they saw her coming.

They stayed at the house, doing what they could for Grace. But it was hard to beat her at her game. She was determined to prove her independence, and she was doing a pretty convincing job.

He ended up guiding occasionally for the local fly shop. An old friend, Rob Lyons, had opened the shop in town and had been bugging him to guide. He figured he wouldn't like the clientele at first—ignorant fat cats from Portland and Seattle, he thought—but the clients actually seemed neither rich nor ignorant for the most part, and he began enjoying his days on the river. There were guys who were wealthy, too, but who he could see loved fishing above all other things.

It felt good knowing Ana and Grace could spend time together. He had wanted her to get to know his mother. If they were lucky, Grace would come to know their child, but that was asking for a lot.

By September, Ana had a tight little pillow for a stomach. At night, the baby did gymnastics for an attentive audience of him and Grace. The baby seemed to give Grace a reason to live. She got out the knitting needles to make woolen booties, a hat and sweater for the first winter. She fussed over Ana in a way he'd never seen. Together, the two of them made him laugh, each jockeying to help the other or be the first one to tell the other to sit, put their feet up and have a cup of tea.

He waited to tell Howard that he would speak at the hearing of the fish commission in October. They would hear plenty of local people clamoring for keeping the dam. He would be one of the few for the other side—a traitor in their midst.

He'd known he would do it since June, when the regional and federal agencies responsible for salmon recovery had announced they would convene in Enterprise to hear what locals thought about their efforts to restore salmon runs. And the issue of the lake dam would be front and center. How people could get so riled by any dam baffled him. They were slabs of concrete, but somehow, people made them into symbols of a so-called way of life. For those who wanted to keep the dams, they seemed to represent everything from anti-federalism to private property rights. These folks somehow ignored or failed to see the irony that the government built, owned, operated and subsidized these dams.

Outside the lake house the day he finally told him, Howard turned red in the face and his jugular bulged. "You can't do that," he said.

"I am going to do it," he said.

Howard was pig-headed and arrogant. But it was more than that. It was his damned jealousy that was at the root of his animosity, always. It was laughable, considering how their lives had turned out. Howard had everything—a good wife, healthy kids, plenty of money. But that didn't salve his wounds. It was as if Joe had taken something from him when they were kids, and Howard would spend the rest of his life feeling cheated, a chip on his shoulder over the favoritism their father showed Joe. The same father who abandoned Joe when he needed him. But that didn't matter to Howard.

Howard's jealousy colored all his dealings with Joe. It didn't matter if it was the dam or the family land—if he was involved, it was a win-lose proposition for Howard, a battle that had more at stake for him than the thing itself. The way he carried himself showed his contempt: his jaw tilted, chin up, chest out. His breath was labored and loud, and a sheen of damp sweat coated his face.

Howard brushed both sleeves with his hand. "I'm going to run for county commissioner soon. I'm on the irrigation district board. I'm a rancher. They want to hear from me. My opinion matters," he said, pulling the toothpick from his mouth. "You. You're nothing. Let's face it. You're an out-of-work fisherman and a drunk."

Joe wanted to deck him but would not give him the righteous satisfaction of being wronged. He clenched his teeth and stared at him, and then he spun away from him. He took a few steps and stopped and looked back over his shoulder. "Go fuck yourself," he said, and he walked away, back into the house, and slammed the door.

"This is not the last of it," Howard yelled after him. "You'll regret the day you do this."

Howard was not the only one to pressure him. When word got around about what he was up to, he got calls at the house. People stopped him on the street. Even Bart called him, not to dissuade him but to warn caution.

"There's people all set to string you up around here," Bart said. "You know how they are about this dam."

A week before the hearing, there was a brush fire outside the cabin. He was lucky to have found it. He and Ana were supposed to have been at a meeting of River's group, but the meeting had been canceled at the last moment. When they got back to the cabin, the fire had been burning down the slope from the road above the cabin. She tiptoed into the cabin and found Grace sleeping while he called the fire department and pulled the hose out as close to the fire as he could.

By the time the fire truck arrived, Joe had a handle on the flames, and the crew had mopped up. The flames had gotten within 15 feet of the cabin. If it hadn't been for the brush clearing, tree trimming and junk cleaning they had done weeks ago, the cabin might have burned.

Tom Crowley, the fire chief and an old friend of the family, suspected arson. His skin was always bright red as though he'd recently come out of a fire. He lit a cigarette with a chrome lighter. "Your neighbors are not driving along throwing burning matches out the windows, unless they want to torch their places, too. No, whoever did it hid their tracks real well. Couldn't find a matchstick. Nothing. Watch yourselves. Someone you know have some kind of grudge against you?"

Joe laughed and shrugged. "Oh, boy," he said. "Where do we start?"

CHAPTER 33

She told him one night in December she thought they were being watched.

He opened his eyes. "How do you know?"

"I can feel it," she said.

They had moved back down to the Imnaha in late October, when the snow was creeping down the Wallowa foothills and dusting the streets of Sockeye at night. Grace had told them to go. She had finished her chemo, and her hair was growing in again, thick, but white, at least until McKenzie brought her to the salon for a hideous coloring job that turned her into a bona fide blue-hair.

Ana lay with her hair spun out across the pillow. "Even the baby can feel it."

On the Imnaha, what they'd lost in sunlight in the depths of the canyon they'd gained in warmth. Their lower elevation and protection from the wind made it feel like another season down here. It was good to be away from town. After his testimony at the fish commission, he had a lot more enemies in town, chief among them Howard.

There was an immense quiet to the place, but at the same time the canyon walls and the winter skies gave it an intimacy. Rather than being dwarfed by the landscape, they felt protected by it.

Her eyes were open but seemed like they were looking off somewhere beyond the ceiling.

She was determined to have the baby at the cabin, even though that idea got a sound bashing from McKenzie. But she wouldn't budge. So McKenzie recommended she talk with Elizabeth Riggins, a nurse midwife. "She's better than the post office at rural delivery," McKenzie had said. "We'll have Life Flight ready, too."

"I know you're serious," Ana had said. "But believe me, we won't need it. Somehow we were fine for a few millennia before Western medicine. We'll be fine again."

Now at the cabin, he sat and slowed his breathing. "What is it?" he said. "I don't hear anything."

She reached for him and stroked his thigh through the sheet. "I don't hear anything either," she said. "I feel it. It's a feeling I get from animals. I don't get this feeling from an animal unless it's afraid of people. An animal can smell fear and can communicate that fear to other animals."

He got out of bed. "I can't just sit here," he said, and he put on his jeans and boots. The clear nights were cold now. He dressed in his chamois shirt and lined jacket. "I won't go outside of earshot of the cabin though."

She pulled on something warm and followed him to the porch. They had talked about whether they should wait to get married after the fish commission's decision and joked about Ana walking down the aisle pregnant. They decided to wait for early summer, when they could throw a big outdoor wedding and people could travel safely and easily from Idaho and other places beyond the valley.

The night was moonless and black. The wind birred in the leafless cottonwoods. The river had its own set of voices, each riffle, pool and tailout a distinct song that he had come to know. He could choose to hear them blended in harmony or pick out their distinct voices separately. And he could tell when the river was high with snowmelt or low. He turned on the flashlight and raked it over the sage and juniper.

"Rex said there'd been cougar sign in the valley," he said. "Scat and prints. Dogs barking."

"If it's a cougar, she's nervous about something," she said. "She's carrying kittens. Or she has kittens and she can't find one."

He slowed the sweep of his flashlight, brushing the outlines of the sage. He tensed and held his breath, fully expecting the sudden appearance of a pair of hot yellow stars to light up in the beam of the flashlight like Leo in the eastern sky.

After half an hour, they gave up and returned to bed.

"I still feel it," she said. "It's still watching us."

"Well, it can watch us all it wants," he said. "If it's a cougar, maybe she'll be our vigilante and keep away anyone who shouldn't be down here."

"I like that," she said.

His guiding work had stopped at the end of the summer tourist season, but he lucked into another job. Bart told him about an upcoming contract doing fish surveys on the Imnaha. Bart helped him with the government paperwork shuffle, and he got the contract. It was a perfect for him. He had to walk specific reaches of the Imnaha and document the location of salmon redds. It got him out on the river every day, yet it wasn't far from home. With his first paycheck, he drove to La Grande and bought walkie-talkies that would keep him in touch with Ana much better than cell phones would do.

She was showing more every day now, but she carried the weight in stride. Being pregnant didn't slow her. If anything, she was busier than ever. She thought nothing of fixing a lunch and bringing it to him at noon. She would show up in her pickup and spread out the lunch on the tailgate or on a picnic table if there was one close by. Sometimes, when she had nothing else to do or she was bored, she would join him on the river. He joked that he should give her his pay since she always seemed to work harder than he did.

She usually stayed ahead of him on the river, often finding things that he had missed. She showed him side channels that steelhead smolts used during high water. They usually had a small gravel dam separating them from the mainstem river. When floods surged downstream, the channels provided backwater refuge for fingerlings. As they explored these channels, they sometimes found landlocked fish that had gotten stuck when the water suddenly dropped. Somehow they had managed to stay alive in these impoundments.

The sensation of being watched continued every night for a week. After a few days, he thought he felt something, too, though he was sure he would not have sensed anything different if she hadn't. They looked for cougar sign but never found it. But they did find horse sign: fresh manure and shoe prints. When they drove up the road to the store at Imnaha, they told Rex about it. He was sitting in his customary bar stool watching satellite television when they came in.

"Folks seen this show yet?" he said, laughing with a wheezy backward pull of his throat. He rose to meet them but never took his eyes off the screen. "It's a doozy all right."

Rex cackled in synch with the laugh track while they moseyed through the dusty aisles. When the show ended, Rex turned the sound down but left the picture on. "How's the pup?" Rex nodded at her. "It's gonna be a big feller. I once heard of a woman give birth to a full-grown boy. Don't know as I believe it, but that's what they said."

She laughed. "Maybe that's what I'm feeling at night when the baby's tossing and turning. He's working on his night reading."

Rex screwed his face and angled his chin. "Seen it on the TV." Rex trailed off, his eyes on the screen. He talked about other things he'd seen, strange weather around the world, conspiracies. He sat on a stool. The screen showed a snowstorm somewhere—stranded cars, snowblowers, flashing lights.

"You want I could turn it up," Rex said. He had the remote in his hand.

"We were wondering whether you've seen people come through here with trailered horses," Joe said. "Someone's been down at our place when we weren't around, or we just haven't seen them."

Rex scratched his head and squinted with one eye. "See any cougar sign?"

"No scat," she said. "No prints. We don't have any animals that might attract a cat. But I get a sense there's one watching us."

Rex changed the channel. It was some kind of violence in Mexico, bodies being carried out of a building and people wailing in the streets. "This is what I'm talking about," Rex said. "I've known of folks been tracked for whole days by a cat till the hairs started standing up on the backs of their necks. Ralston once told me a cat followed him an entire week out hunting down in the canyon. Never seen the cat but said his dogs could smell it and got all itchy about it."

"Someone was riding a horse around the place," Joe said. "Have you seen any of the Macys around?"

She pulled back and stiffened. "You didn't tell me," she said.

"I didn't want to scare you," he said.

"Well, now you have."

"I'm sorry," he said. "I was going to."

She lowered her head and sighed. "Why is this happening?"

Rex ran through more channels, putting his whole arm into the act of poking the remote. He settled on a wildlife show, something about alligators, and made a low chuckling sound in his throat. "Them Macys, like mountain cats themselves. Always moving around in the dark, all quiet like. I always say it was that woman dying the way she did and so young that made old man Macy loony as a jaybird, if you know what I mean. Seen most people keep after their dogs better than that old coot tended to his kids. Left them to figure things out on their own. You know, some people said old man Macy and the wife were blood relatives and that—."

Ana widened her eyes and motioned slightly with her head toward the door.

Joe interrupted Rex. "Say, if you do see any of them around here, can you do me a favor and let me know?"

Rex watched the TV and laughed. "Those gators is sure fun to watch, huh? Just as soon kill you, though."

Joe patted Rex on the wrist. "So it's a deal?"

Rex laughed again, his eyes glued to the TV. "Oh, you bet," he said. "Sure, I'll watch 'em. Just like I watch 'em all. Watch 'em like a hawk."

Ana had turned and started walking away but now she stopped. "All the others?"

"Oh, sure. You'd be surprised the folks come down here. Not just your run-of-the-mill poachers like the Macys. No, sir. End-of-the-roaders think they can hide from the cops. Mexicans looking for some patch to grow their loco weed, can't speak a word of the king's English. And now we got them chemical boys, the cookers, come in here like zombies, all sweaty and bug-eyed and itchy. All of 'em, they're all carrying."

She had crossed her arms and was biting her lower lip. "Welcome to the neighborhood," she said.

Rex cackled and invited them to watch a rerun of *The Outlaw Josey Wales*.

"We've got to go," Joe said. "Thanks for keeping an eye out."

As they were walking away, Rex asked about the rattles. "You put them over your door like I told you now?"

She stopped in front of Joe, and, as he passed her, he tried to gently pull her away. But his hands ran along her shoulders and she didn't budge. He walked to the front door and looked out.

"We sure did," she said.

"Good," Rex said. "I'd advise you get some cougar urine, you see, and spread that around your place. Just don't get urine from a bitch in heat."

"Wouldn't that actually attract cougar?" she said.

"Sure will. Keep the bad actors away. You folks don't worry. I got my eyes open. Ain't nobody comes through Imnaha I don't see. I keep my eyes on 'em all. I'm gonna watch for them Macy boys, like I said, but let me tell you, the ones you want to watch are the ones you think are your friends."

Joe touched the door handle. "Maybe I shouldn't turn my back on my brother."

"Family?" Rex said. He dropped his eyes. "Don't know about family. Out of my league there."

They left, and in the truck on the way back to the cabin, she sat against him. The sky had crusted over with a gray film, and there was a feeling of snow in the air. The grasses had bleached, and even the canyon walls were a dull brick color in the flat light.

"He looked so sad when he was talking about family," she said. "I think he has kids somewhere, grownup. I wonder if they even know he's down here."

He smoothed his hand over her jeans. "I haven't been to the cemetery," he said.

She swiveled toward him for a moment. "What made you say that?"

"Oh, I don't know. It's been on my mind, I suppose."

They drove for a while longer. "Maybe you're ready to go. You could take Grace with you. She might like that."

"Maybe."

***

He visited Grace a week later, and she was in high spirits. Christmas was her favorite holiday, and she had decorated the house in and out with all of the ornaments and trimmings she had collected over the years. But he didn't stay long, and he told her he'd be back.

Bart had just pulled into the lot outside his office. They went for coffee at the Bucksaw. They sat at their customary corner table where Bart could keep an eye on Main Street. Not that there was much to see. An occasional ranch flatbed or pickup rolled by on Main Street. A couple of the tourist places had for-lease signs in the windows.

Dot McGraw came and poured coffee. If the McGraws harbored any ill feelings about him and what he'd said at the fish commission hearing in Enterprise, they hid it well. "Tell your ma hello for us," she said. "You boys just in for coffee?" She stood for a second and waited but knew without a word that they weren't having breakfast. "Hope she's feeling better, poor thing." She put her hands in her apron pocket where the order book was stuffed, smiled and wheeled and walked back to the coffee station.

"You think she hates my guts?"

Bart cradled his big hands around his coffee cup. "She'll get over it. She's a decent woman."

Bart said he'd broken up a couple of fights recently. Not the usual bar fights, though. There was a group that had come into town last summer and had stayed. "Not your peaceful tree-hugger type," Bart said. "Don't know if they're vets; a couple maybe. Not the kind you want to have a beer with. Dangerous. They're part of that gang hanging around your buddy River. Feds are keeping their eyes on them, believe me."

He wiped his mouth with a paper napkin. "He said he was going back to the valley. And he ain't my buddy."

Bart lit a cigarette and squinted through the smoke. "He may be gone, alright, but his friends have stayed on and they're a pain in the ass."

The regulars were in their usual spot, around the big round table in the other corner. Not one of them said a word his way. "I'm getting tired of waiting around for the law to do something," he said. "I've nearly had my house burned down with my mom in it. My dog is dead. We're down there and we're jumping at our own damn shadows."

"You had new trouble?" Bart said.

"No," he said. "But … I don't know. It's stupid." He rubbed the stubble on his chin.

"Most shit I hear is," Bart said. He held his mug with both hands and slurped his coffee.

The regulars were older guys who didn't have to be anywhere anytime soon. There was one, Anderson, who used to be friendly. "I know I'm a little touchy," Joe said. Bart raised his eyebrows and nodded. "Two weeks ago we thought we were being watched. Ana thought it was a cougar. Rex says there's been cougar sign. But I'm not so sure. We didn't find sign at all, but we did find horse sign: fresh shit and shoes."

He told Bart about the number of prints and where he'd found them around the cabin. Bart narrowed his eyes and creased his brow. "How come you didn't say something sooner?"

"I don't know." He shrugged. "What could you do anyway? By the time we can get up here or even make a call—."

"Jesus," Bart said. "I'm coming down and taking a look. Sheriff or no sheriff. Let's see if we can start connecting some dots."

"It's about time, lawman."

Not 12 hours later, down at the cabin, they were startled by a metallic banging and then the sound of a truck spinning gravel and roaring away. She jumped out of bed first and headed for the door. He had been in a deep sleep and stumbled out of bed. He took the shotgun off the rack. She opened the door, but then her body tensed as she screamed, "No!" It was as though a spike had been rammed down his spine. Dressed in nothing but a t-shirt and underwear, he bolted for the porch.

He found her standing in the cold looking at a mass of dead salmon. She was frozen, her arms crossed over her chest and resting on her bulging belly. Her face was pulled down and contorted, her shoulders arched, her body shaking. Most of the salmon were dead, their bodies stiff as planks. But some of them still clung to life, their gills weakly, desperately scratching the air for oxygen, their mouths gasping vainly for cold water. They were all hatchery fish, their adipose fins clipped.

"That's it!" he yelled. "I've fucking had it!" He charged back in the cabin. He took what food he could gather, filled a canteen and grabbed his deer rifle.

He loaded the truck and then helped her collect the carcasses in black plastic garbage bags and threw those in the pickup bed.

There was a distant look in her eyes, sadness and quiet rage. "You're coming with me," he said. "I'm not leaving you here. I'm dropping you off at McKenzie's, and then I'm taking a ride."

He was a lit fuse inside, couldn't stop the burning, the moving forward.

She didn't move. Only stared at him. As indecipherable as onyx. "Don't do this," she said. "You don't know it's them. Even if it is, don't get dragged down with them in this."

He paced. "Who the hell else is it if it's not them? You tell me. Who the hell else! No, it's them. It's them, alright." He kicked gravel. "We're going."

"Don't talk to me like that," she said. "What time is it?" She began to shiver.

He stopped long enough to look at her. "I'm sorry," he said. "It's probably four in the morning. I'm not going back to bed. Please get ready." He didn't wait for a reaction, and she disappeared into the cabin.

Ten minutes later they were gone, Joe driving like a man possessed. He said nothing the whole way, leaning forward and gripping the wheel until his knuckles whitened. They got to McKenzie's place in 45 minutes. He kept the engine going and waited for Ana to get out.

She sat and stared out the windshield. The porch light came on, and the front door opened. In a robe and slippers, McKenzie came down the front walk halfway and stared, arms folded.

The eastern sky was starting to show leaden light. "Let me go," he said finally.

She sat, immovable and mute. McKenzie turned and headed back for the house, and the kitchen light snapped on. After a long while she exhaled and her body deflated like a bag. "How can I let you go?"

He kept his grip on the wheel but turned toward her. She seemed as cold and distant as the snow-capped Seven Devils. He thought of things to say: not to worry, that she would see him, that he had to do this. But they all seemed trite. He only said, "Come on now. I've got to go."

She pulled toward the door and grabbed the door handle. He reached for her but then pulled back. Maybe she would latch on to him and not let go. Or maybe he would lose his resolve. He tried to put the thoughts out of his head.

She opened the door and got out. In the instant before she shut the door, he said he loved her. It sounded like an excuse.

She looked at him. There was sadness in her eyes but something else. A detaching, a letting go. He felt it in his gut, a shock at first but then an acceptance. She had released him, and he was not going to stop her or stop himself. He couldn't. She started up the walkway to the house. He put the truck in gear and guided it out onto the road, alternately looking ahead and watching through the rearview mirror. There was the door opening, the light spilling out. McKenzie and Ana embracing. They stayed put, motionless as a couple of trees, until the truck topped the rise out of town and they disappeared, replaced by the empty black road snaking behind him.

He drove east on Cow Creek and then through the Zumwalt on up to the Buckhorn Road. As he drove, the remembered image of her face stayed with him, as though it were etched into the glass of his windshield. Wherever he looked, he saw her face at the moment before she'd gotten out of the truck. She had seen what was in his mind and knew she could not stop him. He could not stop himself.

CHAPTER 34

He drove north toward Buckhorn Spring as though being pulled toward the Macy place. A calmness inhabited him. He felt as though he were watching himself. He was certain that it was Cody and his brothers. He did not have to put up with cowards who threatened and bullied and intimidated behind his back. Just to look Cody in the eye, that's all he needed. Fuck the legal system. Fuck justice. Was this what it felt like to lose your mind? Or what it felt like to finally know the truth?

It was all so clear to him now as the truck sped north along the empty rolling graveled road. There was only the truck rattling, the wind buffeting the truck from the east, the grass of the Zumwalt, the deep tree-filled canyons, the ice-slashed Seven Devils in the distance. When he was several miles below the springs, he left the gravel and turned west along a dirt road that led eventually to Devil's Run Creek.

The unmarked road soon turned into washboard, and the floor boards vibrated until his back and head hurt. A plume of dust in its wake. Dirt caking his nostrils. He brushed his hand on the dashboard, and it left grit on his palm and a streak where he'd wiped his hand.

He drove on, the road straight and strangely flat up on the benchland. The wind blew hard, the gusts buffeting the truck, the clouds sailing overhead. He pulled his collar and then let go of the steering wheel for a moment to blow on his hands. The vapor from his breath fogged the windshield, then was gone.

The Macy place occupied the high divide near the headwaters of Devil's Run Creek between Joseph Canyon and the Snake. It sat alone back from the road, its boxy shape silhouetted against the big sky. He slowed until the dust trail caught up to the truck and then swallowed it. He stopped and idled the truck, and he sat until he was sure this was the place. He moved the truck away out of sight of anyone approaching.

The old houses like this were nearly all abandoned, these homesteaders' places, their windows all dark eyes, their siding gray and splintered, their porches and roofs sagging or caved in. The only difference with this place was the two columns of smoke rising—one from the chimney and one from in front.

He reached for his rifle from the gun rack behind him. He pulled it down and cradled it in his arms. He checked the action twice, and when he was satisfied he took a case of shells and loaded the magazine and laid it on his lap.

He moved back out onto the road. Dogs barked far away. When he was about to turn he absent-mindedly pulled the turn signal to the left and then caught himself and turned it back into the center position. He dismissed himself out loud: "Why don't you just honk and wave while you're at it?" he said to nobody.

He shifted into second gear. There was some movement outside, and as he got closer, it was a dog. It was a pit bull mix, snarling, chained and standing on the roof of the rusted hulk of a car body, one of several left squatting in front of the house. Another dog appeared, this one a German shepherd straining at its chain and barking, standing on top of another automotive corpse.

The dogs guarded a miserable patch of rusted junkyard. In clumps amid what looked like it had once been an apple orchard, lay a collection of scrap that could have been accumulating since the end of the 19th century. There were parts of old horse-drawn farm implements, engines, whole and partial chassis, stacked engine parts, a mountain of worn tires, cracked bathtubs, sinks and toilets, windows and doors, piles of wood, and an enormous collection of appliances: prehistoric refrigerators, stoves, washing machines.

He passed all this slowly and then slipped by the house and came along the back. Here were the first signs of life: several cars and trucks parked, all of them mud- and dust- and shit-splattered, steps away from the front junkyard. There were several mud-caked motorcycles and ORVs. These were parked haphazardly in the yard, which was nothing more than a dirt-packed enclosure. And then there was the truck whose driver he had come for: Cody's late-60s Ford.

He parked and got out with his rifle. The back door to the house was open but there was nobody in sight. A chain saw buzzed in the distance. He approached the back porch carefully and stopped at a doorless threshold, some kind of mud room leading to steps. It was dark, too dark to see anything. But there was a radio playing. It was coming from inside, pulling in country music. He took a first step, eyes open wide, his rifle angled across his chest. His throat tight and the heart in it.

He topped the stairs and stopped and leaned forward. A thin voice came from within, not more than 15 feet from where he stood.

"Take another step ... I'll blow your head off."

He halted. The voice came from the darkened hallway directly in front of him. It sounded wheezed and mechanical, as if generated by a machine made of rusted parts cobbled from the junkyard outside.

"Put your rifle down," the mechanical voice said and then wheezed with an asthmatic rattle. "Put it down, Wallace."

He pressed the rifle to his chest. The thought of running occurred to him.

"Put it down if you know what's good for you."

He laid the rifle at his feet. There was a click then and the ghostly mug of a man appeared beneath a bare bulb lamp. He was sitting on a stool in the middle of the hallway, one hand waving a shotgun, the other hand now letting go of a long string attached to an overhead fixture. A green oxygen tank sat on the floor with a plastic hose running to his nose.

Old man Macy.

He took his free hand and put it on his throat. He swallowed a gulp of air and then belched a few more words. "Don't try nothing," he said. "I'll take your head off."

He was dressed in dingy cotton thermal underwear top to bottom that hung loosely from his haggard body. His thin black hair fell in greasy hanks and his sallow face wore several days' growth of stubble. There was a tang of rancid scalp and rotten clothing that had not known soap for a long time. He motioned with the shotgun. "Slide it over here, sonny," he said. "Use your boot."

He did as he was told. He'd been holding his breath. "Where is he?" he said. "Cody."

Macy spluttered a laugh, holding onto his breathing hole. Then he aimed the weapon at him. "You kilt my oldest. Won't be another."

"Where is he?" he said. He was dead-set. Let the old man shoot.

Macy wheezed. "You want to visit?" he said, and then grunted and snorted.

Then a voice came from behind. "What's so goddamn funny? You funnin' me, old man?"

He didn't dare turn. He didn't need to. He'd heard that voice before.

CHAPTER 35

"Hands over your head and come on down them stairs backwards," Cody said. "Real careful. Don't want anyone getting hurt that shouldn't. My old man is kinda trigger-itchy. Ain't that so, pa?"

The old man wheezed and put his hand up to his throat. "Wouldn't be neighborly," he honked and laughed.

He eased down the stairs as he was told. His gut ached, and he cinched his stomach to clamp the pain. At the bottom, he stopped. They were outside now. The road was visible past the junkyard. Beyond that, the timbered hills.

"Okay, turn yourself around now, real slow," Cody said.

He found himself eye to eye with the barrel of a rifle. Cody was dressed in full camouflage. He was even shorter up close. He had a mop of reddish gold hair, dark at the roots, and a full, rust-colored beard.

Cody squinted at him. "I could shoot you right now." He said it in a measured way, just the facts. "You come up here with a rifle. Man's got a right to defend his home."

Old man Macy made a gurgling sound above.

"What do you want with a bunch of hillbillies anyway?" Cody poked him with the rifle. "Something big must be up your ass to bring you out here."

"Big," old man Macy repeated. "Real big."

There was defiance in Cody's eye, but not guilt. So much for trusting his gut. "You know something about some fish dumped on my front porch this morning?" What should have sounded angry came out confused.

"Fish was dumped on your porch, huh?" Cody said. "Imagine that, pa. This boy had himself a delivery of fresh fish to his porch, this morning!"

"Fish?" old man Macy said from inside the dark hall. Joe and Cody were standing outside now at the foot of the porch.

"You know something about that?" His ears rang with blood. "You know something about a fire at my mom's house? My girlfriend being harassed? My dog butchered? You know something about those things?"

"That girlfriend of yours—full-blood Nez Perce, ain't she?" he said.

He stiffened. "What's that supposed to mean?" he said.

Cody cut him a look. "Don't mean nothing," he said. He had sharp, ice-blue eyes.

The junkyard dogs started barking. Out on the road, there was a dust trail and then the sight of a Cherokee with a flashing blue light on top.

"Well, boy-howdy," Cody said. "That lawman friend of yours coming to pay us a visit. Ain't that neighborly? Now, go on and get back up those stairs and into the house, friend."

Cody poked him with the rifle and prodded him up the stairs, where he was met by old man Macy, still with his trembling hand on the shotgun.

"Don't do anything stupid," Joe said.

"You hear that, pa?" Cody headed down the stairs. "Take care of this boy, while I take care of the law. And like he says, don't do nothing stupid."

He stood in the darkened hallway. The old man motioned for him to sit on the floor to one side of the door. He could see outside, but he was in shadow and so could not be seen from the outside. He sat, and Macy waggled his rifle at him and at the door.

As his eyes adjusted to the darkness, the metal of his rifle shone on the floor of the hallway that led off into another room of the house. He might be able to slip the old man, pull the shotgun from him and get his rifle. But that could expose Bart, too. Bart's Cherokee rattled up the drive and stopped. A door slammed.

"What brings an officer of the law out to pay us a visit?" Cody said. They were outside the door, within earshot.

"Things would go a lot smoother if you laid down that rifle," Bart said.

"I've got a right to protect my property," Cody said. "You got business here?"

"Just put it down, sir, and let's start there." There was a pause, some small sounds and then quiet. "Good."

Some low conversation followed, out of earshot, but he clearly heard Bart say his name.

Macy spoke next. "Go ahead and look around," he said. "I guess he dropped in to say howdy while I was out in the woods. Ain't that neighborly now?"

The old man wheezed softly but then tensed. The shotgun lay heavy in his lap.

"Where is your father?" It was Bart, much closer now.

"In bed," Cody said. "Ain't feeling too good these days."

"Anyone else home?"

"No sir," Cody said.

There was another silence. The radio snapped with static.

"Careful of them steps," Cody said. "Some of them's a little shaky."

It was only a matter of time now. Bart would show in the doorway, blind to what was inside. Old man Macy had raised the shotgun off his lap and angled it unsteadily across his chest. If he shot Bart, he could claim he was protecting his property from an intruder—a defense that local juries were partial to. But they'd have to kill him, too, to eliminate a witness. And what did the dying old man have to lose, anyway?

The choices were grim. Do nothing, and put Bart in harm's way. Go for his rifle, with any number of scenarios playing out. Or try and warn Bart, with the likelihood the old man would shoot him first.

There was a footstep and then Bart appeared, head and shoulders. He was squinting into the doorway, leaning forward. Bart had on his heavy coat, which meant he was wearing bullet-proofing. But that still wouldn't stop his head from being blown off by a shotgun blast. He wanted to yell, but he held tight. And where was Cody? Did he have his rifle trained on Bart's back?

Bart took another step, then another. The old man's arms were shaking, trying to steady the rifle. It would all be over in a moment, one way or another. If he did the wrong thing, either he or Bart might be dead.

"What's the matter, lawman?" Cody said. "Something got you jumpy?"

Bart had stopped. There was trouble in his face, the set of his jaw, the tightness in his brow. It was the way he looked when he was out hunting.

"No," Bart said, and he turned to face Cody, who was still outside. "There ain't anybody in there."

At that moment, old man Macy turned the barrel of the rifle toward the door.

CHAPTER 36

Joe lunged for the firearm, yelling at Bart, "Jump!" The shotgun fired the moment he hit it. There was a flash and a blast, and for several seconds he lay in a daze on the floor, blinded and deaf. The kick from the rifle had knocked Macy off his chair, and he was sprawled against one of the interior doors as though he had simply placed himself there and fallen asleep. He looked dead.

He got up, running to get his rifle from where it had fallen from the shock of the blast. He groped for the hanging pull string of the overhead light and yanked it. He picked up his rifle close to old man Macy's feet. As he did, a figure darkened the light of the open door.

"You okay?" Bart said, and he ran in with his sidearm drawn. "Anyone else here?"

"Nobody but the old man, far as I can tell," he said. Macy was as lifeless as a Halloween straw man. "I don't know about him. What about you? Where the hell is Cody?"

Bart kneeled and checked the old man's pulse. "Let's get this oxygen tube back up his nose. See if there's a blanket around here."

Outside, there was the sound of an engine roaring and gravel flying. He sprang up to run, but Bart put a lock on his wrist.

"You're just going to let him get away?"

"He ain't going nowhere," Bart said. "Besides, what am I supposed to charge him with?"

"How about attempted murder of a police officer?" he said.

"He never aimed a rifle at me," Bart said. He turned to look back at the old man. "Now let's just clean up this mess and take care of this miserable old fart. And get the hell out of here before the rest of this half-wit clan shows up for dinner with pa. And don't think I will let you just waltz away from this before I chew your ass. You're lucky I'm not carrying your dead butt out of here."

They carried the old man with his oxygen tank and gear and put him into the back of the Cherokee. Bart got behind the wheel. He rolled down the window as Joe walked to his truck.

"Lead the way," Bart told him. "I'm following your ass all the way home."

He stopped and searched his pockets for his keys. He turned to face Bart. "Ana told you, didn't she?" he said. "She told you about the fish?"

"Sure," Bart said. "There was a break-in at the federal hatchery last night. Someone stole a truckload of spawners."

"I figured that's what happened," he said.

"Yeah, and it had nothing to do with the Macy boys, you dumb shit," Bart said. "So just get in your rig and drive."

Bart's Cherokee stayed in his rear view the whole way back down to Sockeye. He should have felt relieved. No one had gotten hurt. And maybe he'd been wrong about Cody Macy. But if it wasn't Macy, who was harassing them? River? It still seemed too far-fetched. And now he'd given Macy another reason to hate him. And what of Ana? Maybe she'd seen something in him that he'd been trying to prove all his life, that he wasn't worth saving. Just as he was getting control of his life, there was a gnawing ache in his stomach, something that told him he didn't have it in him to hold on, that it would slip from his fingers again.

The Wallowas rose on the south horizon. A small plane moved across the sky in the distance. Was that what it had been like for his father? One moment floating, seemingly weightless. The next moment, falling like a stone thrown from a cliff. It was as if something had dropped inside him, descended through the middle of him and down in his gut like a lead fishing weight. So Ana was right. Beyond the anger was sadness, sorrow for what he'd wanted but never gotten from his father, regret for his stubbornness when he could have reached out to him in the last few years, grief for realizing he'd never have that chance again. She'd told him that many times before but it hadn't sunk in. Or he'd been too pissed off to see beyond the anger.

In the rearview, Bart's Cherokee kept pace behind him, with the silhouettes of two figures, one tall behind the wheel and one slumped low, barely visible. He caught a glimpse of his eyes, bloodshot and watery. It was like he had never fully comprehended his father's death, and then, *bang,* he'd finally gotten it. He wiped his eyes on his sleeve. The plane that triggered the memory had disappeared. He'd been holding the steering wheel in a death grip, he realized, and so he inhaled deeply and then he blew out. He relaxed his grip, while nodding to himself how a person would when they've figured something out after a long time. Maybe he could move past the anger now, but what about the sadness? Anger was hot and had a way of making him feel like he could blame his shit on anyone else but him. But sadness felt cold, and it seemed to have a way of making him turn in on himself like a snake in the shade.

CHAPTER 37

Howard called two weeks before Christmas. "I've got some things I want to show you," he'd said, and he was at the lake house in his white Ford Expedition within an hour. When he pulled in front of the house, he blew the horn and stayed in the truck.

Joe figured it had something to do with their land. He'd heard the talk about a zone change for the lake property. But people were always talking about ways to cash in on property values around the lake, and nothing ever seemed to come of it. Howard had seen the family land as what he liked to call an "asset," a thing whose value could be quantified by what it would fetch on the real estate market. He hadn't forgotten what he'd promised Grace.

He came out on the porch with his palms up. The passenger-side window rolled down, and Howard ducked to avoid eye contact. "Hop in," Howard said, chewing on a toothpick. "You'll see."

He climbed onto the leather seat. Howard always kept his vehicles immaculate, and it was a temptation to put his foot up on the dashboard to piss him off. He settled for needling Howard about the purpose of the call. "Boy, you must really want to convince me of something. You plan on taking me out for a steak dinner, too?"

"Can you just shut up till we get there?"

"Get where? And that's not very Christian of you, now, is it?"

Howard grumbled. "No, it's not. Just. Please just be quiet, okay?"

"Sure." He folded his arms across his chest. "Let's go for a ride."

The family land was zoned for exclusive farm and forest use, with a grandfathered exception for the little cabin resort and home on the lake side of the road. Anything on the moraine above the lake road was off limits to development. And the Wallace family owned nearly the entire slope above the lake road. But Howard did not see himself as the future caretaker of a slope of ponderosa, grass and cow pies. Not when the land could be put to so-called greater economic use. And all it took was one hike up the old jeep road on the spine of the moraine to see that this land offered the kind of views that resort developers lusted for: a view all the way to Idaho, mountains in three directions, blue lake below, and a hilltop location that would guarantee those views forever.

There were those in the county who considered the zoning for the Wallace land to be etched in stone, as eternal as the mountains themselves. Not Howard. People created that designation, by God, and people could change it. He'd heard Howard say it often: If mountains crumbled and rivers ran to the sea, zoning designations could be changed. Howard despised Oregon's strict land-use protections, even as he benefited from the favorable tax treatment they afforded his property.

Howard drove to the foot of the old moraine road and stopped in front of the gate. He handed Joe a set of keys. "Get the gate, would you?" Howard said, rubbing his hands.

"What the hell are you up to?" Joe said.

"Just open it, would you?"

"You want to get your nice clean SUV all muddy, huh?"

Howard slapped his forehead. "Just do it, okay?"

He slid out and swung the gate and watched the Expedition lumber over the cattle guard and then shut the gate behind them. He climbed back in and sank into the heated leather seat. Howard put it in four-wheel drive. The road was at first muddy and deeply rutted. He had bounced and banged up it many times in different pickups, but the big SUV climbed smoothly and quietly. The mud turned to snow as they ascended through a small wooded valley in the middle of the moraine. The road crested the hill and ended near a microwave radio station. Howard turned off the ignition, and instantly the quiet was breathtaking.

They got out of the truck. The snow-crusted palisade of Joseph Mountain dominated the southwestern sky. Due south, the view up the old bed of the glacier opened into the heart of steep, snow-covered granite peaks. To the east, across the uplifted slab of plateau that hid Hells Canyon, the Seven Devils scraped the sky. And below, Wallowa Lake fingered ice blue out of the mountains.

The snow crunched below their boots and glinted in the sunlight. Their breath made small clouds.

Joe blew on his hands and rubbed them. "I never get tired of this," he said. "It's a slice of heaven."

"Okay then," Howard said, waving his toothpick. "Tell me what you see when you look out at this little slice of heaven."

It was one of those Howard-style questions with an agenda. But if that's what Howard wanted, he'd give him a piece of his mind.

"It's one of the last great places anywhere," he said. "And hardly anybody knows it exists. Which suits me just fine."

Howard stood stiffly, hands in the pockets of his sheepskin coat. "Now let me tell you what I see. I see a crossroads. I've told you this before. All that land below served our folks pretty well over the last hundred years or so. Now we've got a choice. People want to hold on to the past. But we can't do that. The economy is changing. I keep telling people that, but they don't seem to want to listen."

Joe blew into his hands and rocked on his legs. "I think you're right and you're wrong. People aren't going to throw themselves at the first thing that comes along. They know there's got to be change. But they're not sure we have to go from one extreme to another. You've seen Ketchum, Aspen. There's more than one way to get forced out of your homes. A place can get so's the only ones can afford to live there are the fat cats."

"Don't forget, there's people who sold them that land, brother. Hold on a second." Howard turned and walked to the back of the truck. He opened the rear doors. "Come on over here. I've got something I want you to see."

He came around back. On the carpeted floor of the cargo bay lay a set of architectural renderings. He leaned in. "What the hell?"

"Go ahead," Howard said. He stuck his finger on some print in the upper left corner of the sheaf of papers. "Read what it says."

"Sockeye Ranch? A conceptual master plan? What the hell is this?"

A gust of wind drove drifting snow up the little valley.

Howard snorted with laughter. "Take a closer look," he said. "Recognize anything?"

He thumbed through the sheets. It was their land, of course. But in place of meadows and trees, there were the outlines of buildings with labels: a hotel, restaurant, condominiums, boat dock, tennis courts, pools, riding ranges, bicycle paths.

Howard folded his arms and put a foot on the bumper of the Expedition. "It'll be a regional destination resort," he said. "There's a market for this, yuppies from California, Oregon and Washington, people who take week–long vacations with their families. Even people from back East. The Midwest. They can play tennis, ride bicycles and horses, hike, paddle, swim, fish, water ski in summer. Snow ski in winter. We'll build a ski area that will blow their minds. You name it, they can do it here. We're sitting on a gold mine. We just need to find a developer willing to come in as a partner."

Joe flipped through a few more drawings. "Jesus, Howard," he said, shaking his head. "You don't kid around, do you? When did you do this?" He straightened and dug his ungloved hands deep into his jean pockets. He blew out like he was blowing out the first drag of smoke from a newly lighted cigarette.

Howard patted him on the back and put his arm on his shoulder.

He stiffened. He could see his brother with the good old boys at the courthouse. But they're the ones who ran the county. He was an outsider. Always was and always would be.

"Relax, for crying out loud," Howard said. "Do you want to be poor all your life? Look, I'm serious about this. You can be the chief environmental officer, or whatever you want to call it. Invite Robert Redford and his pals over for a ride and raise funds for the Sierra Club. We'll all be rich, of course, but I'm not just thinking of ourselves. This place could be the economic savior of this county. We all know it isn't timber or livestock or mining anymore. This is clean industry—you should like that, right? It would bring jobs and money year–round. It would attract other businesses and industries. It would bring in the taxes we need to build a town where people could live and work. This is a once–in–a–lifetime opportunity. Think of your … child."

He let go of the drawings and then turned his back to them and kicked snow. "I'll tell you what I think this is," he said. "This is bullshit."

Howard took his foot off the bumper and stood back a step. "What?"

Three ravens caromed off imaginary bumpers in the cold sky above the moraine.

He took a hand out of his pocket and ran his fingers through his hair. "Bullshit. B.U.L.—."

"I can spell," Howard cut him off and then pulled his mouth back in his toothpick–spiked smile that wasn't a smile. "How can you say that?"

He turned back to the drawings. With his finger, he traced the outlines of a road. "I don't know if it's worth telling you," he said. "No, I take that back. It's not worth it."

Howard tilted his head and lowered his voice, his mouth open in a mixture of pain and disbelief. "Try me," he said. "Come on, tell me. I want to know."

He stopped and turned toward Howard. "You always do this," he said. He folded his arms across his chest. "I tell you what you don't want to hear, and then you think you can persuade me that I'm wrong and you're right. I've played this game before. It's getting cold. Let's go back." He turned to walk away.

"No, no, wait," Howard said. He grabbed his shoulder. "Just give me one reason why you think this is a bad idea. Give me some feedback. This is only a plan. It can be changed."

He stopped but didn't turn. "Jesus," he said.

"You don't have to take the Lord's name," Howard said.

"God dammit, then," he said. Now he turned to face Howard. He brushed a spot in the snow with his boot. The ponderosas thrummed in the wind. "You don't stop, do you? Alright, I'll tell you what I think. I also happen to think this land is incredibly valuable. And that's why I wouldn't touch it."

Howard turned his palms upward and made a face of mock pain. "Oh, come on, you haven't gone that far with this environmental stuff, have you?"

"Here we go," he said. "Call it what you will. In a couple of generations, I'd rather be remembered for what I saved, not what I fucked."

Howard cringed, chomping the toothpick. "Do you have to? You're sounding like one of the hippie wackos. We're not destroying anything. We're saving it. We're making it better." His face was blotching red already. "And we're making sure we won't become an endangered species ourselves. What are you going to do? What are your kids—what are they going to do when they grow up and there's no job for them here? They're going to leave. Is that how you want to be remembered? As the guy who refused to allow them to make a living?"

"They can still make a living," he said. "There's plenty of things to do here."

"Then why do we have the highest unemployment rate in the state?" Howard said. "Tell me that."

Joe leaned forward and crossed his arms over his shins. His boots were stained wet from melting snow. "This place isn't meant for everyone, and you know it," he said. "It's never been easy to make a living here. It's not supposed to be. There's just more people coming in, and there isn't much work to go around. It's the nature of the place.

"You used that word, 'crossroads.' Hell, we *are* the crossroads. I agree you can't go back. But I think we've got a chance to reach back to the past. We can right some wrongs. We can go in a new direction."

"You're not making a whole lot of sense to me," Howard said. "You sound like one of my college professors at Oregon State. You have to give me something to grab hold of."

"Okay, grab onto this," he said. "But keep in mind, Ana had nothing to do with this. This is my own thinking."

"Spill it," Howard said.

"We've got plenty of land. Let's return some of it to the Nez Perce."

Howard stiffened and seemed momentarily stunned. Then he turned and faced him.

"What?" he said, his face twisted like he'd bitten into a grapefruit. "Did I just hear you say what I thought I heard you say?"

"You heard me all right," he said.

"What the hell are you talking about?" His face got redder. "Let me get this straight. You're talking about giving our land back to the Indians? I should've known when you—."

"When I what?"

He began rolling up the drawings. "I should have known," he muttered.

"You were going to say something about Ana. Go ahead. Don't hold back."

He stopped and looked back over his shoulder. "I have no problem with her," he said. "But I just think those people are looking for a way to get back here."

"Those people?"

"Indians. Native Americans. Whatever the hell they're calling themselves these days." He closed the rear doors of the SUV. "I can't say as I blame them. But I'm not the one who's going to bring them back. Not unless they want to pay me for my land."

He spit. "Your land? Fuck, it's not your land."

Howard punched his gloved hands in his coat pockets. "You are, my brother, hopelessly naïve. But I should have known better. An outright giveaway. Tell me how anyone would be better off for it—the Indians or the Wallaces or anyone in this valley."

The wind was howling over Joseph Mountain, away to the south, blowing windrows of snow off the cornices that grew along the ridge.

"I'm freezing-ass cold," Joe said. "Let's get out of here."

"Oh, so a little creature comfort, huh? This Expedition isn't such a bad idea after all?"

"I'd take a fucking garbage truck right now, if it was warm," he said. He turned and began walking around the side of the Expedition toward the passenger door. "Let's go."

Howard stayed put. There was a sudden *click* and the beep of the horn. He'd locked the doors with the key fob in his pocket. "Who do you think you are?" His voice was high and cracked.

He leaned against the SUV and exhaled.

"Get off my car," he said. "The favorite son."

"Oh, Christ." He kicked snow. "Don't start with that bullshit."

Howard came around and unlocked the doors. He grunted as he got in the driver's seat but didn't start the engine. He opened the door and climbed up into the cab and sat. Clouds had obliterated Chief Joseph Mountain, the sky platinum and shedding flakes of sailing snow.

Howard gripped the steering wheel with both hands and looked out the windshield, the toothpick protruding from his mouth like a splinter. Now even the nearby ponderosas were obscured in snow and luminous cloud. "I want to present this to the planning department soon," Howard said. "I want to get the zoning changed. And you'll agree to it."

"Mom will never allow it," he said. Their breath fogged the windshield.

"That's why I need you and McKenzie. You can convince her."

"Forget it," he said. He pointed at the windshield. "Case closed. Drive."

"Mom's not going to live much longer," Howard said. He wore that stupid smile and flushed face.

He glared at Howard. "You sonofabitch," he said. "That's it. You know what? I'm walking back. I've had enough." He started to open the door but Howard reached across and held his hand over his. "What the fuck you think you're doing?" he said, and he flailed at Howard's hand as if it were a horsefly. "Get your fucking hands off me."

Howard held on. "You can't do this," he said between his teeth. "You can't do this to me, to our family."

"You're wrong on both counts," he said. And now he returned Howard's stare with his set jaw. "I can do this. And it's not our family you're talking about. It's not even your family. It's you. You want to build a monument to yourself. You want to be lord of the manor. Now let me out of this fucking tub before I have to break the damn window."

Howard withdrew his hand and lowered his voice. "Okay, okay, wait," he said. He took a breath and exhaled. His forehead was flushed and beaded with sweat. "Wait just a second. What do you want? I'll make you an offer. I'll buy out your share of the property."

His eyes flashed, and a jolt of electricity shot through his veins. It was over. He grabbed Howard by the collar and pinned him against the window. "For the last fucking time, I don't want your money."

He released Howard, and then he unlocked his door and got out. He started to walk down the road through the tire track that Howard's Expedition had made in the snow. Howard turned the rig around, spinning tires and gunning the engine. He kept walking. The SUV pulled closer. He didn't budge. Howard laid on the horn, and it boomed out into the stillness and echoed off the boulders down the valley, likely the only car horn sounding for a hundred miles. There was no other way down the blasted hill. Finally, Howard pulled the truck up until its cold chrome bumper rode on his ass. The horn blared once, twice, three times, and then it stayed on. He wanted to stop his ears but wouldn't give Howard the satisfaction.

"Get out of my way!" Howard screamed out the open window.

Joe never turned around, but he could imagine Howard's face turning crimson, the veins in his forehead and neck bulging, eyes popping.

"I will run you down!" Howard screamed.

Howard kept the bumper on him, and Joe leaned back on it, letting it push him ahead. At one point, the engine roared and he braced himself. He imagined falling and at least trying to sink below the surface of the snow and not get scraped off by the truck's oil pan. Howard hit the gas and the engine revved like it would tear down the hill with him underneath, but the truck only jumped up and not forward.

Finally, at a wide spot in the road, Howard laid back, and Joe got ahead of the bumper. He was determined not to turn around. Moments later, the tires whined as they spun in the snow and the engine snarled. Then the tires stopped spinning and he knew it was coming on hard. When he did turn, the giant grille and the headlights were bearing down on him. His brother's face was frozen in rage. But the SUV swerved and then plowed into the snowy meadow to his right, weaving and tearing out sage and juniper until it found the track of the road again.

Howard tore down the road, the truck fishtailing. Then the brakes lights glowed red, and the SUV slid to a stop. He jumped out, slipping on the ice and then standing, shaking and pointing his finger. "I don't need you!" he yelled. His face was contorted and as red as the SUV's taillights. "I don't need you! Don't ever ask me for help! I disown you. You're not in this family. You're not a Wallace. Not you or your fucking squaw or any of your damned offspring!"

He fell, struggled to his feet, fell again. Then he climbed back in his truck, banged the door shut and stomped on the gas. The SUV swerved crazily and at one point hit what must have been a large rock, because there was the crunch of metal on stone. But the truck kept going until its taillights sank below a rise.

And then it was as though the SUV had penetrated back out through a bubble surrounding the little glacial valley. Snow fell from a tree branch and then blew to dust in the wind. The wind blew through the ponderosas. He stopped to take off his boots and shake out the snow, now and again blowing on his hands and then shoving them in his pockets. Then he walked as fast as he could back down the road and to the house on the lake.

He'd always known his brother to be determined, driven, but he had never seen him like this. He'd turned into a monster. In his mind's eye, Howard's face returned, spitting mad in the windshield as he bore down on him from above. The face of a maniac. He remembered how his hands would shake with the DTs. But now they were still. He had assumed once that his family's property would somehow last into perpetuity. But now he saw how fragile it was. It wasn't going to survive on its own, not with Howard scheming to take control. Howard's plan was crazy, and it had to be stopped.

"That fucking squaw," Howard had said. The fat bigot. Maybe he was the one who'd sprayed the little welcome sign on the cabin door. It didn't seem possible until now. Hell, Howard had more at stake than Cody Macy, didn't he? Cody Macy could never bring his dead brother back. But Howard wanted something that Cody could never have and that Joe stood in the way of: 160 acres of prime real estate to develop. And he was probably blaming Ana for Joe's turn. Hell, for all he knew, given that it was his fool brother, maybe it was bigger than that for Howard. Maybe it was some kind of God-and-country delusion, which was an excuse for naked greed. Howard was no different from the government agents who'd stolen the Nez Perce's land back in the 19th Century and then justified it all as manifest destiny for God's self-appointed chosen people.

Joe was dead certain. He would never agree to the development of their land. Never.

CHAPTER 38

In the last week of January, the cold that had eluded them all winter came throttling down out of Canada. It burned nostrils and cracked wood and froze dirt.

The deep Imnaha country, usually spared, could not escape this time. It was even colder down there, the heavy air sinking into the canyons. After their well froze and the power went out, Ana left for the lake. The power was more reliable up there, the water supply stable, and Grace could use the company in the dead of winter.

He stayed behind. He needed to take a gas torch to the pumphouse pipes before they cracked. On top of that, he had more stream surveying to do. The steelhead season started with the new year, and this year was expected to be one of the better steelhead seasons in recent memory.

On the last day of January, he rose early to get to the upper Imnaha at first light. He checked the thermometer on the front porch: Ten below. He made a fire. He put on his warmest fleece underwear and heavy socks and the old Russian fur hat he'd brought with him from Alaska.

He dressed in the dark and ate the last two slices from a loaf of bread, loaded with stiff peanut butter. When the water boiled on the wood stove, he poured it through the ground coffee in a funnel atop his old Stanley Thermos. He drank a cup and then topped off the bottle. Lunch would be a can of stew heated over a small cookstove he kept in the truck. He loaded his pack with the fish-survey forms, the coffee and lunch, along with his pants, an extra pair of gloves and a safety kit. Over these, he put on a fleece pullover and then covered that with a goose down coat. When he was ready, he pulled on his dry waders and wading boots.

Outside, he loaded the back of the pickup with firewood. It would be good to stop at lunch and make a campfire.

He arrived at the start of the reach before the sun crested the eastern ridgeline. He pulled the truck into a meadow interspersed with thick, puzzle-barked ponderosa that glowed in the thin light. He put on his pack and descended through the brush to the river. The water was low and clear. At the edge of the water, the cottonwoods stood leafless in the raw dawn. Tall spruce shot out between the cottonwoods.

Down here, he could get distance from his pig-headed brother's plans, his stupid confrontation with the Macys, the unanswered questions about who was harassing them. Even his worries about Ana could fade for the moment, confident that she was safer with Grace, with McKenzie nearby and under the watchful eye of Bart. He could just be here, do what needed to be done.

He walked only yards before he saw his first steelhead. It was moving upstream, its dorsal and caudal fins barely submerged and making a chevron on the surface. The stream temperature was warmer than the air, but if this weather held, the fish would stop moving. The steep gradient helped keep the water from slowing enough to freeze, but its south-to-north flow put it at a low angle to the sun—a blessing in the summer but not much help now when it could use some solar energy.

There was ice along the edges of the river, and as he moved upstream, he continually crushed the ice with his boots. At times it sounded like glass breaking; at other times it was like hollow plastic shattering. In places, the ice had formed above the level of the river. Attached to a cut bank or a log, the ice grew outward like fungus on a rotting stump.

He worked his way methodically, stopping at each redd. They were easy to spot, the gravel scrubbed clean. He removed his glove and scribbled an entry in his yellow Rite in the Rain, noting the number of fish, their sex, estimated size and condition. Then he took a bright orange plastic ribbon, tied it to a rock and threw it in the river to mark the redd for future surveys.

By 10 o'clock, when the sun had climbed over the canyon walls, he had recorded 23 redds. It was good news. Spawning had only begun. More fish would be entering the river over the next several weeks.

For a moment, he imagined him and Ana and their child—boy or girl, it didn't matter—doing the same thing on the Wallowa River.

He found a log in the cold sun and sat. He pulled out a cold-stiffened English muffin that he'd buttered and spread with cream cheese. The fish had a smell for home waters, but what did that feel like? Was it an obsession that ached? Was it a sense that something was incomplete, missing, unfinished, and that they had to close the loop above all else? They must have sensed the nearness of the end. Did they know they were going to die? Did they care? Of course, they were just fish being fish. Every moment was an eternity, and eternity was every moment.

From that time as a kid on the Deschutes, he'd sensed a bond with salmon, something about them that touched his core. It was this, wasn't it? This longing for connection, this pull for home. The problem with people was they'd lost that connection, most of them. They thought they could live without it, by wits and will alone. He bit into the muffin. It was a miracle, a stroke of unbelievably good fortune, how he'd found Ana, or they'd found each other. Maybe it wasn't so different from the force that brought together two fish, male and female, in the spawning grounds, a chemical attraction. Finding Ana was the end of a journey for him, too, but it was the beginning of a better life, the way it was meant to be lived. He had to make it work.

It was time to move. But as he got up, he sensed that something was watching him, or that there was a presence. He sat back, kept still. Without turning his head, he noticed something to his right, something big and unmoving, but not a tree or a rock. With the caution usually reserved for a rattlesnake, he turned toward the mass.

It took a moment for it to register, but when it did, the nausea rose in his stomach. It was a young calf, dead and frozen. Its eyes were gone, pecked out by ravens or vultures or eaten by yellow jackets, and the meat had been gnawed out of it to the bone.

It had fallen in the river somehow and drowned. Or somehow gotten separated and lost and then found by a pack.

He threw his muffin into the brush. Why had he chosen to sit here, out of anywhere else on the river? How is that he never noticed the dead animal? Its mouth was frozen in a cartoon grin. It was stupid, but he wanted to kick the damn thing for its helplessness. Why the hell couldn't it have done something to save itself? Then he was mad at himself for getting so worked up about it.

He walked into the water and skirted the carcass, trying to ignore its agonizingly peaceful, stupid gaze. When he was past it, he wanted to wash his hands and his face, get the stench out of his nostrils.

He got back to his stream survey. But something felt wrong. He walked a long stretch without finding a redd. It was a poor stretch of river, too fast or not the right gravel for spawning. That damned dead calf seemed to color everything.

At 11:30, he turned back for lunch. When he got close to where he'd found the dead calf, he got off the river and circled through the brush. In half an hour, he made it back to the clearing where he had started the day. He was happy that Ana's truck was there in the lot, next to his. But she wasn't in it.

His gut tightened and his head raced. The dead calf was still messing with him. He returned his pack to the bed of the truck and jogged down to the bridge.

"Joe!" Ana was behind him.

She was coming out of the brush close to where he had just been. He ran to her, the cold air sharp in his lungs. She was wearing a down parka without a hat, and her hands were stuffed in the pockets. She held her lips tightly against her teeth and drew her eyebrows up in a sad arch.

He reached for her and she put her head against his shoulder.

"I'm so glad I found you," she said.

"Is it the baby?" he said. There was an ache in his stomach that was ready to explode.

She shook her head, looked down and then looked at him. "The baby's fine. Joe, it's Grace. We better go."

CHAPTER 39

Three days later, the cold began to loosen its grip. There was a change in the air and the light as soon as he awoke that morning. It was a muffled quiet, a gauziness in the gray sky, and he knew in his bones that it was snow.

He got up and found Ana in the kitchen, sitting at the table chopping celery. The coffee was made and a pot of oats sat on the stove, next to a boiling soup kettle. Even Ana appeared different, as if she too knew and sensed what he'd felt. He came around behind her and bent to kiss her neck. He wrapped his arms over her belly, holding her quietly for a long time, feeling the baby. When she turned her head and looked in his eyes, he knew what she knew, that this was the end.

"Did you sleep?" she said. She returned to chopping. "Get yourself some coffee."

He filled a mug with coffee and sat beside her. "I got up to check on mom a couple of times. I know you did, too. It was around three I guess, and I could feel the snow coming. Did you feel it?"

"I did," she said. "It's different today."

He picked up a knife and started in on the carrots. Howard and Sue would be coming later in the morning, and McKenzie would come after her shift at the hospital. He had avoided Howard each time he'd come around. But it was hard with what was happening. They'd been doing this each of the last two days, keeping vigil at their mother's bedside. Grace had been in pain, but now she was on morphine. She drifted from sleep to moments of clarity, then to delusion and confusion.

"She's peaceful now," she said. "I think she's ready."

He sipped coffee from his mug and nodded. "She's been waiting for something, I guess," he said. "People say that happens. Maybe it's true."

She sliced a yellow onion in half. "Yeah," she said, and when she bit her lip, there were tears.

"You okay?" he said. He thumbed a tear trickling down her cheek. She nodded and sniffled. "Onions," she said, and laughed, but then she held the knife against the cutting board and leaned into his chest. He pulled her close, and she sobbed. The sadness rose in him like a lump of undigested food, but he wasn't ready to let go, and so he got hold of himself and put his mind on comforting her.

He kissed her hair and held her. "When dad died, I was in shock, for a lot of reasons. But I didn't see him like this. It all happened so fast, it was unreal. It was like he was burned out like a cigarette. But I think of mom, and I think maybe she's got this other part of her that is calling the shots now. It's like her body has to finally give it up and let go, and for mom, that's no easy deal. She never gave an inch in her life."

She reached for his hand and squeezed it and raised her head off his chest. "No, she didn't," she said. "If and when she has a moment when she's lucid today, take that time with her."

He leaned into her hair. Holding her and breathing in her smell grounded him. "She'll come around if she has anything left to say," he said. "But even if she doesn't, I'm okay with it. I think I'm ready, too."

She lifted his hand and kissed it. "I think you are," she said. "I've been watching you. I've seen you change. It's not easy to see your mom like this."

"No," he said, and the word stuck in his throat. He pulled his hand from her and touched his chest as he choked on his words. "Not mom. Damn it."

He caught himself from crying again but when she looked at him he couldn't hold it back any longer. It started low and deep, like a cold engine shuddering to life, his body wracking hard, still resisting. But then, finally, he let it go, and it was like falling in deep water, the tears and the heat and the grief engulfing him until there was nothing but pain and acceptance and gratitude.

She held him the whole time, as if she were trying to make sure the pieces of him would hold fast through the shaking.

He tried to say something even though he couldn't form words, but she quieted him with a kiss and looked at him. It was like he'd melted into her and there was no separation any longer between them. "You're a good man and a good son," she said. "Grace knows that. She's proud of you."

He buried his face in her black hair. Something had changed. It was as though he'd shaken off a heaviness, and he realized that he'd come to accept that Grace was going, and he was ready to let her go. But it was something more. Ana had taught him how to open his heart. He'd always been afraid of that, but now he sensed that, rather than taking something away from him, or losing something, he felt lighter. And the word *grateful* came to him. Grateful for Ana. Grateful for his mother and the love she'd shown him. Grateful to be alive.

As Grace lay in her bed, they each tiptoed in throughout the day and closed the door behind them. At times she spoke fantastical medicated gibberish. But when his time came, he bent over her, and she whispered to him with a fierceness that must have taken all her strength, her hand delicate as a bird's wing. "Promise," she said. "Don't let him."

It was as though she was only half in this world, her skin so pale and thin, her eyes shut, her mouth drawn back. The room was warm with heat from the wood stove, but she was cool to the touch. He pulled the blanket higher on her. "Okay, mom," he said. "I promise." She nodded slightly, but enough that he knew she had heard him.

She closed her eyes. He sat in silence, his hand on the sheet over her arm. Dry snowflakes ticked against the window. At one point, she startled and frowned, and he pressed her arm. He leaned his forehead on the bed, and only then noticed the rasp of her breath. Then he picked his head and arm up and was about to stand.

"Leave it open." She breathed the words.

"Mom?"

"The door," she said. The sheet moved where her hand was.

"You want me to leave it open?" He pressed the sheet.

She closed her eyes but nodded once.

"Okay," he said. "I'll come back. Do you want some water?"

But she had already drifted into her narcotic sleep. He got up and walked toward the door but stopped and turned. He inhaled deeply. He bit his lip and closed his eyes and a wave of sadness came over him. When he opened his eyes, the light in the room was drained of color. He returned to her bedside and touched her forehead. Her eyelids fluttered briefly and then stilled.

He left and sat back down at the dining room table. Through the open door, the lower half of Grace's bed showed, her bony legs and feet barely making a ripple under the placid surface of the blankets. She never moved, and he knew they were all thinking the same thought.

She hadn't asked him anything else about Howard. She knew what had happened that day up on the moraine. He'd talked with her about it. She handled it well, consoling him for the pain he'd experienced but at the same time doing her motherly best not to seem to show favoritism. But as much as she tried to love her children equally, it must have been hard for her with Howard. He was such a damn fool. Ever since that fight, it was like Howard had experienced a break with reality. His quest to develop the land had turned into an obsession, some kind of high-stakes personal battle that Howard had to win at all costs.

She never asked him to get along with Howard or to somehow put it right with him. Still, he decided that today would be the day he'd suck it up and accept being in the same room with the jerk. And, maybe his brother would have the decency to do the same.

They drank coffee and ate Sue's ham and cheese sandwiches. He tended the woodstove. He got up to get more wood from the pile he'd stacked in the fall, welcoming the chance for a moment of solitude and a break from the overheated house. Back when he was drinking, this would have been the time to take a pull from a bottle, and the thought was never far from him. The lake was frozen now, the entire landscape, except for the ponderosas, white with snow and ice, the sky like gray stucco. The door opened, and it was his brother.

"Need a hand?" Howard said, an ever-present toothpick drooping from this mouth. He walked to the stack of cut and split pine. He picked up three logs and then approached. He had that look of his, the little grin and upturned eyes that meant he wanted something. "Could use a drink, huh?" he said, and then put his hands up. "You quit, right?"

Joe tipped his chin up. "Not a problem." Then he turned back to the lake. "She's not going to last the day." He sank his hands in his jeans. He was wearing a Pendleton shirt and had turned the collar up.

Howard put the wood down. "I can bring this in in a second," he said. "Believe me, if there were another time to do this," he said. "But I'm not choosing the time. Someone else is."

He didn't turn. He didn't want to see Howard's smarmy face. What could he possibly want on this day, at this time? Did he have the gall to bring up his plan?

Howard drew closer and put his foot up on the porch railing. "Cold," Howard said, blowing on his hands. The branches of the ponderosas sifted the wind with a rushing sound, and a gray jay swooped above and scolded. Then the wind stopped and the stillness returned. Finally Howard came out with it. "I want you to come back in the house. I've got some important things to show you."

He turned slightly. Howard's face was drawn tightly in his "this–is–serious" look.

"You're pathetic. You know that?" he said. Then he rubbed his eyes and blew out through the side of his mouth but kept his hands on his stubbly chin. "You don't get it. Mom's dying in there, and you want to sell me fucking real estate."

Howard stood between him and the door. He made to go around him, but as soon as he did, Howard stepped in his path.

"Wait," Howard said.

"Wait? Hell, no, let me pass," he said, and he moved again.

But Howard put a hand on his shoulder. "One last time."

"Jesus Christ. You're insane." But he stopped. His heart and head raced. Not here, not now, he thought. For Ana, for McKenzie and for his mother, he would not do what he wanted to do, which was to pummel Howard, starting with his slimy face. "I am going inside. Take your hand off of me, and show me whatever the hell you want to show me. Just let mom die in peace."

Howard's face lit up. "Now you're talking sense. You'll see." He inhaled. "Lord, it's cold out here," he said as he blew out through curled lips.

Joe followed Howard into the kitchen. McKenzie was putting away dishes. Howard had stacked a pile of documents on the table. He motioned them toward the table, but she kept her back to him, and he leaned against the sink with a cup of coffee in his hands. Howard picked up the first document and read the legal jargon aloud from it.

"What in the hell did you just say?" he said.

She looked over her shoulder, gave a quick, dismissive shake and returned to the sink of pots.

"It might make more sense if you sat here and I showed you these," Howard said.

Joe grabbed a dish towel, picked a pot out of the rack and dried it. "Get to the point," he said. He opened a cabinet door and put the pot away.

Howard placed the document down neatly over the others and folded his hands over them. "Okay, I have an investor who is making us an offer," he said. "It's … well it's the best we could ever hope for."

She turned and dried her hands on a towel. "Are we really talking about this now?" she said. She looked sideways at him, as if to ask why he was putting up with this.

"I know you may not understand all this business talk," he said, grinning. "I'll try to make it simple."

"Don't patronize me," she said. "I can read a contract."

"Okay then," he said.

He thought to check on Ana. She'd been in there a long time. It had been a dumb idea to come in here. Howard continued to blabber, but he was checked out of the conversation. When he was a kid, he used to play with his father's workbench vise, turning the wooden handle and watching the big threads spin and open the clamps, like a ferry leaving a dock. Now, it felt like the room was on one of those vises, opening and widening. He remembered the smell of machine oil. Howard seemed far away.

"Joe!" Howard yelled.

He jumped. "Jesus Christ."

"Keep your voices down!" She raised both hands and glared at them.

"He hasn't heard one thing I said," Howard complained. "You said you'd listen."

She walked over to the table and sat. "For the love of God, I don't know why you are doing this now. But get on with it. I've got to get back inside." She turned to him. "Get over here, too."

"If you say so," Joe said, playfully. She evidently didn't see the play in it, and he sat.

Howard huffed and started again. His forehead was damp. "He's offering to finance up to 90 percent of the development costs. We form a corporation and, with the proceeds from the sale, we become partners in the development. Our share—."

"Whoa, whoa," he cut him off and raised a hand. "You said 'the proceeds from the sale.' The sale of what?"

He screwed his face into something between a smile and a scowl and smoothed his hand across a document. "You know very well what I'm talking about."

She grabbed the plans and turned them toward her. "Our land?" Then she shoved them away, pushed out the chair and jumped up. "End of conversation. Our mother is dying in there, and you want to talk about selling our land." She wheeled and marched out of the kitchen.

He stayed put. When she was gone and the door was closed, he put his chin in his hand and leaned his elbow on the table. Then he rubbed his temples and squeezed his eyes, shaking his head. "A master of timing, aren't you?"

"I already said—."

"Fuck what you already said, okay?"

Howard's eyes got big. But before he started in, Joe cut him off with a sharpened glare. His stomach felt like a nest of snakes. "Take those plans, put them away, and don't ever show them in here again." He spoke low and through his teeth. "If you don't do it, I swear I'll take them myself and throw them in the fucking lake, you along with them. You heard her, and now you're hearing me. You know ma doesn't want this land touched. I don't care what kind of a deal you've cut with some fat cat, but your deal is dead. You need our signatures on this, this deed or whatever the hell it is, and you're not getting them. Case closed. Done. Finished. End of story."

Howard gritted his teeth, the toothpick jutting out. But his lower lip was quivering, the way it did when they were kids and he was about to cry. "I can't believe I was born into this family," he said, and his eyes narrowed. "I hate you. You, you've always gotten away with murder. You were their favorite. It was always, 'Joe this,' and 'Joe that.' No one ever said anything about me. I got the grades. I went to college. I married a good Christian woman and gave them grandchildren. I made a success out of myself. You, you're nothing. You're a nobody, a fool, a drunk. You and your Sacajawea fantasy—."

The door swung open, and it was Sue and Ana, together. The women looked at them in silence. Their stone faces told it all. And in that moment, the bile that had been burning his stomach was transformed into a sinking loss, a drowning.

"Joe?" Ana said.

"You'd better come in here," Sue said.

He plodded in and shut the door and sat in the chair next to the bed. She looked smaller than he'd ever remembered. The same body that had always been a refuge to him was now empty. When he was a kid, he'd seen a drawing in some Sunday school book of disembodied wings and he'd come to think a person's soul was in the shoulders, attached to wings. And when a person died, those wings would fly off, soul and all, to heaven. That memory came to him now, and he touched her shoulder. When he felt that delicate but unmoving resistance, the muscle nearly gone from the bone, the grief came, and he let himself go into it.

He sat with his eyes closed. The clock on her bedside ticked. There were voices outside the door, low and muffled. The wind outside the room sighed through the branches of the ponderosas. That was a sound he remembered. He was sitting on the ground under the trees. His mother was up on the porch calling down to his father at the dock. They'd created a little paradise, and for a brief and wonderful time, he knew no separation from them or the place. It had felt as though everything—his parents, the trees, the lake—was a part of him. And now a hint of that feeling returned. As though his mother's dying enabled him to finally forgive his father, and allowed his father's presence to come into the room. But it was the father he loved, the one who could be so gentle and kind and patient. He had clung to his anger with his father all this time, but now he was ready to let it go. The tears came. He bit his knuckles as he sobbed. Finally, he was able to love him again. He'd wanted that so badly, but it was something he had to feel in his bones. That had been Grace's final act of kindness to him.

There was a gust outside, and, with his eyes still closed, he felt the room sway as though floating on water.

He opened his eyes. She was gone, but then again, she wasn't. There was a sadness like weariness, but there was a calmness. Grace had taught him not to fear death, and she had shown him how to do it. He was at peace with her death the way he never had found it with his father. The clock ticked. He'd lost track of time, nearly forgotten where he was or what had happened, even forgotten who he was, as if the outlines of his body had somehow blurred into the warm room.

Her body had become an empty vessel. It was time to go now. He stood and began walking away. Then he stopped and turned back to face her. He drew near and touched her cool cheek with the back of his hand, as if to make certain that indeed this no longer was his mother. He shut his eyes and inhaled, nodding briefly and exhaling as he did. And then he opened his eyes once more. She'd always worn makeup, including that crazy purple-blue eye shadow that she loved. But now her face was clear of anything but her pale skin, and she seemed luminous as limestone. She had loved life and had left it satisfied that she'd accomplished what she'd wanted. He turned and walked to the door, and then closed it gently behind him.

CHAPTER 40

After they'd gotten the lake house cleaned up, he and Ana moved back to the cabin on the Imnaha. It was her wish. He could see she was right. It was good to get away from the lake house, at least for a while. And spring was returning to the Imnaha.

The day after they moved, they got up early to go fishing. They were on the road before sunrise, headed for the upper river trailhead.

He had originally thought of going alone. She was due in three weeks, and he'd dismissed the thought of bringing her. But she was having none of it. The steelhead were in the river, the cold had finally broken its grip, and, by God, she would make the trip. She was hard-headed and irresistible like that.

She drove while he scanned the sky for signs of what daybreak might give them. The dry weather was supposed to hold for a bit, but there was a front coming in that could bring snow to the higher elevations.

"You think being pregnant is some kind of affliction?" she said, one hand resting on top of her taut belly. She could have steered the wheel with her bulge. "I was born fishing, and I'll probably die fishing."

"Don't go talking about dying and fishing."

She laughed. "A Nez Perce does not stop her life because she is going to have a baby. We are incredibly strong, and fishing is easy. And besides, it will be good for the two of us. Your mom, and now this weirdness with Howard. We need to spend some time together, alone."

"Well, not exactly alone," he said, and he touched her belly. It was rock hard. The road followed the curve of the river. "You sure you'll be okay?"

"Don't worry," she said. "Instead of worrying, just make sure you're prepared."

"For what?" he said.

"To catch fish."

For the past two weeks, he hadn't done much more than see to it that Grace's things were put in order. Now it was time to let go and consider what lay ahead. Grace was gone. In another two weeks, the federal commission was scheduled to make its ruling on the dam. About that time, Ana would probably be delivering their baby.

She was right. They needed time together. What he'd felt when Grace died had stayed with him, the sense of an opening, a lightness, a wholeness. He told Ana about it, but there hadn't been enough time with everything else going on. Up the trail, out on the river, they could talk.

They arrived at the trailhead half an hour after sunrise. She would park in the trailhead parking lot, but he touched her arm before she had a chance to turn off the ignition. On the way there, where the river road intersects with the mountain loop road, he'd seen a Ford pickup parked beside the road. It was the only vehicle he'd seen that morning, with the exception of the few trucks and cars parked in Imnaha, but he hadn't said anything to her at the time and she hadn't seemed to notice. The truck belonged to Cody Macy. And even though Cody may not have been harassing them, he still remembered what Bart had told him. Don't trust them, especially if you come across them alone. He'd said more than that, though. He'd said to call him.

"What's the matter?" she said.

He motioned across the dash. "Park over there, behind those trees," he said.

She looked at him, twisting her mouth into a question. "What's wrong with right here?"

"I'd just as soon not let on that we're here," he said.

She shrugged but then took her hand off the ignition and put the truck back in gear. She pulled off the road and into the woods a short distance and parked. They put their rods together. He had put his pistol in his pack without her knowing. They left their waders in their packs so they could hike more easily.

They got their packs on and headed up the trail through the trees, each carrying a rod. Here the river hugged the trail to the left. Before long, he stopped.

"What?" she said.

"Just looking," he said.

"I know what you're looking for. Or who," she said. "I saw it, too. Cody's truck, back there. I figured you'd seen it but didn't want to say anything."

He blew out, his breath vaporizing into a small cloud. "Yeah. Just wanted to see if he'd followed us," he said.

"You do need to relax, don't you?" she said. "You're wound tight as a rattlesnake. Besides, I've already encountered him in the woods once before, and you know what happened then. Nothing. After all that's happened. He could have killed you, and what did he do?"

She was right. Still, there was no way he could trust Cody Macy. They waited a while longer in silence. Finally, he turned and began walking again. They headed uphill and into a small clearing. Ahead of them was the spine of the mountains. Thick, old-growth ponderosas towered to their right in an open grove, their bark a bright cinnamon in the lightening sky.

In early summer, this meadow would have knee-high grasses and wildflowers. Now the grasses were brown and matted from the snows and the cold. Ana walked as quickly as ever, not slowed by the weight of the winter emergency gear they had packed.

The trail generally took a straight line while the river snaked back and forth in a series of riffles, pools and sandbars. Always there was the sound of the water, at times overpowering when the trail skirted the river, at other times a whisper like wind in the trees when the river bowed away from the trail.

Once more, the feeling of being followed returned. He resisted turning to look, yet he felt it, like a cold draft on his neck. The rushing of the water in the background only made him more alert for sounds that might not rise above the din. Would Cody walk in without a horse? Why? Or was it a cougar stealing along, watching them from a distance?

He told himself it was his mind playing tricks. He had been on this trail dozens of times, from the time he was barely old enough to walk. No one had ever followed him then, and no one was following them now. What was different, of course, was that he was now with Ana, and she was carrying their child. He felt a gut urge to protect her. She sensed this and even respected it, yet it also seemed laughable to him and he could imagine her scoffing at the idea that she needed anything like protection.

He did not talk about being followed. He tried to put the thought out of his head.

They passed an ancient, dead ponderosa at the head of a grove. It was leaning like the mast of a sailboat into the wind, most of its bark stripped bare to reveal the straight-veined, glossy interior. They skirted giant boulders that either had been left behind when the last Ice Age glacier melted or had fallen from the ridgeline above. They traveled through a stand of lodgepole pine, many of which had their lower reaches charred black from fires, as if their bottoms had been tarred. This stand soon gave out into an open burn area, where the trees had not been so lucky.

The dead trees were mostly spindly and short. Some stood like burned matchsticks stuck in the ground, black and twisted. Most simply had died from the intense heat, their heartwood cooked until it bubbled. In some cases, trees had exploded like bombs, they'd heated so fast. Yet some trees had survived. These were the biggest and fattest of the bunch, their crowns high enough to avoid the flames and their skins thick enough to insulate them against the heat.

She had been walking ahead of him, but now he caught up with her. She was sitting on a rock with a stick in her hand. Her face was flushed and sweating.

"You all right?" he asked.

She smiled a smile that could melt ice. "I'm perfect," she said. "We're perfect."

"It's not much longer," he said. "We'll go in a little ways and work upstream to the falls."

She reached out her hand and he helped her up. "I'm going to have to bring a winch with us soon enough to get up," she said. She laughed hardest when she made fun of herself. "I'm so round you might be able to turn me on my side and start rolling me down the trail if I get tired."

He patted her on her head and mocked. "My fat little squaw," he said, and she punched him in the stomach but laughed.

"Next time you say that, I'll kick you in the *cojones*," she said.

They continued up the trail through the burn. A large understory of mountain mahogany had colonized the open slope beneath the burned trees, their spice strong even in the brisk air. The old fire had jumped the river to their left and then burned up and over the opposite ridge.

Soon, the trail hemmed the water where the river opened up into a wider floodplain. Here the river cut huge looping meanders through the burned-out meadow. They took a side trail down to the river's grassy edge.

The water ran clear, fast and silent, its surface broken only by an occasional eddy. The river bed lay nearly flat, its bottom a fish-perfect blend of spawning-sized cobbles and an occasional boulder. Fallen trees, some charred, others sun-bleached, lay across the stream, the water pooling and cascading over them.

They sat in the dry grass and removed their shoes. They pulled dry waders out of their packs and wiggled into them. He slipped on his felt-soled wading boots and then watched her attempt to get close enough to her feet to place the boots on.

"Are you just going to watch or you going to do something?" she scolded.

"I don't know," he said. "You got to admit; it is kind of hilarious. You look like a beached walrus." He then cradled each boot and slipped them on her and tied the laces. He'll be doing this for their kid in a few years, he thought.

"You'll pay for that remark, you know," she said. "Anyway, you're wrong. I look more like a beached whale."

He removed the fly box from the backpack, opened it and offered it to her. "Chocolate, vanilla or strawberry?"

She slipped her finger over the flies. "I'm sort of a traditional girl, but it's been so cold. I think we need something to wake them up." She fished out a Glo-bug, a simple puff of bright yarn along the hook shank below the eye. "Plus, girls like pink. Maybe I'll get myself a hen." She took the fly and tied it to her leader.

He rummaged through the box and picked a fly that one-upped hers for color. "You're right about the cold." He took the orange-pink fly and held it between his fingers, inspecting it with the river as backdrop. "What do you think? If you were a steelhead, would you have to have this?"

She had already started to walk toward the stream. She stopped and looked over her shoulder. "That's pretty good," she said. "Like cotton candy."

He slipped the tippet end through the eye and tied a knot. "Looks like you know where you're going," he said, and then he laughed. "Maybe I'll go up ahead and drive the fish down to you."

She started walking downstream. "No, you're just going up there because you always think it's better to fish the higher hole," she said.

"You want to fish it?" he called after her.

"I can do fine down here."

"Well, call me if you can't do it alone."

"Likewise, rookie."

He followed the river's edge, walking back out and around the brush to avoid throwing shadows and spooking fish. His heart jumped in anticipation of making his first cast. He fought the urge to run to the next hole. Ahead, he took the first cut back to the river above the head of the lower pool.

He found the riverside trail and then turned downstream, careful to stay back and low, until he arrived at the point where the pool built up against a fallen log and some boulders. The steelhead often could be found here, resting after having negotiated the riffle below. He moved farther downstream. Ana was already in the water, making quartering casts. He waved, and she returned his wave quickly without breaking the rhythm of her casting. He walked back up to a spot where he could cast.

He waded out until he was up to his hips and turned halfway between downstream and the opposite bank. The only way to fish this pool was to let the fly drift down into the tailout and swing across the face of the current until just before it would go over the logjam. It was less important to get a big cast out into the river than it was to get the wet fly quickly down to the fish, which would be hugging the bottom in the cold, and work it slowly across the steelie's field of vision. On top of that, he had to be ready for a strike.

He decided to work the pool from the outside in. From where he was standing he could accomplish this simply by pivoting and working shorter and shorter casts. When he ran out of room to make a good cross-water cast, he could take five or so steps back toward the bank on his side. In this manner, he could efficiently sweep the entire pool. If there was a fish in it, it would at least get a chance to examine his offering.

He was using a sink-tip line, and so he stripped enough line for his cast and then gathered it up in coils in his left hand. He did a roll cast to bring the tip to the surface, then backcasted and let it fly. As soon as the line landed, he quickly mended upstream to give the tip enough slack to sink. He followed the line downstream with his rod held at about 11 o'clock until he felt the tug of the fully extended line and let his rod drop. Then he swung the line through the holding water, holding his breath at the end of the drift, ready for a strike. He loved that moment of fishing more than any other, that sense of being connected and alive, completely suspended in time, focused on what was happening in the moment. Especially that first cast and drift. He waited until the last moment to pull up the fly as it rose and gained speed and the line tightened. He exhaled, the familiar realization that a first-cast fish would not happen today. Then he stripped line back upstream and readied for his next cast. He worked the stream this way for five casts and then stepped toward the bank to repeat the process. He had not gotten a strike, but he was satisfied with the action of the fly in the water.

The mountains above them were covered with snow, and they were like great ships plowing through spindrift. If this is all there is, he thought, this is enough. Out here, in this place now with Ana, their child cocooned in safety. He was amazed she had stuck with him, especially through the drinking. He did not believe in luck, and he did not believe in a personal God; so he didn't credit his finding of her to either of these. It was more than luck, more than mere coincidence that had brought them together and that had enabled him to stay sober for these months. Was he finally at peace with himself because of her? He hoped so. It was his good fortune.

When he had fully worked this spot without a strike, he waded close to shore and began walking upstream. Midway, he heard Ana shout with that unmistakable hoot that meant she had a fish on. He placed his rod carefully on the bank and ran downstream.

She was standing mid-thigh in the current, her big belly lapping the water. She held her rod up at nearly a perpendicular angle to the water, but the rod tip was bent in a tight gooseneck. Then he saw the fish jump, its silver sides flashing as it burst from the water and thrashed to try to throw the hook.

"Hoo-ee!" he yelled as he ran down the beach. "It's a beauty! Hang in there!"

The glowing green fly line ran tightly out toward the fish before disappearing underwater. The line was electric, alive, pulsing. It held firm as though anchored on a snag, then suddenly shifted, moving crazily against and across the current like a thing with a mind of its own. Of course, it was attached to a creature with a mind of its own. He reached the bank abreast of her, his heart pounding.

"She's going to make a break downstream soon. I can feel it," she shouted.

"Keep that tip up when she does," he said. "Be ready to strip line if she comes at you."

With her left hand, she held a loop of line out beside her hip. She stood poised, ready to let the fish run. But the steelhead refused to budge, holding tight and still against the current. She shifted her position slightly in toward shore.

"I'm going to have to tire her out before she tires me out," she said. "That's the only way I will land this girl."

Suddenly, the line went slack. She jerked into motion, quickly but calmly stripping line to maintain tension against the hidden force on its other end. She pivoted, keeping her body roughly square to where she estimated the steelhead was. He made his way out on the gravel behind her.

"Ha!" she cried. "I may have lost her. Where are you, girl?"

"Don't give up," he said. "Pull—."

He didn't get a chance to finish. Suddenly, opposite them in the current, the fish breached again. The hook was still set, and she was able to strip in line to cut slack. The fish seemed as big as his arm.

"She's a beauty!" he yelled. "Yeah!"

She turned and quartered the stream at about 7 o'clock to the opposite bank. She held the line between thumb and index finger and let the steelhead play it out. In her other hand, several large loops of line caressed the water's surface.

"I hope I've got enough," she said. "She'll snap this line so fast."

The big fish blazed again on its way downstream. There was a pile of boulders below. Unless she could keep the tip high enough, the steelhead would be able to scrape the line against the rocks and break free. She had already begun wading downstream, tip held high and stripping line in, to make sure she could clear the stones. He followed her.

"Easy now," he said. "You got it?"

"I'm good."

Just as fast, the fish changed direction upstream. The green line ran madly up the stream, slicing back through her fingers. At one point, the silver-green fuselage of the fish shot by like a turbocharged submarine.

"This is it!" he yelled. "It's her last run!"

"Don't be so sure. This is a native girl I've got here. We're tough bitches."

He laughed at the truth of it. She was as tough as they come; tougher than any woman he knew, even more so than Grace or McKenzie. She could endure more pain, work harder and go longer than anyone, including himself. She was a force of nature.

"Go get 'er!" he yelled.

"Which girl are you cheering for, me or her?" she laughed.

"Don't matter!"

Once again, the fish flew upstream. But Ana must have noticed a change. Walking backwards until the slack was taken up, she began reeling line back onto her reel, one click at a time. As she did this, she kept gentle pressure on the tip and walked upstream now toward the fish.

"She's coming in," she said. "She's tired."

"Just be careful. She's probably got a couple of punches left."

Soon, the long torso of the fish appeared. It was finning languidly upstream, allowing the current to take it down.

"When it sees us it may bolt," he said.

"I'm ready."

But the fish continued to let the stream take it down. She carefully moved in toward the shallows.

"You're almost there," he said.

"Almost," she said.

In a moment, she brought the steelhead within reach. He had pulled out his net, and with one scoop, careful to start from the fish's snout, trapped the steelhead. The fish jumped but only farther into the net and, then, exhausted, seemed to relax and accept its fate. Its back shone like blue metal, its pectoral fins out and its tail waving. Its sides were as silver as a jet's. The fish's gills pumped harder than its slow pace, suggesting that it truly was tired.

"She's a hen all right," he said. "She's wild, a fighter, and boy was she pissed."

"Yes, but she's bleeding. Damn hook," she said. "No wonder she's tired."

A trickle of blood streamed from the steelhead's left gill. She squatted to remove the hook. He moved closer and bent over the fish. He wet his hands, and then carefully cradled the fish at the base of the tail and belly.

"Good girl," he said. "Easy does it."

She leaned in closer to the fish until she could nearly kiss it. With more pressure, she slipped the hook out, grunting and then sighing.

"Sounded like you took that hook out of yourself, not the fish," he said.

"Believe me, it felt a little like that," she said. "Here, let me do this."

He moved out of the way and she took hold of the fish in the water. She gently moved it back and forth and then let it go. It swam a bit but then began listing slightly, showing its silver side to the sky.

"No!" she screamed. "Don't do that! Swim!"

The current carried the fish downstream, the fish letting the current take it. She stood, grunting to straighten herself. Finally, the steelhead righted itself, wiggling its tail a few times. Then, in a flash as though it had touched a hidden electric prod, it sizzled like a shooting star and was gone.

"Thank God," she said. "I did not want to kill that fish."

"I had no doubt she was in good hands. You were something else out there. You were really amazing. Now, come on in and take a breather and get something to eat."

"I'm starving," she said.

They waded to the bank and made for their backpacks, which they had stashed in the brush. He pulled out a plastic tarp and spread it on the river bank. She brought out the tuna salad sandwiches she had made that morning. They unwrapped them and devoured them with the ferocity of hunger that only seems to come from outdoor exertion. "You forget this is fish sometimes," he said. "Tuna from a can." He leaned back on his elbows.

She seemed drained, the blood gone from her face. He sat up and got her an apple from the sack. "You look a little pale."

She labored a grin. "I'm tired, is all. That girl took something out of me."

He shifted so he could cradle her back against his knees and shins. They sat quietly, and he thought she might be sleeping. The sky was clouding up, and it must have been snowing up in the mountains because they were obscured by the low ceiling. Then suddenly her body tensed and she threw her hands out as if something had hit her and she was trying to balance herself. She let go a little surprised whimper.

"What?" He reached to grab her. "What's the matter?"

She bent over and grabbed for her stomach.

"I just felt a pop. And then, whoosh, I'm all wet."

"The baby?"

"I think my water broke."

CHAPTER 41

His stomach tightened, as if he were the one feeling the cramps. He searched her eyes for clues to how she was holding up. Those dark eyes could be so inscrutable, like looking into the depths of the lake. When she exhaled, he relaxed slightly. He had never been around a woman in labor. He would have to make some important decisions, maybe life and death. The thought scared the hell out of him, but he would not let her see that. She needed him strong.

"We've got to get you out of here, fast."

The sun was gone. The wind in the trees drowned the gentler sound of the running river. His watch showed 11:45.

"Looks like snow could be coming down the mountain soon," he said. "Should've known. Let's move this wagon train."

He helped her out of her wading boots and waders. When he pulled them off, he could see she was soaked through the crotch and legs of her jeans.

She pulled off the wet jeans. She stood naked from the waist down and never so much as once shivered. She had brought a pair of thermal underwear, in case it got cold, and insulated rain pants. She pulled them both on and he helped with her boots. He carried the rods in one hand and lightly supported her elbow with his free hand. But she pulled her arm away.

"I really can do this myself," she said. "You worry about the rods."

"Let's get the packs and get out," he said. "Forget the rods. We'll have to come back for them."

He smoothed her forehead. The sweat beaded on his forehead.

"We can carry them," she said. "We don't want to leave them."

"Forget about them. We need to get out of here fast. Can you walk?"

"Of course, I can walk. I can run, too."

He laughed. "I'll bet you can."

They hiked out of the river bottom and found the main riverside trail and started down, she in the lead. She set a fast pace. From behind, you wouldn't know she was about to have a baby. His confidence rose. Maybe there would be no problem. They could walk out the five miles in an hour and a half if they held this pace. Once they got to the truck, they could be to the hospital within an hour—45 minutes if he floored it all the way to Enterprise.

She was cheerful, even chatty at first, like she'd drank a cup of coffee, but after a while she quieted and slowed.

Suddenly she stopped, frozen. "Not so fast," she said. Her face drained of blood and she held her mouth open and stared straight ahead at nothing, not at him, at least. She held her breath and then made halting gasps.

"Oh, baby," he said. "I am so sorry. A contraction?"

"You better believe it. You have no fucking idea."

He put his hand on her head, and she started walking. He willed a calmness over himself, a steadiness he could pull from somewhere deep. It was like he'd done often on the *Jenny A.* out in the gulf. Just go to a place in his head where he could shut out anything that didn't serve him. The fear was like metal in his mouth. He hadn't felt this way in a long time, this *real*, and it took some time to do it, almost like pulling on a new skin. He'd been responsible for other crew members' lives before. But this was the one person who meant everything to him. He knew exactly what he had to do, and the first rule was to stay level-headed at all times. Second rule was stay safe. And third was to get the hell out ASAP.

She stopped as though a snake lay across the trail. She threw her arms stiffly out to her sides, her fingers splayed out like clothespins. His watch read five till noon. He caught up with her and massaged her shoulder and neck. She was hard as a tree. In about 15 seconds, she exhaled deeply and softened to his touch.

"I'm thirsty."

He got out the water bottle and gave it to her. She tilted it and drank hard. She wiped her brow and returned the jug.

"Onward," she said, not waiting for an answer, and she started in again, this time even faster than before she stopped. They walked through the burnt timber. She chatted the whole time about the fish, about the weather—anything but what lay ahead. The trail was rocky and, at one point, she stumbled but regained her balance. He ran to grab her.

"Slow down," he said. "You're going too fast. You're going to burn out."

"Speak for yourself, slowpoke. We need every minute."

It was now five after. He held his breath and waited for the next contraction. But it didn't come. He said nothing out of superstition. If he said nothing, maybe nothing would happen.

But the superstition only worked for another 10 minutes. At a quarter past noon, she again stopped. She leaned against a trailside ponderosa. She bit her lip and contorted her face, her eyes closed, her breathing fast and shallow.

"Try breathing deeper," he said.

"Fuck you," she said, but she laughed a haltering laugh. Then she shivered as she inhaled and blew out. A cloud of vapor wreathed her head. "Don't take it personal, but fuck you anyway." They both laughed.

"Yeah, okay, fuck it all," he said.

"It's like someone just stuck a white-hot poker in my fucking cervix."

"Ouch. I don't even have a cervix but I don't think I'd want anyone sticking a poker in it."

The sound of the snow came first. It made soft ticking sounds as the dry flakes slanted out of the sky and hit the brush. Within only a few minutes, the snow had begun to show white on the ground and on the tree branches.

He joked about the snow but inside he calculated the new challenges. At best, it would make the walking slower. Depending on how much snow accumulated, it would slow the driving, particularly over the shorter mountain route. At worst, who knew? He didn't want to think about how bad it could get. He had to focus on right now.

A second alternative struck him. There was a ranger station on the river downstream of the trailhead about seven miles. The station would be warm, if anyone was there, and it had a phone and a police radio. If Ana started slowing down, it might be best for him to run out, drive to the ranger station and get help. Different scenarios played out in his mind. He could hike back with the ranger. They could call 911 and maybe get a Life Flight helicopter in from La Grande or Lewiston. Could Life Flight even fly in this weather?

They started in again, but her pace slowed. The latest contraction had taken a piece out of her. She's tiring, he thought. She looked at him, and the worry was drawn up in lines around her eyes. "Maybe you ought to go ahead," she said. Her shoulders sagged and her face had melted into a look of stoic endurance. "I'm so pissed. Look at me. I can usually do this without breaking a sweat."

He came alongside her. "You're not usually in labor."

"Oh, you're so smart, aren't you? Well, I'm not so dumb that I can't see the truth. You can go a lot faster than me. You can get help at the ranger station."

The snow swirled ahead of them. "I thought of that," he said. "We'd have to fix you up so you were comfortable. I don't know, though. The thought of you here alone. How can I leave you? What if—."

She raised her hand. "Just shut up. How many days and nights have I spent in the woods? If there's one thing I can do, it's survive alone in the woods. You're going to go, and you better go quick. But before you go, help me build a fire."

She was right. There wasn't time to analyze things anymore. "I can do that," he said. "You sit for a moment at least."

They found an old campsite in a grove of ponderosas out of the wind and snow. He took the tarp out of the backpack and spread it on the ground. She sat for only a second before the next contraction wracked her body. But within five minutes, she was up and helping him scour the surroundings for dry wood, of which there was plenty. Within 30 minutes and another contraction, the two of them had gathered enough fuel to burn for about five hours. With a small axe and backpacking saw, he cut a mix of wood from kindling to logs.

He lit the fire while she sat on the tarpaulin. He hung her wet jeans on a nearby branch. She put on an extra hat, thick gloves, a scarf and every piece of available clothing, including an extra fleece jacket that he'd brought. Over all of these clothes, he draped the gold foil space blanket from their emergency kit.

"You look like one of those campfire popcorn setups," he said. "Maybe you shouldn't get too close to the fire."

"Get out of here," she laughed, but then turned serious. "Go! As fast as you can, get your ass going and let's have this baby. Try to get a hold of Elizabeth Riggins through the hospital."

"Don't go having no baby without me. I still don't know. Is this crazy?"

"Don't make it any harder. What good would you do for me if you stayed? Believe me, I have seen teenagers deliver their own babies. Go!"

He kissed her hard and hugged her.

"Are you sure you'll be okay?"

"Joe Wallace," she yelled. "Git!"

"Yes, ma'am," he said. He stood and took a long last look at her and then he turned and broke into a trot. When he met the trail, he turned once more. Her bulky frame was silhouetted by the orange glow of the fire through the trees.

"Don't go anywhere!" he yelled back. "Stay there. I'll be back."

She said something but he couldn't make it out. She was smart. She'd stay put. It was 1:15. He pointed himself down the trail and ran at a fast but sustainable pace. At this rate, he figured he would hit the trailhead within an hour or less.

The drive to the ranger station would take 10 minutes, tops. He'd make his calls and then head back with the ranger and a litter. If the ranger had a sled, they might need it. That would put him away from her for maybe two and a half hours. In this weather and at this time of year, it would already be turning dark.

"Hang in there," he said out loud, the words hammered by the concussion of his jaw shaking as he pounded down the trail.

He narrowed his focus to the trail ahead of him. He just ran. He hardly paid attention to the river to his right, or whether he was running through thick woods or open glades. About all he noticed was that the snow was accumulating in the open areas. He ran through a few spots on the trail where the snow already had reached over the toes of his boots. Then, when he came back in under the cover of thick stands of young trees, the ground was dry.

When he next checked his watch, it was 1:35. He was not yet halfway. He decided not to look at his watch again until he hit the trailhead. He picked up his pace until he was running with such momentum downhill that he didn't know if he could stop. Several times he doubted the wisdom of what he was doing. He thought of going back: At least he would be with her. But he kept telling himself, he had to get help. Trust Ana, he told himself. She can take care of herself.

He reached the trailhead at 2 o'clock. The truck had about an inch of snow on it. He felt for his keys. Panic: Did he bring the keys? They were not in his pants pocket. He tried his backpack. Nothing. He searched every pocket of his shirt and jacket. No keys. He felt his pants pockets again from the outside. A lump of metal stood out. He reached down and found them and exhaled.

He pumped the gas and turned the key in the ignition. The engine turned over once, twice and weakly a third time before dying, like someone trying to get out of bed on a Sunday morning. He waited a few seconds, and then tapped the steering wheel with one hand while holding the key in the ignition with the other hand. "Come on, girl," he said. "Don't let me down."

He turned the key. The engine started fast, him pumping the accelerator to try to keep it going, but it died again. "Ah, shit," he said, and he banged the steering wheel. *Stay calm.* He gave it another few seconds and then took the key up to his mouth and blew on it like he blowing on dice. "Come on baby," he said, and he put the key in the ignition again and turned it. The engine caught and fired, this time responding to his foot on the pedal. "All right, girl," he said. "Good girl." He petted the dashboard.

He let the engine idle fast and warm, and then he put it in gear and swung out onto the road, the tires spinning in the snow and the back fishtailing. He tried to slow himself, but his heart and head raced. The road lay before him like a dream, untouched. The truck moved silently through the stillness. He turned on the lights and the wipers, the flakes whisking away like dust.

He felt his way along the road, using the truck's gears to brake his momentum on the curves. He kept his foot off the brake pedal as much as possible. He did not want to end up in a ditch. Easy does it, he told himself. Don't rush. He was in a state of pure forward momentum; it was impossible for him to stop.

He reached the junction with the mountain road, which veered to the left. He hooked right, staying on the Imnaha River Road. Another mile and there it was, on the right: the ranger station. But as he got nearer, his heart sank: no green truck outside, no smoke curling from the chimney, no sign of life inside.

He pulled in front of the station, a modular one-story building with drab plywood walls and a metal snow roof. His head dropped to the steering wheel. He leaned his forehead on the wheel and sank into a moment of despair. Why can't there be someone here? Then his picked up his head and inhaled deeply, held it, and then blew out. *Keep going.*

He tried the front door. Locked. He banged on it. Inside, through the window, it was dark, but it bore the signs of work. There was a desk off to one side with papers on it. A yellow coffee mug occupied the middle of the desktop. He traipsed around back and tried the door. No luck. Then he heard a voice, followed by static: The police-band radio.

He had to get in. Even if it meant breaking a window or breaking down the door, he had to get in the station and get help. There was a snow-capped, turtle shell-shaped rock on the ground to the right of the door. He could break one of the panes of the back door, reach in and unlock the door. What if an alarm sounded? Fine, he thought. so much the better.

He picked up the rock and blew the snow off it. As he did, a glint of silver shone from the black spot where the rock had sat. The key lay there, attached to a keychain. He picked it up and tried the deadbolt. The key slid in effortlessly and then turned the bolt out of the jamb. He put the key back and opened the door and entered the station.

He picked up the phone on the desk. It was dead. But there was still the radio, and he knew how to use it.

He made the call, and it felt like Ana's life floated in the static of the radio. Mountain rescue was on its way. Get back to her as soon as you can and wait, they told him. And be prepared to deliver the baby yourself.

As soon as he got in the truck and pulled out onto the road, he felt the panic tearing at his stomach. He was more than an hour away. Going back would be tougher now, uphill and in the snow. The thought of her alone, in pain, seared him till he broke out in a sweat.

"Please God," he prayed out loud. "Please get us out of this. Please let Ana be okay. Let the baby be all right."

He was not one for prayers. He didn't believe in God. But he had to pray now. He'd done it before, up on the boat in Alaska when he'd gotten into a jam. He thought of Grace, and he asked her to look out for Ana.

The severe purity of the snow hurt to look at. When he got close to the junction, he noticed a set of tire tracks emerged from a spot on the left and then merged with his old tracks.

He doubled over both sets of tracks the whole distance. When he approached the trailhead parking lot, he saw the truck. It was Cody Macy's. Was this really happening? Had Macy lain in wait, knowing this would happen? Was this what he'd been waiting for all along?

He slid to a stop and slammed out of his truck. He ran to Macy's truck. Judging from the snow that had fallen over the footsteps and paw prints around the truck, Macy must have gotten there right after he'd left. The thoughts raced through his head, different scenarios, none of them good. He felt as though the world was closing down on him, the walls of the canyon pressing in and down, the leaden sky lowering. His view narrowed. Life was this trail, and he had to get up it as quickly as possible.

There were not only a single set of boot prints and the paw prints of a dog, but also a single tire track, thin and straight. The wheel track belonged to a hunting cart for carrying heavy loads in and out, including carcasses. He stopped and opened his pack. He'd taken his Smith & Wesson .38 Special from the beginning, but now he took it out of the pack and put it in the pocket of his coat.

He ran. He broke into a sweat. *Run*, he told himself. *Don't stop. Run like your goddamn life meant something. Run like the goddamn hounds of hell are on your heels.*

He slipped and fell, slipped and fell, dusted the snow off and started running again. He was hot. He hurt. His lungs burned. He didn't care. He had to get through. *Fuck the watch. I'm not looking*, he said. *Get there as fast as you can.* The thought of stopping, resting, getting his breath arose. He kept going.

Oh, please God, he prayed. *Make it right. Save her. Save our baby.* He didn't care if there was no God. He had to say it. He had to call to something beyond himself.

His joints ached. The trail plowed relentlessly uphill. His clothing was soaked with sweat but he didn't dare stop to remove anything. *Where is it? Must be close. Don't think. Just run.*

The incense of wood smoke came on the wind. Maybe her campfire. He quickened his pace. The wheel track and footprints continued to run up the trail.

He crested a rise. There, past the clearing, where the woods started again, was the smoke. He remembered how the woods he'd left her in were above this clearing. He didn't think he had it in him to run faster, but he did. He got through the clearing. And there, about 30 yards up the trail, was the fresh blaze he'd cut on a spindly tree. He turned in to the right. And so did the track and prints.

Ahead of him, through the trees, a campfire was blazing. And silhouetted against the flames was Cody Macy's hunting cart. A dog barked, one of Macy's dogs.

"Hush up, animal. Who goes there?" It was the unmistakable chain-saw growl of Cody's voice.

CHAPTER 42

He pulled his revolver from his coat. He slipped behind a fat ponderosa. Macy stood with his back to the fire looking out into the woods toward him, a rifle braced across his chest. His shadow and the shadows of the trees around the camp fidgeted out across the glowing snow. A camouflage poncho spread from Macy's shoulders like wings. His face was dark against the firelight.

"Macy!" he yelled. "Where is she! Put down the rifle."

"Wallace!" Macy yelled back. "For Chrissake, get a handle on yourself. I see you over there behind the tree. I was wondering when you were going to show. Point that gun of yours in some other direction and come on in here. Your girlfriend is here with your kid and she would just as soon have you for company than me."

Macy put his rifle on the ground in front of him and put his hands up in the air. He hushed his barking dog. He laughed as though Joe were just some kid playing at cowboy. Joe eased out from behind the tree but kept his revolver trained on Macy. He walked warily toward Macy, trying to see behind him and past the fire, looking for Ana.

"Don't move," he said. "Don't so much as pick your nose."

"Have it your way," Macy said. "But speed this up. It's getting late and I'm not planning on spending the night."

"Ana?" he called. "Can you hear me? Are you all right?"

He kept the gun pointed at Macy while he scanned beyond the fire. Where Ana had lain, there now stood a lean-to of cut poles and a tarp. The ground under the trees had only a light coat of snow.

"She's inside," Macy said in a hoarse whisper. "Tired as a 40-mile mule after what she's been through. The two of them, sleeping like bears."

He moved in a circuit with Macy at the hub. He squinted at the rumpled mass on the floor of the timber structure. There was the bronzed foil of her space blanket. He headed straight to the shelter and the pile of blankets.

Ana lay on her back, asleep, her head tilted into a layer of fir boughs that had been spread beneath the blankets. Her hair covered her face. He knelt and leaned over her, pressing close to her face. Her breath was easy and warm, like a steeping cup of tea. He looked at Macy, who hadn't budged, and put the gun away.

In a hollow of the blankets, the baby adhered to her body as though attached. He saw the head first, with a mass of matted black hair like seaweed, and then the tiny wrist and hand, the thumb already in mouth, sucking away. The baby was dreamily awake, and its dark eyes seemed to flash before returning to a blissful gaze.

He sat on his haunches. Macy stood, silently watching, outside the confines of the shelter. He did not know what to say.

"It's a boy." Macy tried whispering but it came out like the rattle of a broken speaker. "Would offer you a cigar if I had one."

Ana didn't stir. His wet clothes steamed in the heat of the fire. He put his hands down. All the forward momentum that had pulled him up the trail was stopped now, and he was dizzy and hot, the sweat dripping from his hair and stinging his eyes. Macy stood at a distance.

"You delivered the baby?"

"Hell, no," Macy cackled. "She did it herself. I come along and hear this caterwauling. And your girlfriend there is on her elbows and knees and she's taking care of business. Nothing to it. She's reaching down with one hand and trying to catch that little sprout." He reached toward he fire. "You mind?"

"No, go. Please." It was as if Jim Bridger himself had walked out of the woods and found Ana and the baby.

Macy walked to the fire and held out his hands. "I come along and in the middle of dropping this baby your girl here picks up a damn hunting knife and points it at me and says she'll cut my balls off if I come any closer and I sure as hell believe she'll do just that."

He smiled for the first time since that morning. "The old castration threat— works every time."

Macy shook his head. "So I back off and tell her I don't mean any harm. She puts down the knife. But the little guy is stuck. One shoulder out but not the other. So it's her that calls me over and asks if my hands are clean. And I say, 'no,' and she orders me to go wash up and pull this baby out of her. So that's what I done.

"I dropped that little guy right there on that blanket. Then I boiled my hunting knife and used that to cut the cord. You'll see it's a clean cut, tied off with boiled twine. He's a keeper, Wallace, I'm telling you."

He crouched in silence a while longer, his elbows wrapped around his knees. The sweat had soaked his clothes, and his back chilled.

"I was wrong about you," he whispered. He turned toward Macy at the fire. It didn't sound right yet, like it came from his heart. He closed his eyelids and blew out and let his gratitude speak this time, and it felt right. "I was so wrong. I was convinced you were the one. I was sure you were the one."

Macy turned from the fire and cocked his head.

He stood and approached Macy. "All this time, I thought it was you."

Macy scratched his scalp. "You can't apologize if you didn't do nothing."

He took off his wet jacket, laying it on fire-warmed rocks. "I thought you were the one harassing us. I mean spray paint on the door and dead fish on the doorstep. And then someone killed our dog, poisoned him. All this time, we thought it was you. At least, I did. It's why I went up to your place looking for you."

Macy laughed. "Nearly got yourself killed, too," he said. "I guess you don't know my old man all that good. Ol' boy was itching for a fight, and you come along." Then he creased his brow. "Poisoned your dog? Son of a bitch, whoever did it. Killing a man's dog—we got our ways of dealing with that kind of scum. You ever need help, you let me know. Got a handle on who did it?"

Joe grabbed a stick and poked the glowing coals. "Thought I did." But it was not what he wanted to think about now. He wanted to focus on Ana and his son. "I'm sorry your father got caught up in all this. He had a right to protect his property."

"Don't pay it no mind," Macy said. He lifted his hand to wave it off. "He's getting better treatment on the county's dole than he gets at home. Three squares, clean bed. Hell, they even got cable TV."

Behind this talk, there was the thing that couldn't be spoken about. What could he say? That he was sorry he'd killed his brother? That would've been a lie anyway. The unspoken thing stalked outside the circle of light. He had felt this wordless kind of agreement with other men before, and he looked now for a sign from Macy, a light in his eyes or the way he held his mouth.

Macy rubbed his hands and inspected them. "Look, if I was going to pick a fight with you, I'd come looking for you and drop you. No questions asked. A person has to protect their self and his people." Macy looked back at him then for a moment, nodding, his jaw held gravely, and he recognized that as the signal he was looking for that there was no blood to be avenged.

Ana stirred and opened her eyes. He rocked to his knees and met her face with his lips. He kissed her on her forehead, then her cheek and nose. She smiled dreamily.

"How long have you been back?" she said. "I feel like I've been asleep forever." She closed her eyes, reopened them, and blinked as if to focus and awaken herself. Joe brushed hair from her face. "How do you like that?" she said. "He came awfully fast. I don't know what I would've done without you, sir," She raised her head. "Are you still here? Thank you."

He nodded in the direction of Cody, who was facing the fire. "We're eternally grateful to you," he said.

Cody again turned toward them, his frame silhouetted by the fire. "It wasn't anything that anyone else wouldn't do," he said.

He shook his lowered head. "We're lucky you did."

She moved in her blankets. "Do you want to hold your son?" she said.

He'd held just–birthed animals but never a newborn. "Do I ever. Is he sleeping?"

She slid the bundle out from her and into his arms. "Here. He's wrapped in so many blankets he could get lost in them. He'll be all right."

The bundle felt surprisingly light, almost like there was nothing inside. But there in the center was the small head with the dark shock of hair. Still on his knees, he brought the baby up to his chest and with one hand cleared away the blanket from his face. In the flickering firelight, it was like looking down into the surface of a still pond and seeing a reflection in water. The feeling of joy and gratitude and humility stunned him. It was lightness, softness, openness, wholeness, a coming together of everything good.

The boy looked remarkably like her. A boy version of her, with her knowing dark eyes, broad and flat face, and determined lips.

There was a rustling of bags and ropes. Cody had slipped away from the fire and was packing up.

"You're heading out?" He rocked the bundled baby.

Cody paused, then started back in to packing. He worked fast and smoothly. "You folks are set for a while with wood, and you've got help on the way. Not much more I can do here."

The baby had opened his eyes in half-sleep. Joe started to stand, but Cody waved at him and told him not to bother. "We're grateful for all you've done. Indebted."

Cody dismissed that with another wave of his hand. "Anyway, I like to keep one step ahead of that law officer friend of yours." He began loading his one-wheeled cart. "Keeps us all occupied."

She sat up. "Make sure you take enough food for yourself," she said. "You've left us with more than we can eat."

He laughed. "Not to worry. There's a lot more where that came from." His cart packed, he began moving off but then stopped in front of them. "Keep the tarp," he said. "I've got a bunch of them. You've got plenty now to keep you for a while, and it looks like the weather's going to clear. You folks take care of yourselves. Best of luck with that boy of yours."

He grabbed the handles of the cart and wheeled out from the camp toward the main trail. Before he got to the trail, he stopped again and called back. "What's the name of the boy? What do you call him?"

She was already smiling at him with a bemused grin. He shrugged as if to acknowledge that neither of them had a clue. "No name yet!" he called out, not taking his gaze from her. "Not decided!"

There was a laugh and then, from far off, came Cody: "A boy like that's got to have a strong name!" And then he was gone.

It was like Cody had walked out of a zipper into another world beyond, and then the zipper closed up again, leaving them alone together. Joe stoked the fire and then lay next to her and the baby. He was perfectly warm and completely at peace.

"Are you hungry?"

She dropped her head and exhaled. "Starving! And thirsty."

They ate smoked salmon and elk jerky and waited for Bart and the rescue team. Then he lay beside them again. She drifted down into sleep. The boy's eyes were like pools of water, their surface dark and calm. What lay behind them? People spoke about seeing the world through a child's eyes. He shut his eyes and then reopened them, imagining what it could be like for the baby. He tried to imagine a world without names, without ideas, without his stupid fears and desires. Just to be. To see things for the first time without a name for them. Was that how it was for the baby? There was a swaying above them that he knew as trees in the wind but could just as easily have been kelp waving under the sea, or even a feeling that couldn't be described. The wind was blowing beyond the trees, rushing through the passes and ridges high above them. The sound came down through the trees like the far-off whisper of the river. His eyelids closed and he could not keep them open. If he had died then and there, he would have been satisfied and would not have wanted anything more from his life. The sound floated away and he drifted down into sleep.

When he awoke, she was nursing the baby. He got up and stretched. Cody had left enough wood for several days. He put another log on the fire.

He stood facing where Cody had walked out. "How long was I asleep? I have no idea. Was it just a few minutes? An hour?"

She sat and burped the baby. "I'm not much help. I've completely lost track of time. I don't even know what day it is. Is it early? Late? The middle of the night?"

He came and knelt by them. He hadn't looked at his watch since he'd been on the trail. He turned his wrist toward the fire. "It's the seventh of February. A good day for a birthday. And Jesus, it's almost seven o'clock. Where the hell is Bart?"

He touched the boy's cheek, and his eyes glimmered. "What is your name, little man?" He placed his finger in the boy's hand and gently tugged on it to feel his grip. He smiled. "He doesn't know he's separate from you, right? So who am I to him?"

"Only the king of Thebes," she laughed. "Come to take him away from his mother."

"What?"

"Oh, just an old tale about a boy who kills his father and marries his mother, is all. You know, Oedipus?"

He squinted through one eye. "Never heard of him. But remind me not to name him that."

She leaned on her elbow. "I will have to get up soon. God, I'm dirty and disgusting and smelly. The first thing I'm going to do when I get home is take a hot bath."

He rearranged some of the logs that were smoking. The flames flared for a moment. "Is there a Nez Perce name for 'delivered by hunting knife'?" He laughed. "How about, 'delivered by mountain man,'?" He helped her sit.

"I'm sure there's Nez Perce for that." She tilted her head and looked off and up to the trees. Or maybe she was thinking. "How about Red Fish for a name? He's the young sockeye come back to his homeland."

He folded his arms and cocked his head as though listening for a sound. "Red Fish. I like it," he said. "Kids'll call him Red for short, you can bet that."

She twisted her mouth to one side and then the other and looked off again. Then she placed her finger on her lips. "Hmm. Not so sure I like that. Maybe we need a so-called Christian name to go along with it. Something with a story.

I always liked the story of Moses. How he was hidden by his mother, then discovered in a basket by the river and adopted by the pharaoh, you know. Then he led his people back to the promised land. How about Moses? Moses Red Fish Wallace. I kind of like it."

He nudged the baby's cheek. The baby cringed, and it was as though a cloud had passed over his face. Then as quickly as sunshine on a spring day, he changed to an angelic beaming. Half a minute later, he bent his lip in a terribly sad face and whimpered. "I don't know that he likes the name," he said. "Or maybe he's just getting hungry."

"Hungry fella. We can name him later. I've got dinner ready."

He handed the baby back to her, and she pulled him down below the blankets and turned on her side and nursed him.

He rested his hand on her hip. "No, I like Moses," he said. "Moses Red Fish Wallace. I like it. It's an important name. Somebody that people will look up to. But I think I'll call him Mo for short. What do you think of that, little Mo?"

Soon after, there were the beams of flashlights coming up the trail, and then the clanking of gear and men's voices. He sprinted out to meet them where the path from their camp joined the trail. There were half a dozen of them, dressed for backwoods travel and carrying a couple of sleds full of emergency medical and survival gear. Bart's tall frame stood out from the others.

When he told him the story, Bart shook his head. He kept repeating, "I'll be damned. I'll be god-*damned,*" down the trail.

They got to the trailhead and loaded them in the big emergency truck. They drove out in the light snow, Joe and Bart trailing behind in their trucks, an envelope of brightness in the dense night, all the way through Sockeye to Enterprise.

CHAPTER 43

McKenzie eyed Joe sideways. "You're scared."

He hadn't thought of it that way. "Scared? No. Maybe a little. It's all pretty new, you know. Let me give you a hand."

He walked around to the back of her Blazer and opened the rear hatch. She'd come down to the Imnaha cabin to spend a few days helping with the baby. It was February 20, bright and sunny and approaching 50 degrees along the river.

"You want coffee?"

She hugged him. "That's my job now," she said. "This is going to be fun. How's mama and the baby?"

"They're doing great." He touched her wrist for a moment. "Thanks for coming down. Hey, I think she could really use the company of a woman. Especially you. You don't mind if I ride up to Sockeye?"

"I could've brought some things down if you'd given me a list." She took a loaded backpack out of the passenger seat. "Of course not. You should go. We'll be fine. Let me see that little darling." She walked away.

He grabbed her suitcase and set it down heavily. "What the hell you got in this, bricks?"

"No, lead weights," she yelled, laughing, over her shoulder as she bounced up the porch steps. "Just some extra things. You know, there's always stuff you need with a little one."

There was some kind of itch in him. It had started even before they moved in. Something seemed off kilter, maybe the newness of everything. He loved being with Ana and little Mo, but something still felt wrong, like he didn't deserve all this good and that it was all going to fall apart. He'd told himself he could've died happy up there on the river when Moses was coming. But living day to day was harder, and now this incompleteness had crept in, as though a chunk of him was missing. If only he could find it, it would be like completing a puzzle. The ride up the canyon might do him some good.

He had the back of the truck unloaded and everything on the ground when McKenzie came back out and stood beside him.

"I ain't dumb," he said. "If I stick around here, you two've got me at your beck and call. You've got plenty to talk about."

"Sure you don't want to stick around for a while?" She kept her eyes fixed on him.

"What? I'm—. I just need some things."

"You've been sober now, how long?"

He cut her off. "Can't believe you're bringing that up. Do you seriously think I'd drink when I have everything I want right here?"

"Of course not," she said. She could never know how hard it was.

He set the suitcase on the porch and then carried in a cooler of food and a box of clothes for the baby. Ana was sitting in the rocker and had handed Moses to McKenzie. The little guy was in a state of bliss, his eyes closed and his lips parted in a circle. McKenzie rocked and patted the baby. There was an instant bond between his sister and Ana and the baby. He was grateful for it, with Grace gone now. And he was sure he could never provide that kind of thing to Ana. No man could. Ana could take care of the baby stuff on her own, but this was not about taking care of the baby. It was about the world that women create when they are together, especially with a baby. As a man, you could witness it, but you could never take part in it. Mothering seemed to come naturally to women—certainly to Ana. Fathering? There was nothing natural about it. Clark had failed him. Even Ana's dad had fucked it up with her brother. He would have to figure it out on his own.

His kissed Ana and Moses and gave McKenzie a hug. "Be good," McKenzie said.

"Oh, I'm a saint, don't you know?" he said, and then he left.

***

He parked in front of the hardware store. As soon as he got out of his truck and stepped onto the sidewalk, there was River, moving down the sidewalk like a shadow. River continued walking toward him, but with his head down, guilty as sin. All along, it'd been him—the spray paint, Bud, the carcasses. All due to some crazy delusion he'd had about Ana.

"River," he said.

River stopped and looked up.

"Heard you were out of the valley." He could've punched him in the face right then. "Nobody seemed to know."

River's eyes shifted, and then looked past him. He nodded with a sort of forced calm. "I heard about the baby. Good for you," he said, all sarcasm.

River's face and body locked into defiance, and his smirk resurfaced. It must have pained him dearly to see his fantasy about Ana fall apart. "If I'm ever down your way," he said, "I'll have to come and see what life's like for the new parents."

Joe put his hands in his jacket pockets and squeezed them into fists. "Cut the bullshit, okay?"

But River cut him off. "You know, Wallace, it's just a mystery to me why anyone would choose to have kids these days. I mean, think about the world they're inheriting. It seems to me to be an incredibly selfish act. Or just incredibly—don't take this personally—stupid. Was adoption ever in the mix? Or was this an accident?"

"Goddamn you." Joe stepped toward River and looked down on his face.

But he didn't flinch. "Hey there, cowboy, don't take it personally. It's just that we don't need any more people. We need less. Now, if you don't mind."

River made to move past him, but Joe blocked his path. "You know, you're a sick fucker," he said, and then he poked River in the chest. He'd had enough of this pompous fool. He'd put up with this ass for far too long.

River stumbled momentarily, then recovered his balance. He stood motionless, but there was a coiled loathing below the surface.

A couple of ranchers in boot-cut Wranglers and Carhartt jackets, on their way in to the hardware store, paused on the sidewalk.

"You just insulted me, my wife and my kid," he said. "Is your head stuck up your ass?" Something in him wanted to make this animal bite back. "It was you all along, Goddammit. Ana said so, but I didn't think you had it in you."

The vein in River's forehead purpled. "I don't know what you're talking about."

"The graffiti, the fish, my goddamned dog," he said. "No one would've suspected you, and you knew it. You knew Macy was a convenient scapegoat.

You're a sly son of a bitch; I'll give you that. No, you're a sick bastard. All along, they warned me about you, but I didn't believe them. And you knew it, didn't you? You killed my dog. You tried burning my fucking house down, with my mom in it. What the fuck is wrong with you?"

River's eyes bulged, and then he seemed to go inside himself. He stared at the ground. "You and Ana," River said, almost trancelike. "You're fakes. You're like all the rest." When he looked up, his eyes were dark. There wasn't a trace of the naive kid he'd met back on the tracks along the river almost two years ago. His face turned ugly and he screamed. "The commission. It's a fucking farce. They'll delay. More study! More study! Fuck study! We don't need more study, we need action. Get the fuck out of my way."

"Hey now, fella," the rancher with the cowboy hat tried to stop River, but he was too late.

River rammed into Joe's shoulder. Joe grabbed him by his collar, his fists balled under his chin. "You leave my wife and son out of this!" he screamed. "Do you hear? Do you hear me?"

River spat foam. "Fuck you. You and your little fucking Sacajawea!"

"Whoa, whoa." The other rancher moved between them and put his palm up to River. "Hold your tongue there."

"Fuck you, mister, get out of my face."

God, Joe wanted to pound his snotty face. But he turned and began walking away and hoped the rancher would take care of what needed to be done. By this time, there were more people on the sidewalk. "Look out!" someone yelled, and Joe pivoted as River came at him hard and lunged for his neck. Joe got his hands around him, and then they crashed to the sidewalk. Then both of the ranchers were standing above them. The bigger of the two pulled Joe off, and the other rancher took care of River. A trail of blood and snot snaked from River's nose. Joe wiped his hand across his neck and it came away bloody from where River had scratched him with his nails.

Then there was a siren. Bart burst out of his Cherokee.

"What in the hell?" Bart said.

"It's okay," he said.

"I didn't ask you," Bart snapped.

CHAPTER 44

He was late and it was dark and he couldn't account for the time. It had started with one drink at the Glacier Tap, to settle him. Then, he didn't know.

He tiptoed up the porch steps and held on to the post. He swayed across the decking and reached the door and leaned his forehead on it and chuckled and found the handle and turned it and thank God it was unlocked. The cabin was dark and still warm. He turned to walk in to the main room of the cabin, and as he did, the room rolled and he stumbled. He laughed quietly and then said in a low voice, "Can't see shit."

A light came on. Ana was on the sofa, and she squinted in the light. She was in her heavy pajamas and robe and big socks.

"You're late," she said.

He mumbled.

"Don't say anything." She put up her hand. "The baby's sleeping in the bed with me. You can sleep here. I'm going back to bed."

She got up without looking at him and retreated to the bedroom and shut the door. It was suddenly quiet again except for the creaking of the stove. He pulled off his boots and jeans and got a blanket out of the closet and pulled it over him. He turned the light out but stayed awake a long time, the room spinning and the familiar old floodtide filling him with its fleeting but empty promise.

He awoke in head-splitting brightness. He got up to check the bedroom but he already knew. The bed was made. The baby was gone.

No note. His stupidity pooled like black bile in his stomach. Did she go up to the lake house? McKenzie's? He fixed eggs and took a bite but it wouldn't go down, and he retched in the toilet. He had nearly killed himself with a gun in front of his father once. Now he had managed to fuck up the best thing that had ever happened to him.

He could go down to the river, down where Buddy had been shot through the head. Wade into the cold water, feel its pulse on his thighs one last time and rest the barrel of the pistol against his brain. Think about how he'd be doing them a favor. There would be the report of the gun, a pop like a branch breaking in the vastness, so puny that no one would hear, then a splash and the click-clack black tongue of a raven, and he would be gone. Or use a knife. That might be more fitting, to turn the knife on himself. Float for a while, maybe catch in a snag with someone's fishing line, as the blood trailed dark downstream and drained him as white as the carcasses of spawned-out Chinook. But his face would not reflect the agony and ecstasy of the heroic Chinook, the face of the warrior. No, his face would reveal the spineless coward that the sheriff would retrieve from the river with a grappling hook, like the dead heifer he'd stumbled on last winter.

CHAPTER 45

By nightfall, he was back in Sockeye at the Glacier Tap Room. He had spent the day working hard outside the Imnaha cabin so as to avoid thinking about himself and alcohol. But as the day wore down, the pull of booze on him was like the pull of moon on water. He did not want to spend the night alone down there. He cleaned up, put on a clean dirty pair of jeans and shirt, and drove to Sockeye. She wasn't at the lake house, and he left messages on McKenzie's phone.

At the Glacier Tap, the sourness of the room, the stale dimness, felt like a kind of home. There were people he recognized from River's environmental group sitting at a table. He had lost track of whether they were meeting any more, and he didn't care.

He didn't hold their association with River against them. They'd been snookered like he had. One of them, a talkative middle-aged woman with short hair and a Southern accent, waved him over. He picked up a double Jack Daniels from the bar and sat next to her. There were seven of them.

She extended her hand. "Billie. Like the holiday." She had strong hands, no nail polish. She introduced her friends around the table. "Y'all remember Joe?" He forgot their names as soon as he heard them. But he remembered Billie. She liked to laugh, and she was putting down the sauce. She was a short-haired jock like his sister, and she must've grown up around brothers because she seemed so comfortable around him.

He was not yet drunk. He was pacing himself. If he could have no more than two drinks, he'd be okay. Ana was gone. There was nothing he could do about it now. He would start clean tomorrow morning. He would spend the night at the lake house. If she showed up there, he'd sleep in an empty cabin and try talking to her in the morning.

There was one part of him shutting down. It was the part that stopped him from doing stupid things, from seeing consequences. But when it shut down, he loosened up, let down his guard. The alcohol worked on him like oil on a rusted hinge. Was it his real self or some genie that came out of the bottle? He didn't give a shit.

One of the group, a beefy thing who seemed like a small person trapped in a large body, had heard about Joe and Ana's baby. She toasted Moses Red Fish, and they all raised their glasses and drank. Another JD arrived at the table, courtesy of Billie, and he drank it.

Talk got around to River. The big woman said the group was concerned that River might have gone over the edge and joined up with the Earth First! people. There was talk about them working in this part of Oregon again. "It's just a rumor," she said. "We haven't seen him much, but when we have, he's been weird."

She leaned in and whispered: They'd heard some people were going to do something big if the commission didn't agree to remove the dam. "The gossip is they'd blow it up," she said.

"Good luck," he said. "It would take Special Forces to take out that rock."

Then the big woman—Barbara was her name—hit the nail on the head about River. "We could see he had a thing for Ana. We all knew it. Do you think he is capable of something stupid like that?"

"I think that rich boy's capable of a whole lot more than I ever thought he was. He ain't the person he let out to be, that's for damn sure."

A third JD arrived. He raised it to toast the buyer and he drank it. Then there was a pitcher of beer, and soon a full glass was in his hand. He lost track.

He had slipped into a tunnel. The tunnel was dark and warm. He was stuck. He could see a light way off. He couldn't tell where the light was coming from, whether it was above or to the side. He couldn't tell if he was sitting, standing or lying. He stayed in this position for maybe a few minutes or a maybe a few hours. He didn't know.

Then there was laughter and the touch of someone's hand tapping his shoulder. There was the face of the woman, Billie. She was holding hot coffee to his lips and saying something to him. But it was like a bad recording in which whole portions were missing from the tape.

"Drink," she said. "You going to be okay? You need a ride home?"

"Must … have … fallen—." He couldn't finish.

"Asleep. Yeah, you passed out." She punched his shoulder playfully. "Man, what a lightweight. I don't think they have taxis in this town or else I'd call one. I can give you a lift. Or I could call Ana?"

He was tired. He closed his eyes. "No, no. I'm okay. I'll be fine."

When he opened his eyes again, Billie was gone. He put his head on the table. It was cool and wet in places. He wanted to soak his head in ice water.

"Closing up, bud." It was the voice of the night bartender.

He drank the rest of the cold coffee. He got up and lost his balance slightly, but only because he had been passed out. He would be fine, especially when he got a taste of the cold night air outside the bar on his face. He staggered to the bathroom, peed and splashed his face with cold water. He felt better, awake, if not completely sober.

"You want me to call somebody?" the bartender said. "Want the rest of this coffee?" He lifted the pot from the Bunn warmer and held it up to him. "Going to throw it out anyway."

"Nah," he said. "Gonna walk it off for a while."

He found his keys and fumbled for the ignition. Just have to drive to the lake house, he thought. Sleep this off. Get up tomorrow. Start clean. Apologize to Ana.

He started the engine and sat for a while, waiting for it to warm up. He rested his head on the steering wheel and dozed while the engine idled. He turned on the heat and put the fan on high. Then he rolled his window all the way down. He put the truck in first gear, clutched and then carefully released the clutch until he could feel the tug of the transmission. He rolled the truck out onto Main Street, his truck the only vehicle that he could see on the road.

What gear was he was in? He cursed. He jiggled the stick shift to get a feel. Even looked at what he was doing, like he was a teenager learning a stick. "First," he said, and he laughed at his stupidity. When he raised his head, he was on the opposite side of the street, headed on a diagonal for a row of shops on the left. He pulled the wheel to his right, hit the gas instead of the brake, and the truck lurched.

He jerked the wheel left and got a foot on the brake. The engine died, and the truck straddled the center line of the road. No problem. No cars. He stayed there for a while, resting his forehead on the wheel. The only sound was the ticking of the cooling engine. There was a smell of gasoline in the cab. He was tired and wanted to sleep. If he could make it to the lake house. He tried starting the truck but it choked and died. He tried again and it coughed to life. He put it in gear and began to pull away.

A pulse of flashing lights. The short whoop of a siren. "Ah, shit," he said. He banged the wheel with the heel of his hand and rattled his downturned head. "Fuck, fuck, fuck."

It was Bart's rig. For a moment of bleary stupidity, he considered giving him a run for it. But he couldn't outrun him sober, no less drunk. He pulled over in front of the Indian Lodge Motel. Bart got out of the Cherokee and approached.

"Hey, pal," Joe said.

"Shut up and listen," Bart said. "Get out the truck and give me the keys. Shut the engine off."

He turned the key, and the engine died. Bart shined his flashlight in his eyes and blew out a huff of disgust. "Damn you. Damn your idiot brain."

His head hurt, and the lights of the cruiser were dizzying.

"If she wasn't here I'd beat your ass right now."

She? Bart marched him back to the Cherokee, its cherry top hurling shafts of blue, red and white with sickening speed and brightness. There was someone in the back seat, but it was too dark, and the flashing lights too jolting, for him to make out a shape.

"Get in front."

Ana did not look at him when he slid into the seat. Moses was strapped into his car seat beside her. She was composed, as though meditating on some distant object beyond the plane of the windshield. He said nothing, nor did he attempt to engage with Moses. There was nothing to say. He let his shaking hands drop in his lap. The police radio crackled. Outside, the obnoxious lights raked the buildings of Main Street. A part of him wanted to sulk and feel sorry for himself. But he refused to do it. This was it for him. It was clear as water. It was either the bottle or Ana and Moses. And maybe it was too late. Whatever happened, he deserved it. He had chosen this, and now he would pay the price.

Bart got in, pulled the door closed and then sat for a while massaging his forehead and temples. He pinched the taut skin of his forehead between his thumb and forefinger and rocked his head sideways. Then he nodded.

"I'm taking them back to the lake house," he said. "You? You're coming with me."

CHAPTER 46

In the night, he was roused by a siren. It moaned, then revved up to a high pitch, so loud it sounded as though it was outside the wall next to his bed. He lay still, eyes shut, not sure if he was hearing an alarm or if he was dreaming. The siren started up again. Then someone was shaking him and shouting in his ear.

"Get up! Get up! Out of bed!" Bart was dressed and in take-no-bullshit mode.

The nausea was still in him. He ran to the bathroom and retched. He sat on the floor of the bathroom, sweating cold and shaking. His sweat smelled like gasoline. His mouth was a filthy gutter. His head ached. His body ached. He wanted a drink so bad, it was one of those moments when death seemed a kinder alternative.

"Take off your clothes and get in the shower," he ordered.

He knew not to complain. He should have been in jail. He kept his mouth shut, undressed, got in the shower and braced for the water. Bart turned it on, cold. He yelled as the cold water assaulted his face and chest. He leaned on the shower wall with his hands and let the water wake him out of his stupor. He opened his mouth and drank.

Bart disappeared and then was back in a minute, his face in the crack of the door.

"Get dressed fast," he said flatly. "There's clean clothes on the toilet. No time to eat."

He had placed a pair of washed jeans, socks, underwear, t-shirt and Pendleton shirt on the toilet before he left. The clothes felt good, like another skin Bart was loaning him. He was not hungry. The little surge of feeling good from the shower would not last.

Bart stood outside the door, jacket on. He looked grim, his face dark, skin sallow, eyes baggy and red. He picked up his shoes and his coat and hurried to follow Bart out to the Cherokee.

"Where's the fire?"

Bart turned and stared over the roof at him. There was a sadness in his eyes, but also a weariness, a look of resignation he had not seen before. He bit his lower lip, and then got in the Cherokee. He followed without a word. He didn't speak until they were out of town, headed down the Imnaha road.

Bart reached his big hand across the cab and placed it on the dashboard in front of him. "They couldn't save it," he said. "It's the Cummings place—your place. Torched."

He squinted in the dark cab, Bart's face lit by the dim light of the dash. The pit of his stomach formed a fist, and he was grateful there was no food left in him. He searched for the right words but there was just Bart driving. Then the question formed in his mind and he spoke it out loud. "It's gone? Burned?"

He kept his eyes on the road. "'Gone,' is what Crowley told me. Nothing could be saved."

They drove the rest of the way in silence. Bart put the cherry top on and hit 80 on the straightaways, the canyon walls flickering as if lit by colored lightning. They slowed at the Imnaha bridge and passed Rex's place and made the left turn down the canyon road. Soon, the smell of burning wood penetrated the Cherokee. They were still about a mile away from the cabin when they saw the circling red lights of the fire engines throbbing in the night sky and illuminating the cliffs on either side of the canyon.

Bart pulled into the drive and moved forward as far up as he could. The beams of the headlights cut through a fog of smoke and dust. There was a tanker parked on the hill, lights whipping through the smoke and hoses splayed across the ground. Beyond the truck, there were flickering orange flames, but it was impossible to make out any kind of structure. He turned off the ignition and opened his door, but he stayed put, frozen and watching.

"Well?" Bart said, his hand on the armrest.

Joe sat shaking his head. "I don't know," he said finally. "I don't think I want to see this."

Bart got out and shut the door and then leaned in through the open window.

He could sense Bart's stare. "You go ahead," Joe said. "I'll come. I need time."

"I suppose you have that choice," Bart said.

Bart walked up the drive and nearly disappeared in the smoke. Then a flashlight beam swirled and found Bart. A firefighter with his helmet off walked toward Bart. It was Crowley, the chief. The two began talking, Crowley gesturing at the spot where the cabin had stood.

Joe leaned forward and put his forehead on the dash and closed his eyes. His stomach gnawed at him like he'd swallowed dry rope. His eyes, already tearing from the smoke, filled and began to drip. A wave of nausea rippled through his body, a puking, gut weariness that mixed with fear and sadness. And still, there was the burning desire for a drink. He had crossed that line, and it would be harder than ever to go back. The cabin was gone, and he couldn't help thinking that a part of him had been destroyed along with it. Whatever he'd had there with Ana, what they were building—maybe that had been wrecked too, along with the meager contents of their life together.

He inhaled wearily, his lungs filling with smoke. He opened his eyes, exhaled and then let himself out of the truck. The nausea hit him again, and he kneeled and dry-heaved. He was thirsty but there was nothing to drink.

He had a mind to walk away, to walk down to the river. But he walked straight up the drive toward Bart and Crowley. The night air was thick with smoke, and as he walked, it became clear what "gone" meant. It was a total loss. The only thing left standing was the chimney.

Bart and Crowley stopped talking as he approached. What could they say? He inhaled and then coughed. Finally, Crowley extended his hand. "Real sorry, Wallace," he said. "It's a damn shame."

"Don't—," he said, but the words got caught in his throat.

Crowley turned toward the smoldering rubble. A few charred ends of the crossbeams remained on the concrete pads, but in reality, there was nothing left. Scattered about the yard were the remains of their possessions: part of the kitchen table, its steel legs melted; the baby's crib; the stove; the stainless-steel sink; the toilet—all blackened and lying where they had fallen through the floor.

"We tried to salvage what we could but there was nothing we could do," Crowley said. "It must have gone up fast. By the time we got here, there wasn't much more standing than what you see now."

"I appreciate whatever you guys did," he said.

Crowley nodded and walked away.

Bart stayed watching the charred remains. "There's going to be an investigation," Bart said. "Whoever did this, there'll be signs, some evidence they've left."

Joe kicked the dirt, and a cloud of ash blew up. "You know who did it," he said.

"Well," Bart said. He put his hands in the pockets of his jacket. "As soon as I got the call, I sent a deputy out to bring him in."

"Good," he said. "Should've done it long ago."

"He was gone," Bart said. "He'd taken a bunch of things with him, like he was going on a trip. There's state cops and county mounties in three states looking for him."

"Jesus Christ," he said. "What the fuck got into that guy?"

They walked the perimeter of the cabin site. He tried to picture the cabin. Suddenly it seemed so small. Yet while he and Ana and Moses were there, it was the biggest thing in his world.

"Gone, man. I can't believe it. Gone."

They stayed for an hour. But there was nothing to do, nothing to save. Now it was time to try to pick up the pieces he'd broken with Ana. He wouldn't blame her for leaving him. He was a fuck-up drunk, and she deserved better. But he'd had enough of resolutions and final straws. He'd had enough of thinking but not doing. This was the bottom for him. It was time to shut up and do.

Bart drove out of the canyon and up the ridge, the air inside the truck getting colder as they climbed. The sky brightening. It always felt to him as if he were climbing to the top of the world on that drive. But on this morning, it felt more like he was climbing out of a hellhole. What lay ahead of him was the question. He'd already screwed up enough. Maybe he'd crossed the point of no return.

When they reached the lip of the canyon, the Wallowas tore the southern horizon with serrated teeth. It hit him how hemmed in this spot was, their little world, ringed by mountains on one side, hell's own trench on the other.

"It's going to be tough," Bart said. "She was pretty damn upset last night."

"She deserved to be. I was a goddamned idiot."

"You said it yourself," he said. "What the hell's gotten into you? You've got a beautiful woman and a kid now. So why are you trying to throw it the hell all away?"

They passed the wind-blown stubble of the winter fields. Irrigation wheels stood frozen, awaiting spring. Drifts of snow lay in the lee of the wheels and behind piles of pipe.

"Did you ever think they could have been down there in it when it went up?" Bart looked across the seat at him.

"I thought about that," he said. "I thought about that a lot down there. Is that what he wanted?"

"Who in the hell knows what went on behind those eyeballs?"

They seemed to float over the road. "I'm done with drinking," he said. "The drinking's over. That's all I'll say. I'm done. I'm sick. I'm going to the next AA meeting at the fire hall."

"Good," he said. "You can plan on me picking you up and dragging your ass down there myself."

He blew out what could almost count for a laugh for the first time in a long while. Something felt different, lighter. The landscape opened before them, the lumpy carpet of the plain falling away to the northwest from the shoulders of the mountains. They had lost the cabin, he'd fucked up with alcohol, and he'd abused his relationship with Ana. But it occurred to him that these were his mountains. Or, he was theirs. For better or worse, this was where he belonged.

He had left and thought he'd never return. Now his parents were both dead. But he had found Ana. They'd had a beautiful son together, and they were living in a place where they belonged.

If only she'd take him back.

He was done with alcohol. Done with letting it control him. Done with allowing it to run and ruin his life. Done with searching for something outside himself. Done with blaming his father for his shit. Done with being his father's hurt little boy. Done with his brother and his stupid plans. Done. He was ready to build a life that was not a reaction to his father any longer but a reflection of what he wanted for him and Ana.

As they neared Sockeye, he remembered what he'd heard old-timers say about first coming into the Wallowa country. Which was that, as soon as they saw it, coming over the Smith Hill from the Grand Ronde, they knew it was where they wanted to live. The early settlers had seen waist-high bunch grass, plentiful deer and elk, and streams and the lake filled with a kind of fish few of them had seen before and that they called the redfish. Now only about 125 years later, the bunchgrass and the sockeye and the Nez Perce were gone. But in other ways, it wasn't so different. The mountains still ruled and remained wild. And one day the sockeye would return if he could help it. This was where he wanted to spend the rest of his life with Ana and their son.

When they got into town and passed the Glacier Tap Room on Main Street, a nausea and longing came over him. They stopped at McCully's and he bought a bouquet of mixed flowers from their picked-over collection. He buried his nose in the bouquet and inhaled. He closed his eyes. He wanted a drink, and he knew he would feel this way many times more, and worse. But he focused on Ana and the baby. And he mouthed the word silently again, "Done."

They crested the small hill of the old ski run road where the shoulder of Joseph Mountain vaulted up out of the plains. Then they sank down the trough of the hill and crossed the cattle grate and drove down the side of the moraine. His hands shook. He pictured himself giving the bouquet to Ana, her smile, her warmth, and, yes, her forgiveness. He was ready to start again, sober.

Bart downshifted into the rutted entrance to the lake house compound. The drive was snowy in the shade of the trees. But there was something strangely quiet about the place. There was no car, no sign of life, no smoke from the chimney. He broke out in a sweat. Bart said nothing, but he knew he was holding back.

Bart left the engine running while he got out. There was a bare patch where Ana's truck normally was parked. There were footprints in the snow from the steps to the parking space. His heart clogged his throat as he climbed the steps. On the door was a note on a piece of yellow scrap paper in her handwriting: "Took Moses to rez. Can't do this anymore."

He turned, walked down the stairs and, without looking at Bart, stepped through the snow to the edge of the lake. The lake was frozen solid against the snow-crusted banks. He took the bouquet and threw it as hard as he could into the wind. It broke up as soon as it left his hand, the flowers hitting the edge ice and scattering.

He walked back to the truck. Bart was looking straight out through the windshield, gripping the steering wheel as though he were driving and looking for something in the distance. He blew on his hands. "Thanks, Bud," he said. "You can go."

"I can't leave you like this," he said, and then waited. "Look, you know you're going to drink, and I wouldn't blame you. Come back to my place."

He turned and looked back at the lake and then at the house.

"No, but you can do me a favor," he said.

"What's that? Whatever you need," he said.

"Hold on a minute. I'll be right back.'

He strode down to the workshop underneath the porch. He kept the whiskey in a couple of places: behind a draw under the workbench, in an old pair of fishing waders hanging on a nail, above a rafter in a far corner. There were five bottles in all. They were some of the same hiding spots his father had used and that he'd discovered so long ago. He found a black plastic garbage bag for them. Then he walked up to the porch and took the beer out of the refrigerator. Inside, he took a bottle of wine out of the cupboard and a bottle of cooking wine from the refrigerator. He placed all of these in the bag and walked back out to the Cherokee. His hands shook, and his stomach ached. "That's all I know about," he said. "Take it and dump it down your drain for me, would you?"

"I will," he said. "You sure you don't want to stay with me for a while?"

"I'll call you if I need help," he said. "Call me later."

"You sure?" he said.

"To hell with promises. They're just words. I've got to shut up and do this on my own."

The truck ground up the rutted drive and onto the lake road, its taillights spilling red onto the snow. He walked up to the porch, grabbed an armload of logs for the woodstove, went in and made a fire. He had to get her back.

CHAPTER 47

He got in his truck at 3 a.m. and left Sockeye for the reservation. He took the old Thermos full of coffee. He had to see her and Moses and beg her to come back. He was certain beyond anything he had ever felt in his life about that. He never stopped. He pissed in a mason jar held between his legs.

He'd been to every AA meeting in the valley in the past three weeks. He saw Rex Parson and Tom Crowley, the fire chief, at one of the meetings, and Crowley became his sponsor.

It was nearly 8 when he got to the little trailer park. He pulled in to a spot where he could see if she got in her truck, but far enough away that she wouldn't see him. She would have to leave at some point. She couldn't stay in that cramped trailer for long. He waited: one hour, two hours, three hours. He lit three candles from the emergency kit so he could heat the cab and stay warm. He peed in the jar again. His mouth was dry and his stomach growled. He nodded off but jerked awake each time and rubbed himself to create some warmth.

Before noon, she came out of the trailer with Moses in a backpack. She had on her green winter coat and white fleece hat. But she didn't get in the truck. She turned at the foot of the porch steps and disappeared behind the building.

He waited several long minutes before getting out of the truck. She must have gone up the high trail. Behind the trailer, a narrow path led uphill through the sage and juniper. She had told him about it. She used to hike the trail and see how far she could go. He made a wide circle through the sage flat around the trailer and then headed for a point to intersect the trail.

She was on the path, going fast. She was challenging herself, he thought, trying to get back in shape for hiking. He had to work to keep up. Sweat ran down the spine of his back and down his temples and cheeks into his mouth.

She was higher up, about a quarter of a mile distant. But she stood out clearly, her coat and backpack dark against the grass, which had begun to green. He pushed his pace, his lungs burning in the cold air. He had to gain on her, keep her in sight.

She stopped. He dropped to his hands and knees. If he could see her, she could see him. What would she do if she saw him? He held quiet and stayed low until she turned and started up again, and then he jumped and pressed uphill. The blood drummed in his ears. He unzipped his coat.

He kept at it. He was gaining on her. He got within earshot of her voice. She was singing something, her voice coming down on the breeze, a Nez Perce children's song he'd heard her sing before. Her voice pure and deep, not shrill.

She stopped again. The singing stopped, too, as though she had heard or sensed something. He didn't care anymore. He stood still in the middle of the trail.

When she turned toward him, she said nothing. It was as if she had expected to see him. She stared down at him, rocking slightly to keep the backpack in motion. She was about 150 feet away.

She stood silently. He didn't move. Then she turned and began walking again.

"Ana!"

She stopped only long enough to shout, "Leave me alone!"

He started after her but then stopped. She moved up the trail, the only sound now the rush of wind in the grass. No more singing. What was he doing? He should have stayed in Sockeye, kept at his recovery, proved he could stay sober. What did he expect? That she would let him back in her life? That she would suddenly fling open her arms and embrace him? It was reckless and stupid of him. Deluded.

She continued up the trail, now nearly out of sight. Three ravens wheeled in the sky above the hill. At least she had seen him. She'd know he still loved her. Maybe that's all she needed. He inhaled deeply and let go. She disappeared behind a bend in the trail.

He turned and began walking down.

He counted his steps. One, two, three. He got to twenty-one before he stopped. Every step felt wrong. Every part of him told him, screamed at him, to stop. Leaving her like this might have avoided conflict and tears, but it was his hide that he was protecting. This was a test. If he continued down, it would be over. He would never see her again. And he needed her in his life. Needed to be a full-time father to their son. She completed him, made him whole, made him a man. She'd shown him what it was like to live by the strength of conviction. He could not let her go.

He turned and ran up. His heart pounded. The ravens circled hundreds of feet higher, motes of black in the blue sky. Ana was still gone over the lip of the hill. It was as if he were looking through the wrong end of a telescope. Everything seemed so far. He lost his balance and had to look away from the sky. Maybe the ravens were gone, too. His gut and head tore at him. He had to stop. He leaned over and held his knees. The sweat ran off his forehead. The world was enormous, and it was swallowing him. It was stupid to think he could change her mind. It would be better if he returned to Sockeye and avoid the drama here. She would believe him when he proved himself.

He started down the trail once more. But it was like walking against the current of a river, like pulling against gravity. His body wouldn't allow it. He had to turn away. He had to go back uphill.

He found her sitting on a broad, flat rock, surrounded by brush and out of the wind. She had taken the backpack off and was nursing Moses. He let his breath come back to him. A lightness came over him, a weightlessness. There were so many things to say, starting with how deeply sorry he was and how he wanted her to come back with him. But there was no right way to say those things. So he stood and waited.

"He's hungry," she said. She took Moses from her breast and burped him over her knee. His cheeks were bright. She kept her eyes on the baby.

There was a chinook blowing, and though the air was dry from being wrung out over the Cascades and the dry country, it still carried the mineral scent of wet stones. "He's getting bigger," he said.

She glanced at him and then returned her gaze to Moses. "He eats and sleeps, pees and poops, eats and sleeps. It's some life he has." She smiled and then, without warning, picked up the baby and held him out to him. "Take him."

He hesitated. The wind hummed in the brush.

"Take him. He misses his father." She started to get up, but he had Moses in his arms before she could.

"And his father misses his mother," he said. She glimpsed at him when he said it, but he couldn't read her face. He wasn't trying to get a reaction from her anyway. He held Moses on his forearm, cradling his head in his hand. She'd dressed him in the blue and white pajamas that McKenzie had given them. "Hey, little man. You getting enough to eat? You treating your momma okay?" He swayed with the boy like he had sea legs. Moses felt heavier already, solid.

She got up and started packing her stuff. He had no idea whether she wanted him to come or leave. But then she placed the baby's backpack in front of him. "I'll help you put it on," she said. "I could use a break."

She took Moses from him and put him in the pack. When she helped him hoist the pack on his shoulders, her hand ran along his neck and lingered briefly. His entire being warmed to her touch, a book's worth of meaning to decipher. This was it: Move up the trail with Ana and Moses and get his life back, or head down alone and go nowhere.

She said something but he didn't hear. There was her face and her voice, and then the wind and the sun and the birds.

"I just said, are you ready? So, are you ready?"

"You lead and I'll follow. Anywhere."

A half-smile puckered the corner of her mouth. She turned and headed down the trail. They walked in silence, the wind in the grass, their breathing and their footsteps in the trail grit. The baby slept. He sweated against the pack.

"I love this trail," she said, continuing her pace. "Used to walk it when I was a girl. Just go and go. Sometimes I didn't come back till dark. Sometimes out all night, walking in the moonlight."

"And your parents, they were okay with that?"

"Are you kidding? It scared the hell out of them. But they knew they couldn't stop me and I could take care of myself. Wouldn't you want that for little Mo?"

"I must've gotten a worry gene from my ma. Sure, I guess it'd be alright. But you gotta admit, there's a lot more crazies out there."

"Like you?"

"Like me."

It was early spring. The Chinook roared over the ridge ahead and huffed down its flanks toward the valley. The baby leaves of the sage were beginning to show. The wind was warm and wet and hinted at rain.

They hiked another hour, neither of them saying more than an occasional comment about a flower or bird. They passed through patches of wildflowers. She knew all their names, and she pointed out the ones that would flower later, the aster and yarrow and sedum, the wild onion. They stopped at the top of the ridge of dark basalt. The wind had shifted from the south. A curtain of rain dropped in the valley. Forks of lighting broke out of the bruised clouds in the distance, and thunder bounced down the ridges. The baby had awakened and needed to be changed. He knelt so she could lift Moses out of the pack. The baby sniffled and wiped tears from his eyes.

"He's hungry already?"

She laughed. "Oh, probably. That, and he doesn't really dig hanging out in a poopy diaper all that much." She handed him a clean diaper and pins.

After he nursed, Moses was as content as a little Buddha. They sat, the warm wind and scattered drops of rain dampening their skin. He tucked Moses on his arm and swayed with him. Had he ever been this content as a child? It occurred to him that the knot in his stomach, the constant ache, was gone. It was as though it had been some physical thing in his body, like a baby crying to be fed. His craving for booze would never be completely gone. But right now it felt gone, dissolved and flushed out of his system. He wanted nothing else in this world but to be a good father to his son, and to love Ana the way she deserved to be loved.

Storm clouds scuttled above them to the northeast. "A lot of people don't realize how pretty these hills really are," she said. Her face darkened. "Why did you come here? What do you want from me?"

He'd rehearsed this scene in his head obsessively. "I don't know how to say it to come out right."

Her eyes blazed. "Bullshit, bullshit, bullshit." She grabbed a stick, and she scratched out a space in front of her as if she were erasing a blackboard. "It's time. Time to talk. Fuck it, Joe. I don't care how it comes out. You can't piss me off any more than you already have. This is reality, goddamn it, and it's scary, isn't it? You can't run from it. You can't hide from it." She grabbed him by the wrist, shaking them, her nostrils flaring and her eyebrows drawn. "It's going to be okay, damn it. You'll be okay. You can do this. Now, for Christ's sake, tell me what you want." She let go and fell back.

He was holding Moses, and the baby began to cry. "It's alright, little guy. It's alright." He stood and bounced Moses in his arms, his body rolling like he was on the *Jenny A*. It calmed him to hold Moses and to try to settle him.

"He'll be fine," she said. "You're doing fine."

He touched the boy's cheek, and it was as if he'd wiped away a cloud. Moses stopped crying. His eyes brightened, and he smiled. What did Moses think? Did he think at all? Did he picture himself as separate from them, or even from the earth around him? The idea of being a self hadn't even occurred to him. And maybe he had it right. Maybe it was all something people made up to make us think we'd been tossed out of the Garden of Eden when it was here all along.

"What's going on with you?" She touched his shin and let her hand slide off him. She seemed farther away than an arm's length.

He shut his eyes and inhaled and then let it out. When he opened his eyes, he squinted in the bright light. "Oh, so much. You. Moses. Us. Adam and Eve."

"Huh?"

He shrugged. "A lot."

"Not what you're thinking. What you're feeling."

He toed the gravel.

"Don't give me that. We've had this talk before. Look at me." She took hold of his chin. Her eyes were red, and she jutted her jaw. "What are you feeling, in your body?" she said, and she squeezed him, her lips pressed together.

He reached for his temple with his free hand and rubbed it, closing his eyes. Then he placed his hand on hers. His hand was quivering. He held his stomach and his breath and he bit his lip.

"Let it go," she said. "Just let it go." She pulled herself in to him and Moses. She pulled up his shirt, took his hand in hers and placed them on his stomach. She was sobbing, her body shaking.

He had seen pictures of a dam breaching, and it was like that when he felt a wall giving away in him. He tried to hold on, scared, but then it was too much, and he let it go. He took his free hand and reached for the dirt and held his hand flat as if feeling for a pulse. It came pouring out of him. Grief. Regret. Sadness. Like tar that had heated and liquefied and was now flowing out. She held him and took him down with her, the baby in his arms still, and they were now sitting in the grass beside the trail, the two of them holding each other with the baby between them, both sobbing, sweating, rocking. But it was more than sadness or grief or regret that was escaping. It was something that had fallen away, some sort of shell, built over the years, that he'd created, imagining it could protect him from the world, the hurt, his father, the memory of Jenny's murder, Kyle Macy, all of it. And now he saw it was a trick he'd played on himself. It had existed only in his imagination. He'd invented it, it wasn't real. It had never done anything for him except separate him from life.

"You wanted feelings?" He laughed. "You may have got more than you bargained for." There was a lightness, as though the tears had been a weight that had been released from him. "I've never felt this safe before. That's what I feel, is safe." He held her and tasted the salt on her cheeks. "Come back with me to Sockeye," he said. "That's what I want. I want you and Moses back. I want to spend the rest of my life with you. I want to keep my folks' place going the way they wanted it. I want to build a life with you. I want more babies."

She was sobbing, he thought at first, her body shaking. But it turned out she was laughing, too. Laughing and crying at the same time. Tears ran from her swollen eyes and down her flushed face. "Slow down. One thing at a time. Now you're talking about more babies?"

He laughed with her. "Yeah, I guess." He smoothed her tears. "Yeah, that's what I want. It's all I ever want." He kissed her again, her salt on his lips. "I love you, Ana. I love you so much."

She exhaled and sat back, sinking into the grass as if she were in pain.

"What's wrong?"

She shook her head and then bit her upper lip. "I love you, too, goddammit. But, you know what's wrong." She stared at the ground and then looked up at him and crossed her arms. "You've made promises to me before. I can't go through it again. Do you realize the pain you've caused?"

He closed his eyes. "Yes, I do." She was absolutely right, and the pain even now was a foulness inside him that made him want to retch. Instead of clenching and resisting it, though, he let it be. She had taught him to do this when she was getting ready to have the baby. "I know I can't undo what I've done. I hurt you, and I'm sorry. When I say I'm done with drinking, I don't expect you to believe me just because I said it. But I'm done, I promise you. I'm done with drinking. I hate even saying it because it's just a bunch of words. But I've been going to AA. You'll never guess who's my sponsor. Tom Crowley."

"The fire guy. That's appropriate."

"Been dry for 18 years. A flaming drunk before that—his joke, not mine. I've been dry now since you left. Look, I'll always be recovering. I know that. I'll never touch it again."

She fingered his cheek and brushed his arm. She looked at him and then out at the horizon, biting her bottom lip. Alcohol had tried to break her father, she said. It killed her uncle, and then, when it took hold of her brother, it tore holes in her parents, maybe even killed her mom. She had vowed never to be a victim to alcohol herself. "I tried not to fall in love with you," she said. "But I told myself, 'No, he's not like the rest of them.'"

The storm was turning east and melting over the plateau. He reached for her cheek but she pulled away. She began to cry quietly. He pulled her to him, and she sobbed in his shoulder. "You were wrong about me, but I'm glad you were," he said. "I was wrong, too. About a lot of things. I thought I didn't have a drinking problem. Thought I'd never come back home. Thought I'd never find someone I could love and who'd love me. I guess I thought my life was over before it ever began." He kissed her hair. "Now I'm sure. Surer than I've ever been sure. I love you. I would do anything if you took me back."

The sun reappeared, and the valley below was marked by crisp lines of light and shadow from the slanting rays. He kissed her. Then he turned her face gently.

"I will never let you down again," he said. "I love you. I love our son."

He kissed her eyes. But there was a distance in them, a separation, silence. She rubbed her face and then left her hands clasped against her lips like she was praying. She told him that she loved him and that she knew he loved her. But there was sadness in how she said it, like it was a departing, a drawing away. She hesitated, closing her eyes a moment and shaking her head slightly. Then she opened her eyes and he knew it before she said it. "But I can't do this."

It was as if a wound had been reopened. A shock of pain first, and then a slow cutting that serrated from his head to his throat and left metal filings in his gut. But he stayed with it, refusing to run from it.

"Listen to me," she said. "I need time. I believe you when you say you have stopped drinking. But I need to see you sober. I need time."

Now he knew what the pain was telling him. He knew the part of him looking to run or hide or take the easy way out. But he knew, too, that she was right. She deserved that. She had a right to see him prove himself.

CHAPTER 48

He waited for her on the newly painted green porch for an hour. The sky was big and infinitely blue. His heart bounced with the passing of every car or truck coming down the road. Clouds of apple-green pollen from the ponderosas drifted down in showers. The air was alive with insects and birds, and there was the mineral scent of the snowmelt as it crashed down the mountain streams, into the big lake.

He'd been getting the place ready while she was gone. McKenzie helped him with new curtains and other touches, and they turned his old room into the nursery. The walls were still knotty pine, but he'd gone out and gotten a few new lamps to brighten things. The whole place felt lighter and cleaner and more open—not only a reflection of how he felt now but more like an extension of himself.

When it was her, he leapt from the porch and cut straight across the grassy clearing. He got to her before the truck had bumped over the last rut of the sloping drive.

She stopped and leaned out the window, eyes wide and mouth open. It was as though she couldn't find words. Then she said his name, and he reached through and took her face in his hands. It was the her-ness that struck him, the object of his longing now in the flesh and blood, so real that she was almost unreal. Her hair was in pigtails and she was dressed for the road in denim, her face the color of bright agate. Moses was strapped in his car seat and appeared to be waking from a snooze.

"Goddammit, kiss me," she yelled at him, and then laughed, drawing his hands to her. And he did kiss her, his eyes open, his body electric and grounded at the same time, full but light. The world was just this moment for him now, just her, and not so much a narrowing as an opening up.

He held her through the open window a long time, until McKenzie's Blazer appeared behind them. She honked. "Get a room, lovebirds!"

McKenzie had brought things including a few dishes she'd prepared, but she didn't stay long—she hadn't planned to crash their party and knew when it was time go. After she left, they put Moses in the backpack and walked the little path through the pines above the lakeshore. She was tired, though, and when they came back to the house, she took a shower and headed for bed. He followed her with Moses in his arms. She nursed the baby in bed, and the two of them fell asleep, Joe spooning her back, holding her and longing for her but happy beyond words simply to have her back beside him.

They made love in the morning, the baby cooperating, asleep in his room, the air cool and delicious and alive, the robins busy since first light. It would be one of those endless summer days when the glow of twilight stays past 11. After they ate and fed Moses, she drove them up to the dam at the lake outlet.

They parked at the cemetery, and they walked first to his father's stone marker in the old cemetery. She'd picked paintbrush and balsamroot, and they laid the flowers on the stone. He kept his hand on the slate cube and traced his father's name.

She put his hand on his. "You just weren't ready when he went. You had so much to say to him. So much bottled up."

Her hand was warm. "Bottled? Interesting choice of words. You're right. But I can do this now. I don't hate him anymore. Everything I put him through. I guess I thought he was supposed to be perfect. It's like I can connect with him now, touching this. It doesn't make sense."

"Sure it does."

"I think I felt all that before," he said. "Or at least I had some notion of it. But shit, it scared the hell out of me. Still does."

She extended her hand and helped him up. "Come on, I want to show you something."

She led him from the cemetery to the bluff overlooking the lake and the dam. The lake level was high, and water flumed over the spillway. While she was gone, she said, she'd driven to Coquitlam in British Columbia. The Salish people there, the Kwikwetlem, had held a celebration, and she'd gone with a few other Nez Perce to see for themselves.

There was a lake up there, too, and a dam. The dam had wiped out the sockeye run around the same time that the run had disappeared on Wallowa Lake, in the early 1900s. But when she and the other Nez Perce got there, they saw why people were so excited. In a trap at the base of the dam, a single male sockeye had come the day before. And the day they arrived, a hen had followed. After more than a hundred years, the first sockeye had returned to Coquitlam Lake, male and female, ready to spawn.

"If you had been there, you would have cried."

He held her against his chest. "Because I'm such a sensitive guy, of course." He laughed, enjoying the self-mockery. He was taciturn—a word she'd taught him—and would always be. But while she'd been away, he'd changed, and she would see it and hear it. And probably she'd already noticed. In those AA meetings, he'd learned things about himself. About walking right up to the edge and letting go. About putting yourself in someone else's hands. About trusting yourself. About something bigger than himself. He wasn't ready to accept any kind of religion but he knew there was something else, some mystery that connected everything, something invisible but real anyway.

"Those people," she said, "they got a piece of themselves back when those fish came back home. You know, their name in their language means 'red fish up the river.'"

"That's why we'll keep this thing alive," he said. The fish commission's ruling on the dam had come out the week before. It was no surprise: They decided not to decide. Instead, they decided to fund more study.

"We don't need the fish commission. We don't need River. This is for Moses. It's for our kids and their kids. It's for the tribe. Anyone who calls this place home. River—this was never home for him. I don't know what was. Those sockeye are going to come back home here one day, and I don't know if we'll see it, but Moses is going to be here to see it."

She had the baby in a cloth sling in front of her, and Moses was sleeping. "They had a ceremony to return those spawners back up to the lake," she said. "The elders told their stories. They talked about the old days, how there were so many salmon the river would turn black. You'd see a shadow come up the river, they said, and the fish were so thick, if you threw a rock it would skip on their backs. I would like to be alive to have a ceremony like that here."

"And you will. We will."

She nodded toward the dam. "He hated that thing."

River had been arrested while she was gone. Joe called her the day it happened, but she had found out from her friends. He'd been caught with explosives after crossing from Nevada into Oregon down near McDermitt. He was in a federal prison, awaiting trial on domestic terrorism charges.

"I think it started to mean a lot more to him than just a dam blocking some fish." She narrowed her eyes. "I think it was like, if he could destroy that dam, he could destroy his father. After a while, I started to realize we'd never get anywhere with any of the regulators or the irrigators. Because he hated anything to do with authority. They were his father all over again. He never got the approval he wanted from his father, and so he was going to get back at him in his own way."

He picked up a rock and hefted it. "In the end, I guess, it was all about him. Poor bastard. I just can't picture him adjusting all too well to prison." Then he tossed the rock over the cliff.

"Oh, I don't know," she said. "He's going to meet plenty of others just like him there. He might get along fine."

CHAPTER 49

He wanted to take them to his spot up by Billy Meadows, in the hills above the Zumwalt Prairie. It was a place he'd stumbled on years ago while following a herd of elk but had nearly forgotten, and he knew she'd like it.

They made the drive north of town up through the Zumwalt, and on the way he told her about the aspen grove. He'd gone up to camp near the old guard station, and he'd seen the aspens when he'd first arrived, tall and white on the far edge of the meadow, their leaves dancing in the light of the late afternoon. He'd seen them before, and he'd wondered about them because there weren't many aspens up there in that part of the country. After two days of looking at them, he decided to hike in to see them up close.

He'd crossed the yellow cattle grate at the edge of a gravel road, and then into the meadow where the elk herds sometimes gathered. He headed for a stone pence post. When he got there, he set a boot on the top line of barbed wire, and then with one motion, pushed off and launched himself over the fence.

He was on the other side then. "It was a marsh, and my boots were getting sucked down in the ooze," he said. "But the closer I got, the bigger those aspens looked, like some kind of castle or cathedral. I had to go."

He'd made his way to the end of the marsh, he told her, his feet wet. Then, behind sun-bleached snags that the marsh had killed, there were the aspens—about a dozen, with more behind them. In front of them was a small rise of earth filled with the brightest green grass. The aspens were big, 60 or 70 feet tall, their lower trunks clean of branches and only their crowns filled with shimmering leaves. He sat at the foot of those trees and stayed for at least an hour.

Joe and Ana entered the woods above the Zumwalt, climbing steadily on the road leading to Billy Meadows. They stopped at the Red Hill lookout, and they got out and walked down to the east-facing slope of windblown rock and grasses.

They sat together in silence. Then he returned to his story about the aspen grove. There had been a family of sapsuckers living in the trees, he said. The nest was a round hole halfway up the big tree in front of him. There was a chick in the nest, whimpering like a baby's squeeze toy, and every few minutes the parent returned to the nest, shoving its body into the small opening or dropping by to deliver a few morsels from outside the hole.

They sat where wild onion and yarrow grew in the spaces around the rocks. Below them lay the big prairie. Long, flat-bottomed clouds, their bellies in blue-gray shadows, their backs bright, drifted over the country like silent fish finning in a blue lake. Off to the north, the country rose gradually, its far ridge meeting the horizon. All that country was filled with the dark green of the trees, with bands of meadowlands spaced out in stretches of light green. From their vantage, the meadows looked like parks. Toward the south, the country dropped, with the trees petering out in long columns following the contours of creeks or hugging the north sides of small hills. And then the country mostly ran out of trees and was an expanse of prairie with the shadows of clouds moving along the ground. To the east, breaking the far horizon, the Seven Devils rose gray and toothy, crusted in snow.

"I must've sat watching those woodpeckers for an hour," he said. "After a while, it was like I was in a dream. A really nice dream, the kind where you feel like you're in heaven, wherever that is."

She smiled and touched his arm. "Sounds like heaven to me."

He held her hand. It had been still in the aspens, he said, still and quiet except for the birds. But then the wind came up. "It was like the sound of water rushing over stones in the river, or like applause," he said. "And then those leaves started fluttering in the breeze, and it was like they were alive, like the leaves were butterflies suddenly, fluttering their wings. And you know, I was so damn happy in that moment, I could've died right there and then, and I would've had a goddamned smile on my face."

She got up then and reached down for him. "What are we waiting for? I want to see this place."

When they got there, it was exactly as he remembered it. And if she'd had any idea of why he brought her, she never let on. The soft carpet of grass was there still, like an altar at the foot of the trees. They sat, and he produced a ring from out of his pack. A friend of Bart's whom he'd gotten to know, a sculptor and jewelry maker, had created the ring. It depicted a woodpecker carrying a bit of food home to its chick. Instead of a worm or a bug, though, it was the diamond from Ana's mom's wedding ring.

He took another ring from his pocket. It was the one Grace had given him, his father's ring.

CHAPTER 50

The wedding was a small affair at the courthouse with the justice of the peace. After the ceremony, they drove back to the lake house for a little party—very little: McKenzie and Sue, Bart. No Howard. No kids, except for little Mo.

They gathered on the bluff over the lake. The robins sang loudly. The ponderosas spilled clouds of pollen in the wind, settling on the water in yellow–green mats along the shoreline.

Before she died, Grace had left instructions about her ashes. She didn't want any kind of marker, but Joe and McKenzie convinced her to let them put something next to Clark's in the cemetery. She wanted her ashes spread over the lake, and she wanted them mixed with Clark's. She had saved out a portion of the ashes from his urn for this reason.

Howard was out of the picture. After Grace died and Joe and McKenzie refused to develop the land, Howard had disappeared. He might have gone over to Baker City or up to his millionaire friend's ranch up on the Grande Ronde. Nobody knew, including Sue. He came back after a couple of weeks, but when he did, he told her that Joe and McKenzie were no longer part of his family. Henceforth—that's the word Sue said he'd used—henceforth they were "dead to him." He forbade her to see them or to bring the kids to any of their gatherings. Sue put her foot down and came anyway, but she didn't go so far as to defy him about the kids.

He held the urn containing Grace's ashes. McKenzie cupped a simple pottery jar with Clark's ashes in her hands. He took a teaspoon and ladled three spoonsful from each container into a bowl held by Sue.

He walked to the point where the bluff dropped down into the lake. He lifted the bowl in the air, waiting for a breeze that would take the ashes out over the water. Below and off to the right, three boys—brothers staying at the cabins with their parents—fished from the dock. A couple of boats dotted the immense blue lake. The lake seemed to hover in the sky, framed on both sides by the moraines. The moraines led to the mountains, turning from green to dazzling white all the way to the peak-filled horizon.

A breeze brushed the trees, and an osprey hovered over a spot and *yewked.* He took the bowl and whipped it through the air. The ashes separated, the heavier pieces falling like sand and the rest rising in a puff of dust. The small cloud drifted over the lake. It billowed against the sky-reflected blue of the water for a while, and then it was gone, swallowed by the air and inhaled by the water.

The dust of his parents would go its way. Some grains would be carried on the wind and make their way back up into the mountains. Some would fall as film on the water and be carried over the dam. Some would melt in the water and drift in suspension and perhaps be carried off or float down, passing through the gills of the kokanee on their way to the soft muck below. One day, he would join them.

They would all make their way to the ocean, as the sockeye had done for millennia before and one day would do again.

NOTE FROM THE AUTHOR

Word-of-mouth is crucial for any author to succeed. If you enjoyed the book, please leave a review online—anywhere you are able. Even if it's just a sentence or two. It would make all the difference and would be very much appreciated.

Thanks!
Michael

ABOUT THE AUTHOR

Photo courtesy of Jim Clark

Born and raised in New York, Michael F. Tevlin is the grandson of Irish immigrants. He studied journalism at the University of Oregon and worked as a reporter before turning to freelance writing. In *Sockeye*, he combines two personal passions: the recovery of native salmon runs and the wild places of his adopted state. He and his wife have two sons and two grandchildren and make their home in Portland, Oregon.

Thank you so much for reading one of our **Literary Fiction** novels.

If you enjoyed our book, please check out our recommended for your next great read!

The Five Wishes by Mr. Murray McBride by Joe Siple

2018 Maxy Award "Book of the Year"

"A sweet...tale of human connection...will feel familiar to fans of Hallmark movies." *–KIRKUS REVIEWS*

"An emotional story that will leave readers meditating on the life-saving magic of kindness." *–Indie Reader*

View other Black Rose Writing titles at www.blackrosewriting.com/books and use promo code **PRINT** to receive a **20% discount** when purchasing.

Make bridge to insiders into
eg., Minsun, the Blues

CPSIA information can be obtained
at www.ICGtesting.com
Printed in the USA
FSHW011947250320
68487FS